Salutations.

It's been a long time, and a long road. I'm pleased we're still in touch, and hope you can swing a fly-by through Ecuador & come visit one day.

Best wishes always.

Nick

Roppongi

a novel by
Nick Vasey

Roppongi
©2012 by Nick Vasey
All Rights Reserved
Printed in the United States of America
ISBN-13: 978-1467954730
ISBN-10: 146795473X

This is a work of fiction. While, as in all fiction, the literary perceptions and insights are based on experience, all names, characters, places, and incidents either are products of the author's imagination or are used fictitiously. All characters appearing in this work are fictitious. Any resemblance to real persons, living or dead, is purely coincidental.

Roppongi Cover
Concept: Nick Vasey
Artwork & Design: Laura Ainscough
Graphic Design Alchemy: Diego Ganazhapa

Author's Note and Acknowledgments

The first words of *Roppongi* were written in a furiously creative spurt in early 1999, after I had completed my second year of working in Tokyo, and was relaxing in the bayside suburb of St. Kilda in Melbourne. By word count, it was nearly half-finished within one year.

But then life took over, and both the manuscript and my writing took a long ride in the back seat. Incredibly, it was not until late 2011 that I finished the final draft and sent it to the publishers. Twelve long years of gestation; years which as ever, were full of work, travels and adventures.

To tell the truth, I never really believed I would finish the manuscript. Life simply got busy and I lost the momentum, energy and even the desire for writing. Other things always seemed more important than that mouldering silent file hiding in a dark corner of a hard drive somewhere.

But eventually, I faced the realisation that I guess most authors face at one time or another: I would always be unhappy *with myself* if I failed to complete it (are there any bigger clichés than 'the unfinished novel'?). I realised that even if I didn't ever publish it, I would at least have finished my book, to my satisfaction.

Accordingly, some of the people who have given me a push and a prod in the right direction along the way deserve my heartfelt gratitude, for without them, there would be no *Roppongi*.

Firstly, my love and thanks go to my mother Dianne Lesley, for her tireless reviewing and editing efforts and overall support and encouragement throughout my life. Secondly, to anyone who ever read the draft, loved it, and told me I was crazy if I didn't finish it. You know who you are, and your positive feedback was more important than you know. Thirdly, kudos must go to Rosanne Dingli (www.rosannedingli.com), who in 2002 wrote a professional manuscript appraisal which cheered me greatly and revived my interest in my laptop's keyboard. Fourthly, thank-you to Diego Ganazhapa (diegueis87@gmail.com) for his invaluable graphic design alchemy with the *Roppongi* book-cover. Fifthly, a thank-you to the crew at CreateSpace, who helped bring this book to market.

And finally to my remarkable wife Laura Ainscough, whose artistic energies and abilities are seemingly without limits. It is Laura I must thank for the design, lithographic work and aesthetic sense involved in *Roppongi's* book-cover. Likewise for her editing and proofing assistance. In short, Laura's work-ethic and creative output in all things is truly inspiring, and left me in no doubt that not finishing my novel was no longer a credible or viable option. Laura has stoically endured the many instances of grumpiness, tiredness and duress which were necessary for me to bring this book into the world. Thank you my love; I am blessed to have you.

A word now about the subject matter. The Roppongi experience holds an incredibly special place in my heart. And I know the thousands of other people who have run Roppongi's gauntlet over the years feel the same way. Roppongi scars people. In good ways and bad. It gets under your skin, and stays there. And as with all the best drugs, life inevitably seems dull after Roppongi.

But make no mistake – it makes you grow. You are different at the end of it. I had two of the most incredibly fun and intensely mad years of my life there. I met many extraordinary people from all walks of life. The closest I can come to describing it succinctly is that it was like living in a movie. A very fast-moving, unpredictably surreal blur of a movie. There was no off-switch. During this hyperactively hedonistic time I made lifelong friends under the most outrageous circumstances.

The Roppongi diaspora now spreads all over the world; members enjoy a special bond of understanding, of shared experience. Doing Roppongi justice in print was always going to be a daunting task. For there are uncountable 'Roppongis' – everyone's Roppongi was 'their Roppongi'. So for those who took the trip like I did, I hope my *Roppongi* takes you back there. And for those who didn't, I hope you enjoy the ride!

In closing, a word of advice to all you other first-time writers out there who may be experiencing self-doubt, angst or a lack of motivation. Just keep on going! Whatever it takes. For as I now know, there is nothing like the satisfaction of holding your own book in your hands, and knowing many others are enjoying it worldwide.

For those of you who enjoy *Roppongi*, please do me a favour and help spread the word about it! The *very best thing you can do* is visit Amazon, and contribute your rating and an honest review. Your opinions count!

There is a list of ways you can help me promote *Roppongi* in the 'Care To Help?' section at the back of this book. I'd also be very happy to receive your questions, feedback or reviews, so I have included my contact details in that section. Please send me your thoughts! Online, visit **www.roppongithenovel.com** and also LIKE the *Roppongi* Facebook page (click to it from the website).

Additionally, the final pages of this book include a Glossary of Terminology, as well as translations for the few lines of foreign dialogue which appear sporadically throughout the novel.

Thank you for having chosen to read *Roppongi*. I very much hope you will enjoy the experience.

Nick Vasey
November 2011

Travel is fatal to prejudice, bigotry, and narrow-mindedness, and many of our people need it sorely on these accounts. Broad, wholesome, charitable views of men and things cannot be acquired by vegetating in one little corner of earth all one's lifetime.

Mark Twain

*If drugs are such an awful thing,
Why do so many choose to enjoy them?
Could it be we've created a way of life so inhuman,
That drugs are the only chance many people have,
To touch base with their souls?*

Zack Morrissey

The trouble with being in the rat race is that even if you win, you're still a rat.

Lily Tomlin

The nail that sticks out, must be hammered in.

Japanese saying

For Laura ...
who is patient, kind, talented and more.
She is the greatest adventure of my life.

Roppongi

One

Zack leaned back, his safety surrendered to the harness, wondering not for the first time in his life how he had wound up where he was. He glanced around, simultaneously brushing away the long strands of hair attacking his face. Even tied back, it still sometimes annoyed him.

The Negev desert stretched to the horizon. Its mottled earth-red mountains loomed toward him, seemingly challenging the authority of this tentacle of the Red Sea that narrowed its way inland to form the Gulf of Aqaba. The kingdom of Jordan was to his right, Israel was dead ahead, and just a short bus ride around the coast to his left was Taba, the border-town to Egypt. He breathed in deeply. This was an amazing part of the world to be in, and he loved it.

He'd got there through his charm, his bullshit, and his looks. Zack could talk a good game, and this was the primary reason he was currently repairing a rigging ladder high above the deck of *L'Chaim*, a thirty-three metre top-sail schooner. She was a fifty year old Danish-built beauty, made of wood. Her Hebrew name meant 'to life'. The phrase was typically used as a toast when drinkers clinked glasses, the Israeli equivalent to 'Cheers' or 'Skol'. Zack thought it serendipitous that he was first-mate of a yacht whose name epitomised his personal credo.

Before arriving in Eilat, he'd had practically no sailing experience. This minor detail had not, however, prevented him from nabbing a job on the most beautiful and prestigious tourist yacht based in the local marina. He had arrived at the dock well-muscled, tanned, fit: perfectly equipped to lie about his experience. Not too much though, just enough. Zack had become expert at gauging where the 'over-step line' was, and always treated it with the deference it deserved. The secret of being a great bullshit artist certainly did not lie in being recognised as one. Well, not initially at any rate.

When Uri, the skipper, realised Zack also spoke conversational Hebrew and his primary reason for being in Israel was to improve it, his employment had been a foregone conclusion. Zack had known his semi-command of Hebrew was a subtle cocktail of flattery, humility and respect Uri would find difficult to ignore.

After all, who bothered to learn a language spoken by only seven million people? The irony was he had picked most of it up during his last visit to Japan. His Israeli girlfriend at the time, and the many other Israelis in Tokyo had been willing teachers.

Zack also had no moral dilemma about temporarily distorting the truth in order to secure employment. He figured all you had to do thereafter was not give them an excuse to fire you, which simply meant learning fast. And as with his speedy Hebrew uptake, this had never been a problem for him. Miraculously, despite his smart mouth and sensitive anti-authoritarian hackles, Zack had never yet been fired.

Israel, specifically Eilat, was one of the more spectacular places Zack had visited – he'd now been there ten months. Eilat combined many of his favourite things: a hot dry climate, fairytale scuba diving, mountains, deserts, every conceivable recreational activity, and a transient population dedicated to hedonistic pursuits. As far as Zack was concerned, Eilat was the promised-land in spades.

Unfortunately, thousands of mostly idiotic tourists seemed to share this view. It amused Zack to watch them, and he wondered endlessly about their lives. They came in droves, always in a hurry. Fat, loud, ignorant, sunburnt and spending megabucks; were they having a good time? He doubted it. He was sure the majority were just going through the motions. Most of them probably wouldn't relax until they were back in their TV-watching, home-improving, fast-food-munching, nine to five domestic routines – this strange, hot, unpredictable and potentially dangerous land far behind them.

As someone who thrived on and proactively sought unpredictability, contemplating their lives depressed Zack if he dwelt on it. In spite of this, and like them with their TV-soaps, he was addicted to watching them.

Crewing on *L'Chaim* gave him an unparalleled opportunity to do not only that, but to do so from a position of power if necessary. To study them. He recognised they were profoundly different to him, and often felt like he was 'undercover'. But an undercover what? Perhaps discovering that answer would be the key to eventually finding himself atop Maslow's pyramid? He smiled, amused that the famous psychologist's hierarchy-of-needs paradigm had stayed with him all this time.

It was the Americans who most frequently left him speechless.

"Is the water cold?" (Why don't you ask the people swimming?)

"Is it deep?" (What's deep to you? – *bonus chuckle*.)

"Is that food for us?" – this, while watching lunch-time food preparation during a day tour on the yacht! (No, another yacht has broken down, and we need to get this food to them. Sorry.) "Then what're we eating?" (Oh dear.)

"Are there sharks?" (You'll never know if you don't go in!)

"Can you speak Israeli?" (No, but I can speak Hebrew.) "Hebrew? What's that?" (Oh dear.)

"Where did Moses part the Red Sea? Was it here, or a little further down?" (I don't know, I wasn't here.)

Some of the things they said often merited such a bitingly sarcastic response that he could not always be sure it would go over their heads (which was unfortunately essential if he were to avoid finding out what being fired felt like). The five other crew-members had long since become familiar with Zack's acerbic, piss-taking sense of humour, and happily aided and abetted his outlandish answers to the inane questions posed on a daily basis by their passengers.

Zack blamed their need for incessant chatter on television culture. He had arrived at a theory that many Americans would rather risk saying something incredibly stupid than just remain silent; they simply felt uncomfortable unless the air was filled with chatter. The expression 'comfortable silence' apparently meant nothing to them. In this respect, and in defence of his own sanity, Zack felt duty-bound to follow the philosophy of the Starship Enterprise: 'To boldly go where no man has gone before' – forever expanding the frontiers of the undetected sarcastic riposte.

His mind flicked back to the reason for his imminent return to Tokyo. Money, he thought gloomily. Always bloody money. He *hated* the fact his freedom to move fluidly around the planet was dictated by money, or lack of it. The construct of money, and its seeming omnipotence, irritated Zack. To get it usually required doing things you didn't want to do, in places you didn't want to be. Living that debilitating a trade-off for too long wasn't living at all, Zack thought. It was dying. It was giving up.

Long considering it his birthright to roam the globe at will, Zack had done so more diligently than probably all his peers. He had completed university, but then chosen to exit the system. Society's 'standard program' of university, job, career, debts, mortgage etc, simply held no appeal for him. Mainly because it seemed to involve spending large amounts of time in the same place, with more or less the same people, with the pursuit of money being the most important pastime. At best it looked boring, and at worst, it was slavery. He genuinely didn't understand why so many people seemed so happy to buy into it. After all, there was a whole planet to explore! If that wasn't at least one major reason for being alive, then what was? Wasn't it obvious that he should want to search for whatever or wherever it was that made him feel right, happy, fulfilled? Shouldn't *everyone* be doing that?

Apparently not. Most people seemed content to fit themselves into pre-defined soul-crushing boxes, thereafter meekly accepting the life of indentured servitude the correlated social constructs of money and debt foisted upon them.

Recalling once more the psychological concept 'self-actualisation', he smiled. He liked it. The pyramidal structure involved not only identifying all the components of one's hierarchy-of-needs, but achieving them. Self-actualisation was probably the closest psychology had come to defining nirvana. Thanks for nothing Maslow, Zack thought. Give us somewhere to go but only the most general of maps to get there. Well, he had a map to Tokyo, and it seemed going back there was to be a pre-requisite of satisfying his own hierarchy-of-needs.

It had been more than two years since he left his bar-manager job in Roppongi. It wasn't that he didn't enjoy working there. He enjoyed it too much. That was the nature of the place; the intensity of the lifestyle eventually just fucked you up. Roppongi was a non-stop party-shop, a crazy rollercoaster-ride of drugs, drinking, partying and gorgeous women. Money flowed freely from a slashed, seemingly limitless financial aorta, and it was actually his job to make every night the biggest party he could. Since everyone was hell-bent on getting as fucked-up as they could as often as they could, his job was perhaps better defined as conductor to this hedonistic orchestra. Lawyers, bankers, brokers, wankers ... it really didn't matter. They'd all come to his bar thirsting for a wild time. And how he'd delighted them! Under his expert helmsmanship, Bongoes had become legendary for excess.

Bongoes was one of Roppongi's longest running *gaijin* bars. '*Gaijin*' translated literally, meant 'outside person' and applied pretty much to anyone not Japanese. Everyone joked that the Japanese only came to Roppongi to watch the *gaijin* get drunk and lose the plot: a sort of nocturnal nature-walk for the natives. Irrespective of this, Roppongi was in truth a place where foreigners could have a wild night in an otherwise tame country, as well as surround themselves with nationalities other than the Japanese.

When Zack left, after leading the party-faithful for fifty-two straight weeks, it had taken a heavy toll. Looking back, he could hardly credit the state of physical disrepair he'd reached. Afterwards, he had travelled through Thailand, India, and Nepal, then swung through London for the summer. He'd arrived in Israel last year. Seeing him now, no-one would have believed he was the same person who'd for a year cheerfully binged his way through the worst excesses Tokyo had to offer.

During his journey he'd regained his ideal balance of fitness and physique through rigorous training, combined with a seafood, vegetable, rice and fruit based diet. Generally Zack had little time for the tourism-wrecked Thai island of *Koh Samui*, but had nevertheless spent ten days there on a program of fasting and colonic irrigation.

Recommended to him by a hostess friend in Tokyo, its results had both impressed and deeply shocked him. He found himself amazed and angry that this cleansing knowledge had not been included in his western upbringing. The focus was on maintaining wellness rather than treating illness, and Zack found himself wondering why it had taken him this long to discover it. During the ten day program, he had shed six kilograms of toxic waste.

The ensuing sensation of overall well-being and clarity of mind had been an epiphany for Zack. Physically, mentally and spiritually, the fast was the most personally transformative thing he had ever done, and he was grateful for it having bestowed a platform for his renewal.

Now twenty-nine, Zack was in the best shape of his life. Eight percent body-fat and eighty-five kilograms of tanned muscle stretched over a six foot one inch frame. Dark blonde hair fell just past shoulder length, and a goatee-beard ringed what many women described as a sensual mouth.

While most people were fixed and predictable entities, Zack was not. Part chameleon, part electrical current, he was a nomad whose magnetism was undeniable.

Two

Sofia was meant to be sanding the bench in front of her but she cricked her neck, looking up at Zack from the deck. She often wondered what went on in his mind. He was one of the sexiest and smartest guys she'd ever met, and as a mid-twenties Swedish stunner, she'd met a few.

He was also one of the most frustrating. He carried the banner of his independence with him like some sort of neutral warning. Sadly, Sofia knew she had no power over him at all. She had become accustomed to wielding the strength of her femininity over men, but Zack was, as far as she could tell, completely unaffected by it.

It was as if there was an invisible, emotionally impermeable force-field surrounding him. She had tried, but she just couldn't get through it. Thinking at first he was unaware of the magnetic effect he had on people around him, she had since come to realise this wasn't true. But it wasn't a contrived or feigned ignorance, more an apathy, she'd decided.

She had fucked him in his hammock the first night he came aboard. At their invitation, he'd joined the crew at their local watering hole *Mastoolim*, got very drunk, and still easily beaten everyone he'd played pool with. Not just beaten them, annihilated them. It was more an exhibition than a contest and Zack had clearly only been amusing himself.

The amazing thing however, was that there'd been no resentment, no arguments, and the opposition whom he hadn't even met before, were all unusually friendly towards him. His charismatic bonhomie, in combination with a self-deprecating air neatly complemented his profound technical skill.

Sofia had never seen anything quite like it. They'd stumbled back to the yacht together, and as she was slightly ashamed to remember, she had practically raped him. Yes. And repeatedly. Still half-naked and jointly hung-over, they'd awoken in the morning to a blast of cold water from Hans, as he hosed down the deck. A chorus of cat-calls and jeers from crew-members of the boats docked alongside only added to their discomfort. Zack had been welcomed to the Eilat marina family in no uncertain fashion!

Nine months later, the degree to which he had favourably entrenched himself in the Eilat scene was nothing short of miraculous. People couldn't seem to do enough for him. And they certainly wouldn't cross him. This, Sofia had concluded, was either due to genuine respect, or a suspicion they'd be the ones coming off looking stupid if they did.

The sexual relationship between them had continued, until, without warning, Zack had slept with a girl from another boat. He hadn't denied it, tried to hide it, or been ashamed of it. Sofia tried to fight with him about it, but he'd been utterly disinterested, countering her accusations with the simple statement that he hadn't promised her anything, and that she too was free to do as she wished. Annoyingly, this was totally true. But Sofia had never been treated so casually by a man before and had not taken it well. Living and working together on the yacht at such close-quarters, however, made it impossible to stay angry with him. Now their relations were merely okay: not only had he mightily pissed her off, he had also unknowingly punctured her usually robust self-esteem.

He was still hanging back in the safety-harness with his arms spread wide as if in supplication. What *was* he doing?

"Zack," she called out. "Are you praying for the second coming or what?"

His head slid lazily around and he squinted towards the deck. "Hey Princess ... you should know from personal experience that's a stupid question."

Sofia was unable to prevent a half-smile. Unbelievable, she thought. The guy was never lost for words.

Hans suddenly appeared from below-decks. "You tell her, Zack."

Then, approaching Sofia with a grin he added, "If your memory's failing, you can put my name on a refresher list."

"In your dreams, Hans," she retorted. "That'd be about the only way you'd get it up."

Hans mock-pouted, turned on his heel, hissed, "Ice Queen!" and walked off.

Simultaneously there was a blur of movement and a splash.

Startled, Sofia reflexively jumped up in fright, scraping her knee on the very bench she'd been sanding.

"You fucking asshole!" Sofia rubbed her knee angrily as Zack's face, grinning beatifically, emerged from the clear green water, the harness floating beside him. Looking up at the yardarm from which he had just executed a seventeen metre dive, Sofia shook her head.

"You ... are a fucking maniac!" she shouted.

His expression feigned hurt, but those hazel eyes sparkled with dangerous energy.

"Sofia, you suddenly looked so beautiful, and it was the fastest way I could get to you!" he dead-panned.

He really was irresistible, but she wasn't going to give him the satisfaction.

"That's a shame Zack, because I'm just leaving." She flashed him a glance, adding, "I guess you'll have to use your hand."

A mocking, "Oh baby, I love it when you play hard to get!" followed her as she headed for the marina, but this taunt was abruptly cut off by a stream of guttural, cursing Hebrew.

Oh, fuck! With all the commotion, she hadn't seen the skipper, Uri, approaching the yacht.

Uri was a hard bastard. Tough, but fair. Ex Israeli Defence Force (IDF). Rumour had it he was ex-Special Forces. Whatever the case, it showed in the way he ran his boat. He worked them harder than any other skipper on the marina, but this dedication was reflected in the *L'Chaim's* appearance and performance and, Sofia had to admit, she enjoyed the kudos that went with being a member of his crew. Uri did not suffer fools lightly.

Oh well, she thought, at least Zack would get reamed out for doing that stupid dive while the boat was docked. To her annoyance however, she watched as Zack returned the skipper's abuse with a volley of Hebrew of his own, and Uri actually started laughing! Sofia could not believe her eyes. Worse, she had more than a fleeting suspicion she was the butt of Zack's joke.

Honestly, she didn't know why it surprised her anymore. Uri's taciturn nature was the stuff of legend, but a few well chosen words of Hebrew from the wonder-kid had made him laugh instead of giving Zack a most deserved tongue-lashing. She knew it was unreasonable, but sometimes Zack's seeming immunity to the rules of the everyday world drove her crazy.

"Sofia!"

Uri's harsh Israeli accent cut through her like a sharp pain.

"You are doing some work today maybe, or just talking dirty?"

That was it!

She bit her tongue and then forced out a, "Sorry Uri ... I'm just going to get some lunch," as she quickly disappeared below-deck.

*   *   *

The interminable day of maintenance now over, *L'Chaim's* crew and a few friends from other boats sat around drinking beers, smoking joints and talking shit. From his hammock, Zack looked at his friends lounging around the deck, and marvelled at the serenity and sense of camaraderie he felt in this environment. The yacht rocked gently in the warm evening breeze, the mountains bordering the Negev desert soaked up the deep red glow of sunset.

It was mid-June, with temperatures extreme by day, temperate by night. Because of the warm nights, Zack had been sleeping in his hammock on deck for over a month now, and had needed only a cotton sheet for protection. Sometimes in life, he thought, came moments like this, ones he wished could stretch out forever. Eyes closed, he inhaled deeply from the joint and savoured the moment, all the more bittersweet because he knew it would soon be only a memory.

Snatches of conversation drifted by:

"… and then the fucking thing just ripped through the line like it wasn't even there." Hans, unsurprisingly, was talking about fishing.

"… a hundred and twenty shekels for an E. That's unbelievable!" Zack knew the French girl Simona from the dive-boat 'Paradise' was so mortified by the extortionate local prices of any drugs other than grass or hash, that she was considering running the risk of importing her own from a friend in Amsterdam.

" … and then I was right in the middle of a sea of phosphorescence. It was the most beautiful thing I've ever seen. The student couldn't believe his eyes." Iris, the Israeli dive-master from the 'Paradise', was completely obsessed with cave-diving.

"So what's wrong with our resident raconteur this evening? Don't tell me you're asleep after all that exhausting diving and swimming today!"

Zack's eyes flicked open. Sofia's sarcasm-laden comment was directed at him. He'd been expecting something from her eventually. The others had now fallen quiet, and there was no easy escape for him. He let the silence hang for a moment, not quite sure how much he should say. Then he decided on the truth.

"Nothing really," he murmured. "I'm just a bit depressed." He'd been putting this conversation off for some time now.

That got their attention. There was a chorus of responses, some genuine, others mocking and disbelieving.

What the hell. He had to tell them sometime. He held up his hand, then let it out.

"I'm leaving," he said softly. There. Done.

A stunned silence ensued.

Sofia was the first to speak. All she could manage was a subdued, "Where to next?"

"Tokyo," Zack replied.

"Well, fuck me with a rusty chainsaw," Hans exclaimed, using an expression he'd picked up from Zack. "How come?"

Zack turned to face them all. "Well, I've never known if it's the best or the worst reason in the world, but the answer is simple ... M-O-N-E-Y."

His announcement sparked a flurry of conversation about Japan, next destinations, and money in general. Zack's mind drifted and he reflected again on the fact that he'd voluntarily left a US$5,000 per month situation in Japan to ultimately land this US$500 per month job in Israel. The world sure was a crazy place, he thought with a measure of satisfaction.

None of the travellers working in Eilat were there for the money. Quite simply, it would be unusual for any of their ilk to land a job that paid significantly. Why? Because it was technically illegal to work in Israel without a permit. And a permit was impossible to get. Notwithstanding this, work *was* still possible in certain areas and industries. Of course, the pay offered was nowhere near 'Israeli-national' standards.

Crews of the various tourist boats in the marina mostly lived on and were fed by whichever boat provided their employment, and regarded the meagre monthly remuneration as nothing more than beer and cigarette money. It seemed the authorities in Eilat had long turned a blind eye to the vast number of illegally working transients. They would make a token arrest and deportation every now and then, but for some reason they'd never once investigated the boat-crews, of whom over ninety percent were very obviously illegal.

Zack believed the only explanation for this could be that powerful marina interests paid the immigration police to look the other way. Accordingly, the Eilat marina had become something akin to a little travellers' principality of its own, another bubble within the tourism bubble which comprised and fed the town of Eilat.

He loved the fact these people, his friends, were on the marina purely because they were enjoying a new environment, new friends and new possibilities in their lives. They were all on a voyage of self-discovery, never quite knowing what the next day, week, or month might bring. Inexperienced travellers often tended towards panic because of this uncertainty, feeling the need to obsessively forward-plan, but the longer you travelled the more you sensed an underlying rhythm to things and just went with the flow.

Zack firmly believed people worried far too much and completely unnecessarily. Not only about things over which they had no control, but things that probably would not even happen at all!

As opposed to worrying over all the possibilities that may or may not later arrive, Zack had become convinced the most advantageous path through life usually involved initially choosing from no more than two or three basic and immediate options. Until that choice was made, it was wasted energy to worry about the myriad events that might transpire much later.

No-one knew what was going to happen in the future. The choice to be made was here and now, based on whatever was deemed important to that decision making process at the time. New choices made themselves obvious as time went by, with the process then being repeated. Even if a decision appeared retrospectively to have been the wrong one, it still didn't mean it was the wrong choice at the time it was made.

Basically life-choices were, in Zack's opinion, very much a dynamic process, fluid and changeable like the weather. To presume a long term forecast could be imposed let alone enforced was not in the least practicable, or even desirable. Chaos-theory opportunities for synchronicity could easily be missed if one's life rigidly followed a premeditated game-plan.

Zack had been making those decisions for over eight years now. Ever since leaving Australia, firstly for England and then for the world. He had developed an intuitive sense of when change was near, and moreso, in which direction he should jump. The fluidity of his decisions had increasingly become second-nature, and he'd only lost what he felt was his natural rhythm, two or three times.

Having travelled through more than thirty countries, sometimes working and sometimes not, his choice of lifestyle had made him an all-rounder when it came to employment. A top-notch bartender, this skill usually afforded him a most enjoyable entrée to any new country. It promised a good time whilst working and always generated wide-ranging acquaintances, who more often than not connected him to other opportunities.

For the fun of it, he'd recently compiled a C.V. that reflected his actual life, as opposed to the mostly fictitious one he maintained for future serious employment, should that ever become necessary. He had picked watermelons in northern Australia and grapes in the south of France. Selling time-share had been the name of the game in the Canary Islands, whilst in Goa he'd hawked silver jewellery, clothing and other artefacts collected further north.

Bars in Tokyo, New York, London, Perth, Tel Aviv, Koh Samui, Paros, Ibiza, and Capetown had all been the worse for his departure, and now here he was, first-mate of a thirty-three metre top-sail schooner in Eilat.

What Zack loved most was the unpredictability of his life, the challenge of continually adapting to new circumstances. The changes in environment, climate, culture and language kept him sharp, and among the many rewards were the amazing friendships that often developed under conditions neither person could previously have imagined.

Solid friendships grew between travellers far more quickly than between people in conventional environments. And they inevitably had a depth and intensity that would otherwise take years to develop in the normality Zack had increasingly come to think of as stagnation. This was, he thought, because travellers understood their time together was limited.

Accordingly, they invariably dispensed with meaningless small talk and trivia in exchange for some up-front no-bullshit discourse, often revealing in a few meetings, more about their real selves than they perhaps ever would to the folks back home. The inevitable downside of having made these brilliant friends was then leaving them behind. It had over the years however, become less surprising to Zack to cross paths with some of them again, and in the oddest places.

These apparently freak reunions always caused Zack to wonder about the degree to which a higher force was operating. In some cases, the nature as well as the timing of these renewed acquaintances was simply so extraordinary he could not continue to think of them as mere coincidences.

During such reunions he typically became more proactive regarding prospects for collaboration with that person, just to explore whether their combination had potential for more complex rewards. The longer he travelled, the greater reason he had been given to believe in karma. And experience had already proved to him the benefits of mining unexpected reunions to the full.

Three

"Arr ye ginna pass tha' thing aroond innyteem todeey, or mibbeh we beh niddin ano'rh?"

The thick Glaswegian accent of Robbo, *L'Chaim's* third male crew-member, always brought a smile to Zack's face. It forever reminded him of the comedian Billy Connolly. He took another hit from the joint before passing it on.

"Ye've bin thirr beforr, am ah reet?" Robbo asked.

Everyone had tuned in now.

"I was in Tokyo for a year, but eventually retired hurt," Zack replied.

"My God!" Simona exclaimed, her eyebrows raised. "What happened to you?"

"Relax Simona," Zack laughed. "It wasn't that bad. I managed a pretty wild bar for a long time. I just kept going for a bit longer than I should have, that's all."

"How do you mean?" This from Claudia, their German crewmember.

Zack paused for a moment, wondering how to explain things.

"Tokyo … well, Roppongi actually … is just the craziest fucking place I've ever been. If you can imagine getting drunk and taking drugs … coke, acid, ecstasy, fantasy, whatever … night after night after night for a year, then maybe you'll begin to understand where I'm coming from. There's just all sorts of wild shit going on over there. You're sleeping four maybe five hours a night, working seventy hours a week, doing lines for fun at first, and then just to get through the night. Life becomes very very different. People are in a pretty special mindset when they hit Roppongi to party … wild … animalistic. The drinks go down, the drugs kick in, and suddenly you've got people fucking in the toilets. People are getting naked, you've got topless girls on the bar, the music's pumping and the place just spins out of control and keeps on going. I've really never seen anything like it … not anywhere … not ever."

"Fucking awesome!" Hans was on his feet. "Sign me up while I'm young and horny," he whooped, doing a little dance around the deck.

"Hate to burst your bubble Hans, but that's not quite the report I got from Limor the other night," Sofia quipped.

Hans abruptly stopped his capering and sat down, muttering something about too many tequila slammers.

Sofia wanted to know more. "What did you actually mean by 'retiring hurt'?"

Zack hesitated. Then pressed on.

"Put it this way, my Swedish princess. When I left that place you would not have recognised me. I weighed ten kilos less. I had big black bags under my eyes and a complexion like the side of this boat. I looked like some sort of vampire AIDS victim. Man, I was ill, ill, ill. It took me about six months travelling and fitness training after I left to get myself *halfway* back to normal."

"The place sounds deadly," said Simona.

Zack looked at her in surprise.

"That's true, actually. It can be pretty scary. A lot of people can't handle the madness. Some completely lose the plot. They can't walk the tightrope between Roppongi illusion and Roppongi reality, and fall off somewhere along the way. It's usually not a pretty sight."

Simona simply nodded her reply. The mood of the group had sombred. Zack continued.

"I've seen hostesses so hungry for money they turn into big-money hookers. I saw drugs turn a sixteen year old model who'd hardly touched alcohol before, into a walking nightmare in the space of three months. She literally had a psychotic break. Her agency had to hunt her down, have her arrested, and forcibly ship her back to her parents. There are con-artists, thieves, and all types of gangsters on the scene. Problem is, for first-timers, none of this is very obvious. But believe me, everyone's got an agenda. Everyone's got something to sell, and if you walk around with your eyes closed for long, you wind up with a pretty hard-core reality check."

Zack stopped. Everyone now looked more than a little shell-shocked.

So, hand on heart, he added with mock seriousness, "However, as a spokesman for the Japanese Department of Tourism, I have to say the only bad things that happened to me, I did to myself."

A couple of laughs defused the tension that Zack's Roppongi-scape had created.

Simona broke the silence. "I thought the Japanese were all supposed to be really honest and polite."

Zack laughed as he realised why his description had left her confused.

"Most of the people I'm talking about aren't Japanese, Simona, but even so, what you said is more the exception in Tokyo than the rule anyway."

"Oh ... right," she replied uncertainly.

Zack wondered just what sort of twisted picture she had of the place in her mind's-eye now. Suddenly, he decided he'd had enough for the night. It was too difficult to explain Roppongi to anyone who hadn't been there, and he didn't know why he'd tried. To know it, you really had to live it.

Standing up, he unhitched his hammock to move it to the bow section of the deck where he slept.

"Let me bid you beautiful people goodnight. In my absence I guess it would only be fair to wish you good luck with any intelligent conversation."

He turned, dodging a couple of missiles and a lot of 'fuck-offs', before there was a final question from Robbo.

"Ah ... Zack, leek ... afore ye gooweh ... ah wis woonderin' how ahd goo fir wirkin oova thir in Japan ye knoow. Wha' deeyeh rickin?"

Zack turned, with a disbelieving shake of his head. "Are you serious? Mate, you've got *no* fucking chance."

"An'whiy wud tha' be?" Robbo retorted, suddenly defensive in front of the group.

"Just *listen* to yourself, for Christ's sake," Zack disdainfully shot back.

He watched Robbo's stoned expression morph from defensiveness into anger.

Remaining silent, Zack deliberately let the pause infuse the moment with even more tension, whilst scornfully continuing to shake his head.

Just before Robbo nearly exploded with indignation, Zack spoke.

"Who would understand you?"

He added a big grin and then hightailed it for the other end of the yacht.

Four

Zack was star-gazing. The sky was unimaginably clear, and in the couple of hours since leaving the group, he'd seen two shooting stars and a satellite.

Sofia appeared noiselessly in front of him. "You got room for me in there?"

Zack, genuinely surprised, auto-cued.

"You didn't suffer any permanent damage last time, did you Princess?"

"I hope not," she replied ambiguously, as she slid into the hammock beside him. Her hand snaked around Zack's waist and when she turned her head, their faces were close. The evening was bright enough for her to see his face. Shifting slightly, he turned his full gaze on her.

"You're thinking about coming to Japan, aren't you?" he said quietly.

Fuck, how did he do that? It was so irritating the way he read her. Couldn't she have just come to fuck him?

"I don't know," she said evenly. "Do you think it's a good idea?"

Zack pursed his lips thoughtfully.

"What I think is, you'd take Tokyo by storm. *If* you went for the right reasons and were a bit careful. Take me for example. I'm going for the money. That's my prime focus. Sure, I'll have a good time along the way, but I'll come out of it with enough pocket-money for another couple of years' travelling. A lot of people forget their priorities once they're in the Roppongi mix, and good fortune has a habit of changing on them when they do. Basically, if you stick to your priorities and stay sharp, you'll do okay."

Sofia paused only a beat. "I just want to make some bucks, really. And maybe see a bit of Japan. You know me pretty well now. Got any tips?"

Zack raised his eyebrows and smiled. "Nothing else really, sweetheart. You'll figure it out quickly enough. But I can hook you up over there. All you need to do is let me know when you're coming."

She squeezed his arm gently. "Yeah, I know … thanks." A moment's silence, then, "When are you going anyway?"

Zack hesitated. "Sunday."

Her shocked reaction told him he might as well have punched her.

"But …" Sofia faltered, unable to find words. "But Uri …"

Zack cut in. "I gave him two weeks' notice last week." He looked away; he already knew he didn't want to see Sofia's reaction.

Sofia could not believe what she was hearing. She jacked herself up on one elbow.

"And the rest of us, Zack? When were you going to let *us* know?" she hissed. A few seconds passed.

Then, very matter of factly, Zack said, "Sometime this week, I guess."

"Jesus, you are un-fucking-believable!" Sofia's voice shook with anger. "Why do you have to be so fucking *cool* about everything? Doesn't it mean *shit* to you that we've been on this boat together for the last nine months?"

Zack turned again, to face her.

Astonished, she saw his eyes glistening with tears. Somehow, she had reached him. Sofia was ashamed to feel a small thrill. Witnessing Zack lose some control was not new, but those other occasions had been anger or frustration. *This* was something new. She could *feel it*. His distress was palpable, his voice hesitant.

"Christ Sofia, it's hard enough to leave at all, without you giving me shit about it. If anyone was going to understand, I thought it might be you." Zack looked away again, and blinked a couple of times. "I ... I didn't want to upset anyone before I absolutely had to. It's difficult to ... I just want to remember this place the way it is, not for what it sort of changes into *because* I'm leaving."

Could this be the Zack she knew, fumbling for words, eyes pleading for her support? In her excitement, Sofia checked herself before saying anything. Then it was too late. They were kissing, words suddenly superfluous.

She rolled herself over him and quickly pulled her skimpy sundress off her shoulders. Zack entered her to the side of her G-string, the hammock not allowing much opportunity for further disrobing. Straddling him, her feet firmly on the deck, Sofia rode him savagely, grinding her breasts into his naked chest. The hammock's ropes twisted and strained in protest at their violence. Kissing him hard on the mouth, she pulled his tongue inside her, then smothered him with her spectacular breasts. His face buried in her soft skin, Zack thrust harder into her. Sofia gasped as he took one of her nipples into his mouth. He clamped his hands hard around her arse, and the angle of their bodies sent waves of pleasure rocking through her, as he ground her clitoris against his groin. Her orgasm hit like a freight train. She felt his body jerking, and distantly realised he too, was exploding inside her. They pulled themselves harder into each other and held position, revelling in the ecstasy coursing through their bodies.

"Jesus Fucking Christ," Zack breathed, after a few moments desperately hunting for oxygen. "Where did *that* come from?"

Sofia hardly heard him. She was wondering how long the whole awesome thing had taken. Great sex was like being caught up in some kind of vortex. It ripped through you, distorting normal perception of time and space, until you emerged at the other end and vainly tried to make some sense of the maelstrom you'd just survived. She couldn't remember the last time that had *really* happened to her. The times they'd had sex before had been good, really good in fact, but the intensity wasn't even close to what had just happened here. She supposed it was proof of just how much of mind-blowing sex is purely mental. Intensity of emotion, she thought. Accept no substitute.

"Ouch," she yelped.

Zack had pinched her, hard, on the arse. "You're alive then ... that's promising."

"Yeah," she said. "I am. I'm probably as alive as I've been for a while now. What about you?"

Zack's body slackened. He remained silent, as if taken over by some striking thought he could not broach openly with Sofia. Tonight's encounter stirred something altogether too complicated. What was going on here ... really? He knew it was pointless to tell her how he felt, especially now: previous experience had proved honesty only brought heartache. Telling the truth *now* would only made it harder to extract himself from an even stickier situation *later*. Just as it was vital to be candid at times, it was necessary to be guarded at others. He looked at her. His stomach churned. This would be hard work. How could he deny Sofia the truth right now? It seemed there was genuinely no escape for him this time.

He caught her gaze, eye to eye. "Sofia, we both know it doesn't get much better than that. Jesus! You know me enough by now."

She stayed silent.

"I live for moments like that." Was this an admission he would later regret?

He told himself to shut up before it sounded as if he was justifying himself, justifying the encounter, justifying the sex. But he was about to blunder on, when Sofia cut him off disparagingly.

"So life is just a series of *worthwhile moments*, is that it Zack?"

Zack sighed wearily. "Not usually Princess. Only if you're lucky."

He had reverted to his reflexive ripostes. He knew he was on a loser now, whatever happened. This wagon was in motion.

"And I'm supposed to feel grateful for being part of one of them, is that it Zack? Hi everybody, I'm Sofia Lyndstrom and my claim to fame is I was once royally fucked over in one of Zack Morrissey's *worthwhile moments*."

She was supremely angry now, and the fucked up truth of the matter was that Zack knew he could only have dodged it by telling her some bullshit fairy tale. Wasn't life a bitch sometimes? Couldn't people just enjoy special moments if and when they came? What did she fucking want from him anyway? He had now had altogether enough.

"What the fuck do you want me to say Sofia? Just tell me so I can make up some bullshit you'd be happy to hear, and then get some goddamn sleep."

She launched herself out of the hammock like a scalded cat, seething.

"Save your breath, Zack. I'm leaving anyway. Hypocrites like you make me fucking sick. *Zack Morrissey ... global adventurer ... risk-taker.*" She spat out the mocking insult.

"You're so full of shit," she continued bitterly. "One day maybe you'll grow enough guts to take a *real* risk."

Grabbing up her sundress and bikini-top, she turned away before he could see her tears. She pulled on her clothes, ran lightly along the deck, up the gangway and onto the marina. Zack watched until she disappeared into the shadows on the beach. There was no point in going after her. He had nothing she'd want to hear. He checked his watch. It was two o'clock. Christ, the crew had to be up in five hours! Fuck the world for the time being. He needed some sleep.

The funny thing about sleep is that when you need it most, it often doesn't come to the party. Zack went through his relaxation exercises three times but had to concede defeat. His mind was racing. This time she'd genuinely got to him, he thought. She was really under his skin. But why? What was bothering him? Was she right about his being gutless? Was his compartmentalised approach to dealing with the inevitable emotional baggage of travelling a front, a sort of pathetic self-justification for his own emotional cowardice?

Goddamnit! He really didn't need this train of thought right now! How was he supposed to know what the answer was? Did she want a declaration of love, expect him to commit to her and then whisk them both away to some fairytale life in Japan? God, some things could get fucked up quick-time.

"Was that another private joke, big guy?" Zack asked the heavens. Jesus! Why was he so bothered about it? With Sofia he'd followed all his rules right from the start, beginning with 'never hold out false hope' ... 'never say I love you' ... blah blah blah. He'd never promised her *anything* ... hadn't even slept with her for months until tonight's little stunt, and now she was busting *his balls*, after talking her way into *his bed ... again!* Well, fuck that for a joke, he thought. He'd been nothing but straight with her. If she wanted to act like a prima-donna until he was gone, she could have the stage all to herself.

* * *

Paradoxically, Zack was first to wake in the morning, and with a surprisingly clear head to boot. He couldn't have had more than three hours' sleep though, he thought gloomily, knowing he would suffer for this before the day was over. At least they had a full day of cruises ahead; another day of maintenance would have been insufferable. He could have done without the additional night cruise though. He put a third teaspoon of coffee and five sugars into his mug, a huge thing featuring Brutus chasing Popeye and Olive-Oyl around the enamel.

Russians, he remembered, his mind returning to the night cruise. He'd have to get the crew trashed for that, otherwise he'd pass out from sheer boredom and tiredness. This train of thought was interrupted by someone struggling up the galley ladder. Struggling was the key word alright. Sofia's head appeared out of the stairwell; it did not appear to be one of her better days.

"*God-morgon Svenska flicka,*" Zack commented cheerily.

Sofia clutched her head, and swayed towards the kettle muttering grimly. "This ... is *all your fault*, you bastard."

Zack assumed correctly, that after having left the *L'Chaim* last night she must have sought solace in a few drinks at *Mastoolim*. Instantly, he felt a stab of pity for her.

"Sit down for a sec Sof, and I'll get you a kick-start," he offered. Zack was sure however, that she wouldn't want to give in so easily.

She glared at him, angrier still because she currently didn't have the strength to argue.

"Okay. Bastard. Thanks. I appreciate it." With a groan, she sank into the nearest sun-lounge.

The 'kick-start' hang-over cure was now legend on the marina. Zack had introduced it inadvertently when he'd made it for himself one morning. The crew's curiosity ensured its fame had quickly spread. There was even a variation of it, predictably named the 'Zack-Attack', now on sale in *Mastoolim*. It was composed of equal amounts of Baileys, Kahlua, and Scotch whisky, combined with a small amount of milk and generous quantities of coffee, sugar and crushed-ice. Shaken or blended to death, it was then either sipped, or knocked back in a few sharp gulps.

When used medicinally however, it also incorporated a couple of crushed Optalgins, the very strong analgesic tablets originally developed for the Israeli Defence Force. If Optalgin was good enough for the IDF, it was good enough for Zack. As long as the suffering hangover victim held it all down, it had never failed. If Uri knew anything about it, he'd probably fire the lot of them.

An hour later, Zack was the recipient of some genuine gratitude from Sofia. Her recovery was sufficient that she even apologised for the night before. Zack responded in kind, acknowledging he'd probably deserved some of it. Then they agreed to put it aside. What a relief, Zack thought. His last week would've been hellish if Sofia and he were warring.

He winced, as a stentorian '*Bokker-tov chaverim shelli*' assaulted his ears. Uri strode up the gangway onto the yacht, reminding all within earshot that their working day had most certainly commenced.

Five

Zack was seated on the aisle.

The stewardess name-badged Anna turned to him with a smile and another Jack Daniels with dry ginger ale.

"Do you always have that much ice?" she queried.

Zack shifted in his seat and smiled back at her. She was flirting!

He replied, "It's an old habit now. I'm used to it. What's your poison?"

"I'm a Margarita girl." She paused before adding, "When I'm in the mood."

Zack studied her eyes intently, searching for something. He enjoyed observing people, and as there had so far been nothing more diverting on this flight, he already knew the rest of her was pretty interesting. There it was! A slight, downward tilt of her pupils in response to his enquiring gaze. Almost immediately she looked straight at him again, a conscious correction of her previous involuntary revelation.

Suppressing another smile he asked, "Are you stopping over in Tokyo, or going straight on?"

With a hint of mischief, she continued their eye contact. "Actually, a few of us have got the weekend off before heading back to London. We haven't a clue what we're doing though."

"If you like, I could show you around. I know the nightlife inside out. At least I did a couple of years ago," Zack replied. "Hopefully there'll be a few surprises for me this time as well," he added.

"You work in Tokyo?" she asked curiously.

"I ran a bar in Roppongi. That's probably what I'll end up doing again this time, but I'll have to check out the scene first. A lot can change in two years."

She nodded for him to continue.

"I'll be in there tomorrow night anyway. Why don't I give you the details, and if you want, we can go walk the wild side."

She smiled at that. "You could mix me a special Margarita."

"I think … I might enjoy that," Zack replied slowly, bathing her in the full beam of his amused gaze. "But first, the formalities." He indicated her badge. "You're obviously Anna. My name's Zack, Zack Mo…"

She cut him off. "Morrissey," she said, with an impish grin. "Yes, I know."

Zack scribbled a mud-map of Bongoes on the sick bag, and handed it to her.

"Very classy," she smiled.

Until that moment, he hadn't been absolutely sure she'd come. Now he was.

"Tomorrow night it is then," he said.

"Sounds good," she replied, and walked off down the aisle.

Zack eased back into his seat, sipping his JD thoughtfully. It appeared his first weekend back in Tokyo certainly wouldn't be boring. Perhaps even as full-on as his departure from Eilat? Surely not; his last week in Eilat had been a blast. Thanks to Hans, bless him. Once the word of Zack's departure was out, Hans had made sure the party in *Mastoolim* would be one to remember.

It had turned into an absolutely epic bender that didn't stop until Zack boarded the bus for Tel Aviv at two o'clock the following afternoon. It began innocently enough, with mid-afternoon beers at a few other pubs: The Underground, The Yacht Pub, The Three Monkeys, so he could say his goodbyes around town. Everyone then migrated to *Mastoolim,* where they dropped some pills.

At about one, they'd all headed to the Roxy, a cave-like club which Zack, Hans and others had made their own. Much later, as soon as he'd felt the unmistakable first 'reality nudge' of the E comedown, Zack shared some acid around, and the night continued sashaying wildly around them. It seemed everyone turned up at the Roxy that night, and the music was great, which made a huge difference. Oddly, many people were saying, "See you in Tokyo." Uncharacteristically, even Uri had put in an appearance and wished him well – an unprecedented demonstration of skipperly esteem.

Zack smiled to himself, remembering the pleasure Uri's attendance had given him.

At dawn, the stayers had moved to Tzion Beach Café for a last few joints. A spectacular sunrise heralded yet another perfect day. Eilat truly was one of the few places that looked better than its postcards. Mesmerised by the LSD-enhanced colours of the bay and mountains, Zack didn't immediately notice the white lines Avi had expertly cut onto the table in front of him.

"Is a goodbye present," Avi had said, in his heavy Israeli accent.

"*Toda raba,*" Zack replied gratefully.

Avi ceremoniously bowed his head, then added, "*Do-itashi-mashite.*"

Zack laughed in surprise. It meant, 'You're welcome' in Japanese. Avi had winked at him, and said he'd probably see him in Japan soon, as he had to visit some friends there on business. The coke was good stuff. Really perfect timing. Zack was surprised it had materialised at all. It was quite rare to find it in Tel Aviv, let alone idyllic Eilat.

The sunrise prompted the last of his friends to say their final goodbyes; they headed back to start their day's toil on the boats. Afterwards, Zack and Avi had chatted for ages, drinking cold Goldstar beers, while watching the bay come to life.

It had been a very weird feeling watching the guys go out in the dinghy without him for the de-mooring, and a strange sadness and sense of loss washed through him when the *L'Chaim* set sail for the day trip to Coral Island. As the yacht disappeared, Zack felt like an amputee. He had changed direction irrevocably: there was no going back. A sort of philosophical melancholy had overtaken him, and he couldn't remember what he and Avi talked about for the next few hours.

He barely remembered getting on the bus, or the five hour journey to Tel Aviv – just vague images of the Negev swirling by and some *Charedim* who'd regarded him as they might a Martian. Those weird looking fanatics had shouted at him in his dreams, or maybe they actually had been shouting at him. He would never know, for his mind and body had collectively shut down, enforcing an involuntary period of recovery.

He'd spent a couple of days recovering in Tel Aviv, chilling out on Banana Beach with another circle of Israeli friends he hadn't seen for a while. Knowing his ex-girlfriend Nurit was out of the country, he'd also found time to pay his respects to her family. They loved him, and he them, which was another of the reasons the break with her had been difficult. Well, for him anyway. He good-naturedly suffered their abuse for his rudeness in not having contacted them earlier. Then he kissed them goodbye, and caught the plane to London.

Ahhh, London, he thought. He loved London in the summer. No other city changed its character so completely for the better simply due to the sun's blessing. Festivals, concerts, beer-gardens, parties: it was a fantastic vibe. Londoners were utterly different at this time of year, and he wondered if science would ever notice it, let alone explain it.

Theories about Vitamin D deficiency just didn't cut it, he reckoned. The summer recovery was too swift. It had to be solely the grim, unrelenting miserableness of the preceding weather that was responsible. Grey, Grey and more Grey ... then Wet then Cold ... then Black, Wet, Cold and Windy. Fuck-all to look forward to in that lot, he thought.

When 'Grey, Damp and Freezing' is all you can expect for months on end, life has reached a new low. Not the case in July however, and it was a pity he'd only had a week to spare. The inexorably mounting total on his credit-card had given him little choice in the matter, he reflected wryly.

He wondered which of his Eilat compadres would materialise in Tokyo. Sofia was a certainty. Hans too. Robbo was at least a probable. Simona too, he thought; all the drug talk would strengthen her resolve to visit. Iris? Maybe not ... no diving. Whoever arrived, observing how they coped with the place would be interesting. Their traveller inhabitants aside, it was difficult to imagine two environments less similar than Roppongi and the Eilat marina.

His situation with Sofia was unresolved. She had taken him to dinner the night before the party. They fucked each other senseless on the beach afterwards. She had a curiosity now that wouldn't go away. Zack wasn't sure whether it was mainly directed at him, or Japan. Probably both, he thought. In any case, it seemed there was unfinished business between them. He looked at his watch. 12.30 a.m. Japan time. He'd be landing in seven and a half hours. Then he'd have to run around like a maniac and find some temporary accommodation: not always easy.

Time to catch some serious Zeds. He struggled with sleeping on planes, so this time had come prepared. In his pocket were some 2mg Rohypnols, one of the strongest tranquillisers on the market. They were generally used by travellers who badly needed to sleep after drug-fuelled partying endeavours. He'd decided that combined with Jack Daniels, they would probably do the trick for the flight. He notified a steward he did not want to be woken for anything, swallowed a tablet and the last of the JD, put his seat back, and commenced a series of relaxation exercises.

*   *   *

The clanking of a breakfast trolley woke him. He stretched slowly, testing the functionality of his limbs before looking around. His watch informed him it was 5.55 a.m. Japan time. He felt a bit groggy, but that was normal after a Rowy, so he dug around in the seat pocket for the plastic pack of orange juice he'd previously secreted for just this moment. It wasn't cold, but it was wet and tasty, which was what his furry mouth needed right now. He would definitely feel better after a few coffees. The caffeine habit he'd developed on the *L'Chaim* didn't look like deserting him anytime soon.

He looked across at the old man in the window seat. The man was still unconscious, a trail of spittle drooling from his mouth onto his shirtfront. Watching its cohesive, languid motion made Zack vaguely nauseous, and he was grateful for the empty seat between them. Pointlessly, he checked his watch again, wanting the flight to be over. Deciding there was time to freshen up before the breakfast cart reached him, he retrieved his toiletry bag and ambled to the back of the plane. And there was the delectable Anna.

"Well, you're a sight for sore eyes," she commented brusquely. Somewhat annoyingly, she looked quite as fresh as when Zack had last seen her. It was actually difficult to imagine her elfin features looking tired, or for that matter disagreeable in any way at all.

Zack regarded her with a mixture of apathy and reproach.

"It's only fair to let you know, that should the misfortune of seeing me first thing in the morning ever befall you again, this is probably as good as I'll ever look."

She held up her hands in mock horror, proclaiming, "Oh my God, I've been warned."

"It's just that I'd hate to mislead you in any way Anna, especially at such an early stage of our relationship," Zack responded silkily, tongue firmly in cheek.

"You're so *considerate* Mr. Morrissey. I don't know what to say," she purred in response.

Mutually amused by their repartee, they hadn't realised they were the cause of a queue.

Zack indicated the waiting public. "I'd better get in there and clean myself up, otherwise they mightn't let me in the country, and ..."

"And that would be a tragedy," she finished for him, squeezing past and gently brushing her breasts against his arm.

I have to agree with you Anna, Zack thought, watching her figure undulate between the rows of seated passengers. Looking forward to the prospect of undulating his way into her, he turned and stooped into the tiny piss-closet.

Half an hour later, shaved, washed, breakfasted, and in a clean shirt, Zack felt very much on top of things. There were two good things about Rohypnol. One, you slept. Two, you slept deeply. As soon as the initial grogginess disappeared, you were fresh and ready to roll.

His thoughts were still on Anna. With increasing maturity and experience, Zack had refined his sexual philosophy to a point where, usually, he didn't really care whether he got it on with a particular girl or not.

The primary difference was that in his younger days he would have slept with some chick just for the sake of it, the 'nothing better to do at the moment' principle applying. But these days he had nothing to prove to himself. Supremely comfortable in his own company, unless particularly interested, he was as likely to leave opportunities alone as follow them through.

This selective apathy, it seemed, now worked in his favour. Women could sense that what they did or thought with respect to him basically didn't bother him. This had the curious effect of making him the hunted rather than the hunter. He liked this role-reversal, enjoying the increased power it was possible to exercise from being entirely cognisant of his 'quarry' status. Years of travel and hospitality experience had made him expert at interpreting the myriad giveaways of facial expression, speech and body-language that his razor-sharp but disarmingly laid-back style of conversation so effectively elicited.

Zack recalled the only time in his life he had been in what he supposed must have been 'love'. Nurit. He shook his head at the memory. Their relationship had ended shortly before he'd left Tokyo last time. He had spent two solid years with her. She was a phenomenal woman. Sexy as hell, strong, spiritual, intelligent, independent. They had done some travelling together, and their bond had been intense. Two similar strong individuals. The highest highs, and the lowest lows, the much clichéd emotional rollercoaster.

They'd eventually split because she'd wanted the sort of freedom only a single state could offer. To travel wherever she wanted, whenever she wanted, with no compromises. His first trip to Japan had been with her, and during that year they'd loved and fought like crazy people. If a relationship survives both partners working nightlife in Roppongi, Zack thought, it can survive anything. So many beautiful people, so much temptation, jealousy and distrust. Throw in drugs, alcohol and hedonism: the hubble and bubble invariably brought trouble. Ironically, their relationship *had* survived Roppongi. She just wanted out at the end of it, so she'd fucked off back to Israel, then dropped out of sight somewhere in South-East Asia.

The break-up had been tough on him. He had struggled for the next six months. Nothing had seemed worth anything. Listless, demotivated and borderline depressed, he had finally got his shit together again in Nepal, refocused, and purged her from his system. He hadn't seen her since. For his own sanity, he was happy enough to keep it that way.

His attitude to women since then was cool, appraising, speculative, and ultimately distancing. For a while, some had needlessly suffered because of his angst, but he'd recognised this attitude as self-defeating, not to mention really bad karma, and summarily scrapped it. It had been the start of his behavioural code with respect to women, a code he believed had since served him well. Notwithstanding this, Sofia's recent fiery accusations had raised some unwelcome questions.

He snared another coffee as the breakfast cart made its final pass, and envisaged the next few hours. Task number one was to get into the country. Last time, he'd entered Japan on his British passport, then significantly over-stayed his three month visa before reporting himself to Immigration in order to leave the country.

He was fairly sure records of those 'over-stayers' were kept only for a year, but in any case, this time he was going in on his Australian passport, complete with a freshly authorised 'working holiday' visa. Once again he silently thanked his father for having organised the British passport for him a dozen years previously.

As a traveller, more passports meant more options, which could only ever be a good thing. He had to assume the entry was not going to be a problem.

Task number two was accommodation. Usually, travellers working in Japan lived in what were known as '*gaijin-houses*' or they shared rented apartments. Both types of accommodation were generally shoddy and cramped, with barely a vestige of privacy.

Occasionally, luckier people, usually pretty girls, talked their way into the spare bedrooms of ex-pat professionals' houses. These were much grander affairs, wholly subsidised by the employer, and as close as it was possible to get to Western-style housing in Japan.

Brokers, bankers and their like were often keen to get extra 'play-money' from a lodger for otherwise 'dead' rooms, or take in a hostess on the condition she did some general cleaning, and the hope she might ultimately perform a more intimate service. Regardless, Zack had to organise some almost certainly shitty short-term accommodation, while he assessed his longer-term options.

A nudge from his right startled him, and he looked over curiously.

"You've to put your belt on son," the old man rasped. "He's taking her down."

Zack smiled at the dated language, nodded, thanked the old fellow and complied. But he was curious. Impulsively, he asked, "What brings you to Tokyo, sir?"

"Drugs," came the wheezy response. He seemed to be smiling, even though he'd now launched into a coughing fit.

When he stopped, and in response to Zack's sustained quizzical expression, he added, "For me emphysema. Experimental treatment. What about you, why are you here?"

Without batting an eyelid, Zack replied, "Sex."

The old man raised one eyebrow dubiously. "Is that a fact? Well, I wish you luck, son."

"Likewise," Zack said.

It was the end of their conversation.

Six

The plane landed fifteen minutes early and without incident. Zack was at his presentable and charming best when he approached the girl at Immigration. He always chose a queue that ended at a young female officer, then affected a good-natured, slightly shy and self-deprecating manner. The only place he'd ever struck trouble, predictably enough, was security-conscious Israel. And that had been his own fault.

One of the senior officers had overheard him joking around in Hebrew, and this mistake cost him about forty-five minutes of additional questioning. How many times had he been to Israel? Was he Jewish? How long did he stay? Where did he go? What did he do? Who did he know? Why did he speak Hebrew? Blah blah blah. Although the interrogation had been a pain in the arse, he really loved Israel and given its brief and turbulent history, he could forgive their over-zealous paranoia when it came to national security.

Immigration was a breeze. No, he had not been to Japan before. Yes, he did know where he was staying. Yes, he did have documented financial backing. Would they like to see his letters of introduction to Nova, the English school he was interested in working for? Seconds later his passport was stamped 'working holiday', and he stepped through the gates for his second adventure in Japan.

Zack headed straight for the 'limousine bus' information bay. Turned out to be half an hour until the next run to ANA Hotel in *Akasaka*, the easiest and cheapest way to get to Roppongi. He waited in a little café, sipping what passed for iced coffee in Japan: a highball glass full of cold black coffee with a few lonely ice cubes, a tiny plastic pack of UHT creamer, and another tiny plastic pack of sugar syrup. Milk apparently had nothing to do with the concept. Zack had finally discovered that to get it to taste anywhere near the way he wanted, he needed an extra glass, extra ice, six creamers and six sugar syrups. He then poured half the coffee into the second glass and distributed the ice, creamer and sugar-syrup evenly.

Apart from this being how he enjoyed the coffee, he also got a kick out of the bemused, nervous reactions of the waiters as he made his bizarre requests, but who then watched in fascination as he carried out the ritual. Quickly looking up, he'd catch them all gawking. Making a crazy face, he'd grin like a lunatic, raise the glass and loudly say '*Kanpai!*' Usually the result would be an outburst of nervous looks and laughter followed by self-conscious scurrying around, as if by watching for too long, one risked infection.

This display illustrated a Japanese saying which particularly fascinated and appalled Zack. It translated something like, 'The nail that sticks out, must be hammered in.' This Orwellian perspective was perpetuated daily in many ways. 'Big Brother' was effectively anyone, and therefore everyone ... the system in general. Consequently any deviation from convention, the smallest expression of individuality was, for an average Japanese person, in the context of their own future, a potentially dangerous step. By extension, sameness equalled safety, and individuality equalled danger. Being in Tokyo really was like visiting another planet, Zack thought, because the Japanese as a race, were just *so* different.

Nurit had expressed it well in a letter to him once: 'I admire them as robots, but pity them as human beings.' Zack had still seen nothing to challenge the truth of that statement. The extent of their conformity was fascinating, their contradictions were baffling, their work ethic was incomprehensible, their misogyny was legendary, their racism was appalling, and their social ineptitude was staggering. If ever a nation was sexually and socially maimed, Zack thought, it was Japan.

With a few notable exceptions (language barriers notwithstanding), the only genuinely interesting and *open-minded* Japanese people he had met had been travellers (as opposed to tourists) outside Japan. Rare examples of Japanese youth, they were the recalcitrant nails, refusing to submit to the enormous pressure of the hammer of Japanese conformity.

Such audacity usually carried a heavy price. Dishonour, ostracism, reduced job opportunities and the possibility of being disowned were potential penalties for marching out of step with the rest of the country. Zack had only the utmost admiration for anyone who valued their individuality enough to risk these consequences.

He checked his watch: 8.37 a.m. One upside of their anal nature he reflected, was their obsession with punctuality. In Japan, if it ran, it ran on time. You could just about bet your life that his bus would pull out of Narita on the dot of 8.45. London Underground should be sent over here for a few pointers Zack thought grimly. Quaffing his second glass of coffee, he made a quick toilet stop before boarding the bus.

Traffic was surprisingly light, and fifty-five minutes later he was in the foyer of the five-star ANA Hotel. He had no intention of actually staying in the hotel, but they had a useful luggage-drop facility for users of the limousine-bus service. So, his main backpack safely in storage, Zack made a few phone-calls. The first was to Madden Corporation. Madden, a crazy forty-five year old Jew, professed himself American, but his frequent use of Hebrew army slang suggested a strong Israeli background.

He'd married a Japanese woman and lived in Tokyo for over fifteen years, right through the bubble economy of the eighties. He owned *gaijin-houses* and small apartments, all squalid, but cheap enough to appeal to the travelling market.

Madden was the archetypal bastard landlord, notoriously hard to contact when things went wrong, which they always did. Even the Israelis couldn't stand him. It seemed withholding rent and enforcing a face to face meeting was the only way to get to see him. Zack's memories of him were uniformly awful. He was hyperactive and childishly impulsive, with a swarthy, unkempt appearance, all of which was very much at odds with Japanese culture and unnerving to people with whom he did business. He was now loaded, but you'd never guess it.

Zack thought much of his demeanour contrived, but also suspected Madden was manic-depressive. He and Nurit had lived in one of Madden's apartments for about six months last time, before moving to a better place.

"*Moshi mosh* ... Madden Corporation," chirped a girl's voice on the other end of the line. She was probably one of his tenants getting a cheap deal for a few hours phone-work a day. Her job would be just taking endless messages for Madden to sift through later.

"Is Madden there?" Zack thought it was worth a try.

"No, he's out at the moment. Can I ask what it's regarding?"

Zack asked if they had any 'by the night' accommodation, and was told the minimum stay at any of the *gaijin-houses* they ran was one month. God, the guy was a money-hungry bastard.

"I want you to pass on a very important message to Madden," Zack added.

"Of course."

"Tell him he's fucked too many people over lately, and he's going to get hurt," Zack said. "He won't know where, he won't know when, but night-time will be dangerous for him. This is not a joke. Make sure he gets the message."

He hung up amid her protestations, grinning at the image of Madden looking nervously over his shoulder of an evening. Might make the guy think twice about being such a prick to people.

His second call was to Shunit, an Israeli girl working in the office of another landlord called Sasaki. After small talk and the welcome back stuff, he explained his accommodation needs. She was helpful, giving him contact details of a *gaijin-house* situated in the back-alleys of *Harajuku*, somewhere behind the *Kiddyland* toy store on *Omotesandō*. He was quite lucky, she said, because it was closing down, soon to be re-furbished as a porn-studio. In the meantime, they were taking guests at 1,800 yen a night, or about US$18. He should speak to an English guy called Mark.

Zack thanked her, adding he'd be in Bongoes after nine o'clock if she wanted to catch up. The room was super cheap for Tokyo, especially *Harajuku*. He was not overly enthusiastic about dragging his arse over to what was probably a rat-hole, but beggars couldn't be choosers and it would only be for a week or two. Besides, the location was unbeatable.

Omotesandō, was the Champs-Elysees of the very trendy *Harajuku* district. It ran more or less from *Yoyogi-Park* up to *Aoyama-Dori*, where it changed its name into something else. Zack had only ever heard that next section called 'Designer-Dori', in testament to the outrageous number of luxury-label boutiques that resided on it. *Omotesandō* was a wide boulevard, lined either side with a row of traditional 'cherry blossom' trees and crammed full of fascinating shops, boutiques and pseudo-bohemian art galleries and cafes. It was an area of privilege and wealth, a great place to hang out people-watching on Sundays.

Zack knew it was early. Most *gaijin* travellers in his scene in Tokyo worked nights and slept days, except models and English teachers. Mark, whoever he was, would probably have had fuck-all sleep, but Zack had no choice. He had to find out if there was a space available, so dialled the number. It rang for a long time. Finally, it was picked up by someone who sounded like they were talking through a wardrobe.

"Yeah, is Mark there, I'm calling from England, it's urgent," Zack said. He figured if Mark was there, that would get him out of bed and to the phone.

"MAA-AARK!" the girl screeched. "Someone from England."

Wincing, Zack jerked the phone away from his ear. He'd always hoped there was a special karmic debit which applied to people who chose not to move the phone away from their mouth before emitting primal noises at serious decibels.

He heard a lot of thumping and bumping in the background, then a voice.

"Allo ... ooziss?"

"Mark, sorry to ring so early, but I had no choice. I don't know why that chick said I was calling from England ... I asked for Mark from England. Anyway, I've just flown in, and my friend Shunit said to call you about a room. I'll probably only need it for a week or two."

"Aaah fuck ... yeah okay. We gotta cuppla spaces. You bin 'ere before?"

"What ... Japan?" Zack queried.

"Yeah."

"I used to run Bongoes back in '95."

"Really?"

Zack sensed a new respect in the response.

"Well, getchaself round 'ere anytime today and yer in."

"I'll see you in about an hour," Zack replied. "And thanks."

"Sawright," Mark said. "Seeya soon."

Zack hung up, leaned back in the luxurious armchair and yawned a half-smile. Fucking cockneys! The guy seemed alright though. Missions one and two accomplished. He was quite pleased with himself. Accommodation in Tokyo could be your worst nightmare. He'd been lucky again.

Looking outside and seeing it had turned into a sparkling day, he decided on a brief walkabout. He strolled up *Roppongi-Dori* towards its intersection with *Gaien-Higashi-Dori*. Known as *Roppongi Crossing*, it had the Almond coffee-shop on one corner, which was the main orientation and meeting point for anyone describing a nearby location, or coming to Roppongi.

The gigantic structure of the *Shuto Expressway* nearby towered about six storeys above *Roppongi-Dori*. Zack had been in Tokyo at the time of the *Kobe* earthquake. It had killed more than six thousand people, but he hadn't even known about it until his brother phoned from London to check he was okay. Apparently it had been all over world news. Zack didn't watch TV in Japan, just videos. He certainly didn't waste time fretting over the likelihood of impending natural disasters, although one of the quakes last time had scared him shitless.

He and Nurit had been asleep in the *gaijin-house* when it started. Generally, the tremors rumbled and shuddered for a few seconds, then stopped. Zack usually quite enjoyed them. Atypically, this one had woken them both up, and then decided to seriously rock their world. It was the real deal. The bed was shaking. Pictures fell off walls and toiletries off shelves. As it went on and on and on, he and Nurit huddled under the bed-covers, holding each other tightly. Zack had honestly thought it might be 'the big one' and that his short life could well be over. Then it stopped as suddenly as it had begun. Just like that. Very. Fucking. Scary.

In that sort of terror-vacuum, with Dali-esque time distortion, it was difficult to be sure, but Zack reckoned the quake must have lasted for at least forty-five seconds from the time they'd woken up. Since then, Zack had always envisaged the huge concrete pillars of the *Shuto Expressway* crumbling, and the whole thing sliding sideways, toppling over into nearby buildings like some sort of huge drunken snake. It would happen one day, the big one in Tokyo, and it was believed that over a hundred thousand people would die. Zack could only hope neither he nor his friends would be there to experience it.

During this cheery mental segue, Zack found himself surprised to realise just how much he was enjoying the sensation of being back in Tokyo. Paradoxically, even though the Japanese approach to life couldn't be more diametrically opposed to his own, he felt completely comfortable, relaxed and at home here.

Probably some of the reason for this was their predictability. On the whole, he had a pretty good grasp of how they thought, and additionally, the Japanese were often intimidated by foreigners. Sometimes physically, but more importantly on a mental level, precisely because *they didn't know* what the 'crazy *gaijin*' might say or do next.

A further reason for his easy state of mind was the large number of travellers working in Roppongi at any one time. Apart from the wankers and wannabes, who were easy to weed out, he'd met some amazing people last time, and they'd had a blast. By the end though, he'd really been ready to leave. He'd been completely Tokyo-ed out, and didn't intend to return anytime soon. Everyone had told him he would be back, but he hadn't believed them. He'd been wrong. Tokyo was like that.

Roppongi had always seemed a strange and somewhat disquieting place to him during the day, when it was undeniably ugly and dirty-looking, a dormant but hungry vampire waiting for night to fall so feeding could commence. Under its preferred cover of darkness however, Roppongi shone as brightly as a fresh-faced Vegas showgirl, and had many times the allure.

There was a Japanese term for small-time betting operations, which translated as 'money-drinkers'. Zack thought the word, whatever it was, most apt for Roppongi. A few restaurants and cafes opened during the day to cater for tourists and office-workers, but most of it didn't show any sign of life until after six in the evening. He turned left at the crossing towards Tokyo Tower, an uninspiring replica of the Eiffel Tower. Originality counts for a lot, Zack thought. To him, that tower fully epitomised the Japanese ideology and approach. They were great replicators, but rarely made any bold masterstrokes themselves.

Marvelling at the number of sinister-looking crows in the vicinity, he crossed to the other side of the road and reversed direction. Nothing seemed strikingly different to when he'd left, but by day it was pretty much impossible to tell. The bar business was nothing if not fickle. New looks, new concepts, new music, new girls and new customers made for a constant state of flux. It was rare for any one venue to remain consistently popular. In this respect, Bongoes was one of the few exceptions. Since its inception around six years previously, it had maintained a popularity that was the envy of other Roppongi bars.

The reason was in fact fairly simple. Good bar design, but moreso, people like Zack. The owners consistently picked good people. Real people, with intelligence, personality, charm and wit. The all-important staff of Bongoes was now a sort of diaspora ... an extended global family whose members typically arrived for a work stint between travel jaunts. These days it was uncommon for Bongoes to need to recruit a 'virgin' employee.

Zack stopped briefly, leaned forward and peered into the gloom of the Bongoes window. He wondered how many cockroaches were crawling about in there; they ran rampant all over Roppongi during the summer months. Then he stepped back again. New neon sign in the window, more photos on the walls, but otherwise it looked the same. He smiled. If it ain't broke, why fix it? One of the owners, an English guy called Steve, knew Zack was due to arrive, and Zack was hopeful of catching up with him later in the evening. In the meantime though, he would give Victor a call.

Zack had helped Victor, a Russian, last time by pointing him in the direction of a job at a newly opened strip club called 'Cloud Nine', whose defining edge was that nearly all the dancers were *gaijins*. This had not been done before in Tokyo. So recently, Zack had not been too surprised to hear that the concept club had since borne four offspring, but *had* been very surprised to learn that not only was Victor still in Tokyo, but was now a major power-broker in the company's complex web of management. It would be good to see him, not to mention useful to pick his brains. Zack got his backpack from storage and jumped in a cab to *Harajuku*.

"*Kiddyrando onegaishimasu*," he commanded in Jap-lish, confident the driver would be familiar with the giant toy-store on *Omotesandō*. It was certainly easier than giving step by step instructions, Zack thought.

"*Kiddyrando ... ah ... kiddyrando. Hai hai*," came the response, and Zack was on his way.

Seven

Zack located the *gaijin-house* quickly, and immediately met a few of the occupants who were lounging around in the mid-morning sun on the veranda. Shep was a chef from Sydney, and currently worked at the trendy Las Chicas eatery just up the road.

Yitzhak was an Israeli didgeridoo player and '*basta*-worker'.

Beth was Canadian, and working as an English teacher for Nova, the expensive multi-branch English-school Zack had used as part of his immigration patter.

Zack saw Mark before Mark saw him, and could not believe his eyes.

"Hey you evil East-End scumfuck!" he yelled.

Mark turned quickly, saw Zack and burst into laughter. Jumping the last few steps, he wrestled Zack to the ground and almost dragged them both off the porch.

They sat staring disbelievingly and joyously at each other for a moment. Mark wasn't quite as tall as Zack, but probably weighed about the same. His hair was bleached blonde, and dark, dangerous eyes flashed out of an over-tanned face. He'd been a regular at a bar Zack had part-owned back in London's Earl's Court years ago, and they'd quickly become good friends. It seemed a lifetime later, and now here he was again! It was amazing, Zack thought. What karmic twist had brought him crashing back into Mark?

"Fuck, if I'd known it was you, I'd have rung even earlier," Zack quipped.

"You fuckin' worthless shitsack! If I'd known it was you I'd 'ave stayed in me fuckin' bed," Mark gasped breathlessly.

"What, and missed a call all the way from home?" Zack parried, with a chuckle.

"I told you he said he was calling from England," Beth said self-righteously.

"You are still a right fuckin' bastard no doubt," Mark replied, simultaneously acknowledging Beth's comment with a nod. "Less go get a coffee 'n' pass the guff."

"Can I at least get my stuff inside first?" Zack protested. "I've got to make a phone-call as well."

"Yeahh yeah yeah," Mark complained. "You're juss like an old woman."

Zack ambled across to the public phone in the lobby and dialled, while Mark stashed his bag in a room somewhere.

"Victor," came the answer.

"Ahh, you're just a Cold War fucking refugee. You wouldn't know your arse from your elbow, would you?" Zack responded.

"Zack, it is you! You are a dirty mongrel bastard, this is right yes?"

"Oh, I must have taught you well, Vic. Have a guess where I am right now?"

"Well, maybe Israel, maybe London, maybe fucking maybe? How I would know?" Victor chuckled. "Where are you?"

"Try *Harajuku*," Zack prompted.

"You are in *Harajuku*," Victor repeated uncertainly, still not sure if Zack was fucking with him.

"Yes, I truly am," Zack confirmed.

"So I am winning the bet," Victor answered triumphantly.

Bet? What fucking bet was Vic on about? Suddenly a vague memory drifted around the fringes of Zack's mind's eye. His last night at Bongoes. Lots of shots. Lots of cocaine. Shaking Victor's hand. Five years. Twenty thousand yen.

"Oh no!" he groaned. "You must be practically a millionaire these days, and you'd take money off a struggling traveller?" Zack now clearly recollected their wager on his returning within five years. God, he'd been so sure he wouldn't!

"Oh yes!" exclaimed Victor gleefully.

"Okay, okay," Zack relented. "I want to see you anyway to get an update on what's going on in this crazy fucking place. Can you come to *Harajuku*, or shall I come to you?"

"Your timing it is good, I think. Maybe there is something interesting for you," Victor said.

"Keep the good stuff coming Vic. Where are we meeting?"

"I see you in Shakey's Pizza three o'clock, and you will buy me the lunch no? Hee hee hee," Victor snickered, still amused by the betting win as well as by Zack being back in Tokyo.

"Okay ... cool ... brilliant ... see you then," Zack said resignedly. He hung up. "Fuck, I can't believe that guy."

"What's the story?" Mark asked, reappearing at the bottom of the stairs.

"He's got a memory like a fucking elephant," Zack complained. He related the story to Mark, whose undisguised mirth did nothing to improve Zack's humour.

"Well that's one to him, nowt to you! Now, less get out of 'ere, I'm 'ungry," Mark urged.

Five minutes later they each bought two overpriced but delicious gourmet pies from the Sisley shop, and Mark scooted across the laneway to extract two large beers from a vending machine. Zack had forgotten about beer machines ... admittedly, a very cool Japanese idea.

Mark flipped the lid off both cans, and handed one to Zack. "Better'n coffee! Well we're celebratin' aint we?"

Zack nodded, but had his mind on something else. Always when travelling, he kept an eye out for ideas, concepts or products that looked both profitable, and were conspicuously absent from other parts of the world. Last time in Japan, he'd been instantly excited about the possibilities that beer-machines, and to a lesser extent canned coffee machines, had in Australia and the UK. Thirty seconds of euphoria ensued before he'd realised that in just about any country other than Japan, the beer machines would simply be stolen or broken into. So he'd let the idea free-fall, crash and burn. The instance had, however, provided another lesson in the commercial potential of thinking beyond a cultural mindset.

They went up the stairs on the corner and sat themselves at one of the outside tables just below the massive video-screen, giving them a panoramic view over the *Meiji-Dori* and *Omotesandō* intersection. The novelty condom store, Condomania, was still in business, Zack noted.

He turned his attention to Mark, who had already launched into his first pie. "What the fuck are you doing over here anyway, you maniac?"

Rolling his eyes portentously, Mark replied, "Juss the usual ... anyfing and evryfin' ... y'know."

This meant, Zack discovered, that Mark was bartending and occasionally DJ'ing at the bar Déjà Vu, as well as working as an extra on some TV shows when he could get up early enough. And some dealing of course.

Zack focused on the drugs. "Is there much decent stuff around at the moment?"

"Mos' is comin' in fru vem fuckin' Iranians," Mark replied, again rolling his eyes. "Tossers they are. Shit coke, no acid, great *Ice*, and run o' the mill eckies. I got some awesome *Doves* though. Oh, and the big aitch of course." He continued ploughing into his pie.

"There's heroin in Roppongi now?" Zack asked, surprised. He took another swig of beer, wondering how on earth Mark could wolf his down so quickly. His own pies were scalding.

"Fuck yeah!" Mark looked up, clearly taken aback by Zack's query. "Oh okay ... you got me."

Jesus, he actually thought I was taking the piss, Zack realised. Roppongi must really be hitting the high road these days.

"Can I get a couple of *Doves* off you for tonight?" Zack asked, remembering his imminent assignation with Anna.

"Fuck, you're right quick off the mark aincha! Yeah don't see why not, I'll give ya two for eight. They's usually five large a pop," Mark replied.

"You're too kind," Zack replied absently, wondering where the *Doves* had come from.

"What, you goin' 'ard right from the off geeze?" Mark quizzed.

"Yeah, I thought I'd give it a bit of a nudge tonight at Bongoes, see where it leads me. One of the hosties from the plane is coming in, so ..."

Mark cut him off. "You've only bin in the bleedin' country two seconds, an' you've already tuned one o' the 'osties from your fuckin' *plane* ... thass bang out of order thattis." He scowled into his food.

Zack ignored this outburst, and munched his pie thoughtfully. "She'll almost definitely bring her mates. Why don't you come as well?"

Mark pondered as he chewed, eyes narrowed. They suddenly lit up. "Thass a brilliant idea. I'm off t'night, an' a good pal o' mine's DJ'in' openin' night at this new gaff the Big Apple. I'll blag us in. Perfect!"

"Let's do it then," Zack affirmed.

"Fuckin' oaf guv'na," Mark replied, raising his beer. "To Roppongi!"

"To Roppongi," Zack replied with a grin. It had begun!

They drank and reminisced until Zack departed for Shakey's, telling Mark he'd be back at the house by five.

Shakey's hadn't changed a bit. It was a favourite of his and Nurit's last time, as their shitty Madden apartment had been just around the corner. They had been regulars for the all-you-could-eat pizza and salad deal at lunchtime. Zack's eyes swept the room as he commandeered a vacant table from where he could see everything.

The usual assortment of teenybop *Harajuku* crew was there. Girls with '*ka-wy-ee*' paraphernalia hanging out of their curled, coloured hair, and off their bags and from their phones. They were re-touching their makeup, giggling, chatting, eating and doing whatever homework they had that week. It was depressing to envisage the lives that awaited most of them.

Zack still hadn't slept with a Japanese girl, and had no real inclination to do so. Granted, he *had* been in a relationship with Nurit most of his last time in Roppongi, but even if he'd been single, he didn't think it would have happened. Even out of curiosity.

Their subservience to men did nothing for him, and from what he had heard, despite or perhaps because of all their obedience in bed, they lacked imagination and were dead boring fucks. The sad thing was there were plenty of western guys who enjoyed the feeling of superiority they got from such sexually and emotionally malleable women. The US-Forces who regularly forayed into Roppongi sprang to mind. And the Africans, he thought.

A wry smile formed as he remembered the R&B club, Vietti's, that had been popular with all the black guys last time around. He had worked a few nights there, before moving on. The scene had been disturbing to say the least. Young, naïve Japanese girls flocked there in search of their black dick fantasies. Before they knew it they'd have had their drinks spiked and be out of their heads. Often, as their subconscious took over, they would have accommodated more than one dick by the night's end.

Be careful what you wish for, Zack thought. The toilets were basically fucking booths. Roppongi folk-lore had the DJ famously remarking, 'Please don't rape the girls *on* the dance floor'.

Only in Roppongi.

Regardless, Zack thought, he would have ample opportunity this time around to reconsider whether an anthropological adventure into Japanese sexuality might be on the cards.

Victor's arrival interrupted these musings. He walked in looking almost as Zack remembered him. Shorter hair now, a little more weight, but otherwise the same. He was however, wearing an enormous grin. Zack knew Victor didn't give a fuck about the *niman* yen ... he had to have a tidy pile stacked away by now. Having Zack back, and simply having won the bet would be more than ample satisfaction. Zack would give him the money anyway of course, because it was his nature. In Zack's book of life there were Sayers and Doers, and he had zero tolerance for the former.

"Well, well, well," Zack intoned. "Looks like a self-made man heading my way. From what I hear Victor, congratulations are most definitely in order. Oh, and just so I don't have to listen to you gloat any more than is absolutely necessary, there's your money." Zack pointed to the two *ichimans* he'd placed on the table.

"Zack, Zack, Zack, my friend, you know I cannot take this money from you." Victor had his hands in the air in protest. Zack had known Victor would feel a bit embarrassed if he pushed the money thing, so he pushed it.

"You can and you will and that's all there is to it. A bet's a bet. I apologise for forgetting about it. You know that's not like me." Zack stood up and stretched his arms out. "Take the money, give me a hug, sit down, and tell me what's what and what's not in Roppongi. I've got a bit of catching up to do."

After they'd embraced, Victor shook his head resignedly at Zack, sat down and put the money in his pocket. "I never could argue the points with you Zack, but I am taking this money now only for two reasons. First, and this is from my country … it is bad luck to have money on the table between friends. Second, because I can give this to you back many times."

Victor had been looking forward to seeing Zack. Three years back, as manager of Bongoes, the coolest bar on the strip, Zack had been on top of the game in Roppongi. Everyone knew him, and it seemed like he knew the movements of Roppongi almost as well as he knew his own bar. They'd met because Victor's wife, Sacha, had worked at the same club as Zack's girlfriend Nurit.

At that time Victor had been struggling, labouring and painting for a shitty six hundred yen an hour. Effectively poverty wages in Japan. Zack's timely advice had led him to his current position, and more than US$150,000 in the bank. That amount did not include what Sacha had made from managing a *hostess-club*, which was only a little less. So he'd come from being a flat-broke, freshly married Russian in a new and difficult country, to a situation where he was on the verge of being set for life. Victor knew he could never repay Zack for his useful recommendation. So if Zack needed help of any sort, he would do his best to make it happen.

He was pleased to see Zack at least seemed a little calmer now than before. Last time, as his departure date had drawn closer, Zack had spiralled out of control, especially once Nurit left Japan after their break-up. Victor knew Zack had been emotionally pole-axed, but in response, he'd become larger than life. Nobody could say no to him, and at least once that Victor knew of, he'd kept an after-hours party going in Bongoes right through to opening time the following night. He'd then looked at his watch, said, 'Oh fuck, time to work,' kicked everyone out for an hour to clean the bar, and then worked through the night as normal. Most of those barflies had gone for 'breakfast' and then come back to continue drinking into the night!

Zack's multifarious abilities were unquestionable, but his unpredictability was one thing that worried Victor and had often troubled others. He had to admit Zack now looked amazing: rejuvenated, re-energised. Victor wondered how long it would take for Roppongi to suck it all out of him once again. Well, he'd do anything to help Zack, so they might as well get on with it.

"Tell me some stories mate," Zack said.

Victor turned his mobile phone off. They talked without pause for almost three hours, before Victor left to organise the night ahead.

"Watch this," he said, turning his mobile back on. Instantaneously it chirped imperiously. Shrugging his shoulders resignedly, he waved a goodbye and left with the phone at his ear.

In three hours Zack had learned a lot. But now he felt drained. Everything was on course. Victor had an excellent job for him if he wanted it. He'd have to decide within a week. Enough was enough for the moment. He returned to the house, asked Mark to wake him in two hours, and crashed onto his bunk.

What seemed like only seconds later, the lights were on. Music was blaring, people were shouting, and Mark was leaping around like a lunatic telling him the shower was free and to get his shit together.

"Where *is* the shower?" Zack groaned. Mark pushed him along a corridor into what felt like a sweatbox. It was a sticky night, and Zack was sweating profusely. The cool water felt so good he closed his eyes, leaned up against the wall and wished he could stay there. His peace was short-lived however; the incessant banging on the door soon reminded him of the joys of communal living.

"ALRIGHT FOR FUCK'S SAKE," he shouted. The clamour ceased. He got out, dried himself off, wrapped the towel around his waist, and opened the door to see a striking blond girl as tall as himself drumming her fingers impatiently against the wall.

With a theatrical bow, Zack said, "Welcome to the bathroom. To your right you'll see some fine examples of seventies retro styling, and to your left …"

"Very fucking funny. Who are you, the new comedian?" she snapped.

Not so easily deterred, Zack put his fingers to his temples. Closing his eyes, he sombrely intoned, "Yes. I sense already that you and I are to be lovers. So it was written … and so it shall be."

"You're off your fucking head," she said, pushing past him. He stepped forward, and the door slammed shut behind him.

Zack smiled. He was feeling better already.

He dressed quickly in light cotton pants, singlet, and his trusty CAT boots. Painful experience had taught him that if you intended to get *FUBAR*, at the very least, protect your feet. He found Mark out on the patio, smoking a joint.

"Who's the freaked out Darryl Hannah stress-head?" Zack asked.

Mark exhaled a cloud of blue smoke into the still night air. "That … would be Melanie."

"And her role in the scheme of things is …"

"Strippa wiv more front 'n Brighton. She's only 'ere coss no-one else'll 'ave 'er I reckon. Sheeza right cunt that one," Mark replied.

Zack took a wild guess. "Just because she wouldn't fuck *you*," he said, "is no reason to …"

"'Ow the fuck would you know anyfink …" Mark snapped reflexively. Then he stopped, realising Zack had to be winding him up. "You don't fuckin' let up do ya? 'Ave you saved up four years of pisstakin' for me or wot?"

"Whoa there big boy!" Zack had his hands in the air and his eyebrows raised. "I can't help what some maniac chick babbles on to me about the moment I walk into your house."

It was fair to say this comment hit the spot. Mark exploded.

"WHAT !" Mark was on his feet now. "Did she fuckin' tell you about …?"

Zack quickly cut him off. Mark was too wound up. There was no fun left in this.

"Fuck me dead Mark! C*hill out* for fuck's sake!" Zack waved him away annoyedly. "It doesn't matter anyway. Let's go, and perhaps *not* continue this conversation in the cab."

Zack took the stairs in two leaps and looked askance at Mark from the street. "C'mon mate. We're gonna have a *great night*. We'll start with a few quiet ones at Bongoes. How's that sound?"

"Yeah, yeah okay. Less get out of 'ere," Mark muttered, only slightly placated.

"You've got the gear?" Zack checked.

"Yes m'lud," Mark replied, doing his eyes-rolling-in-disgust routine.

They walked through *Harajuku's* back streets to *Omotesandō* and collared a cab.

Eight

Mark was deep in thought. Fucking Zack wound him up like no-one else could. Effortlessly. He'd always been able to, and Mark couldn't for the life of himself understand why.

Zack always seemed to know stuff he shouldn't, people he couldn't, and he pulled off stunts that normal human beings would get beaten up for. He always seemed a few steps ahead, and sometimes, like just now, it got on Mark's nerves.

Zack was a good bloke though. Great fun to be with. You never knew what was coming next with him, except, to expect the unexpected. Mark shook off his remaining irritability and focused on the night ahead.

At Bongoes, the current manager, Jacko, had his back to them as they entered.

Zack said loudly, "Christ, what's with this shite music?"

Jacko spun around, ready to engage an adversary, then saw Zack smiling broadly. He sped out from behind the bar.

"Fuck, Zack, welcome back man! Great to see you! How are you?" he said, simultaneously nodding enthusiastically at Mark.

"Thirsty," Zack answered. "Mark, Jacko, Jacko, Mark."

"I've seen you round I think," Jacko said.

"Déjà Vu probably," Mark replied, unaware of the irony of his response.

"That's right," Jacko said, vaguely remembering. "What are you drinking Zack?"

"Beer thanks mate. Draught's fine." Zack proffered his hand to the other barman. "I'm Zack. You are?"

"Jarrod," the younger kid replied.

"Good to meet you. How's Jacko here treating you?"

"He's okay." Jarrod looked puzzled.

"Just make sure he never gets you in the back room after hours, or mark my words, you'll be walking like a fucking cowboy," Zack said, straight-faced.

"Zack, cut the shit for Christ's sake. You've only been here two minutes," Jacko protested.

Raising his hands in mock-surrender, Zack gave way. "Okay, okay … fair enough."

Jarrod looked like he didn't know what to believe.

Zack glanced around the oval-shaped bar-room. They had the attention of all the bar's customers. "Here's to the night ahead, ladies and gentlemen," he said loudly enough to be heard with ease. "Cheers."

Most of them joined him in the glass-raising ritual.

"God, you'd think they'd be a bit happier given it's Friday," Zack commented to Jacko. "You might have your work cut out for you tonight."

"It's actually been pretty good lately," Jacko responded. "Doesn't kick off until after ten though."

More people drifted in. Mark fell into conversation with a group down the bar. Jacko quizzed Zack about Nepal, and after a while Zack thought it was time to test the waters.

"So what's the story with staff here at the moment? Steve's fed me all the usual lines, but what's actually going on?"

"Well, I'm leaving in two weeks, and Steve knew you were coming. So I can't see a problem with you taking over," Jacko replied.

"Right," mused Zack. "I'll have a chat to Steve later on tonight I suppose, and see what's what."

He mulled over his options. It seemed he would have a choice. Victor had offered him the dance-manager's position at Cloud Nine. This in effect meant overseeing and keeping in line a big bunch of money-hungry strippers. Given that guys' salaries in Roppongi were generally a fraction of what girls made, the position was highly prized. At 350,000 yen per month, the base salary was already 50,000 above Bongoes' top rate. Moreover, Victor had assured him that by working the angles through the girls, he should easily clear over half a million each month. As a mere male, in Roppongi, Zack knew it would be pretty much impossible to do better than that.

He also understood the extra earning potential inherent in Cloud Nine's system of tips, kickbacks and bribes. Additionally, the hours were less punishing than Bongoes' ... *and* he wouldn't have to drink as much. Leave that mostly for after work. The fact he'd be surrounded by a naked smorgasbord of stunners certainly did the job's appeal no harm either. In short, Victor's offer was a clear winner. Zack would still be drinking at mate's rates in Bongoes, with access to his old network, but he'd also be able to develop a new circle of contacts at Cloud Nine. Zack was afraid he'd have to disappoint Steve. Of course, he'd wait until he was definitely 'in-situ' at Cloud Nine.

When Aya walked in, Zack realised it must be ten o'clock. She spotted him immediately. "Zack, you're here!" She raced over to hug him. "Wow! It's so good to see you again!" she enthused.

"It's actually really good to be back, though I never really thought I'd hear myself say that," Zack replied.

"That's because you were a naughty boy and almost drowned in this place last time. I'll have to keep a closer eye on you this time," Aya remonstrated.

Aya was a total sweetheart, Zack thought. She effortlessly combined the best of her Japanese culture with the more relaxed approach of a westerner. She was a bright-eyed breath of fresh air, a real pleasure to be around. Five formative years in Hawaii had saved her brain from a traditional Japanese fate.

The bar was filling out and Mark had rejoined them. "Zack, where are these birds anyway?" he asked.

"How would I know, Mark?" Zack hated stupid questions.

"I bet she doesn't come."

Ah! An opportunity. "Alright Mark, if she does come, you give me the E's for nothing. If she doesn't, I'll pay double. How does that sound?"

"The fact you're so bleedin' confident is music to me ears geeze. Okay, you're on. Let's have some shots." Mark was apparently warming to the evening.

"Yep, it's time to up the pace a bit," Zack agreed. He turned to Jacko. "Guess what time it is Jacko!"

"I suppose it must be shot o'clock." Jacko was resigned to his fate. "You wanna do the honours Zack?"

"I'd be delighted, my good man." Zack cruised behind the bar and grabbed a couple of shakers.

"I think we'll start with a real loosener. Jacko, didn't this used to be your favourite?" Zack asked, holding up a bottle of Jack Daniels.

"Oh shit. We've got Lynchburg Lemonades coming our way," Jacko said to Mark with a grimace. "I never should have trusted him."

Zack was in full swing behind the bar. Fuck, it felt good to be back. Joking with the crowd. Vibing with the music. Mixing up shots. He spun around.

"You're going to love this shot, Mark. It's the preferred wake-up-call of the French alcoholic. Just like a citron-pressé ... only bitier!"

"Wot is he goin' on about?" Mark raised his eyebrows at Jacko.

"No idea," responded Jacko laconically. "I don't think he does half the time either."

They'd just downed their third shot, when something caught Mark's eye.

"MMMM-mmmmm, look wot the cat brung in."

"Shit man, she is *hot*," Zack agreed, watching Anna come through the door. "By the way, have you got those E's mate?"

"Wot? Wottyer talkin' about?" Mark hadn't twigged yet.

"The E's. Our bet." Zack grinned at him.

"No! No Zack, yer 'avin a fuckin' laugh." Mark stared incredulously at Zack, then at Jacko. Zack looked with satisfaction at Anna gliding sexily into the bar. He heard Jacko say to Mark, "You idiot! Did you actually bet with him?"

Zack wondered if Mark was more stunned by the fact that she'd turned up and he'd lost the pills, or that she was just so fucking beautiful. Both of the above, probably.

She'd seen him, so Zack made his way through the parting, and increasingly admiring crowd.

"Welcome to my humble abode," he greeted her, with a kiss to either cheek. "It is embarrassingly good to see you."

Anna looked around the bar. "It's very small," she replied.

"As you've possibly experienced Anna, size does not always the event make, and good things do sometimes come in small packages. Even so, I hope I don't hear you use those words again tonight."

Zack winked, then looked over her shoulder at her two companions, and upped the ante further. "These must be your fellow workers of the air. Come up here, have some shots, and let's do the introductions."

Rachel was a petite, large-breasted, dark-eyed brunette from Leeds. Birgit was Swedish, slim, and inevitably blonde. All good looking girls, but Anna was the runaway star. Champagne was popped, shots were shook, and the party got properly underway. The Bongoes boys were well impressed, and Mark and Rachel were already trading traditional English barbs about northerners versus southerners.

Zack wangled stools at the bar for Anna and himself and offered her a private toast. "To you having made it here tonight, and to my first night back in Roppongi."

"I'll drink to that all night," she said, flashing him a cheeky wink.

It turned out the girls were staying just up the road at the Ibis Hotel. Excellent news!

He outlined the tentative plan for the evening to Anna.

"Can you get any E's?" she asked.

"Funny you mention that," Zack said. "The moment you walked through the door guaranteed me two free pills."

"How do you mean?" She looked both curious and amused.

Zack explained how the bet had come about.

"So you were pretty sure I'd come, weren't you Zack?"

It was not a question, Zack realised.

Her eyes locked on his, flashing a dangerous invitation. Zack couldn't believe it. She was actually making him hard.

"Weren't you, Zack?" she repeated. More urgency this time.

Drowning in her eyes, her mouth, her face, he vaguely heard himself saying, "Yes Anna, I was pretty sure." The next moment, they were kissing.

It had been instinctive for both, and they reluctantly broke it off as the inevitable cheers went up around the bar.

Anna wore a wicked grin. "Ohh yes," she whispered. "We are going to *party* tonight!"

Party they did. Shots, beers and champagne flowed until Bongoes was rocking. Zack started drinking water at about one a.m, anticipating the party and the pill yet to come. They left Bongoes around two a.m. Zack, Mark, the three girls and some Swedish banker that Birgit had dredged up. Jacko told Zack the guy was a bit of a jerk, but Zack was in no mood to rock the boat at this point. Let the guy fuck things up for himself.

He and Anna downed their Eckies on the street outside Bongoes. Mark and Rachel had taken theirs minutes before. Mark offered to sell the Swedes some, but apparently they weren't into it. Accordingly, Zack guessed their paths would later diverge, and was delighted. That's that problem solved, he thought.

The Big Apple crew were very happy to see them, and a crowd was still building. Zack, eyes closed, rested against the wall in the foyer while Rachel went with Mark to confirm their complimentary admission.

Zack's arms snugly encircled Anna's waist as he pulled her closer to him. An ambient techno beat was vibrating from within the club. Zack could hear the Swedish guy complaining about something. The E hadn't kicked in yet, but Zack already knew he didn't want this guy's energy anywhere near him tonight.

He opened his eyes. "Look mate, if you don't like the music, and," looking up and down at his suit, "the scene, take Birgit back to Bongoes or Motown or somewhere else in Roppongi. There's no sense you guys being here if you're not going to enjoy it. Birgit, you've still got the whole weekend with the girls, and the hotel's just around the corner. What do you think, Anna?"

Zack hoped Anna had picked up his telepathy. He needn't have worried.

"Yeah Birgit," she echoed. "That's a good idea. We don't all have to stay together for the sake of it. There's a million clubs and bars you and … I'm sorry what was your name? Oh yes, Peter, could go to if you want."

Anna's remark resulted in huddled whispering, which Zack broke into by detaching himself from her, to ask Peter for his business card.

He gave Zack one automatically, then hesitated. "Why do you want it?"

"Oh, just in case Birgit goes missing or something tonight. I mean, you might be some kind of psycho," Zack said lightly, while simultaneously pre-empting their departure.

The situation was interesting. Anna knew what Zack was doing. Birgit was clueless. As was Peter, who wasn't sure how to respond without going totally on the offensive. He decided not to risk it, settling for a face-saving, "Don't be fucking ridiculous."

Mark and Rachel returned with their entry-clearances, but Birgit and Peter were in a whispering huddle once again.

"Come on … fuck's sake … less go." Mark was pumped.

"Just a sec Mark, I think Birgit and Peter are going somewhere else," Zack prompted.

Birgit decided. "Yes, I think I will go back to Bongoes for a while with Peter. You don't mind do you guys?" She looked apologetically at her workmates.

"No darling, you go. It's fine, enjoy yourself." Anna and Rachel were unanimous.

And that was that.

Nine

Inside the club, Zack began to feel absolutely bloody amazing and he knew Anna was feeling exactly the same. That was the great thing about Ecstasy, its telepathic nature. The sense of oneness, all anxiety and external trash gone, and the total immersion in each millisecond of pleasure.

He had first told Nurit he would marry her if she wanted to, during one such moment. But that was a long time ago. Now Anna was here for him. This simplistic train of thought made him realise the X-factor was kicking in strongly.

"Anna, I've got to …"

"I know. Me too."

He led her unsteadily to the side of the room. Thankfully there was an empty couch. They sank into it gratefully and the E head-rush stormed their sensory castles.

"Fuck, this stuff is amazing," Zack breathed, pulling Anna's exquisite, shining face closer to his, revelling in the smoothness of her incredible skin. Her mouth was close to his, then closer, her tongue alive against his. Everything around them melted into the throbbing tribal backbeat which urged their appetite for each other onwards.

Zack didn't know how long they'd been melded together like that. It could have been thirty seconds or five minutes. Time had melted into that surreal meaninglessness he loved so much on Ecstasy. Nothing to worry about except being in the moment. He became aware of Mark shaking him.

"We're 'ere as well you know mate," Mark said.

Zack looked around. The expression on Mark's face was probably a match for his own euphoria. He jumped to his feet, whooping with excitement. Picking Mark up in a giant bear-hug, he danced him around the floor. Both laughing like maniacs, Zack finally broke away, becoming aware of his surroundings and the people around them. He couldn't stop laughing at the wonderful weirdness of everything as they made their way back to the couch. The girls were laughing together as well, pointing at them as they approached, then handing them some water.

"The music. Fucking brilliant, don't you think?" Zack said.

"Oh yeah. Well cool," enthused Rachel.

Zack realised he didn't know whether Mark and she had got it together yet. He hoped they had, or did. He wanted everyone to have a good night.

The initial rush of the E hitting his system had abated. He was now in the floaty mainstream of euphoria, but with more of a grip on things than before.

"Jesus Christ Mark, that thing hit me like a fucking train man. These pills are awesome," Zack exclaimed.

"You can say that again," Anna purred, and Zack instinctively moved closer to her.

"Yeah well I told ya they woz wickid gear," Mark replied. He was barely listening, his eyes shut, body grooving along to the backbeat.

"Very wicked," Anna echoed dreamily into Zack's ear. She was wearing a skin-tight cutaway dress, and Zack's fingers were around her finely sculpted ribcage, massaging her soft skin. He couldn't stop gently kissing her neck, and the sensation of her firm arse up against his semi-hard groin was pure anticipation.

The club filled up as Roppongi's hostesses finished work. The music intensified. The floor was packed, everyone dancing together, in themselves, mixing it with the all-consuming vibe. Most of the crowd were E'ing or tripping, generating an exhilarating wave of hedonistic community and beatific goodwill. Zack finally took a break, body-signing to Anna where he'd be.

Sitting down, he let his vision drift, blur and shudder through the lasers and the smoke. Someone sat close to him, and Zack instinctively turned to see who it was. He smiled uncertainly at the heavy-set, swarthy man. The guy looked familiar and wore a grin like the Cheshire Cat.

"Hello Zack, my old friend."

That did it. "Fucking hell! Ban ... my God, how are you man?" Zack's face split into a grin at the sudden rush of recognition.

"As you see, Zack. As you see, my friend."

An Iranian hard man in the drug-dealing world of Roppongi, Ban had been on friendly terms with Zack last time. They hadn't really done business together, but after Zack helped Ban into some good customers, complimentary E's and coke had always come Zack's way.

"Not retired yet mate?" Zack shouted.

Ban grinned, shrugging his shoulders. "Where are you working this time?"

"Dance Manager at Cloud Nine Roppongi. I start next week." Zack yelled back.

Ban raised his eyebrows, acknowledging the accomplishment. "You and me should talk sometime Zack." He got to his feet. "But not here. Call me soon." Having given Zack a *meishi,* Ban extended his hand once more. When Zack shook it, he felt a little package in his palm.

"Ban, you don't have to ..."

"I know I don't have to Zack. But you the only one who never ask me for nothin'. Chill my man, enjoy it with your girl, an' I see you later."

A pat on the shoulder, then Ban disappeared into the throng of bodies.

Anna replaced him almost immediately and wrapped her sweating, sexy body around him.

"You are fucking gorgeous," she whispered. "Let's get out of here. I want to be naked with you while we're still flying."

And that was how Zack found himself in the double bed of a four star hotel with a stunning, fully E'ing sex-goddess along with what seemed like a bit more than a full gram of half-decent cocaine. When Anna saw the coke she squealed with delight. Zack explained about Ban while they both did a couple of very healthy lines.

"Nice friends," was all she said. Her mind was elsewhere. So was Zack's. They ripped each other's clothes off, Anna pushing him down, forcing her tongue deep into his mouth. Seizing his rigid cock and working it expertly. Zack moaned and writhed. The pleasure was unspeakable.

"Wait a minute," she said, pulling him into a sitting position on the side of the bed.

"What …?"

Zack trailed off as he watched her tap little puffs of coke onto the end of his dick. The burning was followed by an amazing tingling sensation as Anna worked her tongue around the glans of his penis. She packed more coke onto his cock, and still holding him in her hand, began some deep licking and sucking.

Zack closed his eyes, the pleasure vortex swirling around him violently. Then opened his eyes, forcing himself to watch her. Fascinated at the sight of his cock pistoning in and out of her mouth. Moaning ecstatically as she switched tempo and fellated just the head. *Fuck she was incredible!* Abruptly, he pushed her away. He didn't want to come just yet, but a few more seconds of that and it would be all over.

She looked at him in surprise. "What's up?"

"Time out," Zack replied. "Refreshments."

He took a bottle of champagne from the mini-bar. Returning, he saw, as if in hyper-reality, the scene as it was at that moment. Anna, her beauty only heightened by the night's exertions, lay with her head arched back over the pillow, oblivious, her fingers gently manipulating the soft pink flesh of her clitoris. It was probably the most erotic thing he'd ever seen.

Without interrupting her, he popped the champagne, letting it fizz and drip down onto her shaven pussy. He straddled her in reverse, feeding his cock back into her mouth, tensing with the pressure she applied. Pouring more champagne over her already glistening mound, he then passed her the bottle. She gulped a couple of mouthfuls, and then took him back inside her mouth.

Zack gently worked a finger just inside her and flicked his tongue over her exposed clitoris. The bubbles fizzed deliciously around his cock, and he felt her back arch and contract with the pleasure of his tongue. He spilled a little more coke out of the packet onto her clit and the top of her lips. He massaged this in gently, hearing her sharp intake of breath, then pushed two fingers deep inside her and went back to her clitoris with his tongue. She bucked and let go of his cock, overwhelmed by her own pleasure, but just as he'd thought she was about to come she pushed him off.

"Turn around," she gasped. "Get inside me now."

There was no messing with that attitude. Zack lowered himself onto and into her, pushing himself upward and taking one of her rock-hard nipples in his mouth. Fuck, she was spectacular! He bit down on the nipple. She grunted like an animal, thrusting him deeper inside her. Her hands dug into his arse, and she pushed one finger just inside his anus.

Zack felt an enormous burst of intensified sensation, and kept pumping uncontrollably into her, hands on her breasts, tongue deep inside her mouth. Anna's body stiffened. Her climax slammed home, racking her body with a series of shuddering convulsions. This visual triggered Zack's own explosion. They finally came to a quivering halt, sweating, kissing, and crazily, deliriously together.

"Champagne, champagne." Zack gasped. He grabbed the bottle, gulping greedily, before splashing some onto Anna's breasts and into her mouth. He put the bottle aside to kiss her breasts and flatten her body under his. Their tactile sensuality heightened, the sensations were like electrical charges: out of this world. Zack fleetingly considered the fact that relatively few people experienced such supremely enhanced sex, but that they probably still thought their sex lives were pretty good. The thought was gone in an instant, along with the flash of pity he felt for them.

"That was unbelievable Anna," Zack said, still breathless. "You are amazing ... really fucking amazing,"

"*I'm* amazing?" She raised an eyebrow.

He lay sideways on the bed, using her shaven sex as a pillow, and looked up at her along her curves. She looked magnificent, her tawny blonde hair matted with sweat and champagne, clinging to skin.

Her eyes were closed, but Zack could still remember the feverish, animalistic spark that had flashed through them as she'd ordered him to fuck her. Now she reminded him of a big jungle cat, after a kill. Well-fed, purring contentedly, the danger gone. It was a delicious sight.

Anna's thoughts were with Brian, her husband, and about how guilty she ought to be feeling. Coming onto Zack on the plane. Doing this with Zack now. And for what she would do later with Zack.

But it was a distant concern, and for that reason she supposed their marriage was all but over. Brian was an announcer for the Channel Four television network. Pretty high profile in a geeky sort of way, but the hours he kept, combined with her itinerary, had already led her to suspect his seed was being sown elsewhere. She didn't really care anymore; thank God they had no kids!

She'd come to the conclusion that monogamy was basically an unnatural state for human beings. It was a shame, but there was more than enough evidence to back up this depressing realisation. Would it have made a difference to Zack if he'd known she was married? She doubted it.

He was a good-time guy, but one of the last people she'd pick for a relationship. Hard to walk away from, granted, but no long-term fulfilment lay down that road. You might as well try teaching a dog to miaow. He was sexy though. And a good laugh. And good in bed. *Oh, shut the fuck up Anna!*

All that only made him more dangerous, she thought. She had no doubt that many women would happily chance their hand in playing for keeps. In the meantime though, he can keep doing that, just ... *there* she thought, stretching her body in pleasure at his continued clitoral kisses.

Zack snuggled himself in around her body, breathing in the combination of her musky femininity and deliciously sexy *Paris* perfume.

"Penny for your thoughts," he ventured.

"Mmmm ... just floating in the afterglow ... you know."

"Actually," she added, "I'm just dreading the possibility that the girls are going to barge in here later today and want me to go sightseeing or shopping or something else equally stupid."

"You don't *have* to go."

"That's true, of course."

"And probably wise, given what I've got in mind," he added helpfully.

She raised herself onto her elbows. Zack had to concentrate hard not to look exclusively at her perfect tits. He elaborated.

"I thought we'd have an invigorating hot shower, do the rest of the coke, come back to bed, drink some more champagne, fuck till we're totally exhausted, take a couple of Rowies and some Panadol, crash out, then go out for dinner whenever we wake up. But … if you've got a better idea?"

She smiled provocatively. "I think I'll go with that one for the time being."

By the time they finally succumbed to a drug-fuelled unconsciousness sometime around midday, there wasn't much they didn't know about each other's sexual appetites, preferences and equipment. The 'Do Not Disturb' sign on their door remained firmly in position until eight o'clock that evening.

Ten

Zack felt grotty wearing the same clothes, but declined the underwear Anna jokingly offered him, telling her he might've gone for it last night, but thanks anyway. She then disappeared to Rachel's room, no doubt to get all the juicy details. Mark had already left to go to work. Birgit had returned alone the night before, but then gone off sightseeing with Peter much earlier in the day.

So Zack, Anna and Rachel went to *Harajuku* for a meal at Zest, a long-time Mexican favourite of Zack's. Zack was thinking that as he'd failed to catch up with Steve last night, maybe he'd do an after-dinner drink with Mark at Déjà Vu, then cruise down to Bongoes on a Steve-finding mission.

"Wow, this is beautiful!" Rachel exclaimed.

Zack had deliberately stopped their cab early at *Aoyama-Dori*, so they could walk the rest of the way down the famous *Omotesandō* boulevard.

He agreed with her. "You should see it during the cherry-blossom week. Then it's spectacular."

"They only flower for a week?" Rachel asked.

"Yep … just a week." Seeing her dismay, Zack added, "It's good in a way though. Makes people appreciate them more. It's actually a tremendous cultural event here."

"I still think it's sad," Rachel said limply.

They walked down the hill, past an impressive stone-walled fashion emporium, past the Tag Heuer flagship store and museum, towards *Kiddyland*, finally making a left at Café de Rope. Zack suggested they come back tomorrow, for the 'Sunday People Parade' and to explore the shops and galleries. Rachel was keen to see inside the seven-storey toy-store, *Kiddyland*.

Personally, Zack hated the place. It was too claustrophobic. All manner of things whirring, ringing, clicking, screeching and moving all around you … not to mention yapping kids everywhere and so much kitsch rubbish you could throw up just looking at it let alone playing with it. It had been his experience however, that girls loved the place. Go figure. But he supposed everyone should see it at least once.

He was far more interested in the narrow alleyways that snaked around *Harajuku*. They retained some of what he imagined 'old world' Japan had been, but were now fused inextricably with money, progress, and modernity. The contrasts however, could be striking.

For instance, peeking through the fence of one dwelling might reveal a small shrine set in an exquisitely cultivated bonsai garden. The adjacent structure might house an ultra-hip, urban-chic hair and beauty salon, whilst the other neighbour would be a '*sentō*', the old-style Japanese public bath-house. The whole area was a fascinating melting pot of incongruous styles, eras and influences.

Last time in Tokyo, *Harajuku* had been Zack's first home, and because he finished work at daybreak, he'd often seen it wake-up of a morning. Amongst other oddities, he'd been transfixed by the sight of tiny, ancient, Japanese women, hunch-backed after years of toil, brushing the laneway at six in the morning with their quaint miniature besoms. They'd reminded him of his school-days studying the poetry of Wilfred Owen – 'bent double like old beggars under sacks'.

Given that similarly miniaturised street-sweeping machines moved daily through the laneways, Zack had concluded the besom-wielding was more a comforting daily ritual for them than a practical necessity. From early days of his last stay, he'd tried never to be without his camera. Scouting around in the dawn hours had been a great way to steal some above-average shots. The black and whites he'd taken of the ancient women were still amongst his favourites. So many wrinkles! And so much history! Zack had wondered at their lives, their loves, their tragedies and triumphs.

He'd always given them an enthusiastic '*Ohayou gozaymashita*' and they'd always acknowledged with a smile and a nod the greeting of this crazy *gaijin* with long hair and sunglasses, who might as well be from another planet. In spite of their being walking anachronisms, Zack had a great deal more respect for them than he had for the younger Japanese people he routinely encountered. The older generations at least had their tradition and culture, as well as a deep sense of the importance of honour and respect.

The attitudes of Japanese people brought up post World War Two had invariably been subverted by the admittedly necessary task of re-building; a preoccupation which subsequently mutated into an insatiable hunger for money, success, and economic power, seemingly at any cost. Unfortunately, these people had never known another Japan, except in the stories of their parents and grand-parents.

They passed a traditional-style noodle shop with its coloured lanterns and a wooden facade, then crossed another laneway and entered a modern building comprising numerous restaurants. Zack pointed out the stairs going down to 'Oh God' and explained it had previously been a favourite of his and Nurit's on Sunday nights.

By Japanese standards it was a large bar-restaurant, and had a couple of pool tables. It had however become more renowned for its cinema screen and surround-sound system, for the movies they regularly showed. It was a cool place to chill out with friends. Up the stairs on the opposite side of the atrium was Zest.

Zack suggested they start with drinks, either frozen daiquiris or margaritas. Both were excellent at Zest.

"God, I don't know if I can face alcohol," Anna muttered. Rachel quickly concurred. Zack looked from one to the other, utterly aghast.

"But you must! You don't understand! If you don't drink now, you'll feel raggedy all night. Just two margaritas will have you feeling good again. You absolutely have to trust me on this. Remember, it's my specialist subject!" Zack's face had become an improbable blend of pathos and indignation.

Anna laughed. "Jesus, I suppose we'd better. What passion! And that look on your face … do you *practise* that look Zack?"

He grinned sheepishly. "I am serious about the drinking though," he said. "Jesus, you're only here for a couple of days, you might as well live a little."

"I did more living last night than I'd expected from the whole weekend," Anna quipped, with a sideways glance at Rachel.

"Seconded," Rachel added. The two of them were once again giggling like little kids.

"Well, Tokyo can do that," Zack observed.

The nervous Japanese waiter hovering nearby didn't know how to make his move without interrupting them, so Zack made it easy on him and got their drinks order organised. Feeling better after a couple of strawberry daiquiris, Zack noted the girls were now sold on the frozen margaritas, bemoaning the fact no equivalent existed in England.

Zack knew food was going to be a tricky issue. He advised the girls not to over-order, although they all felt starving. Too often after drug-partying, he'd ordered half the menu somewhere, only to be able to squeeze a few bites down, then have them bag the rest for later. So they shared a nachos main, then poached portions from each other's chimichanga, quesadilla and burrito.

"God, it's brilliant!" Rachel enthused. "Why's it so good over here, and so crap in England?"

"The Japanese are great replicators," Zack offered.

The conversation meandered into the girls' work environment, and they regaled Zack with shocking stories about some of the arseholes they dealt with at thirty-nine thousand feet.

They then insisted on picking up the bill, explaining that their meal allowance made it practically free. When Zack suggested Déjà Vu for drinks, neither hesitated for a moment. So they taxied back to Roppongi.

At midnight, Roppongi was clicking into gear for another Saturday evening of ballistic hedonism. Zack observed the Japanese touts: androgynous pretty-boys, their bleached hair varying shades of rusty orange. Each proffered voucher proclaimed a more amazing offer than the previous one. Prettier girls, cheaper drinks, free entry, variations on these themes.

The touts' main targets were ex-pats, tourists, and the ever-present swarms of *salarimen*. They had a highly developed nose for money, and although Zack didn't understand a lot of Japanese, he knew their spruiking was of the most obsequious kind: most of these touts were awful, ever-hopeful, cringing symbols of desperation. God save him from ever suffering such humiliation, he prayed.

They strolled along *Gaien-Higashi-Dori* towards Tokyo Tower, the fused odours of stall-fried tofu and exhaust-fumes assailing their nostrils. Taking a left at the large corner sushi shop, they swung immediately into a short dead-end right. Hello Déjà Vu!

The usual mixed bag of nightlife flotsam and jetsam were out the front. Zack was ever-amused by these scenes, and when he wanted some fresh air, would often just hang out there chatting to the doormen and watch the show. Afro-American and Nigerian drug-dealers attempted peaceful co-existence. A group of young Japanese-Brazilians sat on a stair-rail opposite, passing around a spliff, and two huge *gaijin* doormen were planted like gargoyles outside the stairs descending to a club called Gas Panic 99. A new Gas Panic, Zack registered, and wondered what the story was there. There had been only two, previously. He made a mental note to ask Mark what was going on with that.

They walked in to Déjà Vu. Zack marvelled at how little the place had changed. He had nearly ended up working here last time around, because one of Nurit's friends was the bar-manager. The bar still went halfway along the left side of the long narrow room, leaving standing room two or three people deep between the bar and the booths down the right side of the room. It opened to a compact dance-floor at the back, with an even more compact toilet facility beyond that.

Most weekends it was impossible to get in either of the toilets without an interminable wait. These were the only places people could take a private moment to snort, toke, cry, vomit, break up ecstasy, or whatever. Sometimes they were even used for their intended purpose.

It was too early for the main crowd, but Zack was glad to be there while it was still relatively laid-back. After last night, and in spite of the alcohol during dinner, he was feeling pretty subdued. It crossed his mind that he might just be getting old. Mark leapt from behind the bar to give Rachel a big hug. She must, Zack reckoned, have been pretty good last night.

Not that Zack had any recent knowledge of Mark's behaviour or success with women, but any half-decent looking guy working the bars in Roppongi routinely got laid by women far more beautiful and willing than most would ever get elsewhere without paying for it. Then again, Mark knew she'd be gone tomorrow, so he might as well make the most of it. No scenes, no recriminations, just new horizons. Zack smiled. In Roppongi, nightlife was king, and bartenders were gods. That was just the way of things.

"Good to see you guys made it," Mark said, detaching himself from Rachel.

They settled at the bar while Mark fixed their drinks. Zack passed over a 5,000 yen note. Mark gave change of 3,000. The round of drinks was technically worth 4,000. With management possibly watching, you always had to go through the motions. Mark could get away with comping a few drinks, but there was only so far you could push your luck. Heavy-pouring the spirits measures was another easy way of fudging the system.

After the traditional clink of glasses, Zack sipped his Jacks and dry and assumed his customary observation mode.

"Check out that babe on the dance floor. She is one sexy creature," Anna commented.

Zack had always thought it a curious anomaly that women could compliment and appreciate their own gender sexually, without being tagged as leaning in that direction. For men, such comments still seemed to be the preserve of the gay and bi community.

He followed Anna's eyes. There was no doubt about it. The girl was very fucking sexy alright. There were four other people on the small dance-floor, but she was apparently dancing alone, her sinuous and very feminine figure sensually undulating to the rhythm of low impact trance music. Her hair was long and dark, and she was garbed simply in a white cotton singlet, Thai fisherman-pants and sandals. A cobra tattoo swayed on her left shoulder-blade, and in the smoky intimacy of Déjà Vu, her freely expressed sexuality packed a powerful punch. Zack wondered where she was from. She looked Israeli, he thought.

"Okay, okay that's enough." Anna punched Zack lightly on the shoulder, and pulled his head around for a kiss. "I said look at her, not get hypnotised."

Zack took the hint, and turned to face the bar. "Mark, what happened to the old Gas Panic Bar?"

Cocktail shaker in hand, Mark replied, "Far as wot I know, they juss wontid ta relocate tha fucka to a bigga space. Iss ontha utha corna now, an' ninety-nine is their new place wot opins til nine in the mornin'. Nine 'til nine ... hence the name."

A row of kamikaze shots magically appeared on the bar, to just as quickly disappear as the four of them made light work.

Another four were on the way when Zack felt a hand on his shoulder. He heard a female voice saying, "Is Zack ... no?"

Looking around, he found the face of Anna's sexy creature just a few inches from his own. Totally surprised, and with Anna watching on, he found himself momentarily lost for words.

"You are Zack yes ... I am sure. You do not remember me maybe?" Her eyes smiled, playfully.

Zack's mind raced. Was it possible he had known, and then somehow forgotten this woman? Surely not!

"No. Wait. Give me a sec." Zack's battered memory entered warp overdrive. "You were ... one of Nurit's friends, and your name is Da ... Dari ... no, it's Dorit. Dorit!" Zack announced triumphantly.

She beamed with delight. "So you *do* remember me!"

He felt Anna tense a little beside him.

Zack's composure returned. "Of course I do now, Dorit. But I saw you dancing before and didn't recognise you at all."

"Yeah well, I been in India for long time in the mountains. In Manali you know, and I lose all this bullshit weight from Tokyo. Now I'm feeling *esser* ... you remember *esser,* Zack?"

Dorit had explained her metamorphosis with that typical in-your-face bluntness Zack loved about most Israelis.

He answered her in Hebrew, explaining he'd been in Israel for a year and a half, and understood the language better these days.

Her face lit up again. "Im-press-ive, Zack," she answered, accenting the syllables for effect. She clicked her tongue appreciatively a couple of times, acknowledging with a glance Anna and Rachel, who had been giving her the once, twice and thrice-over. Zack hastily made slightly strained introductions.

Anna and Rachel were cool, and remained so, while he and Dorit did a quick catch-up: what had happened with him and Nurit, what he'd been doing since the break-up, his travels, his time in Israel. No-one else said a word during this time; Anna and Rachel had exchanged sideways glances.

Picking up on the vibe that she was perhaps not entirely welcome, Dorit scribbled her phone number onto a beer-coaster.

"Call me," she said with a smile. "When you're not so busy."

She moved back towards the dance-floor. Zack quickly tucked the coaster into his pocket; he was already looking forward to that meeting.

"Mr. Popular," Anna remarked caustically.

Zack sighed. "Don't give me a hard time Anna. She's just a friend of my ex, who I almost didn't even recognise." He wondered why he was even bothering with this justification.

"She certainly recognised you though," Anna responded icily.

Zack finished his drink. "I've got to see Steve down at Bongoes," he said. "Let's get out of here."

Eleven

Bongoes was absolutely packed. There were almost as many people drinking outside on the road as in the bar. Rachel had stayed on at Déjà Vu, so Zack grabbed Anna's hand and they plunged into the crowd together, making their way to the back of the bar. Zack saw Steve first: he looked heavier, especially in the face. Not surprising really, after all that time in this environment. Then he was spotted in return.

"Ahhh, the long-haired delinquent finally returns to Tokyo. Just like I knew he would. It was only a matter of time Zack. I mean, how could you leave all this behind?" Steve's greeting arrived with a strong handshake.

"Yeah, I really missed you too, Steve. Even if you didn't pay me so much, I'd have come back just to see you," Zack sarcastically retorted. "Anna, this is Steve the boss-man, Steve, meet Anna."

Steve eyed her curiously. "You do *know* this individual is a dangerous lunatic?"

Anna met his gaze and raised an eyebrow. "He hasn't disappointed so far."

"Unlike his performances here, which were always a disaster!" Steve exclaimed. "Seriously though Zack, it's going to be good to have you back. Lately we've had some enthusiastic, but pretty green kids running around in here. We really need someone who knows what they're doing again, especially with the music."

Zack held his hand to his heart. "Steve, I'm touched."

"Enough of your bullshit. What are you drinking?"

"I'll have a Brown Dog. You remember those, don't you mate?"

"Jacks and … dry, wasn't it?" Steve ventured.

"Memory serves. Impressive."

"I was a barman too, once upon a time you know Zack," Steve admonished.

"And one of your best Margaritas for Anna," Zack added.

Ordering done, Steve turned to Zack again. "So have you got a work visa this time?"

"Yes-sirree, I'm squeaky clean, stamped, authorised, vetted and verified. I'm ready to rock and roll." Zack hammed it up with a Yankee drawl.

"How long do you reckon you'll hold out?"

"I'm going for the whole year again," Zack replied, as he deftly relieved Jacko of their drinks.

Steve whistled slowly through his teeth. "You might have to take things a bit easier this time. What do you think?"

"Probably," Zack replied, ignoring Anna's quizzical glance.

This was Steve's way of letting Zack know he didn't want the bar getting *quite* as out of control as it had before. Too many drugs (and he hadn't known half of it), too much nudity, too much setting things on fire, and too much of everything else that was too much fun.

"You're looking much better anyway," Steve added, before he allowed himself to be drawn away to talk with someone else.

"What was that all about?" Anna asked.

"Oh, not much. Steve gets anxious easily ... a few people were a bit worried about me back then," Zack replied. Suddenly he felt a little weary, and wasn't in the mood to be squashed in by all these people.

"Look Anna, let's chill out back in the hotel. I mean, we'll stay if you really want to ... or go somewhere else. I know you've only got tomorrow before you leave and ..."

"Sshhhh." Anna put a finger to his lips. "I'd be happy to get out of this sweaty mess of drunks and into bed with you. Let's go."

They left, waving goodbyes to Jacko, Aya and Jarrod, with Zack signing to Steve that he'd call soon.

Zack took the lead, and wove them a path through the teeming Roppongi streets. Thousands of people of different nationalities, all getting fucked up. Israelis, Iranians, Nigerians and others manned their '*bastas*', selling everything from crazy dance-party hats to laser pens to 'bug-in-a-nut' novelties, as well as the usual range of designer rip-offs.

Four Japanese girls in Budweiser swimwear were passing out free beer in plastic cups. Zack grabbed two, and they continued walking. Skirting a drooling wild-eyed *salariman* with vomit on his tie outside Almond, they crossed *Roppongi-Dori* underneath the enormous Shuto expressway. In less than two minutes, they were back in the Ibis hotel.

The sex was restrained, less frantic, and more tender than the previous night. As a couple, they had melded very quickly. Zack felt like he'd been with her for weeks and wondered if she had this effect with every guy. They dialled a wake-up call for ten, giving them six hours to sleep pressed up against each other like a couple of spoons.

*   *   *

Waking up proved difficult. Zack dragged himself into a sitting position, drank two bottles of mini-bar orange juice, and promptly regretted it. The acidity bubbled ominously in his aggrieved stomach, as he realised he was starting this, his third day in Tokyo, in the same clothing yet again.

Fortunately however, they would have more time in *Harajuku* today, so he could pit-stop at the guesthouse and change, before any further adventuring. Zack showered to wake himself up, told Anna he was going to his place, and arranged to meet her in front of *Kiddyland* at midday. Squinting in the bright sunshine outside, he wandered dazedly to *Nogizaka* station, got a train to *Meiji-Jingumae* and found his way back to the guesthouse.

The first person he encountered was manic Melanie.

"Oooh look who it is. Mister Comedian," Melanie cooed sarcastically.

"Fuck off, you psycho," Zack replied as he headed upstairs. He was not in the mood. He heard stifled laughter from others in the kitchen. At what, he didn't care. Zack lay down on his bunk, holding his head. Just half an hour more sleep, he thought.

Knowing he was kidding himself, he got straight up again. He did not want to miss their midday meeting. Donning some clean clothes, he consigned the others to a plastic bag under the bed, grabbed some B-Group capsules, some Optalgin, his sunglasses, and headed to the kitchen for water.

Two guys and a girl were at the table. Yitzhak, Zack had already met, but the other two he didn't know. "*Bokker-tov Yitzhak … ma-inyanim?*" Zack poured himself a water and sat down.

"*En baya*, Zack," Yitzhak replied.

Once he'd swallowed his medicine, Zack addressed the other two. "My name's Zack. I hope you guys aren't best mates with the psycho."

They laughed, and the guy leaned forward to shake hands. "Antonio, and no, I do not like her."

The girl nodded noncommittally in his direction. "Hi," she said. "I'm Ella."

Needing to stay awake, and with an hour to kill, Zack was happy to chew the fat with his housemates. It turned out Yitzhak ran a couple of *bastas* in *Shinjuku*, near the red light zone of *Kabukicho*. He was pissed off because business had been slow, and he'd been getting more attention than usual from the police.

Zack guessed he had overstayed his three month visa: more than eighty percent of Israelis and nearly all Iranians in the *basta*-business were illegal. Once on overstay, two things could happen. You either handed yourself in voluntarily to Immigration in order to leave *legally*, or you eventually got caught, imprisoned, then summarily deported. The advantage of handing yourself in? No imprisonment, and two weeks leeway to organise your affairs before leaving.

Antonio was Venezuelan and Zack guessed he was also overstaying, although this information was not offered. In Tokyo, clever *gaijin*s played their visa status very close to their chest, as informants in grudge situations, as well as for reasons of job competition, were not uncommon. Antonio was a waiter and Latin-American dance teacher at the popular Roppongi Latin bar 'Salsa-Central'.

Ella was German, not particularly communicative, and worked as a hostess in BlackJacks, the largest *gaijin hostess-club* in Roppongi. Zack reflected briefly on the misfortune of the poor punters who actually paid to keep *her* miserable company.

At eleven-thirty Zack farewelled the group. On *Omotesandō*, the sun was bright, but at least his tender eyes now had some protection. Needing something hot and nourishing, Zack called in at the *tempura* shop opposite *La Foret* on *Meiji-Dori*. *Tempura* was one of his favourite Japanese meals; various delights deep-fried in a light batter.

He ordered prawns, vegetables, rice and *miso* soup. Ice-cold water was freely available in jugs, and for 720 yen or US$7 it was one of the cheapest and most tasty meals around. *Miso* soup especially, was good for hangovers. He ordered another bowl and finished it quickly. Feeling vastly improved, he returned to *Omotesandō* on schedule.

On Sundays, the section of *Omotesandō* between *Meiji-Dori* and *Aoyama-Dori* was usually blocked off in favour of pedestrians. Street-entertainers proliferated, although Zack doubted their presence had featured in the original decision-makers' rationale.

He'd heard the home-grown bands that used to operate near *Yoyogi-Park* had been shut down by the authorities, which was depressing, but unsurprising. Far too much anti-authority individualism for the government to tolerate, he guessed. Their increasing popularity with Japanese youth would only have tightened the governmental noose.

He crossed *Omotesandō* and sat on the low railing opposite *Kiddyland*, watching an evil-looking clown fold balloons into various shapes and sizes.

His thoughts however, were of Anna. She was a cool chick ... it was a shame she had to disappear so quickly. He'd asked how often she came through Tokyo, and she'd said that for the moment she didn't know, and wouldn't, until she got back to London and sorted a few things out.

So be it. Long ago he'd pragmatically accepted that regularly losing friends and lovers was inevitable for a traveller. Best to enjoy the pleasures life offered up and be grateful for them, rather than morbidly mourn what had passed. There was ...

"GETCHASELFUPMAN !"

The hands came down hard on Zack's shoulders and went around his neck. Instinctively, Zack grabbed them and somersaulted forward in fright. Mark flew through the air and landed heavily on the footpath, a thunderstruck expression on his face. One of the clown's balloons exploded. Dogs and passing shoppers scattered. A child began to cry.

Zack got up off the pavement and stretched his body, checking for damage. "You're really a fucking idiot sometimes Mark," he said laconically. "You'll get hurt doing that to someone one day you know."

Also back on his feet, Mark rubbed a couple of sore spots. "Jesus Christ, Zack. Remin' me not ta fuckin' sneak up on *you* again. Wot a great idea Anna." He glowered in her direction.

Stunned Japanese bystanders had finally realised it was just 'crazy *gaijin* being crazy *gaijin*' and continued belatedly on their way. Most of them would probably tell the story for days, Zack thought gloomily.

"I said give him a little fright, not jump on him and try to strangle him," Anna rebuked.

"Where's Birgit?" Zack asked.

"Gone to Disneyland with Peter," said Rachel, dusting Mark down.

Zack sighed dejectedly. "Good fucking luck to them on a Sunday like this."

He knew they would queue for hours on a fine weekend day. It was bad enough on a weekday. As far as he was concerned, if you weren't a child, the best way to enjoy Disneyland was to be tripping your head off. That way even queuing could be a laugh. The last time he'd gone, they'd all been on some really good acid. The day and night that transpired had been one of the funniest and most entertaining of his life. His stomach hurt for two days afterwards from laughing so much. It was even better than going as a kid.

"Wherever we're going, can we eat first?" Rachel asked.

Mark and Anna were hungry as well, and they ended up at Denny's, an American-style eatery, which was a short walk down *Meiji-Dori* towards *Shibuya*. They passed the rest of the afternoon as sightseers, wandering into art galleries, handicraft and antique shops, checking out the different *bastas*, and pausing to watch street-entertainers.

The girls were particularly amused by the rival groups of Japanese Elvises. These performers, evicted from *Yoyogi-Park*, had re-emerged at *Omotesandō*, their numbers and rivalry undiminished. Today there were two distinct groups. One group was larger, with a contingent of fifteen. The other consisted of only seven.

All wore blue denim jeans faded to varying degrees, tight white tee-shirts, big-buckled belts, and black cowboy boots. Wallets in back pockets were chained to a belt-loop. Hair-gel was obligatory and the amount of it used here would keep some multi-national in the black for years to come.

Each group had its own ghetto-blaster, and to watch one lot hip-swivelling to *Hound Dog* while the others gyrated to *Return to Sender* only twenty yards away was comical to say the least. Not all the Elvises of each group danced at the same time. Rest periods were often taken; this time was primarily spent grooming, looking tough, learning moves, and scowling at members of rival groups.

What fascinated Zack was the obvious gang hierarchy ... sort of like a troupe of monkeys. Watching, it was easy to spot the 'apprentice' Elvises, those not yet fully-fledged members. Zack could all too easily imagine the sad rituals these alienated youths were prepared to suffer for full acceptance and inclusion.

As they watched, one of the 'apprentices' bumped into his 'master' while being taught a new gyration. The master slapped him hard on the side of the head, then strode off a few paces, gaze averted, seemingly trying to re-establish his 'cool'. The scorned apprentice scurried over bowing, scraping, and repeating '*Gomenasai*' over and over again in his quest for forgiveness.

"Jeez, thass one sad fucka!" Mark jeered contemptuously.

"Sometimes, if you're really lucky, you get to see fights between the groups," Zack commented absent-mindedly. "And that," he added, "is really funny."

They paid their respects at the *Meiji-shrine* shortly before dark, and the day finished with dinner, a movie at Oh God, and a slow stroll through the streets to the hotel. A bit of awkwardness followed. Neither Zack nor Mark were sure whether to impose themselves on the girls for their last night, but it turned out the girls didn't want them to go, so after a few 'don't be stupids' and 'are you sures' the new couples headed for their respective rooms after agreeing to meet for breakfast in the morning.

Inside Anna's room Zack asked again if she genuinely wanted him to stay. Perhaps she wanted the last Tokyo night to herself? He was taken aback by the vehemence of her reply.

"God, you're so damn *nice*, aren't you!" she fumed.

Zack frowned, and let a few seconds pass, to better emphasise the unwarranted bitchiness of her comment.

"Ahm, just a moment babe. If I've missed something here, feel free to fill me in anytime you're ready. Didn't we just have a kick-arse weekend together?"

Zack was deliberately playing dumb. But fuck it … he'd make her work for it. She was the one suddenly getting shitty.

"Oh, it's all just so easy for you, isn't it Zack? This week you've had me. Next week it'll be that Israeli chick, and the week after, God knows who!"

She wasn't crying yet, but she wasn't far from it. He guessed it was a combination of fast-living, lack of sleep, and the drug comedown. It tended to result in overly fragile psyches: he'd seen it a lot. She was just a little frayed around the edges. But despite feeling slightly sorry for her, he didn't give in. He wanted to see where she planned to take this, or if there even was a plan.

"It's the way of the world I'd say, wouldn't you?" Zack quipped offhandedly, quickly slipping into his standard self-protective stratagems.

She looked across at him with a pained expression. "You're disgusting," she said quietly.

"You can really talk Anna! You're an *air-hostess* for Christ's sake!" Zack shot back. He switched to sarcasm and a falsetto voice. "Mmmm, I wonder which nationality I'll chip into the old bedpost *this week*." He stared accusingly back at her. "For you it must be like going to a fucking *restaurant*!"

She looked at him hard, for what seemed like a long time. "I'm married, Zack. I have been for six years. And you're the first time I've been unfaithful."

Zack sat down abruptly on the bed, mentally pole-axed. Fucking hell! What a turn up for the books that was. Little surprised him these days, but not for one *second* had he thought she might be married. No wonder she'd turned him inside out in bed. He'd probably been on the receiving end of God knows how many years of sexual deprivation!

"Why?" he said.

"Oh I don't know." Anna shrugged unhappily. "The usual reasons I suppose. Boredom, frustration, he's probably doing it. Right time, right place, right guy. All of the above. Take your pick really. But I just didn't expect *not* to feel bad about it. I mean, what the fuck does *that* say about the marriage I'm in?"

She walked over and sat beside him on the bed, pulling a pillow onto her lap and hugging it to her.

"I'm sorry Zack. I shouldn't be putting this on you. They're my problems and I'll deal with them. I wasn't going to tell you until maybe my next time through. But I couldn't help it." She sniffed morosely and wiped a couple of tears away. "I'm sorry."

Zack put his hand to her cheek, then around her shoulder. "It's okay babe, I hear you."

With a grimace, he added, "I'm not much good for advice I'm afraid. The marriage thing is ... ahhm ... sort of out of my league, if you know what I mean."

"No, not really. What does that mean exactly?" Anna was unconsciously picking at the tassels on the duvet, but glared at him nonetheless. "Haven't you ever got close to being married?"

Zack lay back on the bed and sighed. He supposed there was no option but to give a bit here, even though he found it pointless.

"At one point I would have said yes to my last serious girlfriend, if she'd wanted to, but she didn't."

"Why not?"

"Ahh, she was even worse than me." Zack's voice took a slightly harder edge. "Travel. Independence. Freedom. At the end of the day, all those things were more important to her than I was. So she left me to go looking for them." Zack smiled, remembering his heated arguments with Nurit, their circularity, their increasing frequency, the periodic truces. Once, she had even set his clothes on fire ... in a wooden *gaijin-house*!

"Have you seen her since then?"

"No."

"How long's it been?"

"Coming up three years."

"Do you want to see her again?"

Zack wondered about that anew. "No, not really. I mean, I wouldn't go particularly out of my way *not* to see her, but I'm also not interested in seeking her out."

"Why not?"

The question snapped Zack out of his reverie. This pointless conversational tangent had quickly become an interrogation, and he had now had enough of Twenty Questions.

"Because. For what it's worth, it took me about six months to get her out of my system. And I've been pretty happy since then. That's it. I'm happy she's out of my system. I've moved on. Period." Zack's expression and tone clearly brooked no argument or further conversation on the matter.

"Okay, okay, I'm *sorry*. I was just interested that's all. No big deal." Anna sulkily lay back on the bed, staring pointedly at the ceiling.

Zack went to the bathroom for a piss and a think. Oddly, a little graffiti-ditty on the toilet wall years ago in primary school, popped into his head.

Some come here to sit and think
Some come here to shit and stink
I come here to scratch my balls
And read the writing on the walls

'Writing on the wall,' he thought. Good tip. He decided to say his goodbyes and leave, and was washing his face when Anna came in. She had changed into a negligee. She pressed herself up against his back and hugged him gently.

"Zack, I want you to stay. I don't care whether we have sex or not. I just want to be with you tonight. Will you stay? Please."

Jesus! Was the woman a fucking mind-reader?

Zack closed his eyes. Her breasts were warm and soft against his back, and he was already getting hard. Would he stay? Christ, as Mark would say, 'It'd be rude not to.'

"You promise to be chilled?" Zack asked.

"Zack, I said I was sorry, I was just angry with my situation," Anna replied softly.

He turned and kissed her. "I'll stay."

Their nine o'clock wakeup call came around all too soon, and the four of them headed to the restaurant. Breakfast was not an upbeat affair. After they'd waved the girls' courtesy bus goodbye, Zack and Mark trudged wearily along *Gaien-Higashi-Dori* to *Nogizaka* station. It had certainly been some re-introduction to Roppongi, Zack thought.

"Iss a shame they 'ad to go, ay," Mark commented breezily.

"What? Why, Mark? Did you want her to settle down here and have your kids? Is that it?" Zack's tone was bitter.

"*Wot*, is up your fuckin' arse?" Mark stopped to glare at Zack.

Zack just kept walking. He knew his comment had been harsh, but strangely, these days it seemed that the *impermanence* of things was starting to irk him. It was a peculiar reversal. Usually he *celebrated* the continual state of flux life offered, deriding the opposite state of affairs of permanence and routine, which led to boredom and apathy.

But eventually, he had to know. Did anything really *mean anything* in this life? It seemed you just couldn't win. Stick with something or someone, and it inevitably got boring at best, unbearable at worst. Did anyone ever really have their cake *and* eat it?

Zack did not believe most of the fifty or sixty year marriage celebrations he'd seen were the everlastingly blissful accomplishments they were made out to be. That was just what onlookers *wanted* to believe. In reality, the long-wed couple didn't know, and had never known, any fucking different. Locked in for years to the same routine, they wouldn't know how to change anything even if they wanted to.

So how could they know what they'd missed? And that what they'd missed wasn't ten times better than what they'd had? Was it *human nature*, Zack wondered, to crave something else, desperately want someone else, or just need to be somewhere else? Or was it just his nature?

Stopping to let Mark catch him, he apologised for his outburst. They returned to *Harajuku* together in silence.

Zack had talked with Anna until about four in the morning. They'd covered an awful lot of territory. Family, careers, travel, sex, love, partners, marriage, children, drugs, happiness, and the future. Anna was truly at a crossroads in her life, and had a lot of thinking to do before she saw her husband again. It had been great talking to her with all the barriers down. They'd really established a connection, and an understanding of each other's problems and hopes.

Now she was gone. They'd exchanged all the usual details, and promised to stay in touch one way or another. But she was still gone, and Zack felt empty. Intellectually, he knew it was wasted energy to feel this way, but he also took some heart from it. It proved some aspects of his psyche were still working like those of a normal human being.

Twelve

Victor threw Zack to the lions on Thursday night, effectively one night's warm-up before the weekend madness. The job of Dance-Manager turned out to be a lot more complicated than Zack had imagined.

Picture the scene. Forty money-hungry strippers competing for the money of a limited number of customers in a limited number of hours. Customers and dancers from many different countries. Gender barriers. Language barriers. Culture barriers. Alcohol, egos, desire, jealousy, drugs and sex.

All were weapons, triggers, or just plain trouble.

Disputes amongst customers. Disputes amongst dancers and customers. Disputes amongst dancers. Nervous breakdowns. Substance addictions. Psychological problems. Relationship problems. Attitude problems. Money problems. Dirty tricks. Slur campaigns. Bullying. Violence. The permutations for potential disaster were pretty much limitless.

And just for good measure, it turned out Melanie, the psycho from the guesthouse, worked there. Zack had laughed out loud at her reaction to his new position. Her about-face in attitude had been predictably nauseating. He'd have to keep an eye on the bitch though. One bad apple and all that. Nevertheless, it was good to be the king.

The first two weeks were complete mayhem. Zack almost expected to be fired. Then to his surprise, he learnt the majority of people who mattered, were highly satisfied with his performance. Apparently mayhem was normal. It was just keeping it within acceptable parameters that required a gifted manager.

By week four, Zack pretty much had the hang of it. His main priorities were the collection of nightly agency-fees from the girls, and the accurate calculation, processing and reconciliation of all dance-related credit-card transactions. First and last, make sure the numbers were right. Deal with the headaches in between.

The girls were all employed by the agency of which Victor was second-in-charge. It was owned by an ignorant, loud-mouthed American called Chad, whom Zack had disliked on sight. They paid a substantial nightly 'tip-out' fee to the agency for the privilege of taking their clothes off in Cloud Nine. The club's money came from high entry fees, extortionately priced drinks and snacks, as well as a twenty percent cut from the girls' credit-card earnings.

The girls made additional pocket-money from 'drink-backs' which were commissions on over-priced drinks purchased for them by customers. However, the bulk of their income came from either doing topless table dances, where the customers were not allowed to touch them and they kept their genital area covered, or from private dances, where they were obliged to flash their genitalia at the customer, and he could touch them anywhere except between the legs. This included kissing their tits and bodies. Lip to lip kissing however, was prohibited.

As far as Zack was concerned it was more or less prostitution without penetration. And he wasn't even too sure about that, sometimes. With the sort of money on offer, it was always a slippery slope.

The big money was in private dances. A security-guard monitored the private-dance-room to ensure the rules were followed. Zack was surprised to learn this scrutiny applied more to the strippers than the customers, but his naïvety didn't last long. After all, if one of the girls pushed it a little further with a customer, he might stay loyal, meaning perhaps thousands of dollars extra earnings for her.

But this sort of behaviour disadvantaged other, more principled girls, and along with many other possible indiscretions, was a fineable offence. Part of Zack's job was to liaise with the security guy to ensure as level a playing field as possible for all the girls. However, with such big money on offer, this was never an easy task.

This is not to say he did not have power. He did. He could fine them, send them home, restrict their alcohol, transfer, suspend or even fire them for a serious enough breach of conduct. In the meantime, the girls tried anything to pull the wool over his eyes, or get on his good side. Given the possibility of his 'interests' becoming conflicted, it was technically forbidden for him to have sex with any of them. Victor had told him that of course it happened, but warned against it. Zack figured he could live with this. There were plenty of other babes in Roppongi.

For the most part, sex for the strippers was just another commodity, another thing to trade for what they wanted. It seemed pretty obvious to Zack that if he didn't put out sexually, he was more likely to get money from them for his 'favours'. Realistically, what else did they have left to give? Accepting bribes for favours was common practice and the girls weren't stupid; most were adepts at this game. Much to his financial advantage, Zack was, as ever, a quick learner.

*   *   *

Meanwhile, he had moved out of the guesthouse, and in with Shunit. They shared one room of a two-room apartment in a block owned by her boss, Sasaki. Their room had a jerry-rigged 'curtain' part-way down the middle – the barest vestige of privacy. But it was a good enough set-up. And because she worked for Sasaki, they had the place at a serious discount.

An English couple, James and Teri, shared the other room. He was a waiter at BlackJacks and Teri hostessed at an upmarket club called Cadeau. They'd been together for a year in total, and in Tokyo now for two weeks. Zack gave their relationship another month at most, hoping that when it fucked up, they didn't get really vocal or violent. Work was enough of an emotional war-zone; he could do without living in one as well.

Shunit herself, was as cool as ever. It was just like old times. She laughed a lot at Zack's stories about 'Silicon Valley', his nickname for Cloud Nine. Her lifestyle was very different. She was studying Japanese full-time on a student visa. So she was up early in the day and sleeping at night, the opposite of Zack. When on their first meeting she'd mentioned needing a new room-mate, Zack had got lucky again.

He'd also been bumping into Dorit quite frequently. Zack was having an unusual amount of trouble pinpointing his feelings towards her. For better or worse, he now had an inbuilt wariness when it came to Israeli women. She was so goddamn sexy though, and he'd always been pretty wasted on one thing or another when he'd seen her.

But something had always stopped him; he'd always found an exit. She reminded him far too much of Nurit for his liking. Not so much in looks, but definitely in attitude and sex-appeal. Zack knew his evasive tactics were wearing thin; he would probably be forced into making a decision fairly soon.

First and foremost however, his income was looking good. Money was flowing in from four sources. His Cloud Nine salary, tips from the girls, pool-sharking, and commissions from Ban for all the drug hook-ups he organised. His expenses were low, his drugs were free, most of his drinking was free or ridiculously cheap, and if he concentrated on maximising his cash-flows this time round, he'd be on easy street for years to come.

*　　*　　*

Potting the black-ball, Zack reached over to shake Tanaka's hand. It was four-thirty in the morning on a Thursday, and they were at Zack's favourite after-hours pool bar, the Seventh Floor.

"That's *niman* yen you owe me now, Tanaka-san." Zack spoke courteously, without a winner's satisfaction. He didn't actually enjoy taking money off this easy-going, elderly Japanese gentleman. In fact, he'd come to quite like him. But, if he wanted to play ...

Tanaka bowed stiffly and said, "It is enough for me tonight, Zack." Opening his wallet, he passed Zack two *ichimans*.

Taking the money, Zack suddenly felt a little flat. "Let me buy you a drink before you go," he impulsively suggested. "Come on. It's only four-thirty."

Tanaka looked at him quizzically. "You don't want to play pool?" He indicated the next eager challenger, a serious-looking Japanese kid of about twenty-two, who was eyeing Zack off whilst screwing the two pieces of his own cue together.

"Fuck the pool. All I ever seem to do is work and play pool. Let's just have a drink and chill out."

Tanaka seemed surprised, but acquiesced.

Zack ordered a Tom Collins and his usual Jacks and dry. They settled at a table in the corner nearer the bar, away from the pool table's magnetic pull.

"You very good pool player, Zack. You must make much money here in Roppongi," Tanaka commented politely.

"Not really," Zack said. "Not in here anyway." He paused. "Sometimes down at the Sports-Café though, I make good cash off the Americans. A lot of them really think they can play, and want to show off their money." He shrugged his shoulders and grinned amiably at Tanaka. "What can I do?"

Zack liked the bigger mainstream venue for its financial opportunities, but unfortunately loathed its atmosphere: desperate suits with more money than personality, who generally hung around until late, waiting for strippers and hostesses to finish work.

Tanaka eyed him curiously. "When you leave Tokyo, what you do with this money you make here?"

Zack smiled again at the question. The old man was surprising him this evening.

"Well, I'm addicted to travelling, Tanaka-san. I've done quite a bit already, but I haven't been to South America yet. That's my next adventure."

"And what you think of the Japanese, Zack?" Tanaka leaned forward as he said this and dropped a long piece of ash into a scarred plastic receptacle between them.

Zack laughed. "You really want to know?"

Tanaka nodded.

Zack took a sip of his drink before answering. Then he met Tanaka's sustained gaze.

"To tell you the truth, I think they need to lighten up a bit. Just not be so goddamn serious all the time. Work, work, work. What is that all about, Tanaka-san? You only have seventy odd years on this planet. And only fifty or so of those as an adult, free to do what you want."

Zack noticed Tanaka smiling slightly at this. For some reason, the smile was vaguely unsettling. He pressed on regardless.

"You should be allowed to enjoy that time as much as possible, don't you think Tanaka-san? Do what makes *you* happy. Not what anyone else *wants* you to do, or *thinks* you should do."

Realising he'd spoken quite forcefully, Zack shrugged, and softened his tone. "That's my opinion anyway, for what it's worth."

Tanaka considered this. The smile had gone. "You make good point Zack, but if everybody thinks like this, then what will happen in Japan?"

Zack took another swig of his JD, and shrugged again. "Jesus, I don't know Tanaka-san. Maybe there'd be less people here, happily making more money, and the ones who left for a while would be happier at having experienced ways of life and business outside Japan. Who knows, Tanaka-san? Japan might even benefit from that fresh knowledge."

Zack glanced down at his drink and swizzled the ice blocks around with his straw, before looking back up at Tanaka. "All I know is I'd feel like I was living in a cage if I had to do things the Japanese way."

The old man seemed to have a quiet chuckle to himself, then took another sip of his drink, and leaned forward to stub out his dying cigarette. It occurred to Zack that all he'd been doing was answering Tanaka's questions. Funny, when Zack chatted with folks normally, it was nearly always they who answered Zack's ready line of questions.

"What about you Tanaka-san? How come you're out this late? Are you retired, or still working?" Zack asked.

Tanaka paused, swirling the last of his drink around the glass.

"I still working, Zack. I work for the Government. Administration things," he explained. "It is not so interesting, but it is what my father did."

"You see! That's *exactly* what I mean Tanaka-san!" Zack exclaimed. "You do it because your father did it, and that's pretty much the Japanese way. Not many Japanese seem to do what *they* want to do." Zack's tone again embodied his exasperation with this concept.

Tanaka nodded again. "Perhaps in some things you are right Zack, but now I must go."

He finished the Tom Collins, shook Zack's hand and bowed again, a little more deeply this time. Zack returned his bow even more deeply, wishing to show clearly his respect for the older man. Once Tanaka had disappeared, Zack turned his attention back to the pool players. The Japanese kid with his own cue was still here. He decided to stay. There was more money to be made tonight.

Thirteen

The day Hans turned up from Eilat, Zack's night at Cloud Nine had been a disaster and he was morosely nursing a post-work drink in Bongoes. Thank fuck it was Saturday, he thought. The end of the working week. One whole day's blissful respite from that crazy fucking place! He grimaced once more as he silently played the nasty scenes over again in his mind's-eye.

A normally okay chick called Amy, thinking her client wouldn't notice because he was so drunk, had tried to overcharge him. The guy had cottoned on, and gone totally ballistic. He'd refused to sign the credit-card slip at all. Then, very loudly and unusually passionately for a Japanese, he had slagged the whole place off. There was no shutting him up.

Despite Zack's best damage control it had still got pretty ugly. The Cloud Nine vibe hadn't just been broken, it had been irretrievably destroyed. A fight had started. And that fight started another one. Zack remembered observing that energetic ripple move around the room, as if in slow motion; he'd been absolutely powerless to stop it. In the confusion and chaos that followed, customers had left without paying their bills.

Amy's friends had rallied around her, screaming abuse at the guy, who'd ended up nursing a bloody nose, inflicted by another loyal customer of Amy's. Amy herself had dissolved into a hysterical mess, and then locked herself in the toilets. The guy had eventually been physically removed by security. The night in Cloud Nine had been effectively over at only 12.40 a.m.

Zack shuddered involuntarily and took another hard pull on his drink. What a nightmare. To his credit, the DJ had gamely tried to play on, but the boat had already sunk. Nobody's heart was in it; not the girls, and not the customers, who'd left in a flood. For the first time ever on a Saturday, the club had closed at one o'clock.

The fallout could have been worse, Zack supposed. As it was, he had copped an earful from the manager Marco, for not keeping the girls under better control. That shit rolled quickly downhill. Zack had fined Amy *goman* yen, and transferred her to a sleazy, low-rent satellite club for the following fortnight. Let any other wannabe troublemakers sweat on that prospect, he thought.

To top things off, he'd also finally got an email back from Anna, the air-hostess. She was having a tough time of it with her husband. She didn't say whether she'd told him about the fling with Zack, but her overall tone wasn't positive. She sounded lost, and jaded.

Zack felt for her. He'd genuinely hoped she'd somehow work things out with her husband. No doubt he'd find out more when she came back through Tokyo in a couple of weeks. Zack had pushed her out of his mind, and was concentrating on getting himself and the Bongoes' staff drunk, when Hans strolled casually into the bar.

For a moment, Zack could not believe his own eyes. His melancholy mood vaporised. Leaping to his feet, he skirted a few customers and lifted Hans off the ground in the customary bear-hug. It had been over two months since they'd seen each other. Stepping back, Zack surveyed the Hans he knew and loved.

He was super-tanned, and if anything looked more athletic than ever. His dark eyes darted around the room, trying to quickly get the measure of this place Zack had previously told them so much about.

"When the fuck did you get into town, you old sea-dog?" Zack exclaimed delightedly, releasing Hans and dragging him across to a bar-stool.

"Shit Zack, I think you broke a rib!" Hans complained.

"Can it, you pussy! Jesus, I can't believe you're here. Fucking fantastic!"

Zack pushed him onto the stool next to his. "So when did you get in?"

"Thursday." Hans leaned forward onto the bar.

"And I've only just seen you now! Unbelievable! Why didn't you call me?"

"Yeah, well I got caught up finding accommodation. It was a nightmare, Zack."

Zack organised two fresh beers. "You should have got my mobile number from these guys," Zack nodded at the Bongoes staff, "and given me a call for fuck's sake. I could have helped. Where'd you end up anyway?"

"A shit-hole. Madden International Guesthouse, but I won't be staying." Hans shook his head ruefully. "The guy who owns it's a complete asshole. He'll be lucky if I leave without punching him a good one on the jaw."

Zack tried not to laugh, but failed miserably. So he passed Hans a beer instead. "*L'Chaim, l'chaim* my friend. Welcome to big bad Roppongi! What do you want to do with yourself here anyway?"

Hans took a long, thirsty swallow and let out an appreciative burp.

"Well, I got lucky really. Met this guy on the plane who said I should come work with him. He's what they call a *host*. Works at a club in *Ginza* or somewhere. Gets paid loads to talk to Japanese women. Gets laid sometimes as well. I figured I could handle that, so I called him today and I'm going to meet the boss tomorrow night."

Zack was interested. He'd heard about *host-clubs*, but knew of none in Roppongi. Consequently he had assumed that wherever they were, they were probably all-Japanese affairs.

"Where's this guy from?" Zack asked curiously.

"He's a Yank," Hans replied. "But he seemed alright."

"Well, see how you go but if it doesn't pan out, let me know and I'll see if I can hook you up somewhere else," Zack offered.

"Much appreciated, mate."

They drank a ton of shots and reminisced about their Eilat adventures. Apparently Sofia was on her way over as well. Zack was unsurprised. According to Hans, the crew dynamic had changed once he'd left, with Zack's departure somehow acting as a catalyst for the others' decisions to get on the road again.

Shifting gears, they relocated to the Seventh Floor. Zack and Hans hit the pool-table and played doubles for a while. Hans was just good enough for them not to lose a game. It was now two in the morning, and the place was beginning to hum. Ban turned up for a while, and, as ever, deposited a little gift with Zack prior to leaving. It turned out to be *Ice*. Thoughtfully, he'd also included a tiny glass pipe. Zack and Hans left the game and went to the toilets.

"You had this stuff before?" Zack asked.

"Nope."

"Neither have I. Supposed to be a real kick in the arse. Well, here goes nothing."

Zack dropped a few crystals into the little glass bowl and ran the flame gently beneath it until wisps of smoke appeared. He kept them smoking after one inhalation, drew breath and pulled through again, finishing them off. The rush hit him during his second toke. He passed the pipe and stash to Hans.

"It's ... just have some," he wheezed, unable to explain further.

The room was suddenly too bright. Too sharply defined. Too small, Zack thought. He would have to get out of here soon. The stash and the pipe he thought, and then remembered Hans. He turned and helped Hans finish his toke without wastefully vaporising the crystals. Then he dumped a few more crystals into the bowl. They shared this batch and Zack somewhat unsteadily tucked the plastic bag with the remaining crystals into his sock.

On the way out, he put the pipe up at the back of the locker section. Why hadn't he thought of that before? Was he being too paranoid? Probably. Fuck, this rush was really something else. He'd been feeling a little weary before, a little drunk also. Not anymore. Now he was supercharged, absolutely confident that at the moment he was capable of doing *anything*. He and Hans wafted out of the toilets back into the bar area. Zack turned to Hans. His expression looked strange. Sort of distorted, like an image from a twisted mirror. Zack's body bent with his howl of laughter. Hans cracked up too, and the pair wove their way to the bar. Strangely, although reality was distinctly distorted, Zack's system was on full alert, his senses super-acute. He felt as if he had 360-degree vision and was aware of everything going on around them. Pausing to scan the room, his body seemed to levitate six inches.

Whoooaahhhhhhhfffuuckkkk! Then everything clicked into slow motion. That's better. He could focus on single things more clearly now. There were some absolutely luscious babes here he hadn't noticed before. Oh, and some of his strippers. Seeing them, he laughed again. What a ridiculous job he had! Roppongi was fundamentally ridiculous. Now he couldn't stop laughing ... there was no point to any of it anyway ... it was all just ridiculous. Pool-game, he thought. Let's get back on the table. Hans appeared with two beers, and suddenly they were surrounded by strippers.

"Oooohh, Zack's flying! Naughty boy, Zack! Who's your friend?" the one called Maxie asked. Zack wondered whether it was possible for a cleavage to pout invitingly, because that's what this one seemed to be doing. He imploded into the forced reality and introduced Hans. As if from far away, he heard himself gibbering on about how they'd worked together on a yacht in Israel. Christ, have to get away from this, he thought. He made a break for it and managed to set up the next game on the pool table. The initial mega-rush was subsiding, but time zoomed on, and it was hard work trying to keep out of trouble with the strippers. It seemed to Zack they'd planned a concerted attack ... pincer movements, the whole thing! Once there, he couldn't get this idea out of his head. They were the enemy! Zack did his best to fend off their come-ons, whilst Hans watched on somewhat bemusedly.

"Trust me, I know what I'm doing," Zack assured him.

Hans shook his head in dazed disbelief.

After a few games, they lost one, and re-visited the toilet to finish off Ban's gift. Once back at the pool-table, the events and substances of the night started to take their toll. Everything got more blurred, words and actions more disconnected. Zack was vaguely aware of losing another game, and then doing rounds of body-shots with the strippers.

After that? Nothing.

Fourteen

Zack came to in semi-darkness. He struggled to get his eyes to open. When they finally did, it seemed they weren't working very well. His head was pounding and his mouth felt like a piece of claggy carpet underlay, and tasted worse. Basically he knew he was in bad shape. What *the fuck* had happened? Where was he? A figure moved to the side of his vision, and very slowly, he brought the face into focus. Dorit!

What the fuck was going on?

She gave him a cup with something hot in it. "*Miso* soup," she said. "That's what you asking for when I find you anyway. I 'ope you still want it."

"Dorit, what happened?" Zack groaned. "What am I doing here?" He tried to focus again, but failed. "How did I get here?"

She sat on the bed beside him, gently shaking her head. "I think maybe you pass out near *Yoshinoya*. I was coming from little party in Déjà Vu, and see you in the footpath. The manager wants to call police, but I say to him I take you. That's it."

"Jesus, what's the time?" Zack asked, suddenly panicked.

"Five o'clock."

"Fuck, I've got to get out of here! I'm working at six." Zack moved forward in the bed and felt shards of pain shoot through his head. He closed his eyes and saw stars. He opened them again and shook his head a little. The stars were still there – not a good sign.

Dorit merely watched him with a smile. She appeared quite amused.

"What are you laughing at Dorit?" he snapped. "This is no fucking joke."

"You are usually working on Sunday, Zack?"

Zack looked at her in disbelief. Then he sank back into the bed in abject relief. She was right! Sunday! What a beautiful word. Sunday, Sunday, Sunday. Thank God for Sunday!

They sat in the silence of Zack's relief for a moment. Then, ashamed of himself, he looked back at her.

"I'm sorry Dorit. I shouldn't have snapped at you."

She simply nodded her understanding.

Zack couldn't believe the headache he had, so he sipped the *miso* soup. It was delicious. "Where did this come from?" he asked. "It's really good."

"Thank-you, I do it myself."

"So, not just beautiful ... gifted as well," Zack complimented.

She stroked her hand through his hair and looked down at him.

"And I was beginning to think you maybe don't like me, Zack." Her eyes were black, her features truly exquisite. In spite of his sorry condition, Zack felt his loins stirring.

He looked back at her reprovingly. "Come on. You know I'm attracted to you Dorit, it's just …." Zack trailed off.

"After Nurit, you worry about having something with Israeli girls, Zack? What this saying is? Once bited … umm?"

Zack smiled at her charming English. "Twice shy," he replied. Another fucking psychic, he thought gloomily. "And I'm not worried. Just wary."

She leaned down and kissed him gently on the lips. "You should not to fear from me, *chamoodi*. I want you to be comfortable in my 'ouse." She took his cup. "Let me to get you more soup."

Zack lay there, considering just how differently last night's debacle could have turned out.

Police - Arrest - Confinement - Questioning - Drug Allegations - Work Enquiries. He owed Dorit a lot. Fuck, that *Ice* was evil stuff! He *had* also been drinking for more than ten hours though, he supposed. He wondered how Hans was doing. Zack had no recollection whatsoever of their parting.

"Dorit," he said, as she re-entered the room.

She gave him the soup and sat down on the bed again.

"I owe you a *huge* thank-you, you know." It was heartfelt. "You probably saved me from a bunch of trouble. I really owe you one."

She smiled that incredibly erotic smile, and gently stroked the hairs on his stomach. "So it is fine with you if I am taking it from your body?"

Without waiting for him to answer she added, "First though Zack, you are going to my shower. You are stinking like a beast."

Zack struggled into the shower and ran it hot for a while, before letting icy cold needles blast his skin. Then back to hot again. God, it felt good. The door opened, and Dorit slipped in beside him. Her body was incredible. Flawless, toned olive skin, and not an ounce of fat anywhere. Her small athletic breasts stood proudly, and the large dark nipples were erect and inviting. She took the soap, and massaged it over his body. Zack closed his eyes and once again thanked God it was Sunday. What had he done to deserve to be rescued by this goddess last night?

She knelt down and soaped his now rock-hard member. Zack groaned with pleasure. Then he felt her mouth close around him. He was so turned on by her, he could feel he was about to come already.

Pulling her off and up, he spread her legs and pushed her up against the wall. Rivulets of water cascaded between her legs, and he followed their path with his mouth.

Suddenly he wanted this girl *badly*. His aches and pains disappeared with the sexual adrenalin of the moment. Pushing his tongue inside her he then flicked it over her clitoris. Her body twitched against the wall as he continued probing with his tongue. He moistened a finger inside her and then gently stretched her arse with it, as he ground his face further into her delicious sex.

He could sense the pressure building, through the decreasing intervals between the spasms that rocked her body, and suddenly she pulled him off. She turned the shower off, and in a tangled soaking union, they collapsed onto the bed. He was on top of her and she took his cock back into her mouth. Zack's tongue was already playing games with her, and he again pushed the tip of one finger into her arse and his thumb into her soaking wet sex. He felt her body contract, and she gasped as her orgasm hit. Her teeth pressured his cock as she came, and she masturbated him even more furiously, while continuing to suck his engorged head. Zack spasmed out of control. Then he was coming. She milked every last bit of pleasure out of his orgasm. They fell back into each other's arms, exhausted. Zack felt like he was going to have a heart attack. His system was racing.

With not a word exchanged, they both fell asleep.

When Zack woke up, he was alone. Feeling a little better, he pondered this latest turn of events. It now seemed like a dream, but he knew it wasn't. Where was this little twist going to take him? She was quite a piece of work, he thought. He stretched out and relaxed. For the moment he didn't really care what happened next. He was alive and seemingly intact. Relax and enjoy. Don't think too much.

A moment later, he heard a door open, and Dorit reappeared. She had some bags in one hand, and what looked like a pizza in the other. Zack realised he was starving.

"I thought we 'ave dinner in the 'ouse tonight," she said. "Maybe I take you another place when you are ... aahhm ... better." She smiled as she said the last word.

"You are a legend, Dorit. And don't worry, it's going to be *me* that takes *you* out to dinner sometime soon."

She'd bought coke (the liquid variety), some tuna salad sandwiches and sausage rolls, as well as the pizza. It was a veritable bedroom feast, and Zack couldn't remember the last time he'd appreciated food so much.

Out of habit, he checked his watch again. Eleven o'clock. Then he remembered something else.

"Did you find my phone last night, Dorit?"

"Umm ... no." She finished her mouthful of food. "You didn't have one with you when I ... undressed you."

Ahh fuck! How many mobile phones can one guy lose?

He'd already lost the first a few weeks previously, and he'd lost five the last time he was here. Only in Roppongi, he thought. Maybe someone who knew him had picked it up. He had his name and the Cloud Nine office number on it. After all, this *was* Japan. Someone *might* want to get it back to him.

"Here, call it." Dorit tossed him her cellular.

He dialled, and it rang.

"Allo," a voice answered.

"Who's this?" Zack asked.

"Who's *this*?" came the answer. "You don't sound like a Dorit."

"You know who it is. It's Zack. You've got my phone in your hand. I'm trying to track it down."

"Ah, Zack." The voice was annoyingly familiar. "You were a bit wasted last night I think, yes?" It was an infuriating remark.

Zack took a deep breath and forced himself not to speak. Silence ensued.

"Relax Zack, it's Ranay from Seventh Floor my friend. I saw your name on it so I decided to keep it for you."

"Thanks Ranay, I owe you one. Are you working tomorrow night?"

"Yes, I'll be here Zack."

"I'll come in and pick it up after work around three-thirty if that's okay. In the meantime, just turn it off, so my calls go straight to the answering service."

"Yeah, no problem Zack. I'll see you then."

"Thanks mate."

That was one more thing he didn't have to worry about. He was glad to have such good relations with the guys there.

"Now can you relax?" Dorit asked.

He looked at her warmly. "At this exact moment Dorit, I honestly couldn't be happier."

She dropped out of her clothes and snuggled in close to his warm body. Zack, running his hands over her smooth skin, felt himself getting hard again. Dorit just smiled and put her hand down to stroke him.

Fifteen

The next couple of weeks were full of change. Through Dorit, Zack met an Israeli called Lior, who was basically a more sophisticated version of Ban, except his drugs were much better and the margins much greater. Through chance conversation, it coincidentally transpired that Lior was very good friends with Zack's friend Avi from Eilat. Lior checked Zack out through Avi and subsequently offered him a deal. This deal was much more organised, and more lucrative than anything Zack had imagined possible. On current business, it meant an extra half a million yen or thereabouts a month for Zack, primarily from coke, ecstasy and acid.

Taking up this offer, however, meant summarily cutting Ban out of Zack's now considerable market. Zack wrestled with this dilemma for a couple of days, then decided. He would go for it. It was impossible to turn down that sort of extra money for doing hardly anything more than he already did. The X-factor was Ban's reaction; Zack wasn't particularly looking forward to that conversation.

In addition to this imminent re-alignment of forces, Dorit was leaving for India again, to escape the coming winter. Her visa was up, and she'd already done one visa run, which meant she was unlikely to be allowed in again, at least for a while. The fact she had even scored a second three months was an unusual success for a *Sephardi* Israeli. Why? Because her skin colour wasn't to Japanese tastes.

Anecdotal evidence strongly suggested that many 'turn-backs' at Narita airport were based primarily on skin colour. Notwithstanding this, Dorit also didn't want to risk the consequences of potentially being caught on overstay. For Zack, who had found himself settling into a very agreeable casual alliance with her, it was yet another case of exercising some stoicism and just accepting the loss.

The Gods however, were in benevolent mode, because just as Dorit was about to leave, Sofia arrived. Zack spoke to her on the first night she got in, but was so busy with Dorit's imminent departure and everything else that he didn't immediately have any time for her. She promptly got a job hostessing at a club called Casablanca, and moved into the apartment Hans had found.

*　　*　　*

Zack met Ban on the more or less neutral territory of the Sports Café. He organised a couple of drinks for them, then cut to the chase.

"Ban, the reason I wanted to see you is I'm dropping out of the game. I'm not going to bullshit around with you; we've known each other too long for that sort of crap."

Zack paused. Ban listened impassively.

"Mainly because everything's getting too risky. As you know, the cops have been cracking down lately, but apart from that, the fact is a lot of the stuff we've been offloading recently has just been shit. No offence mate, but people know they're being fucked over and they don't like it. And I don't blame them! People who *were* friends of mine have changed their attitude towards me, and that pisses me off. I'm sick of ripping off friends. It's as simple as that."

"So you've found a new line of supply, Zack?" Ban asked quietly.

"I haven't *found* anything Ban," Zack lied. "Are you even listening to me?"

There was a long silence. Ban looked unconvinced.

Zack persevered.

"At the moment, little birds are telling me to take a step back. You might be wise to lie low yourself." Might as well make him think twice, Zack thought. "Basically Ban, I just don't want to be associated with this shit at the moment. Call it instinct."

Ban pressed his fleshy hands together on the table and leaned towards him.

"You know Zack, it's not just me in this thing we're in. There are people behind me, and people behind them … and some of those people probably aren't going to be very happy. I like you, Zack." Ban paused meaningfully. "But what I think doesn't really matter sometimes."

Zack felt a knot of unease at the pit of his stomach as he considered the invisible forces Ban was referring to. Who were these people in the shadows? Roppongi had to be one of the few places where trying to get out of something only got you into even hotter water. He sighed inwardly. He'd already had enough of this conversation but, poker-faced, decided to brave it out.

"Look my friend, I've tried to be nice. I don't know what more I can do. You'll just have to organise your little distribution ring without me now. That's all there is to it. And you can tell your *people* whatever you like. I really don't give a fuck. They don't *own* me."

Zack finished the remainder of his drink, stood up and put his hand across the table. Ban still hadn't spoken. But they shook hands anyway.

"It's been fun, Ban. I hope it doesn't have to get nasty."

"So do I, Zack. So do I," Ban murmured, more to himself than to Zack, who had already turned and was headed for the exit.

Neither of them could possibly have envisaged what was to come.

* * *

It was Wednesday. It had been another trying night at Cloud Nine. One of the girls had been caught smoking *Ice* in the toilets, then she'd run around inside the club screeching like a banshee. Incensed, Marco had fired the girl on the spot. At which point, she completely freaked out and became hysterical. She started screaming that 'everyone was doing it … why was she the only one getting fired and no-one else …blah blah blah.'

Zack necked the rest of his drink in disgust. Marco had ordered a staff/dancer/management meeting tomorrow before work and it didn't require a genius to deduce the agenda. Given his own plans for the immediate future, Zack couldn't believe the timing of this latest bullshit event. The Roppongi Gods were having a laugh alright! Extreme care would now need to be taken with any of his avenues through the strippers, or the club at all for that matter.

Sitting in Bongoes after this latest nightmare, he chatted with a couple of the old regulars about what hard work most of the strippers were. As usual, it was next to impossible to get any sympathy from other guys about his job. Every male he knew thought Zack had the best job on the planet! What a fucking joke.

Then Dyson walked in. Dyson was a nickname in deference to the gold-standard brand of vacuum-cleaners. He had won this tag as a result of his industrial-strength drug habit. One of Zack's regular customers, they'd been friends since Zack's last tour. Dyson also happened to be a banker, so at the moment he was just the person Zack needed to see.

As a matter of course, and especially in light of the Ban situation, Zack had decided to give himself a bit of extra insurance. He needed to hide any money that wasn't legitimate, just in case he was ever investigated. Bank details would be one of the first things they checked, and he'd surely be an idiot to be caught out on that basis. On the contrary, he'd be able to offer them his bank details as a *defence*. As ever, Zack mused, it was just a question of identifying every potential risk and then doing your utmost to minimise all of them, at all times.

Dyson ambled over, and Jarrod organised a couple of drinks for them. After preliminary chit-chat, Zack told Dyson what he needed. An hour of conversation covering ins, outs, whys and wherefores ensued, with Dyson finally satisfying Zack's exhaustive inquisition. He agreed to set up an offshore banking facility with Zack as sole signatory, at cost through his bank. Account fees were to be mates-rates.

Zack would provide Dyson with a sum of cash twice a month to be deposited into the account. In return for this favour, Dyson would receive two grams of cocaine a month. If Dyson had any idea what it was wholesaling at, he would've asked for five.

This seemed to Zack a reasonable price to pay for a respectable, anonymous and untraceable external fund repository. If he was going to do this thing, he was going to do it properly. Who knew how much his current market might expand in between now and whenever he left? Aside from which, given the life he led, he'd always thought it would be kind of cool to have an offshore account. He left Bongoes at five-thirty a.m. and went home to sleep. Nice to have an early night for once, he thought.

As the elevator-doors opened on his floor, that possibility vanished. Turning the corner towards the apartment, he encountered a monumental screaming match in full swing. James was standing in a pile of clothes in the corridor, holding a wide-open suitcase and a half-empty bottle of *Kirin* beer. Various items of clothing lay scattered around him on the floor.

" ... AND IF I SEE THAT BITCH'S FACE YOU CAN TELL HER I'LL SMASH IT MYSELF."

Teri was crying and screaming, just going nuts. Zack briefly stuck his head around the doorway and was lucky not to have it taken off by a boot that sailed past his nose. He winced, but took the opportunity to jump into the room before she could reload.

Shunit was in the kitchen in a bathrobe, patiently smoking a cigarette. She rolled her eyes and raised her hands in the air. No words were needed. Zack pleaded with her to go into the other room to calm Teri down. Better a woman, he guessed. Shunit screwed up her face at him, but went.

Zack immediately pulled the sliding partition firmly across. He called James into his room. They sat cross-legged on the floor.

"What the *fuck* is going on?" Zack asked.

James looked pretty drunk, but he could speak. "I dunno what to do Zack. Honestly. She's tripping her head off. It's her first time on acid, and she's got it in her head I've slept with one of the hosties from BlackJacks. I admit the chick's been trying it on, but I haven't done *anything* with her. She must have spun some bullshit story to Teri's friends, hoping it'd break us up."

Zack sighed wearily as he absorbed this information. It was a common enough story. Chicks in Roppongi could really be bitches sometimes. He'd had the same thing happen to him more than once last time with Nurit. Half a dozen different girls had tried pretty hard to break them up. It was some sort of power thing, Zack had concluded.

Two things were good anyway. First, was that Teri was tripping. She was hyper-emotional at the moment, and would probably see things differently when she came down. Second, was that James seemed pretty straight-up about not having fucked this chick, whoever she was. Hopefully he could convince Teri of the truth tomorrow.

Zack looked at James and said, "Well, it's obvious you won't be sleeping in there tonight. Get your stuff together and maybe you can sleep in my bed tonight. I'll try to get Shunit to sleep in your room. If that can't happen, you'll be kipping on the floor my friend."

"Thanks mate." James looked considerably relieved at having the decisions made for him so promptly.

Zack left him to retrieve his stuff from the corridor, took a deep breath, and went into the other room. Shunit was sitting on the bed hugging Teri, who was still sobbing.

Shunit raised her eyebrows at Zack and said *"Chaval al azman ... schteim trippim."* Zack closed his eyes in disbelief. *She'd taken two trips?* What the fuck was wrong with people? Without saying a word, he went back to the other room and grabbed two of his own precious Rohypnols. He hated to waste them, but this was the only way she, and therefore he, was going to sleep anytime soon. Re-entering the room, he asked Shunit whether she minded staying with Teri for what remained of the night. He genuinely pitied her: she had a class at nine o'clock. It just wasn't fair.

She shrugged her shoulders and with a resigned expression said, *"En brera,"* Hebrew, for 'no choice'.

After more comforting and cajoling, they persuaded Teri to take the tranquilisers, and Zack got the fuck out of there. James, meanwhile, had got the place back in a semblance of order.

Before turning the lights out, Zack spoke forcefully to James. "Listen James. This is serious. Tomorrow you'll have to talk to her and do two things. First you have to convince her this chick's lying and you've done nothing wrong, and second, you have to explain to her that if something like this happens again, I'll throw both of you out into the corridor for the night, after which I'll get Sasaki to kick you out permanently. It's not fair on anyone, least of all Shunit."

Zack pinned him with a hard look. "Aside from which, I deal with enough of this sort of shit *at work*."

James paused, and then nodded assent. "Fair enough," he replied. "And thanks."

Zack leaned over and grabbed another Rohypnol for himself. "Goodnight," he said.

It was seven a.m.

Sixteen

The drugs meeting at Cloud Nine the next day turned out to be more or less a non-event. There were the usual threats of instant dismissal, as well as a new one of informing the police. Zack had to laugh. He knew they'd never involve the police. He was only half listening anyway. His thoughts were again with Dorit. She had organised her flight for Monday morning. They had booked a room at ANA hotel for the Sunday night. The plan was to go out to the infamous rave club Flower (a.k.a. Geoid) after work on Saturday and then on to an after-party in *Yoyogi-Park* for some sun and recovery, before crashing in the luxury of the hotel.

The weekend at work was busy, but passed without serious incident. A couple of girls were blatantly using the club as a front for prostitution, but there was nothing Zack or anyone else could really do about it. Apart from which, nobody wanted to.

It worked like this. The customer agreed his 'fuck-price' with the girl, then came into the club and paid her via supposed private dances in the club, usually on company credit. The girl would come to Zack asking him to process up to thirty or forty private dances (between two to three thousand U.S. dollars worth), which she obviously hadn't had time to actually do. Zack's role was to formally confirm the amount with the customer, who obviously agreed. Then the corporate card took a hammering. This way, the customer got a receipt from a bona-fide and well-known Tokyo club and could claim the cost as a legitimate entertaining expense. It also made the girl look good in that she was bringing in wealthy customers. And then there was the club's cut. Twenty percent of the credit-card dance total, plus entry, plus drinks, plus food. Ka-ching! Thanks for coming, pardon the pun. Corporate entertaining at its best, Zack thought. Even the shareholders got a fucking. His pity went out to them, whoever they were.

Adamantly refusing to be roped into the customary Saturday night drinks session in the club, Zack slipped out and walked purposefully towards Bongoes. He had arranged to meet Dorit for a couple of drinks before heading to Flower. He stopped off at a less popular bar on the way. Their toilet was usually unoccupied, and had a useful black-topped formica wash-area. He cut himself two big lines and hoovered one up each nostril, mopping up the remnants with a couple of fingers and numbing his gums with them.

Studying himself in the mirror, he felt his pulse quicken and his temples throb as the drug alerted his body to its presence. Not too bad he thought, assessing his appearance. He'd recently joined up at Tipness, the up-market fitness club, and was trying to get in there three times a week. So far it was more like twice weekly. Don't let yourself go this time, he thought.

Ten feet tall and bullet-proof, he headed back onto the street, and by the time he strode into Bongoes, he felt magnificent. He grabbed a beer and moved to Dorit, who was with Lior and another couple of Israeli girls. They were already E'ing, and Zack guessed they'd be pretty keen to get moving. He was right.

"Zack, thanks to God you are 'ere," Lior said in his thick accent. "Dorit 'as been driving me crazy."

Dorit rolled her eyes exaggeratedly. "But really, we must to get away from these alcohol suit-people." She looked around the cramped space and twisted her exotic features into an expression of singular distaste. "*Ezeh magilim,*" she added for good measure.

Zack had to admit that generally speaking, there was a cavernous divide between the normal patronage of Bongoes, and the rave-party crowd. Apart from the obvious image difference, Zack found it interesting that contrary to what constituted the legal state of affairs, most dedicated ravers actually looked down on alcohol and those who drank it to excess. They considered it an unsophisticated drug that was less rewarding, not to mention more physically damaging to their health, than alternatives such as ecstasy or LSD. And looking at the physique of the average raver in comparison to the average beer-swilling barfly, it was undeniable that they had a point.

In addition to this, Zack thought, most ravers had at least incorporated elements of spirituality and an appreciation of nature into their existence, whereas consumerism and a reckless worship of the 'bottom-line' still ruled the alcohol-quaffing world with an iron fist.

"I hear you, Dorit. Come on, let's get the fuck out of here," Zack responded. Flower was just a short taxi-ride away, and Zack swallowed a pill on the way, washing it down with a mouthful of what would probably be his last beer for the night.

As they neared the steps that descended into the legendary dance-club, Zack could hear the 'thump thump thump' of the heavy bass back-beat, pounding remorselessly against the inside of the thickly padded entrance doors. He felt himself quicken with anticipation. Waving a hello to several acquaintances who were hanging around outside, they went through, and those thick doors closed swiftly behind them.

In a few short steps they voyaged to a parallel dimension. A world of darkness and rising mists, of flashing strobes mixed with a sea of UV-enhanced psychedelic colour. Insinuating itself throughout this fantastic dreamscape was the relentless pumping energy coming from the speakers. This energy was absorbed, mutated, and subsequently reflected in exultation by the seething mass of super-charged people crowding the dance-floor. They headed upstairs to check the scene out from above.

"Fuck-Ing-Hell," was all Zack could say. It was going *off* down there. "I'll meet you guys by the bar in a minute," he shouted.

"Are you alright?" Dorit shouted back. She looked concerned.

Zack disarmed her with a huge smile. "Yeah, I'm fine. I just want to watch what's going on from here until this E kicks in. You go. I'll find you."

He watched her disappear down the stairs. She looked sensational. She was dressed in the style of a Native American Indian: hair in plaited pigtails, a brown suede miniskirt and boots, and a midriff-top of ethnic origin. Together with the body paint, the tattoo, and the *bindi* on her forehead, her athletic figure epitomised rave-party chic. She was already on the fringes of the dance-floor, Zack noticed. The way she moved she'd be centre-stage before long.

It was a pity, Zack realised, that establishment forces would never loosen up for long enough to appreciate the more primal 'seeking of self' which was possible through the use of ecstasy and acid in combination with this type of music and atmosphere. No wonder the dance-party phenomenon was an unstoppable force. It seemed increasing numbers of people were sick to death of the shallowness and mediocrity of a life worshipping at the altar of materialism. There had to be something more, they reasoned, and many of them, through parties such as these, often discovered the gateway to that 'more'.

As ever, the paradox lay in the fact the establishment had a massive vested interest in maintaining the status-quo. One could argue their very reason for existence disappeared without it. It could only benefit the world, Zack thought, to one day get all those fucking politicians and bureaucrats into an appropriate environment, shove a load of drugs down their throats, and then watch them venture precariously down the road of true self-discovery and expression.

Politicians were shit-scared of the phenomenon of dance-party culture, and with good reason, Zack thought. Millions of their subjects were gravitating to this side of the fence, and consequently perceiving the rat-race's futility and capacity for self-destruction ever more clearly.

He occasionally tried to imagine the politicians of the day coming up on some good quality MDMA, and then just going for it. It was difficult to visualise, but comical nonetheless.

Speaking of coming up ...

Zack could feel the music's tentacles permeating his senses, and without even thinking about it he was already moving downstairs towards the dance floor. He had to get into that space and get moving, otherwise he'd end up vegetating on a couch somewhere, too blissed out to care. Not that there was anything wrong with that either!

The next hour and a half or so was a fantastically surreal, most beautiful blur of happiness, liberation, and the celebration of life. He danced solidly, near Dorit for most of it. She looked so pure. Like a fertility goddess dancing to some ancient rite, she was blissfully unaware of everyone's admiration. Dancing from somewhere deep in her primal self, she was simply awe-inspiring.

Zack timed out of the dance floor and went to the bar for a change of pace. Lior was already there, sweating and beaming.

"You know Zack, usually I am not really drinking ... for sure not on E. But we should to celebrate I think."

Zack was slightly breathless, and could only nod. The next thing he knew, there was a bottle of Moet chilling on the bar. They charged their glasses, and Zack toasted them both.

"To the success of a Roppongi partnership," he proclaimed. They raised their glasses high for the clink, and at that moment Zack felt everything was perfection. Life was good - he was where he needed to be.

"C'mon! Let us to take something." Lior grabbed the bottle of champagne and they headed for the toilets.

They had to wait for a cubicle, and when the first door opened, two girls and a guy unselfconsciously spilled out as one, joking and laughing. Zack wondered whether they'd been having sex or just doing lines. Maybe both. Who cared? The rules were several worlds away.

Zack and Lior installed themselves in the cubicle and Zack watched as Lior cut four killer lines. As well as the *effect* of the drugs, Zack loved the ritual of snorting the stuff. It was the principle, he thought. It was a symbolic and deliberate rejection of societal norms and establishment law. Who the fuck were *they*, to tell *him* what he could or couldn't do in his own time with his own body? It was an outrageous imposition on anyone's personal freedom.

He was always amazed at how many of the herd unquestioningly accepted and followed those laws blindly, seemingly not challenging or finding out or even caring what was valid, or not. 'Sheeple' he had recently heard them called, and he thought the term apt.

Still, it was just changing times he supposed, more or less like prohibition must have been back in the day. He would be very surprised if the drug legislation in fifty years maintained today's blinkered standpoint. Christ, they'd probably have legalised everything by then. Cut out the black market and the associated crime, and pick up a previously untapped fortune in government tax revenue into the bargain.

High as kites from the drugs, adrenalin and atmosphere, Lior and Zack headed back to the bar, swigging from the bottle of Moet, pumping it overhead, a symbol of hedonistic excess. A few people whooped and cheered as they went by, and Zack felt he could almost explode with freedom and happiness. This was living!

They dropped another E and joined the girls at the bar. The champagne was nearly gone, so Zack ordered another one in Dorit's honour. In Roppongi there was *always* another reason to party. They charged en-masse back onto the dance floor in an orgy of emotion, friendship and ecstasy. Whooping, swigging champagne, cavorting like the Bacchanalian partygoers they truly were. Zack felt the rush of the second E kick in, incredulous it was possible to feel this good. He looked at the shiny happy people around him, and couldn't help feeling sorry for those who would never know this seemingly crazy but completely un-hypocritical world.

A couple of hours later, Zack found himself in one of the chill-out rooms with Dorit. It was full-ish but not packed, and a few people were passing joints around. Zack was leaning on a cushion against the wall and gently massaging Dorit anywhere he could find skin. He slipped his hands underneath her top and caressed her erect nipples through the warm sweaty sheen on her body, the tactile sensations blowing them both away.

The first indication that something was wrong, was when the music just
STOPPED   DEAD.

Even so, Zack didn't snap out of his reverie until a minute or so later, when incredibly, the lights came on.

Christ, what was the fucking time? He looked at his watch but realised he was too E'd up to read it. So they asked the people next to them. It was only eight-thirty! What was going on? He pulled himself up and looked downstairs. What he saw was impossible, surely? The fucking *police* were here!

He watched their pathetic self-important little uniforms run around in circles below, like players in some sort of animated cartoon. It had to be a drug raid, he thought. Zack wasn't personally bothered … he had nothing left on him. But what the fuck were they doing here? Why Flower? Why now? He had never heard of this place being raided … ever!

Most people had left the chill-out room and were curiously leaning over the balcony. Others had bolted for the toilets. Some people would probably be awake for days, Zack thought, with an amused smile. He and Dorit headed downstairs, and bumped into a staffer they knew.

"What the fuck's going on?" Zack asked..

"Apparently they're after some idiot who's got a gun," was the answer.

"*Gaijin?*" Zack asked.

"Don't think so ... maybe Jap-Brazilian. That's what someone was saying anyway."

Zack's first emotion was relief that it wasn't a drug-raid, and the second was amusement for all the product that must have been ditched, snorted or swallowed unnecessarily. So this raid would actually be good for business, he thought. How ironic!

The cops had apparently got their man. The lights went down and the music came back on about ten minutes later, but the atmosphere and momentum of the night had been dislocated. A lot of people were shaken by the sudden appearance of the cops. Jolted by the harsh bright lights and the break in music, many had now lost their euphoric vibe. Oddly, Zack felt strangely buoyant in the face of all this melodrama.

"Let's go to *Yoyogi,*" Zack suggested.

"What ... now?" Dorit asked surprisedly.

"Yeah, why not? Look around you ... it's time to get out of here. It'll give us more time in the hotel anyway. We should find Lior and the girls so you can say goodbye, or see if they want to come."

They hunted around for five or ten minutes, but couldn't find the others anywhere. So they headed outside.

"That's really weird of them to leave without ..." Dorit was saying, as they emerged into the eye-stingingly bright daylight.

Then they spotted the trio relaxing against a wall in the carpark, basking in the glorious sunshine. As ever at moments like this, Zack was suddenly very glad he had his little travel-pack. Water, chewing gum, eye-drops, chap-stick, and most importantly at the moment, sunglasses.

"You really come prepared, huh Zack?" Dorit's friend Maya remarked.

"Yeah, well I'm a professional, what can I say?" Zack shrugged.

The *Yoyogi-Park* idea was greeted enthusiastically and, still buzzing chemically as well as from all the excitement, they jumped into a cab. Zack shot a last look at the chaotic scene they were leaving.

He wondered what all the Japanese people on *TV-Asahi-Dori* thought about this influx of crazily-costumed, drug-affected, weirdo-*gaijin*, wandering around on their street at nine o'clock on a Sunday morning. It was always an entertaining spectacle, and just another of the many contrasts he loved being a part of as a foreigner in Japan.

There must have been something in the water this particular weekend, because when they got to *Yoyogi*, all hell was breaking loose. Instead of families, school-kids and tourists sauntering about, there was complete bedlam. Police cars everywhere. Cops running all over the place. Things were truly going nuts today, Zack thought.

They pulled the cab over near *Omotesandō* and got out. Zack collared the nearest bystander who didn't look like a tourist and asked what was going on.

"It's the Iranians. They had a massive sort of political meeting in *Yoyogi-Park*. Then the police tried to arrest some of them, and they all went berserk."

"Fuck me!" Zack exclaimed. What were the Iranians doing having a rally at all? Legally speaking, the vast majority of them shouldn't even be here. You'd think they'd try to keep a low profile. Sometimes, he thought, they were just too hot-headed for their own good.

Zack wondered if Ban was out there. He doubted it; the guy was too smart, and had too much at stake. A wry smile accompanied his next thought. It wouldn't exactly be inconvenient for him if Ban was arrested and deported.

Leaving his vantage point, he re-joined the group.

"What now?" Lior asked.

"Well normally I'd wander into the park, work on the tan I don't have, and watch the Iranian-sponsored free entertainment, but to tell you the truth I'm a bit tired." He turned to Dorit. "What about you babe?"

"Let's get some coffee first," Dorit suggested.

They camped out at a table on the footpath of Café de Paris, up the other end of *Omotesandō*. By the time everyone had finished their coffees, it was obvious that energy levels were flagging. After what they'd already put through their systems, caffeine didn't quite make the grade. Lior and the girls decided to crash in *Yoyogi-Park's* sunshine for a couple of hours before heading home. Goodbye hugs and a few tears were shared by the girls before Zack gathered Dorit into a cab and directed it to ANA Hotel.

They sauntered in past the door-staff like a couple of rock-stars and headed for the check-in counter. Zack knew he currently cut a daunting figure for them, with his jeans, vest, boots, space-age sunnies, and shoulder-length hair streaming out. Dorit's arresting looks and even more strikingly incongruous outfit turned every head in the lobby.

From the tribal dance-rites of Flower to check-in at ANA Hotel was quite a journey, and the pair of them presented an irresistible spectacle in this elegant polished-marble foyer. Dorit had left her bags here the day before, as had Zack a travel bag. A bell-hop followed them with their baggage cart. Now they had the attention of everyone in the lobby *and* buffet area. Zack found it hilarious. He knew people were thinking, *'They must be famous ... who are they ... what group is in town?'* Astounding what a bit of attitude and self-expression can achieve in this buttoned-down place, he mused.

The poor bell-hop tried his best for invisibility in the lift, but at the same time couldn't help trying to get away with studying them more closely. Zack decided it would be a shame not to give him something to talk about, so he whispered to Dorit, and in the next twenty seconds, they generated some pretty powerful sexual energy. The doors opened to reveal a very serious-looking group of Japanese businessmen.

Their mortified bell-hop hurriedly led the way out, blushing as much as it was possible for a Japanese to blush. Zack and Dorit peeled themselves off each other and bowed theatrically to the stunned group before exiting the lift. As they entered their room, the giggles were starting, and by the time the bell-hop left it was impossible to hold it any more. They simply dissolved into hysterical fits of laughter and collapsed on the bed.

"Did you see the lift-boy's face?" Dorit was beside herself with laughter, and there were tears in her eyes.

"What about the guy eating breakfast?" Zack gasped. "His egg stayed in mid-air for about thirty seconds!"

"And these men at the lift ... *Ya-alla, chaval al azman!*" Dorit couldn't stop laughing.

Zack rolled over, pulled her top off and started kissing her breasts, which made her giggle even more. After a couple of minutes of tussling, she pushed him off.

"The amount we pay this hotel Zack, believe me, we will to *really enjoy* their bathroom."

Zack had a hard-on that wasn't waiting for anything, and needed no second bidding. They expended the last of their energies on some fast and furious sex. Both of them climaxed in the shower, the pent-up tension from Flower's erotically charged atmosphere helping them on their short journey.

Zack watched her perfect, freshly moisturised and powdered, olive-skinned body slip between the pristine white sheets of their enormous bed and smiled dumbly in appreciative wonderment; today, life was pretty good. They each took a Rohypnol, drank as much water as possible, then crashed into dreamland.

*   *   *

Sitting morosely at the breakfast table the following morning on a bit of a post-E-downer, Zack found himself again mulling over the nature of his life. Another breakfast, another departure, and life just keeps rolling on. Fan-fucking-tastic.

He looked across at Dorit. She was in a similarly subdued mood, engrossed in toying with her selection from the buffet. Without looking up, she spoke.

"Zack, usually I am not getting too serious with this stuff, but before I go, I want that you know something."

He waited.

"Because of you, I really love this last month in Tokyo. And believe me I want to leave this fucking place *two* months before. You important to me, and I don't forget that."

Then she did look up. Her eyes were full of tears.

"Just promise that if you ever close by, you can find me. I always enjoy to see you."

Zack was genuinely lost for words. He took her hand and held it.

"You know that I will, Dorit. But it was really good to hear you say it."

"Take care, *matok shelli*," she whispered.

And then she was gone.

Seventeen

Zack looked blankly at the screen in front of him. It said, 'Inbox: 37'

He'd wandered listlessly around Roppongi after watching Dorit's bus disappear, not feeling like going back to the apartment straight away. It had been a couple of weeks since he'd checked his email, so he ended up at an internet cafe. Sipping the sticky bitter-sweetness of his double espresso, he surveyed the screen.

His eyes flicked through the list. Seeing one from Anna, he brought that up first.

'Hey Zack,

*You're probably wondering why you haven't seen me again yet, so I thought I'd let you know. The thing with Brian eventually reached crisis point, and I told him everything. I said if he wants to divorce me, go right ahead because at the moment what we've got is no marriage anyway. Then he broke down, and confessed to two affairs (told you I was right). Bastard! The bottom line is that after a pretty full-on 24 hours of pain, tears and honesty, we both decided to overhaul our situation, and try to save our marriage. This meant a few changes/compromises. He's cut back on any non-essential hours at the station, and I've agreed to work only the European routes (max one day stop-overs if any). Basically give ourselves some quality time – actually just some time you know? So I won't be seeing you in Japan (and Brian would obviously be happier if I didn't see you at all). But I think you and I understand each other, so I've created another email address for myself (*margarita-babe-70@hotmail.com*), because he knows about this one, and I wouldn't put it past him to check up on me (don't worry I've deleted this message!). Anyway, I just want you to know you were (for want of a better expression) 'good therapy' for me, and that I very much appreciated our time together. When you're next in London, let me know. Hopefully we'll be able to catch up and I'll give you a progress report.*
Take care of yourself you lunatic.
Anna XOX'

It brought a smile to Zack's face. He went through the rest as quickly as possible.

- a video short of a great-dane fucking a woman. This was from a travelling friend of his who was now working in Spain for the season.

- one from his brother in France, who had recently started the season as a snow-board instructor. All was well.
- some 'Fwds' of the normal 'circuit email' jokes from old Tokyo friends, many of whom were now in the States.
- one from a Tel-Aviv friend, complaining about how boring it was in Israel, and how fucked it was that Netanyahu was still running the place like an idiot.
- one from a crazy genius friend in Thailand who'd received death threats for running a very controversial website on various atrocities and ongoing political cover-ups in Cambodia.
- one from a guy he'd done the fast in Thailand with. He was back there again, intending to fast for a whole month this time.
- one from his mother, who was proud of herself for having mastered the technology sufficiently to have been able to send him anything at all.
- more pornography from a couple of English friends now in Brazil. They were buying cocaine for $US5 a gram and staying with some local girls in a beach bungalow. They'd put other travel plans on hold indefinitely.

Those were all that mattered. The rest was pure crap, and he dumped it in the trash. Then he composed a response to Anna.

'Hi Anna,

Firstly congratulations! Secondly, so that's what therapy is. I'd always wondered! No, seriously, I hope you guys wake up to yourselves and do make a go of it. Brian must really be something if he got you to marry him in the first place. I guess you just have to go looking for whatever it was you loved about him way back then. A bit of 're-discovery.' I wish you luck. He'd be dumb to lose you.

Things continue over here at the usual breakneck pace you're now a little familiar with. Just the usual you know – alcohol, drugs, parties, sleep, work. That's the famous Roppongi cycle. Rinse, and repeat! You just have to keep yourself and the cycle upright and going forwards ... therein lies true mastery. The Force, Luke. Use the Force!

I will drop you a line from time to time or when I'm next on your shores. Don't forget to check into your new email address at least once every sixteen weeks, or the bastards will shut it down on you.

Best of luck to you Princess Leia.
Zack XOX'

He dashed off a few more replies to the deserving, forwarded the dog's sexual conquest on to practically everyone in his address book (it really was an impressive display), then headed back to the apartment.

James was still sleeping, but he found Teri up and about. It was the first time he'd seen her since 'the night'. From the way she was acting, Zack guessed she was feeling mighty uncomfortable. He decided to make it easy on her.

"So how are you, Teri?"

"I'm okay ... I guess," she replied, eyes downcast.

"That acid can really set your mind on fire, can't it?"

Now she met his gaze squarely. "I am *never* taking that stuff again! I just can't believe what happened. I've been wanting to apologise all weekend."

He grinned at her reassuringly. "Don't worry about it. I could see you were way out of whack. You took too much for your first time, and you didn't know what to expect. Believe me, it's a drug of extremes. As much as you had a shit time, it's just as possible to have a fantastic time. It depends on your environment, who you're with, and the frame of mind you're in when you take it."

She didn't look remotely convinced. "That's what they say. All the same, I don't think it's for me."

"All things in moderation Teri, all things in moderation," Zack replied. Then he went to his bed and crashed. He had to get ready for work in four hours. He set his alarm and for once, sleep came easily.

*   *   *

He arrived at work fairly well rested. As usual his first phone-call was Victor. The question was always the same.

"How many girls?"

They went through this routine every night, double-checking the number of girls Zack was expecting, coincided with Victor's lists. After all, there were four other clubs Vic had to worry about. All in all, a lot of girls.

Victor informed Zack that he was permanently losing three sub-standard girls to other clubs, and that two new girls were starting in their place. This was good news. Zack was glad to be rid of them, and to not have to wear any of the flak for the decision was a bonus. He'd had a lot of trouble from two of them, and the other one had all the class of a rutting dog. Both the new girls were from the States, and according to Victor, they were star quality, especially the one called Crystal.

She must really be something, Zack thought, if Vic was big-noting her. These days Victor was effectively immune to beautiful women. Not far behind him, Zack had often thought what an unfortunate side-effect it was for a profession to have.

He flicked a cursory glance around the club. Monday night. Fuck all going on. The girls were just waiting for customers. Zack went up to the private-dance area, chatted with the security-guy Georgiou and waited for wonder-woman to turn up.

When they did, it was with Chad. Zack usually didn't have much face-to-face dealing with him, which suited Zack just fine. Chad was a classic example of right place at the right time success, and through rounding up women and sending them to Japan like cattle, he'd made a fortune over the last couple of years. Nowadays, unfortunately, he believed his own bullshit and really thought he was something special. He was a big brawny guy full of false smiles and superficial pats on the back, who thought he was a lot smarter than he was.

He rode a gleaming Harley ostentatiously around Roppongi, and was forever telling anyone who'd listen about his 'way with women'. Zack kept his acid tongue in check and just played along like a 'good ol' boy'. So far this had seemed to work okay. But even though Zack was earning good bucks at Cloud Nine, it still galled him that he was simultaneously lining the pockets of an arsehole of Chad's quality. *Ahh, what the fuck!*

Crystal, it turned out, was without question, the poster-girl for America. She was the epitome of Playboy centre-fold material. Blonde hair, blue eyes, incredible body, and those perfect white teeth flashed a big smile at Zack as he listened to Chad make the introductions. Zack offered them a tour of the club, but Chad cut him off.

"Oh don't worry about that, Zack. Believe me, these girls know their way around," he drawled, adding a suggestive wink. "But I want you to take real good care of them, make 'em feel right at home."

"Hopefully, it'll be a pleasure Chad," Zack replied, gazing levelly at Crystal. "Right now, I can really use some girls who know how to behave."

He was sure he detected a hint of amusement in Crystal's expression as Chad left. At what though? He gave each girl a copy of his club-rules and told them to read it thoroughly. Checking their reactions, he added, "Come back to me anytime you've got any questions."

Moving to his desk in the corner, he turned when Crystal spoke.

"How long have you been working here, Zack?"

She didn't say it in a bitchy or trouble-making way, Zack thought. Moreso a natural curiosity, as well as feeling out her new boss.

"Nearly three months now. Why?" he replied, holding her gaze.

"You just seem to have Chad's number, that's all."

"Let's just say I'm good with people."

"Yes, I think you are, aren't you?"

This affirmation was accompanied by a lingering visual appraisal.

"Question is Crystal, has he got your number?" Zack asked.

With a little smile, she replied, "I don't think that's very likely, do you?"

She was still smiling when she let her friend drag her off to the change-rooms.

"Remember to read those rules, or it will cost you," Zack called after them.

Jesus, she was a piece of work, he thought. The way she looked, he hadn't expected too much from the upstairs department. She had his attention now though. Things might be interesting with her around.

After work, Zack went to Bongoes to pick up the package Lior had left for him, and to catch up with Hans. Zack hadn't seen much of him since he'd taken up the *host* position out in *Ginza*. He'd also seen next to nothing of Sofia. There was just no fucking *time*, he thought. Sunday was the only spare day, and usually it was spent recuperating from everything.

"How's it going stranger?" Zack asked, as Hans settled in beside him at the bar.

"Everything is great. It's easy money," Hans replied.

He showed Zack his new Rolex watch and ring, both gifts from a woman whose favourite he'd become. He'd also received an expensive necklace which he hated; he didn't wear it unless he was at the club.

"I think she really wants to fuck me, Zack. She keeps talking about going back to her little apartment after we've been shopping."

"Is she married?"

"Yeah."

"Be careful then," Zack advised. "If the husband gets wind of anything, he could make life difficult for you by threatening the club. Then they'll just fire you."

"I get the feeling the apartment is a spare. They only use it occasionally, or something like that."

"Well, be careful anyway," Zack repeated.

"Do you think I should do it though?"

"Just trust your judgment mate, but shit, if you really want to, then go for it. Life is short. Why the hell not?"

"Yeah, I suppose," Hans mused.

Zack changed the subject. "Why don't you, me, and Sofia have dinner somewhere on Sunday? I feel like I'm already losing touch with you guys. You've really got to make an effort over here sometimes. The time just vanishes."

"As long as you promise not to bring any *Ice*," Hans replied jokingly.

Apparently Hans had ended up in some far-flung train station after passing out in his seat. Upon waking up, he'd then realised he hadn't even picked the right line, and it had taken him another two hours to get himself home.

"No, we'll have a civilised night for a change," Zack laughed. "How's Sofia going anyway?"

"She's doing okay. She hates having to sing karaoke with customers and especially hates having to dance with them, but she's getting good hours and making bucks."

Zack couldn't help but smile at the image of Sofia under this sort of duress. "That's what it's all about," he said. "Give her my best."

The friends parted, promising to be in touch for Sunday.

Zack was surprised to have seen so little of Sofia. She *was* working in Roppongi after all. She must be going straight home after work instead of going out. Weird, he thought, and resolved to catch up with her before the weekend.

* * *

The package from Lior nestled between his feet on the floor of the taxi. Rule number one. If you've got drugs on you, never walk anywhere if you can help it. In the extremely remote possibility the taxi was stopped (let alone searched) by police, he would push the package under the front seat, and deny any knowledge of it. He'd already wiped it clean of prints.

Over the past few months, he'd developed a pretty good system for distributing what had turned into mainly a coke and ecstasy pipeline. During the night at Cloud Nine, he'd call the mobile numbers of key people at various bars in Roppongi, and they'd organise orders on a daily basis.

Everything was in code, just in case: candles, eggs, and apples. *Ice* was still 'ice', which was after all, a normal bar supplies item. For example, tonight he'd had an order from one bar-manager for six candles and ten eggs. This meant that tomorrow, before work, Zack would drop off six grams of coke as well as ten ecstasies.

He much preferred doing his rounds prior to work, as he firmly believed police activity in Roppongi was at its lowest ebb early in the evening. He never took orders from anyone he didn't know, and worked only through people he knew were genuinely into Roppongi's party scene.

It was all about risk assessment. Identify your risks, then minimise them to the greatest extent possible. His micro-economics training at university was serving him well.

Arriving home, he walked in the back way. The other golden rule was no drugs, ever, actually in the apartment. Apart from the few private moments necessary to package the separate orders. This was, inevitably, the most difficult commandment to adhere to, and it had taken Zack considerable time and thought to find a relatively secure nook in the building to stash the main supply.

It had to be somewhere that was quickly and easily accessible, as well as being undetectable and unlikely to be found. It also had to be difficult to observe from anywhere else. Satisfying this set of criteria was not as easy as it sounded.

Once in the building, you couldn't help but notice the large pile of junk at the far end of the second floor. It looked like it had been there forever. The debris consisted mainly of clapped-out air-con units, chests of drawers, and broken furniture. Situated in a corner, most of it was just out of view of both the lift and the apartment doors. Behind the main pile of detritus, wedged up against the wall, was a decomposing mattress. Its stuffing was escaping from several holes which pock-marked the patterned exterior.

Zack had chosen one of these holes as the main repository for the stash. He figured that as it would be the last thing to be moved, he'd at least have a window of extraction time if efforts to clean up the section ever commenced.

The only chance of him being spotted as he deposited or retrieved the stash was from someone using the stairwell, and the inevitable noise they made always allowed him ample time to conceal his activity. Given the mouldering condition of the mattress, he'd acquired a metal box in which to house the product, as rats were certainly around the place sometimes.

Dropping the package into the box, he shoved it securely back into its snug resting place. Tomorrow afternoon he would temporarily retrieve it to put the day's order together. All in all, he thought he'd minimised every risk he could in terms of the mechanics of the operation.

The only other, and unfortunately inevitable weaknesses were human ones, and as ever, he would have to stay on top of those. Zack quietly entered the apartment, and went to bed.

*   *   *

The next couple of days progressed most agreeably. Both the new girls seemed to have settled in alright with the rest, which was a relief. Jealousy and bitchiness were always two of his biggest problems – in some ways, Zack thought, it was like being in a women's prison.

Crystal too, was keeping him on his toes. Even though she must have heard through the grapevine that he hadn't slept with any of the girls, her flirtations were unmistakable.

In spite of himself, Zack had to admit he was attracted to her. Goddamnit, who wouldn't be? It was definitely tempting, but he was giving nothing away, and to date had cursorily brushed aside her not so subtle invitations to play.

Eighteen

Sofia had finished at two a.m, and was waiting for him as he barrelled into Bongoes after work on Thursday. It was great to see her, and they embraced like long-lost siblings.

"So, mystery-girl, where have you been hiding? You don't write, you don't phone, what's the story ... don't you love me anymore?" Zack joked.

"Of course I still love you my darling!" Sofia replied dramatically.

Jarrod, who was behind the bar and had been chatting Sofia up for the last hour, rolled his eyes in disgust, and said, "I think I'm going to be sick."

"Don't be like that Jarrod," Zack said reprovingly. And then to Sofia, "Jarrod's not much of a romantic you know. Unfortunately his job's made him a cynic when it comes to affairs of the heart."

"I heard that you lying bastard," Jarrod retorted from the other end of the bar.

"Oh I don't know," Sofia said. "He seemed quite the romantic until you arrived, Zack."

Zack feigned shock. "Is this true Jarrod? Were you making a move on my *sister* before I arrived tonight?"

"Fuck off the pair of you ... what are you drinking?" Jarrod said resignedly. He poured Zack a beer, and Sofia, a vodka, lime and soda.

"So what do you think of mental prostitution for a profession?" Zack asked, referring to Sofia's hostessing job. "Have you got the hang of it yet?"

Sofia groaned. "I've never felt as repulsed by, yet sorry for, so many men in my entire life. This country is just unbelievable. Most of the men who visit these clubs are pretty sad."

"And you've only been here a few weeks," Zack grinned. "You won't believe the things you'll see and hear as time goes by."

"Last night this one guy wanted to give me twenty thousand yen to go to the toilet and give him the underwear I had on. Can you believe that!"

Zack laughed out loud at her shocked expression. "I hope you took it."

She punched his arm. "Of course I didn't ... that's disgusting!"

"You're kidding!" he spluttered, rocking with laughter. "You really didn't take it?"

She shook her head vehemently.

"Oh Sofia," he chastised. "I've obviously got *a lot* to teach you. By next week, you'll have cheap sets of extra panties in your bag for just those occasions. And the week after, you'll be steering the conversation in that direction."

Clocking her bemused expression, he continued. "It's all a *game* over here Sofia. Remember what I told you in Eilat about Roppongi Illusion and Roppongi Reality?"

She nodded.

"While you're here, the money you make from your salary is only *part* of the money it's possible for you to make. And no, you don't have to prostitute yourself," he added, after seeing her dubious expression. "You just have to *play the game*."

"Which is?" she asked.

"Every one of the customers that sits with you wants to be made to feel special. Right?"

"I guess."

"So all you have to do is tailor your approach to the predilections of each guy, *without* crossing any lines of morality within yourself. Think of it like this. You are an actress, and Roppongi is your interactive stage-show. The *hostess-club* is anyway. It's all just a game."

He checked her expression, before continuing.

"But remember what I said in Eilat Sofia. You are here *for the money*. Get what you can from these guys, for Christ's sake. You have to sit with them for hours anyway. Use the time for *your* benefit. Get them to take you shopping of course. That's normal."

Zack paused again, but Sofia offered nothing. She seemed to be taking his advice onboard.

"But if they're not *too* insufferable you should also get them to take you to things you want to see or do in Japan. *Kabuki*, *Sumo*, traditional festivals, *Fuji*, *Kyoto*, whatever. Fuck, you name it and they'll pay for it. You can get practically whatever you want out of these guys, if you know how to *play the game*. Granted, some of the experiences are less than fun because you're in their company, but at the end of the day, you're still getting well paid for a unique experience of this country."

"What about when they want to sleep with you?" Sofia asked.

"Well, that usually comes about," Zack conceded. "But it doesn't have to, for quite a long time, and that lead-up time can be very lucrative for you in terms of tips, gifts and experiences. But if they finally do push the issue, you just shut them down in whatever way seems the most appropriate at the time. Shout at them and storm off. Pretend to be really upset and leave. Cry if you can – that's always good. Whatever. Be creative!"

He grinned in response to the face she pulled. "More than half the time they'll spend the next few weeks blaming themselves, and try to woo you back with even more expensive gifts. And if they don't, then who cares? What have you lost? Nothing, except a pain in the arse." Zack rolled his eyes before pointedly adding, "Next!"

Sofia considered this. "I guess you're right. I suppose if I'm going to be here, I might as well go for it."

Zack took another sip of his drink. "Just remember, all you have to do is get each of them thinking he's your *special boyfriend*. It's not hard Sofia. That's what he wants to believe, after all."

He held up a delaying finger – he wasn't finished. Sofia deserved the complete picture.

"Eventually of course, the whole sorry cycle inevitably fucks up and dies, but there's always another one ready to try his luck. It's like ducks in a shooting gallery: they just keep on coming."

"You don't like them much, do you?" Sofia asked, regarding him curiously.

Zack looked at her appraisingly. "If you want me to generalise, I would have to say no. I think they mostly treat women like shit, and the majority of them are just desperate, sexually-repressed, socially-retarded fodder for the Japanese GNP. In their board-rooms and offices they're omnipotent and act accordingly. Get them in a social situation where the foreign girl doesn't have to play by their rules, and you've never seen a fish more out of water. It's genuinely sad."

He took a breath. "So if they walk into a *hostess-bar* thinking they can spend their money to get cosy with a Western girl, as far as I'm concerned they deserve to lose it. Fuck, the amount of times I've thought about the money I'd have made in this place knowing what I know, if I was a girl that looked like you …"

Zack trailed off, shaking his head. "Don't get me wrong. I'm not saying it's easy. It's not … far from it. But gender-wise here, the remuneration is more than just a little out of whack."

"It seems like you're doing okay as you are," Sofia noted. "What's it really like being in charge of all those silicon-titted stripper-chicks anyway?"

Zack organised another drink for himself. Sofia's was still nearly full.

"It's funny you know. The first few days in there you're trying not to gawk at all that flesh. It's a normal human reaction after all. The next few, you only notice the girls you think are really hot, and that may well be because of *how they are*, rather than *how they look*. But by the end of about the third week, I was practically immune to the whole thing. You run around and get the job done, and non-stop tits in your face becomes just another part of it."

"So are you sleeping with any of them?" Sofia asked. "I saw you with that beautiful darker-skinned girl once. Is she one?"

Zack told her he hadn't slept with any of the strippers, and explained why. He also explained who Dorit was, and that she'd been a hostess.

"So you're also getting extra money out of what the strippers earn?" Sofia exclaimed.

Zack could see she thought it was low. "Fuck Sofia, some of these chicks are earning two or three thousand US dollars a *night* ... and I help them into some of those customers! If they don't want to play the game, then I'll help some of the other girls *who will*. This is fucking Roppongi, not Sunday School! Everyone's greasing a wheel somewhere, that's just the way it works here."

"It all just seems so sordid I suppose."

"That's because it is," Zack replied with a grin.

"What do you do here for Christmas anyway?"

Shit, Zack thought. Christmas?

"I have no idea," he replied. "I'll have to find out if anyone's having a decent party, I suppose. Christmas doesn't really mean much in Roppongi."

At that moment a couple of arms appeared around his chest, and he felt the unmistakable sensation of two breasts on the back of his neck.

"So *this* is where you hang out after work!" The voice and tone belonged unequivocally to Crystal. Zack didn't have to turn around to confirm this. She was with the other new girl, Paris, and every male in Bongoes was in the process of hiding a double-take.

Zack had a theory that because strippers were accustomed to a looser than average sense of dress, that they often, and even moreso in an environment like Roppongi, blurred the edges between what was merely sexy, as opposed to outright risqué, public attire. He wondered if 'Stripper-Chic' could ever go mainstream.

The pair of them were vamped to the hilt. Crystal could have just walked off a glamour magazine shoot, and Paris wasn't far behind. Zack did the introductions to a clearly amused Sofia while half the bar looked on. Crystal positioned herself closely right beside Zack. For her part, Paris took up 'distraction or decoy detail' beside Sofia.

Crystal ordered more drinks for all of them. Shortly afterwards, a bottle of Dom Perignon champagne arrived, by way of an introduction gift from one of the brokers Zack was faintly acquainted with. Evaluating all the alcohol on the bar, he sighed. It didn't look like being an early night.

"So, am I performing to your expectations so far, Boss?" Crystal asked with an ambiguous smile.

He swivelled slightly to face her. He was still undecided as to whether he would cross the line for this one. "I think it's safe to say you've gone beyond what I expected for your first week, Crystal," Zack responded evenly.

To his surprise, after some more sexual semantics and role-play, they actually fell into an enjoyably real conversation. He learned she was originally English, but had moved with her family to the States when she was eleven. She was now twenty-five, and a genuine Texan beauty. She'd been modelling since she was sixteen, and had been contracted as the Miller beer girl for three years.

Zack was curious. "Why are you doing this sexy stuff now then? I mean, you're beautiful enough to do all the more conventional work."

"Sometimes if I'm having a shitty night, and the guys are arseholes or just plain disgusting, I ask myself the same thing," she said. "Basically though, unless you're modelling the top catwalk shows all the time, the money here is unbeatable. And I'm just not skinny enough to do those shows. It's as simple as that, really."

Zack shook his head in amazement. He'd seen her figure on stage during the week. It was statuesque, incredible. But then, considering some of the stick-figures that passed for beauty in world fashion these days, it was understandable, he supposed. 'Heroin-chic' or 'vampire-waif-child' or something similar was apparently the hot look at the moment. It seemed Crystal's conspicuous curves were simply not in vogue.

Crystal elaborated. "I can *average* a thousand dollars a night in this place, and I have no expenses. If I net less than five grand a week here, it's a bad week. In a good week I can clear ten grand."

She raised a solitary eyebrow, before continuing. "In anyone's language, that's a lot of money. I already own my own house, as well as another large block of land with a river running through it. I drive a brand-new Calloway Corvette back home, and with the money I save from this trip, I'm starting my own business."

"What are you going to do?" Zack asked.

"I'm designing and releasing swimwear. It's my own label ... Crystal Dreams."

"I'm impressed," he said. "Do you want to get married?"

She laughed, then turned listener, while Zack told her about a few of his adventures.

"So you're an opportunistic wanderer," she concluded.

"That, I suppose, is a fair description," Zack conceded.

"So how long are you staying in Tokyo?" She appeared genuinely interested now. The vamp behaviour had taken a back seat for the time being.

"I'm intending to stay until about July next year," Zack replied. "But things change pretty quickly in this town, so I'll just take it as it comes. What about you?"

"Oh, I'll serve my three month sentence here, then take a break to Hawaii or Thailand or somewhere. Then I'll decide if I can stomach the thought of another stint."

Crystal had previously been more or less facing the bar, but during their conversation they had turned towards each other and her right leg had wedged itself between Zack's legs. She knew *exactly* what she was doing, he thought. And meanwhile, her partner in crime was doing an outstanding job of engaging Sofia.

Zack poured more champagne, smiling to himself at the ridiculousness of his situation. He had to admit it. For the first time in more than three months of stripper-evasion, he was very, very tempted.

Crystal seemed to sense this, and pressed her advantage by leaning further into Zack, apparently to get to some cigarettes on the bar. Her breasts rested on his upper arm, and as he closed his eyes he inhaled the beguiling perfume on her neck. Oh, this girl was *good*, he thought.

Definitely time for a piss and a think! He pushed his bar-stool back and excused himself with an apologetic half-smile, before heading to the toilets at the back. Something told him this was trouble, trouble, trouble with a capital T. Just make your excuses and *leave* for fuck's sake, he told the guy in the mirror.

Getting his dick out, he was not surprised to find it semi-hard. Who was he kidding, he thought? He was never *not* going to fuck this girl. He knew it, and worse, she knew it. So how was he going to play it?

Leaving the toilet, he was accosted by the broker who'd sent the champagne over. "Zack, you have to introduce me to those chicks man."

Zack cringed at the 'man' artlessly tacked on to the end of his plea. He really loathed the sorry attempts some of these geeks made at coolness in the bars of Roppongi. His decision arrived instantly. "Your name's Brian, right?"

"Ben, it's Ben."

It was the out he needed for tonight anyway, Zack thought. Give this situation a little more time. He introduced the numpty to the girls, indicating with a roll of his eyes that there was bugger all he could do about it.

He then covertly explained the situation to Sofia while he had the chance.

"Such restraint, Zack. I'm so proud of you," she quipped acidly.

Choosing to ignore her bitchy tone, he added, "We're on for Sunday night, don't forget."

"Yeah, yeah," she replied with a frown.

He flitted over to the dynamic duo and Ben the bonehead, to bid them all goodnight. But as he left, Crystal followed him to the door.

Silly to have imagined he might have escaped that easily.

"Are you fucking that Sofia girl?" she asked outright.

Zack smiled. "No," he replied. "Haven't you heard? I'm not fucking anyone." He looked pointedly at her before casually adding, "At the moment."

God, he just couldn't help himself! He might as well take her home right now for Chrissakes.

"I've enjoyed being with you tonight," she said. "That's not a crime, is it?"

"Not yet, no," he agreed. He checked himself before adding, "But Chad might not see it that way. You do realise he desperately wants to fuck you?"

Crystal regarded him coolly and drew on her cigarette, apparently unperturbed by his bluntness. She took her time before exhaling. "People are allowed their dreams, aren't they Zack?"

The smoke seemed to hang in the air around her words, and Zack had to admit her toughness only added to her allure.

She surprised him by suddenly adding, "Where are you going anyway?"

He reached out and gently touched her cheek before replying, "I'm going … to sleep."

She raised her hands, palms outwards, and smiled again in the manner of someone who must necessarily concede a small battle in order to win the overall war. "Okay okay," she said. "I'll see you tomorrow."

"I'll look forward to it," Zack replied with a grin. "It's been fun."

Impulsively, he leaned forward and kissed her goodbye on the lips. "Goodnight Zack," she purred.

*   *   *

The weekend was relatively uneventful. Zack had resisted the temptation to go drinking, so when he awoke at around two on Sunday afternoon he felt well-rested and full of beans. He jogged up to Tipness, and put himself through a forty-five minute workout before running back home again. Bursting through the door, he grabbed a glass of water and sat huffing and puffing in the kitchen.

The apartment was once again harmonious. James and Teri had so far continued to defy Zack's expectations of a split. In fact, the 'tripped-out' incident seemed only to have strengthened the bond between them.

Shunit poked her head around the corner from their bedroom. "*Ata rotzeh café nudnick?*"

Zack smiled at her good-natured abuse. "*Ken makshefah katana shelli ... toda rabah.*"

He looked out the window, surprised at how bright it was. Pretty warm in fact. Winter had definitely arrived by night, but this day was a little out of character for early November.

Shunit gave him his coffee and read his thoughts. "Is a beautiful day ah?"

Zack nodded, grabbed his phone, and they went up to the roof to enjoy the sunshine. Working nights then drinking late, sunshine was not something one saw a lot of in Tokyo.

He sipped his coffee, then shivered a little as a breeze blew lightly over the rooftops. It was one of those days where as long as you were in direct sunlight and there was no breeze, you were as warm as toast. But if an interfering cloud arrived, or the wind picked up, the underlying chilliness quickly made itself felt.

"So," Shunit asked. "What's going on in big bad Roppongi these-days?"

Because her Japanese learning program took place during the day, she lived completely opposite hours from the rest of the flat, and rarely ventured into the Roppongi scene. As a typical Israeli however, she loved to occasionally hear a few stories, to catch up on what she called 'the gossips'.

"Are you doing anything tonight Shunit?" Zack replied.

"There is something interesting maybe?" she asked, half sarcastically.

Zack was undeterred by her tone. "I'm meeting two friends I worked with in Eilat for dinner at Las Chicas. They're great people. If you want to come, I'd like you to."

Shunit's apathetic expression was transformed to one of genuine warmth. "*Ezeh* charmer." She rolled each of the 'R's' dramatically in that inimitable Israeli way, and added, "Yes. Good. We 'ave not been out almost since you move in Zack. I am getting boring maybe?"

Zack didn't answer this semi-rhetorical utterance, and they sat in silence for a while.

The sprawling metropolis of Tokyo stretched in every direction for as far as it was possible to see. It was like a gigantic grey machine, with trillions of moving parts. The immensity of it never failed to strike Zack, and he often imagined the whole city sinking under its own weight, or systematically breaking down as a result of the excesses of its inhabitants.

The trilling of his phone ended this reverie. He lay back on the warm concrete and closed his eyes to the sun before engaging the call.

"Yeah, hello."

"Hey shitfabrains."

The unmistakable sound of his brother's voice jolted Zack instantly upright. They hadn't spoken since London.

"Josh! How the fuck are you? Where are you exactly?"

"Still in France. I'm at a ski-resort. Everything's cool as, over here. I quit snowboard-instructing and took on managing a nightclub in the village. Just finished work now actually. Means I get time to myself on the mountain for a change, and drink for free into the bargain."

Zack smiled. His brother sounded pretty high and loose. Like Zack, Josh never really slurred his words, even when he was trashed, but Zack could tell by his tone that he'd had a few. They were an unstoppable force when they partied together. He missed having Josh around. It was such a pity he'd never made it to Tokyo.

"Sounds like you've got it sussed, brother. Everything's pretty cool over here as well. Got all the bases covered so to speak, and the money's rolling in. Can't complain."

"Well, I'm not making your sort of money, but then again, you're not carving it up off-piste every day. It's really something out of this world, Zack. You don't know what you're missing."

"Yeah, yeah, yeah, I know. You do tell me this every time, remember. Haven't seen your hairy arse out here in Japan either, brother. Maybe next season I'll come your way and give it a go."

"Time's ticking bro. You're not getting any younger you know!"

Zack cut him off. "Blah blah blah. Fuck off, you cheeky little shit. I'll run rings around you any day!"

Josh was laughing. "Oh well, if you insist. After all, it's not cheap to chat with you. Some would argue you're not worth it."

Zack took the hint. "Actually Josh, give me a number for you over there. I've got a company dialling code here, and I can call you for the cost of a local."

Taking a moment to apologise to Shunit for their interrupted roof-time, Zack then phoned Josh back.

They spent the next forty-five minutes catching up on the last few months. Shunit had long since disappeared back downstairs when Zack was done.

He followed up with a call to Sofia and Hans to confirm they were still on, then called Las Chicas with a booking for four at eight o'clock.

Nineteen

The trendy *Aoyama* eatery Las Chicas, was packed as usual with an arty sort of sophisto-bohemian crowd. This theme was punctuated with a heavy *gaijin* presence, most of whom were either models, artists, musicians, actors or 'Roppongi-kids'. It made for an eclectic mix of egos, attitudes, and appearances.

Except for the chicken-Caesar salad, the food was merely adequate, not exceptional. Zack assumed the enduring appeal of the place lay in its open-plan concept of combining funky bars and dining with a library, an art-gallery, an outdoor cinema, as well as a recording-studio and internet facility.

The décor and art on display was constantly changing. For up-and-comers in the art scene, an exhibition or opening at Las Chicas could mean the difference between spectacular success and ignominious failure. It really had become a scene unto itself. Zack had even heard people describing other people or places as 'Las Chicassy'.

Regrettably, he reflected, this ultra-chic reputation hadn't done much for the service. Specifically because Las Chicas was such a scene, it was now 'cool' to work there. Consequently a number of the wait-staff were 'out of work something or others' and carried themselves with an attitude in keeping with their lofty aspirations.

As someone who'd spent much of his life in professional hospitality, attitude from these pretentious little pricks could really send Zack through the roof. Either do the job and do it well, or don't do it at all for fuck's sake, he thought.

In spite of this, he had to concede Las Chicas was one of the most interesting places to start a Sunday evening. Most people working nightlife in Roppongi had Sunday night to themselves, and many chose to spend it bumping into the rest of Roppongi at Las Chicas. Fuck it, Zack thought. Wine, women, song, and any type of intercourse. What else was there in Roppongi? When in Rome, and all that …

The very black, very handsome man who called himself Max watched as the waitress showed Zack and his three friends to their table. The blonde sure was something special, he thought, and wondered where she was from. She looked Nordic. It was the second time he'd been able to watch Zack since Ban had pointed him out a couple of weeks previously. For what he had planned, he wanted, no, he needed Zack on his side, not running in opposition.

So since then he had made it his business to find out a bit about the man. What he'd learned did not inspire his confidence regarding the likelihood of winning Zack over. The guy seemed to have friends all over the place, and in the sometimes spiteful atmosphere of Roppongi, this was akin to a minor miracle.

He sighed, and considered how much easier this problem would have been to deal with back home. In Nigeria, people disappeared all the time. It was almost a national sport. But everything was different over here. Especially the money. He frowned, contemplating the Chivas Regal in his glass. Unfortunately, given the problems he'd left behind, he couldn't afford to step out of line too much. He was lucky to even be here. If it hadn't been for his friends at the embassy ... but then, they were crucial to his success in Japan full-stop.

But Max was suffering. The relative impotence he felt here, following so closely on the heels of the merciless network he'd run for so long in Lagos, frustrated him immensely. Supposed tough-guys like the Iranian, Ban, wouldn't last five minutes on his home-ground, he thought with disgust. They were just too soft. He took a final glance at Zack, who had his head back, laughing like he didn't have a care in the world. Max allowed himself a smile, secure in his knowledge that would soon change.

Sofia was mid sentence. "... it was like a red worm."

She was telling a 'dick story'. Most hostesses had at least one. Hers had happened in a taxi the previous evening. Her customer had drunk a lot at dinner, then got his dick out on the way to the club. The guy had actually begged her to touch it! Sofia had stopped the cab, exited, and taken another one the rest of the way to work. Then she'd told the *Mama-San* about it, requesting that if the customer did show up, that she not sit with him. Happily, he didn't arrive, so a potentially embarrassing confrontation in the club was avoided.

"God Sofia, what a fucking prude you are! Just one little blow job and he probably would have given you a hundred thousand yen." Zack was beside himself with mirth as he envisaged Sofia's disgusted reaction to the situation.

Hans followed his lead. "These girls just don't know when they're onto a good thing, do they mate. Easy money, and what do they do?"

Shunit, less used to this style of lowbrow conversation than the others, looked distinctly unimpressed. "You guys wanted to have dinner just with yourselves tonight maybe?" Her arched eyebrows and laconic tone bespoke the possibility she might not be jesting.

Sofia responded instantly. "Yeah, solidarity sister!" and they clasped hands vigorously above the table.

"Alright, alright, we're just messing around," Zack offered placatingly. Inclining his head towards the nearby waiter, he added, "Shall we get to the business of ordering?"

"Do you know what you 'aving, Sofia?" Shunit asked.

"Anything without little red worms, I suspect," Hans quipped, earning himself further warning glares from the girls.

And so the night continued. Zack glanced around. Shunit and Sofia had hit it off immediately. This hadn't surprised him at all. Both were strong, independent, and smart. As their meal progressed, the usual table-hopping around the venue was in full swing. Also in attendance were a couple of the Bongoes staff, as well as some of their regulars. And as usual, half of BlackJacks was floating around. A couple of the J-Men's male strippers were doing their customary 'out in public with some female models' routine. This always struck Zack as funny because nearly all those guys were gay. A bunch of Zack's strippers watched their table predatorily from a booth in the corner. Everybody eyeing, scoping, measuring, in this violent sea of over-eager libidos.

It never ceased to amaze Zack how easy it was to become accustomed to the plenitude of extraordinarily beautiful women in Roppongi. His mind flicked back to his schooldays. They had been tough times. His parents had moved a lot, so he'd always been the 'new kid'. The playground fights, the teasing, the solitude. How he'd fantasised about such women then!

Now here they were in abundance, and they were nothing if not easily attainable. It had been that way for a long time now. His schooldays seemed like someone else's life. But as with anything that continually comes too easily, his appreciation of women in general, he speculated, may have been forever eroded. And his current job certainly wasn't helping.

One odd thing about Las Chicas was how early they always closed the restaurant section. About ten-thirty, dinner over, they drifted into the adjoining groove bar where a DJ spun modern beats until about three a.m. Because of good memories with friends who had first introduced him to the place, Zack always drank vodka and cranberry juice (or 'Cape-Cods' as the Yanks called them) in this bar. The girls had more champagne, while he and Hans followed the vodka trail. Shelton, an outrageously pretty and very camp guy worked behind the bar. Zack got along famously with him, so the vodkas that arrived were not without teeth.

Taking a sip, he scanned the bar. There were a few models with attitude, known colloquially as MWAs, some hostesses with the Gas Panic boys, three African-looking guys in the corner, and a few funky Japanese youngsters at the tables.

Judging by their typically wild gesticulations, the Africans were in intense conversation. One of the guys glanced around and happened to catch Zack's eye, so Zack gave him a big smile and raised his glass in cheers. The guy did not respond. He immediately looked back at his friends, then dropped his eyes to the ground. It was almost as if he was embarrassed, Zack thought. Or even ashamed. Weird. Those sort of Africans were usually pretty friendly.

He promptly forgot about it, his attention drawn back to Sofia and Shunit, who were grooving away on the tiny dance-floor as if they'd been practising in the bedroom together since their schooldays.

"So what's up with that married Japanese woman?" he asked Hans. It was the first chance he'd had to talk with him alone. "Any action yet?"

Hans's face lit up. "Yep ... all this week. I've been dying to tell you actually. She's incredible, Zack. I mean, she's nearly forty! But she fucks like a demon. She'll do whatever I want, like a slave or something. I think she really gets off on it."

"Do you?"

"Jesus Zack, I can't complain. She's bought me about fifteen grand worth of stuff, and she told me I should sell the scooter, because she wants to buy me a motorbike. She leaves big tips at the club, *and* I'm getting well paid into the bargain. Where's the problem?"

Twenty

Zack heard about the dead girl shortly after arriving at work on Friday. It had happened in Gas Panic 99. A Filipina girl had passed out in some corner, and never made it back. Rumour had it she was a hooker. Not that it made any difference. Dead was dead. Drugs were obviously suspected, but no-one knew anything yet.

He didn't have too much time to think about it anyway. Friday night was full steam ahead, and his potential dalliance with Crystal had moved in the spectrum of probability from if to when. He had agreed to go out with her for a few drinks after work. Things at Cloud Nine were going really well: he had most of the girls on that fine line where they respected him because they knew he tried his utmost to be fair. The trick was keeping them there.

Admittedly, their antics often made him laugh. Their latest game was to see who could make a guy come the quickest via their private dance ministrations. The record was thirty-seven seconds by a British chick called Linda. She'd come prancing up to Zack's corner bureau, her enhanced chest jiggling magnificently, to tell him all about it between gales of laughter.

Time of course being money, the received wisdom was that if you could get them to come in their pants quickly, that was so much less time you had to spend with them, as the hapless *salariman* inevitably sped shame-faced to the toilet to mop up. It was then onto the next customer. Stripper-logic, Zack thought amusedly. Someone should write a book about this place.

From the moment he and Crystal arrived in Bongoes, the sex was predestined. He'd more or less given in. He knew it, she knew it, and it was all happening. She was a vision of sex. She was wearing a black miniskirt with a sheer white blouse and wonder-bra. She could have walked straight off the billboard.

As if she needed the wonder-bra, Zack thought, but that's stripper mentality. No such thing as overkill. They've flaunted it for most of their life. Was there any other way? He could see other guys' envy wherever he looked. He had to admit that Crystal's sexual self-awareness and obvious desire to fuck him was a massive turn-on.

They charged through a couple of bottles of champagne and a gram of coke. In the toilet together, she did her lines and then got his cock in her mouth while he did his. You had to be happy with that. A glass of Moet in one hand, lines of coke going up your nose, and a Playboy Centrefold with her mouth around your cock. Decadence, hedonism, excess. The rules do not apply.

These thoughts whizzed around his skull until he felt his body arcing into orgasm. She looked up into his eyes, and hungrily took everything he had. After washing his seed down with a quaff of champagne, she grinned at him like a rabid nymphomaniac, then kissed him hard on the mouth. He watched, half-mesmerised as she casually touched up her lipstick. Then they sallied out. He wasn't sure, but it was possible he'd shattered the thirty-seven second record.

He didn't care. It was one of those moments. He supposed it was a 'guy thing'. They walked into a huge cheer as they came out to the packed bar. Zack looked around them. Everyone was clapping. Jarrod was grinning back at him manically. Things were blurring into that zone of surreality where you could sense people, passions and events tilting and then spinning ever-faster out of control.

"LET'S GET OUTSIDE,' he shouted. 'GET SOME FRESH AIR."

Crystal nodded. It was time to leave.

The crowd parted as the sea had done for Moses, and they passed into the chill morning air. You could make a worse exit, Zack thought. Fucking flying at the moment. Yeeh-fuckin-hahh! He pulled Crystal closer to him and kissed her savagely.

"So, where d'ya wanna go Boss?" she drawled, hamming up the Texan in her.

He looked at her shining face. "Have you been to the Seventh Floor? Nope? Let's pay the boys a visit then."

It was five a.m, and the place was filling out. Some of the other strippers were there, and the, '*Oh yeah, we finally got you*' look came over their faces the moment he walked in with Crystal. Melding into the stripper entourage, Zack put his name up on the board for pool.

"Hey Zack, I'll play with you man." It was Mako, a Japanese friend of his. "I'm up next. We'll play doubles," Mako continued, whilst flashing a thousand watt grin. Mako was always the same. He was one of the few good friends Zack had, who was full Japanese. He was unusually tall, very friendly, and had the sort of easygoing confidence that often accompanies serious wealth. Zack had met him back in '95 and liked him immediately, in spite of his money. His family was *Yakuza*, and rumour had it that his father was *Oyabun*. It was a powerful way of winning friends and influencing people. Zack hadn't seen him for about six weeks.

"Where the fuck have you been Mako? Every time I get used to seeing you around, you disappear again."

"Ahh ... I have to move man ... you know ... keep moving." He was swaying around to the music, and his eyes were slightly glazed.

Crystal meth probably, Zack thought.

"Zack." He re-focused. "I been in New York man, and San Francisco. See some friends. Been partyin' a lot man ... a lot, you know."

"Yeah, I know partying Mako. It's good to see you my friend. I hope you're taking care of yourself."

"Yeah, yeah Zack my man ... no worries Aussie." Mako put his arm around Zack and whispered, "You wanna smoke some *Ice* Zack? I got some reeaallly good shit man, really good shit you know."

"Yeah, maybe Mako."

Crystal appeared with the cold beer Zack so desperately needed. He did the introductions.

"Mako, this is Crystal. Crystal, my good friend Mako. Except I only see him once every month or two."

"Hi Mako." Crystal dazzled him with that all-American smile. He immediately put his arm around her.

"Zack's not really that good a friend you know," he said with a mischievous grin. "You and me, maybe we should talk a bit, smoke a bit, you know."

Zack threw his hands up in mock despair. "He never changes, Crystal. What can I say?"

Before Crystal could open her mouth, Mako insisted. "Really. We should smoke a bit. Three of us you know. Quick. Before the game comes up. Let's go."

So just like that they ended up in the toilet together, toking Mako's *Ice* through a strange-looking pipe.

"Traditional Japanese pipe, man," Mako spluttered, between tokes. He passed it on to Crystal.

"Have you had this stuff before?" Zack asked.

She shook her head and looked at Mako, who was bobbing his head up and down and making odd whooping noises.

"Well, get ready for an interesting rush," Zack said. He fired her up, and she finished the crystals off.

"You smokin' your name girl," Mako spluttered, before cascading into giggles. He re-filled the pipe and Zack started sucking the powerful chemical into his lungs. He finished one breath, and took another toke before passing it back to Mako.

WWHHHHOOOOOOOSSSSHHHHHHH !!!!

Everything slipped into jerky slow motion. Crystal's head spun towards him and was laughing about something. She leaned into Zack and started kissing him. Zack felt himself get hard straight away and thought, 'Fuck, that's impressive.'

Mako had put the pipe down next to the basin and was pissing into the toilet. Crystal was watching Mako pissing. Zack wondered if she was thinking about threesomes. Christ, he couldn't deal with that thought at the moment.

"Put the pipe away, Mako." Zack slowed the rush enough to get that much out.

"Oh yeah man, the pipe, the pipe. Ornamental pipe you know. Must not forget."

They headed back out to the bar, straight to the pool table. Amazingly, they played well, and were unbeaten three games later. Sensing Crystal's attention waning, Zack timed out of the game.

"No problem Zack. I understand. You spend time with your woman."

"Yeah, okay Mako. Thanks for the games and the smoke. Much appreciated."

"Zack. It's my pleasure man. See you."

He got Crystal to the bar and they sat down. She pulled her stool close. She had one hand on his crotch, the other on his chest and her tongue in his mouth before he could get a word out.

Finally he managed, "Crystal, d'ya wanna do the last of this coke before we go?"

She nodded, so it was back to the toilet. But the toilet was occupied, with a number of people waiting. Cursing to himself, Zack then had a bright idea. He'd done it before with no problems. They were on the seventh floor of an eight storey building, and whatever operated upstairs had long since closed. He guided her outside, and instead of getting in the lift, they headed into the stairwell. Up the vacant flight. Eighth floor. All clear. Brilliant.

The sun was just peeping over the horizon. Zack knocked the rest of the coke onto the polished stone ledge, taking care to shelter it from an errant breeze. As he was carving lines, he became aware that his cock was once again in Crystal's mouth. He did his two lines, and then with a considerable effort of will, pulled her off his cock to do hers. She bent right over in front of him.

He hesitated only for a second. No-one was going to come up here. Except possibly them, by the looks of it. He peeled her miniskirt up over her arse and pushed his fingers between her spread legs. She was soaking. Pulling her g-string out of the way he launched himself fully inside her. She gasped for a moment, then braced herself against the wall and the railing and started grinding herself back onto his cock. Then she took one hand off the wall.

Zack could feel her fingers on herself and him, as he thrust in and out of her. A low moan began rising from somewhere deep in her throat and he grabbed hold of both her tits. He knew he was about to come, and then they were both coming, bucking wildly.

Crystal let out a feral moan that Zack was pretty sure people on the ground floor would have heard. Who gave a fuck? He eased himself out of her, whipped her g-string back up, then turned her around. They lost their tongues in each other's mouths for a while, and when they finally focused, Zack realised how exhausted they both were.

"Time to go, I think," he said.

* * *

When Zack woke, he was horrified to find his watch telling him it was a quarter past five. He had to be at work in forty-five fucking minutes! Fortunately all his kit was already there. He only had to shower and shave.

"Crystal, Crystal get your shit together." He shook her awake.

"Wha', what's going on?" She stretched herself out like a cat with all the time in the world. In spite of the urgency factor, Zack watched her. She was truly a magnificent animal.

Then he sprang into gear. "Crystal, move your arse! It's a quarter past five. What time do you start?"

There were two start-times for the girls. First group at seven, the next at nine.

"You're seven o'clock aren't you? Come on, move yourself girl!"

Her eyes were now open, and pretty much focused. She pouted at him.

"Zack, I feel like shit. I probably look like shit. Let me start at nine? Please, please, please? Come on, be reasonable." She pulled him down, back into bed, and wrapped those long legs around him.

Zack had known it was coming. He shouldn't give in to her on principle, he thought. But she did have to get herself home, get ready and then get back to Roppongi. He did some quick thinking and figured he could get away with it. Saturday was always a slower starter. What was one less girl for a couple of hours?

"God, you're gonna owe me, girl." He tried to struggle out of her grasp.

She smiled smugly. "I promise I'm good for my debts Zack."

He felt her hand snake between his legs.

"Crystal, I've – got – no – time." He wrestled free, and scooted into the tiny bathroom.

Scraping his face during a lightning shower, he forced some toast and a coffee down his neck, then quickly kissed her goodbye.

"Lock the door on your way out," he warned her.

Once outside, he turned to look at her again. "Oh, and if you are even one – minute – late tonight, you *will* cop a fine. I've already been more than fair."

She pulled a face and blew him a kiss. "Bye."

Zack grabbed the cached drugs on his way downstairs. He was rushed, and he hated it. Haste bred carelessness and carelessness bred mistakes. Luckily, it was the last of the week's consignment, so he was carrying only marginally more than he needed for tonight's drops. He had no option but to race around Roppongi's drop-off spots, and wear the half-hour penalty for arriving after six.

The first phone call once he got to Cloud Nine wasn't Victor, but Lior.

"Zack ehh, I don't want to say too much now, but you can maybe meet me after work?"

"Sure thing Lior. Where?"

"Somewhere different than usual. McDonalds. Yes. I will sit upstairs near the telephone. What time is good?"

Zack thought quickly. "Four o'clock?"

"Yes. See you then. Bye Zack." The line went dead.

Zack looked thoughtfully at his phone before putting it back in his pocket. Lior was usually so laid back, so calm. To say he'd sounded anxious tonight was an understatement. Zack usually rang Lior when he knew the size of the order. Lior hardly ever rang him. What the hell was going on?

The call bothered Zack all night. He was distracted, edgy, and combined with his unforgiving drug and alcohol hangover, work was not altogether too much fun. Marco was on his back for the smallest things, and had given him a hard stare regarding Crystal's altered timetable.

Fortunately she turned up on time, and had successfully made the transition to glamour-goddess. The night crawled by, and he arrived at McDonalds happy only that the week was over. His curiosity however, was undiminished.

Lior, reliable as ever, was relaxing near the phone with a cigarette.

"You look like shit, Zack," he announced matter of factly.

Zack regarded him disbelievingly. "Fuck you very much, Lior. If you'd had my week, you'd probably look like this as well."

Lior shrugged indifferently.

"Well, what's the story for fuck's sake?"

Zack immediately realised he had spoken too loudly. His fatigue and anxiety had momentarily won out.

Lior was unfazed.

Zack sighed and sat down. "I'm tired Lior. Can you just tell me what's going on?"

Stubbing out his butt, Lior leaned forward.

"In the last two weeks, three people in Roppongi have died from bad drugs."

"Three people!" Zack exclaimed. "I'd only heard about one."

"Usually it might not be such a big deal. But I hear one girl she was a good friend of the police chief's daughter."

Lior leaned back again, and lit another cigarette. "Zack, the Japanese are funny people. They don't care too much when the *gaijin*s all the time are killing themselves, but when Japanese start to die in Roppongi, they need somebody to blame."

"So what do we do?"

"We take it easy for a couple of weeks. Then, if things cool down, we go again for Christmas and New Year. Just tell your people there's nothing at the moment because of the police crackdown. And be careful. Tell your contacts absolutely no talking. Someone somewhere will be asking questions. You can be sure for that."

Zack sat motionless, absorbing this bad news.

"Well, it's not us. So who the hell is pushing shit that ugly onto the scene?"

"Don't know, don't know," Lior mused. "But we must to find out Zack, because it can be danger for us. Use your people. We should to find out while we are not selling. Keep your eyes and ears open."

Twenty-One

A relatively uneventful week followed. Zack found himself playing pool with Tanaka again after he left the club on Saturday.

"Tanaka-san, I don't want to take your money anymore. Let's just play for fun, okay?" It was the truth. Zack no longer had the stomach to keep taking money from this old gentleman.

"Okay Zack, but let me buy you drink instead."

Zack knew it was useless to protest, so shrugged his acquiescence.

Tanaka returned with the drinks and racked up another frame. Zack was surprised how quiet it was this week. Usually people would be clamouring to get a game. He wondered if the lack of drugs could be responsible. Maybe people were catching up on their sleep?

"So Zack, you hear about the young people dead now?"

Tanaka's comment zapped Zack back into the room.

"Yes, I heard Tanaka-san. It's terrible, but I think Roppongi will always have these problems."

"But why, Zack?"

Zack looked at the wizened face in front of him and wondered how you could possibly explain the 'E-rush' or the '*Ice*-high' that so many people loved, to somebody who was already an adult during the second-world-war. He gave it a go anyway.

"People work hard in Tokyo Tanaka-san, and sometimes they want to play hard as well. Drugs help them lose themselves for a little while. They don't have to think about their worries or their responsibilities. They want to feel good. Feel sexy. Have fun. Drugs are just an easy way."

Tanaka regarded him intently, but said nothing.

"You come from a different generation, Tanaka-san. A different time. It must be difficult for you to understand."

"What about you Zack? You like to use drugs sometimes?"

"Sometimes Tanaka-san. Sometimes, yes."

"There are many drugs in Roppongi?" Tanaka raised his eyebrows.

"Well, yeah," Zack mused. "There's more now than a couple of years ago, anyway."

Tanaka bowed his head. "I cannot understand these young people and their drugs, Zack."

He shook his head slightly, as he moved to the table and broke the pack.

They played a few shots in silence. Then the peace was banished by a commotion near the doorway.

Zack glanced over his shoulder to see Mako and some friends stumbling in.

"Zack my friend! Hey hey … rock and roll baby!" Mako was flying as usual. "Good to see you so soon you know. What are you drinking?"

"Yeah, good to see you too mate. I'll have a Jacks and dry. Mako, I'd like you to meet Tanaka-san. Tanaka-san, this is a friend of mine, Mako."

Mako ostentatiously assessed Tanaka, but greeted him respectfully enough. Tanaka bowed stiffly, then turned away to the table to play his shot. Mako, momentarily puzzled, shrugged off the snub and headed to the bar.

Tanaka put his cue back in the rack and picked up his coat from the table. Zack noticed he had not played his shot.

"Tanaka-san, what's the matter?" Zack was nonplussed by this strange energetic shift.

"Too many young people for an old man, Zack. I am tired." His tone brooked no argument.

They shook hands, exchanged bows, and Tanaka left swiftly. Zack was still pondering his inexplicable mood-swing as Mako thrust yet another drink into his hand.

Then his train of thought changed tracks. "Mako, can I talk seriously with you for a moment?"

Mako clapped him on the back jovially. "First time for everything Zack you know man!"

Zack shot him an unforgiving scowl, which didn't let up.

Once he'd realised Zack really wasn't kidding around, Mako grabbed him by both shoulders and shook him a little. "Zack, it's me man, whaddaya wanna know?"

Zack led him to a corner table on the far side of the room. "What do you know about the drugs that killed these kids?"

Mako reacted as if he'd tasted something bitter. "Is a tough question Zack, an' we tryin' to find out." He fingered his chin. "Not good for business, you know man."

"Tell me about it," Zack muttered. "Seriously Mako, between us we both know a lot of people around here. Who the fuck is putting this shit out?"

Mako hesitated, glancing around the room before replying. "Our best guess at the moment is the Africans … Nigerians I think. My people are working on it Zack. We find them, tell them to stop. If they do, okay. If not, then …" He didn't really need to finish the sentence.

Africans, Zack thought. It sort of made sense. Everyone else was too organised. Iranians, Israelis, and the *Yakuza*. But the Africans. As well as some random Japanese-Brazilians. They were wildcards. A lot of splinter-groups. More unpredictability. Yeah, it seemed a reasonable enough hypothesis.

"Zack. You want to take something maybe?"

"No. But thanks, Mako," Zack replied. "I've got to get going. Not really in the party mood tonight you know."

"You worryin' too much Zack. Life is short man. Enjoy."

Zack looked hard at Mako. "Shorter for some, apparently." He drained his drink and got to his feet. "See you later Mako."

Mako shrugged his shoulders. "You hear anything interesting Zack, you phone me okay." He popped a *meishi* into Zack's pocket, winked and re-joined his friends at the bar.

Back on the street, Zack ignored the madding crowd and made his way down *Roppongi-Dori* towards *Nishi-Azabu*. The freezing air cleared his head, and he turned the situation over again. Obviously the *Yaks* were as bothered by the unnecessary deaths as every other 'legit' drug dealer on the strip. With their resources Zack figured it wouldn't be too long before 'results' of one kind or another were obtained. He would update Lior soon. For now he just needed to sleep.

* * *

Zack phoned Lior first thing Sunday and brought him up to speed on the *Yakuza* perspective. Lior wanted a meeting, so they rendezvoused at Las Chicas. It was early afternoon. The place was quiet, and Zack immediately spotted Lior outside by the carp-pond. He was sitting with someone else, which surprised Zack. It was usually all business with Lior. As he approached them, the other guy turned around with a big grin on his face. Zack did a double-take. For fuck's sake! It was Avi, from Eilat.

"Hey Zack. 'Ow is everything wiz you? Is great to see you again … long time ah?" He got up to shake Zack's hand and they embraced.

"Fuck Avi, it seems like a lifetime ago. So much going on. You got me so trashed the whole thing was just a blur when I woke up in Tel Aviv." He punched Avi lightly on the shoulder. "Probably best really. I was pretty sad to leave." He shook Lior's hand and sat down.

Lior pushed a packet across the table towards him. Zack picked it up and opened it. Inside was a mobile phone. For a moment he was perplexed, then the penny dropped.

"They are getting heavy Zack, so we must to be more careful. That phone is stolen and we give it new code. It is good maybe for two or three months. Then the phone company wakes up. Keep it out of sight. Use your other phone for normal calls, and don't to answer this one in public. Put on vibrate only, and people leave a message. If not, if you're being watched and they have tag on your phone, they know you have a different one. Even if they can do not much, we don't want that they know. Looks bad. Don't give the number to anyone not involved, and make sure they understand it is business only number. If you making a business call, do it private. Toilet. Wherever. I think they for sure watching you."

It was the most Zack had ever heard Lior say. He hesitated for a moment, before realising it was obviously okay to talk in front of Avi.

"What makes you think so?"

Lior squinted his eyes and smiled. "Zack, you are not the most … ehhh … low profile … person in Roppongi, you know."

"So you still partyin' hard, huh Zack? Lior, ee was bad in Eilat too." Avi put his head back and laughed loudly. A little too loudly, Zack thought.

Lior pissed him off sometimes with this superior crapola. Although, he had to admit it did irritate him that he hadn't thought of an alternate phone. It was a smart move. He could certainly do without this 'too high profile' garbage though.

"You think the stuff just sells itself maybe Lior? Or perhaps you would prefer to be the public face of our little partnership?"

Zack spoke quietly, and held Lior's gaze until the Israeli capitulated and raised both his hands in defence.

"Zack, don't to get shitty. I know it is 'ard to avoid."

A heavy silence pervaded the space between the three of them. Zack let it go on for a while and then turned to Avi. "When did you get over here?"

"About two weeks ago." Seeing Zack's surprised expression, he added "I 'ave been in *Osaka* and *Yokohama*."

"You sticking around for a while?"

"No, I 'ave seen everyone I need to see. I leaving to Amsterdam on Friday."

Zack regarded him curiously. "Amsterdam, huh?"

Avi just smiled, and shrugged his shoulders.

"It is my second 'ome these days you know."

"Pity you're leaving so soon. We could have had an interesting weekend."

"I 'ave one in Amsterdam for you, Zack."

I bet you will, thought Zack. He'd always liked Amsterdam.

The rest of the afternoon progressed amicably enough over a few beers and served to redress the tension that had arisen earlier. When the evening crowd started to file in for dinner, Lior and Avi excused themselves and departed. Zack declined their offer of a ride home. He repaired to the bar. He felt like having a drink and a think by himself for a change.

So, it looked as if Avi was instrumental somewhere in the procurement of their supply. Lior would never have spoken so freely if Avi wasn't intimately involved. Zack cast his mind back. It made sense, he supposed. If he remembered rightly, that last day in Eilat, Avi had mentioned he might be coming over *on business*. He hadn't known Zack would coincidentally hook up with Lior anyway.

Zack had to wonder now whether that *had* been coincidence. The Amsterdam reference, and Avi's expression as he'd made it, more or less confirmed his involvement. It would certainly explain why the stuff was such high quality. He wondered how they got it into the country, but supposed he didn't need to know. His thoughts moved onto what to do with the rest of the evening, when his phone rang.

"Yeah, hello."

"Hey you dirty bastard. What are you doing?" It was Hans.

Zack looked at the beer in front of him and replied, "Drinking. Where are you?"

"Sofia and I are at Las Chicas. Do you want to come over?"

Zack was immediately on his feet, covertly surveying the space. "Yeah, that sounds good mate. You're there now, are you?"

Then he spotted them out on the main terrace, and crept up quietly.

"Yeah mate, we're here now. How long d'ya reckon you'll be? You want us to order something?"

Zack was right behind Hans and bent down to his left ear. He spoke loudly. "I've already ordered actually mate, but thanks anyway."

The reaction was brilliant. Hans rocketed out of his chair, looking back disbelievingly. Sofia glanced around, did a double take, then tried to catch the glass that Hans sent flying. It smashed anyway, as Zack strolled around and took a seat.

He nodded casually towards the broken glass. "That was pretty clumsy, mate. Bit jumpy, aren't you?"

Sofia was laughing. Hans was not.

"Jesus fucking Christ, Zack. You scared the shit out of me. You are a complete *motherfucker!*" He looked at Sofia, who still couldn't stop giggling, and shook his head, before sitting down again. Bending down, he started collecting the biggest pieces of glass.

Sofia stopped laughing long enough to say, "C'mon Hans ... you have to admit, it's pretty funny."

Hans was still a bit off-balance. "What are you fucking doing here this early anyway Zack?"

Zack pulled a spooky face. "Keeping tabs on you, mate. What do you reckon?"

A sour-faced *gaijin* waiter had finally come over to sweep up the rest of the glass, so they ordered more drinks.

"Same again thanks mate," Zack said, still grinning at Hans.

Hans glowered at him. "How long have you been here?"

Zack looked at his watch. "Ooh, coming up four hours now, I think."

"Who with?" This from Sofia.

"I had to catch up with some Israeli friends I hadn't seen for a while. Any other questions?" He wiggled his eyebrows, glancing from one to the other.

Hans looked askance at Sofia. "And you thought it would be a good idea to have ... *this* ... with us for dinner?"

"So how are everyone's lives? What's new, who's who, what's hot and what's not? C'mon kids, I hardly see you anymore. What's up?"

Sofia could see Zack was a bit drunk, but he was obviously in a great mood.

"Things are good actually," she replied, allowing Hans a bit more sulk time. "Took your advice on how to play the game, and it seems to be working well enough. It's incredible actually. There's this one old guy who's absolutely loaded. Always has bodyguards with him. Tips me thirty or forty thousand yen every time he comes in. Calls me his *gaijin* grand-daughter."

Zack waggled his finger at her. "Don't believe that bullshit. They all want sex, baby. Trust me. You make sure you break it sometime before the whole thing goes seriously sideways on you."

Sofia laughed. "Zack, the guy's about eighty for God's sake."

"Doesn't matter. He's definitely dreaming about slipping one into you Sof."

Zack nudged Hans playfully. "And what about Romeo here. How's your woman from Tok-A-Yo, Hans my man?" Zack's delivery echoed the famous Deep Purple track.

Hans could see sulking was futile. "She's alright I suppose," he said grudgingly. "Yeah, everything's cool enough. We've got a little routine worked out now, so there shouldn't be any problems."

"You guys miss being out there in the Red Sea?"

Zack's abrupt query was like an Exocet-missile from left field, and a brief silence followed.

"What? For five hundred bucks a month, and all that slave-labour we did!" Hans exploded. "You've *got* to be kidding, don't you?"

Sofia was studying Zack carefully. "You miss it, don't you Zack?"

"Is it always about the money guys? Really? Is it?" Zack cast his arms around. "I mean, all this Roppongi bullshit, the money, the drugs, the beautiful people, the fucking craziness. Are we happier now, or were we happier then? Whaddaya reckon?"

"Jeez Zack," Hans intoned. "Don't go getting all philosophical on us. We can go back, if you miss it that much."

"Aah, but Hans, we can't go back. It will never … be … the same. And that is what I'm getting at, I guess." Zack's wistful expression remained for a moment, then he appeared to snap out of it. "Oh well. That's enough sentimental shite for now. Let's have some dinner. I think I need some."

*   *   *

Sofia and Hans were riding home together in a taxi. They had left a spectacularly drunk Zack in the bar, chatting with Shelton the gay barman. He had refused all suggestions of a lift, or that he should go home at all. They themselves had only left when Shelton assured them he'd make sure Zack was okay.

"What do you really think of Zack, Hans?" Sofia asked. "I know he's our friend, but what do you really think of him?"

Hans weighed her query for a moment before answering, and checked her face to be sure it wasn't some kind of trick question.

"I love the guy to death. But really, he's a bit crazy, y'know." Hans paused to think some more. "He definitely doesn't see the world like you or me, or most other people probably. He never looks it, but sometimes I get the feeling he's a bit lost."

Warming to the subject, Hans turned to face Sofia. "Not lost in *knowing* what to do. Lost in *deciding* what to do. Zack's problem is everything comes too *easy* for him. It's annoying to watch him sometimes." He looked at her a bit apprehensively. "And you?"

Sofia was lost in her own thoughts. "You're right, I think. Every now and then, I think I've got his measure. Then he says or does something completely out of left field, and I have to start guessing all over again. I agree with you though. He's definitely searching for something. But I don't think he's worked out what it is."

They rode the rest of the way in silence.

Twenty-Two

When Zack regained consciousness, he knew before he moved a muscle that the black dogs of hangover hell were unhappily chained to the inside of his skull. Ample previous experience suggested not moving anything too quickly would be a good idea. Not wanting to disturb the dogs, he spoke to the apartment without opening his eyes.

"Shunit, James, Teri, someone? Can one of you tell me what happened, and what time it is?" He felt himself being prodded, and slowly tried to open his eyes.

"Why don't you ask me?"

The voice was unmistakable. Zack groaned as Crystal came into focus beside him. As he was wondering just how that had happened, she informed him the time was five-twenty. He peered grimly at his watch, hoping against hope that she might be lying, but sadly, it appeared she was right on the money.

Zack focused on his breathing. "I think I might be dying."

"You're just lucky I was even there Zack. I think that pretty boy behind the bar had his sights set on converting you to the other side."

His mind swam. Then he realised she must be referring to Shelton. "No no no ... Shelton's a mate."

"A *mate*?" She emphasised the Aussie term in a peculiar manner. "Well yes, last night he nearly was anyway," she quipped. "I don't think he was too happy with me turning up when I did. Maybe he disapproves of us."

It took Zack a moment to even realise she was playing with his words, and that his brain was in fact seriously damaged. How best to proceed? Time ... was ticking away. Shower. Had to get to the shower. He dragged himself slowly upwards and maintained the kneeling position for a moment whilst marshalling further energy.

"Oh yes, he would have *loved* that position I think Zack."

Why didn't she do something useful, Zack wondered. Like shutting the fuck up. Making a quick mental note never to marry her, he got shakily to his feet. Vision of sorts was arriving, and he struggled unsteadily to the bathroom. The water was a blessed relief, but unfortunately it couldn't get at the dogs, or at whatever that thing was swimming around in the muck at the bottom of his gut. He moaned softly, massaging his temples. If he made it through this night, it would be a miracle.

He went through the rest of his routine like an automaton, mentally willing the pain and sickness to the outer edges of his perception. With nothing more than, "I'll see you at work," he left the apartment. He didn't even kiss her goodbye. Outside in the cold air he felt slightly better.

Once in the cab however, he knew trouble was imminent. He tapped the driver's Perspex screen and held up a delaying hand. Then he turned towards the auto-closing door, leaned out, and threw up violently into the street.

In a cold sweat, and with his stomach still cramping and twitching, he looked up to see James and Teri anxiously watching from the footpath, on their way to the foyer. *Wonderful*! He grimaced a smile at them. "Late for work," he said, and quickly closed the door. He didn't even want to look at the driver. "*Roppongi Crosseten onegaishimasu*."

He knew something was amiss when Chad was the first person he saw in the otherwise empty club.

"Zack, ah, we gotta have a talk. Sorry pal, but we're gonna have ta let you go." Chad wore an expression of brotherly faux-concern, which almost made Zack throw up again.

Zack gave him nothing, simply went behind the bar, and poured himself a large glass of cold coke.

"Some of the girls have been complaining, and that's how it is y'know. I know ya've been fuckin' Crystal, and I don't give a fuck about that, but the girls are bitchin' about you and I gotta keep 'em happy."

Yeah, sure, Zack thought. He was amazed how calm he was. "Okay."

"Y'ain't got nothing else ta say?" It appeared Chad was expecting him to put up some sort of fight, or defence.

He thought for a moment whilst draining the glass of its contents. "I guess if you had a serious reason Chad, then I'd have to take it seriously. But it's a joke. A bad joke. But still a joke."

"But Zack, I can only …"

"Fuck off, Chad."

Zack was in no mood for further bullshit. He walked out from behind the bar, threw Chad the keys, and headed to the store-room to get his stuff. Then he left. On the way home in the cab, Zack honestly felt nothing whatsoever, and wondered what was wrong with him.

He decided not to think about it until he woke up. Upon arriving home, it became apparent Crystal had already left. For this he said a fervent amen. After swallowing more painkillers, another Rohypnol, and some water, he collapsed into bed and slept until midday on Tuesday.

* * *

Upon opening his eyes, he was relieved to find that the dogs had left him. He had another shower and exited feeling pretty much human once again. The recuperative powers of the human body were truly remarkable, he thought. Looking around the flat, he discovered the Poms were still in bed, and as usual, Shunit was at school. He made himself Vegemite on toast, some coffee, and sat at the kitchen table contemplating the ramifications of his unexpected setback. He'd never been fired before. He checked the time. Midday. Then he made a phone call.

"Steve, is that you?"

"Yeah, who's that?"

"It's Zack, mate. Where are you at the moment?"

"Ahm, just leaving *Meidi-Ya* for the bar. Why, what's up?"

"I need to speak to you. You'll be at the bar in ten minutes?"

"Yeah, I'll be there for a while."

"Great. See you shortly."

"Righto."

Zack finished his breakfast with a small prayer to whoever might be paying attention that Bongoes would need him. He'd be able to find work elsewhere if he *had to*, but nowhere else would provide the fun, money and connections that Bongoes could. What to say? He just loved the place. If he could get back in, it would be business as usual.

He shaved, dressed, packed his gym gear, and had a look outside. It was a miserably wet and grey day, so he took a cab, and hoped the weather wasn't portentous.

"G'day Steve." Zack wandered into the bar.

Steve was practically hidden behind the weekly stock order, as well as a bunch of larger boxes.

"What the hell is all this crap?" Zack asked, gesturing at the boxes.

A disembodied voice answered, "Oh, I found a place to get Christmas and New Year stuff early and in bulk." Steve straightened up with a groan, leaned on the uppermost box and looked across at Zack. "I swore last year we wouldn't leave it to the last minute and get fucked over on price and availability again."

"Question is," Zack said, "where are you going to put it all until then?"

"That's true," Steve conceded. "I thought I might be able to get it all in the back, but clearly that's not going to happen." He shrugged. "I'll have to take it back to my place, I guess. Anyway, what's going on with you?"

"Well, you know that girl Crystal I've been seeing a bit of."

"Yeah. Be hard to miss her. Fuck knows what she sees in you though." Steve smiled genially at his own quip.

"Ho Ho Ho. Well anyway, she's the reason I've just been fired for the first time in my life."

Zack went on to explain Chad's obsession and jealousy, and how it had all turned out.

"So I was wondering if you need me down here, as I am now very much available."

Steve looked blankly at Zack over the boxes, his head making the 'No' movement. Zack's heart sank.

"Jeez mate, the Gods must be smiling on you or something. Talk about timing. Aya's heading off to Australia next week and I was going to have to get one of the part-timers from the other bar to fill in, until I found someone else. In fact, Aya's been managing since Jacko left, and I was going to have to let the young kid Jarrod take over. Frankly, I'd rather have you in charge. If you're up for it, that is. The kid will be disappointed, but that's life in the big city."

Zack could hardly contain the relief and joy he felt at his luck. "Steve, you know I'd love to come back! Many thanks mate. I thought that fucker Chad might've really put a spanner in my works."

"No problem, Zack. It works for me. It'll be great to have you back."

"When do you want me to start?"

"I'll have a chat to Aya, and let you know when her last night is. I'm pretty sure she's finishing this Saturday. I'll give you a call."

"I'll be in on Saturday for Aya's party anyway, so I'll see you then. And thanks again."

"Easy done, Zack. See you Saturday."

After a firm handshake to seal the deal, Zack walked out of there feeling ten foot tall and once again indestructible.

Fuck, what a relief that was! And now he had a week's holiday to boot! Yeeh-fucken-haahhh!

He'd been expecting a call from Victor at some point, and got it on his way to the gym.

"Hey Vic, how are you mate?"

"I'm okay Zack. What about you? I tried to call you last night. What happened?"

Zack knew Victor would almost certainly have known of Chad's intentions, but been powerless to change them.

"Well, you know what happened mate. Chad fired me. A lot of girls complaining about me apparently, which we both know is total bullshit. He did however mention the fact I'd been fucking Crystal. It's an ego-decision. Just fucking pathetic really."

"Yes Zack. I could not do anything. I am very sorry my friend. He is a dumb, jealous American. You have no job though, and this is bad."

"Oh, to be honest Vic, I'm not that worried about it. I'll probably be alright. Couple of weeks off might be good for me. How did things go last night anyway?"

"Oh, it was okay. Just a quiet Monday, so okay you know. The girls were very shocked. They really liked you. But you know that. Chad has just made himself look like, well, even more of a motherfucker than usual. I am sorry anyway."

"Don't worry about it Vic. I'm not. I had a good run. Thanks for the opportunity. I hope the whole thing hasn't fucked your position around too much."

Victor laughed. "No Zack, Chad needs me to clean up his mess always."

"Well, I've got some time now, so we should catch up for dinner or something. It's just been work, work, work for ages. Let me know when suits you."

"Yes, we must do this. I will call you later, okay."

"Yep, brilliant mate. I'll speak to you soon."

"Okay Zack. See you."

Once in the gym, Zack put himself through a light aerobic weights circuit. It would be stupid to push himself too hard, with his body still fragile. Moving to the pool-room, he did twenty laps of the twenty-five metre pool at a leisurely pace.

He'd recently taken up lap-swimming again after an extended layoff. Having beaten asthma as a kid by swimming innumerable laps over a period of years, pool-swimming had for a long time given him the shits.

These days however, it had grown on him again; he found it therapeutic. The rhythmic monotony of the stroke easily induced a meditative state. Today however, it was superfluous. He was floating already. He was free. He was on top of things. He was Zack. He relaxed so much in the spa-bath he almost fell asleep.

Leaving the gym he got a shock. As he turned the corner he almost ran into Crystal. Their eyes met and Zack laughed. "Hey, how are you?" he said, before leaning forward to give her a kiss.

She jerked her head away, then took a couple of quick steps backwards.

Zack, genuinely shocked, tried to make a joke of it. "What? I got leprosy suddenly Crystal, and no-one even told me?"

A look of shame crept over her face. "It's not funny, Zack. You lost your job for fuck's sake, and I might lose mine." She was obviously pretty rattled.

Zack was hurt, disappointed, and now angry.

"Don't be fucking *stupid*, Crystal. They're never going to fire *you*. And in case you didn't realise, it takes more than being fired by some insecure fucking loser to rock my boat. But it's nice to know where you stand anyway sweetheart."

Zack stepped past her to continue up the stairs. Then he paused for a moment, and turned around.

"Oh, one last thing baby."

Crystal regarded him uncertainly. They were still just a few steps apart.

"Be sure you don't gag too much when you let Chad shove his cock down your throat. You just *take it*, like a good employee." The bitterness in his voice surprised even Zack.

Her face hardened. "Fuck you Zack." But her voice was shaky.

He regarded her coolly for another moment. "Not … very … likely. Enjoy life on your knees, Crystal."

Turning swiftly again, he left her standing there.

Zack's post-gym exuberance had evaporated. He felt sick to his stomach. Personal weakness was one of the traits he most despised in people. His exposure to it was usually limited because of the friends he chose to cultivate. Misjudging somebody like Crystal disappointed him. He simply couldn't understand the transformation. Technically, he made less than a quarter of the money she did, for fuck's sake!

He shook his head in quiet amazement. All that money, a brain plus looks, all that superficial independence, and she'd compromise the lot in a heartbeat for her job under a fucking loser like Chad!

Fucking Roppongi! Soulless, money-driven, corrupting bitch of a place!

Zack was more upset than he cared to admit. That instant, he decided to get out of Tokyo for a few days. Some time in the mountains. A bit of hiking. Visit a few temples. A few tabs of acid. Hot springs. No *gaijins*. No bullshit. Just what the doctor ordered.

Twenty-Three

The train to *Nikko* left early the next day. Zack had taken a break there with Nurit back in '95, and knew exactly where he wanted to be. It wasn't peak season, so his short notice booking at the 'Turtle Pension' as it was quaintly called, had been no problem.

He watched the urban sprawl of Tokyo flash past the window. It seemed interminable, but gradually gave way to a hotch-potch of semi-urban dwellings. These were punctuated by small vegetable gardens, each with a little rainwater tank. Finally the train sped into rural Japan proper.

It was very weird seeing so much green everywhere after endless nocturnal months of Tokyo's uncompromising urban greyness. The snow-capped mountains in the distance seemed to beckon him. He'd have to get some snowboarding in this winter, he decided.

His thoughts flicked back to Roppongi. He'd had to ring Lior and explain the situation. Business was on hold for a couple of days. He'd also told Lior of his success with Bongoes, and that it would be business as usual when he got back. Lior was impressed with the turnaround time, and had called him a lucky sonofabitch. Zack had agreed with him.

That evening he headed for the cosiness of a famous little noodle restaurant. It served improbably large bowls of various noodle-based dishes. They also did *tempura*, which was a bonus.

The walls of the place were covered in the poetry, prose and graffiti of previous visitors, indisputable evidence of its popular international appeal. It was a nice touch Zack thought, and put his mind to work on what his contribution would be.

Roppongi's now a world away
And thank the Lord for that
How I wish my mind could stay
Here – when I go back on Sat.

It was a silly little ditty, but it sprang quickly to mind and he somehow felt it apt. He signed it with a flourish, and dated it 2/12/98. Only twenty-three days to go until Christmas. Unbelievable!

They'd had a brilliant Christmas party last year in *Mastoolim*. It was all the more interesting because Israel was only the second country he'd ever been in during Christmas, which didn't actively celebrate it. *All the foreigners on the Eilat marina had definitely made up for that!*

He smiled faintly. The irony was that Japan, being primarily Buddhist, shouldn't celebrate it either. Commercialism and consumerism had long since dispensed with such purist ideology however, as he'd discovered during his previous Christmas here.

He surveyed the room. There was seating for about twelve people, no more. It comprised a combination of rickety wooden chairs, stools of various sizes and shapes, as well as a couple of small up-ended barrels. The woman who owned the place was somewhere in the region of sixty, and Zack observed her as she bustled about her domain.

She wore a filthy apron over checked pants which were tucked into dark-green rubber boots. Her hair was pulled back and tied with some incomprehensible scarf arrangement. As had been the case last time, a smouldering roll-up cigarette was anchored to congealed saliva on the bottom right hand corner of her lip. A large bulbous mole on the other side of her mouth sprouted a number of thick black hairs. These hairs were not as thick as those protruding from her ears and nose. She was no beauty-queen. Her three other customers seemed to reflect a similar level of personal vanity. Zack smiled to himself. Roppongi certainly was a world away!

He felt over-groomed and over-dressed, even though he had not showered or changed since his arrival. But that was okay, he thought. After all, he was a *gaijin*. He was supposed to be different. And this was provincial Japan. He wondered whether the woman would exhibit the same extraordinary behaviour upon presentation of his meal, as she had last time.

Amongst the many misconceptions held by Westerners about how polite Japanese people were supposed to be, there existed several anomalies which Zack found particularly fascinating. For example, the Japanese considered it extremely rude to blow one's nose in a public place, whether it be on a train or in a restaurant. However, Zack routinely witnessed Japanese men openly *urinating* in public areas around Roppongi, and would watch as pedestrians passed by as if in complete ignorance of the event.

In direct contrast to this, whereas in Western culture it is generally thought to be good manners to eat one's meal quietly and without fuss, in Japan it is traditionally considered to be actually insulting to the host if one eats any noodle-based dish without an exaggerated amount of slurping, grunting and burping, this apparently signifying relish and appreciation.

This seemed to be even more the case in rural as opposed to urban Japan, and Zack was looking forward to performing the ritual with an appropriate level of gusto.

His chair faced the door, so he looked up immediately when the girl walked in. She caught his gaze instantly, and if anything, looked more surprised than he did. The moment they stared at each other became a little surreal, but Zack broke the spell by looking around the room. Then, as if it was the most natural thing in the world he said, "Would you like to join me?"

She was an extraordinary looking creature. He watched as she regained her composure whilst contemplating his offer. In a way, he had her trapped. She would either have to leave the restaurant altogether, or remain in an uncomfortably close-quartered silence if she chose not to sit with him. Zack allowed himself another little smile.

She continued to survey the limited seating arrangements, and then rested her gaze on Zack's candidly amused expression.

"Why do you want me to join you?"

Canadian or Yank, Zack thought.

"I don't know yet," Zack replied. "But I like to assume the best about people. Isn't that good enough?"

She gravitated into the seat opposite his.

"You must get disappointed a lot then eh?"

Canadian. Good! The 'eh' gave it away.

Zack studied her a moment before replying.

"Sort of part and parcel of life really, wouldn't you say? I think it was Bob Marley who said something like, 'Truth is, everybody is going to hurt you; you just gotta find the ones worth suffering for.'"

At this, she looked across the bench at him appraisingly.

"Have you got a name?"

"Zack." He extended his hand. "Good to meet you."

She took it. *Such soft skin.*

"What are you doing here anyway?" she said. "It's not exactly tourist season."

Zack smiled again. "I'm not exactly a tourist. And your name would be?"

"Very clever," she replied, before adding, "Carla."

She was an aristocratic looking girl, Zack decided. Lean, supple, athletic, and graceful. One of those people who seem to glide, catlike, through life, rather than trudging through it like everyone else. Her face was delicately structured, and she had porcelain skin. He watched her eyes move about the room before they came back to him. They were a clear green, and he wondered if she wore contacts. She had jet-black straight hair, which was cut into a very modern angular bob. She looked like space age technology. She was looking at him now, and he wondered at her thoughts.

Zack gestured to the wall. "Have you thought of what you're going to write yet?"

She looked around as if noticing the graffiti-clad walls for the first time. "I already wrote something last time I was here."

"When was that?"

"A few years ago."

"Where is it?"

In one fluid motion, she rose and twisted, wraithlike, to the left of the doorway. She pushed a *meishi* and a scrap of paper to one side, revealing her previous contribution. A hint of a smile passed her lips as she re-read her words. Zack, unable to read from where he was, joined her at the wall. She was a few inches shorter than him, and he poked his head over her shoulder whilst following her gaze.

'Roppongi - I am calm in the centre of this storm. Amen.'
Carla de Lange - 17 Oct 1995

"Still calm?" Zack queried offhandedly.

"Oh yeah," she replied quickly. "Older, and definitely wiser."

She raised her eyebrows at him. "What's your effort? You don't strike me as someone with nothing to say."

Zack pointed out his contribution.

She moved towards it, laughed, and turned her head. "Trite, but it's cute." She paused before adding, "So you leave on Saturday?"

He grinned. "No, I actually leave Monday but it didn't rhyme so well."

"I see. Poetic license."

"No, I'm kidding. I do leave Saturday. There's a going away party I have to be at."

She sat down again and stretched, her hands clasped high overhead.

The proprietor chose that moment to arrive and plonk down Zack's steaming bowl of noodles. Stepping back a few paces, she stood impassively, arms folded in expectation.

Zack didn't know how he was supposed to slurp the goddamn things up noisily *right now*. They were just too damn hot! So he blew on the noodles, looked up at her, shrugged and made a face in a plea for respite. With a snort, she grudgingly obliged and retreated to her culinary epicentre.

Carla watched her retreat somewhat dubiously. "Don't think you've impressed her too much."

Zack blew some more into his bowl, before replying, "Oh well, you can't win them all."

He started slowly slurping the noodles into his mouth, putting his face very close to the bowl in Japanese style. When he eventually looked up, Carla was watching him in silence.

He swallowed quickly. "You're not having anything?"

"Ahhm, yes. I think ... just *miso* soup and rice."

She turned in the direction of the old lady, and without moving from the table, communicated this order in clipped Japanese.

Zack raised his eyebrows. "I'm impressed."

"Don't be. It's far from perfect."

"Most things are," he replied smoothly.

She tilted her head towards him. "So, it would seem more than a few people come out here to escape that madhouse."

"Makes sense to me," Zack said. "Actually, I'm sort of surprised I don't know you."

"I don't hang out in Roppongi. It makes me sick."

"Well I can understand that, but what I meant was that I was here in '95 as well, and you must have been hanging out there then otherwise you wouldn't have written what you did."

Carla looked like she was about to say something, but changed her mind.

Zack pressed on. "I was here with my girlfriend back then. Maybe you knew her? Her name was Nurit. Israeli girl. Very beautiful. Straight black hair."

He waited a beat. "And eyes like yours, actually."

He followed this up with a series of loud slurps, caught a look of appreciation from the harridan, and nodded good-naturedly back at her.

"She worked at BlackJacks for a while, didn't she?" Carla chose to ignore the 'eyes' bait.

"Yep."

"Yeah, I remember her alright. One of the most stunning women I've ever seen. Didn't get to know her too well though, before she just kind of vanished off the scene."

"Well, she pretty much felt the same about Roppongi as you do. She ended up working in *Shinjuku*. We didn't go out that much eventually, except for when we argued, and then we'd just take off separately with our own friends."

"Were you faithful to each other?"

This caught Zack off guard. He paused momentarily.

"That ... is a good question. Well, I was to her, yes. I think she was to me as well. But I'll never really know. There were just too many fights and too many opportunities."

"She probably thinks the same about you."

"Probably. We did actually last the distance over here though, unlike most couples. We split up at the end of our Japan adventure, and she dropped off the map in India. I went to Thailand, then India, then Nepal. But I haven't seen her since she left Tokyo."

"Do you miss her?"

"I was in love with her, if that's what you mean, and that's only happened once. It took me a while to get over it, and get on with things, but I'm probably a better man for it."

"I'll ask again. Do you miss her?" A patient stare.

Zack expression hardened a little. "You don't give up, do you? There must be a gig on a current affairs show waiting for you somewhere."

She remained silent and held his gaze.

Zack regrouped. "I still think about her sometimes, but I wouldn't say that I miss her, no."

"You came here with her, didn't you?"

"Yes, I did actually."

"And I'd also bet that you're staying at the same place you both stayed before."

Zack looked at her in astonishment. "What are you, psychic?"

"You miss her."

Zack suddenly realised that she had just done to him, what he always did to everyone else. She'd controlled the conversation, and had somehow inveigled more out of him in three minutes, than he'd offered anyone else in three years.

He had no explanation for her prescient insights, and again had cause to wonder why women didn't rule the world. Then, at some invisible cue, they were both laughing.

"Well, maybe I have sentimental lapses," Zack conceded.

The cigarette-lipped woman brought over Carla's food, and apart from the obligatory slurps, they ate in silence until the food was gone.

Carla re-opened the conversation. "What do you plan to do here for the next four days?" she asked.

"I've been working my arse off for the last five months," Zack said, "so I plan to do a lot of relaxation. Take some mellow acid and do some mountain walks. A bit of temple-gazing maybe. Definitely some hot springs as well. What do you think?"

"It sounds like a good plan, except I don't have any acid."

"I've probably got enough for the pair of us, if you're up for it," Zack replied. "When are you leaving anyway?"

"I've got to be back at work for Friday night, more's the pity."

"I forgot to ask – where do you work?"

"The same place I always have."

"Jacks?"

"Yep."

"Hostessing?"

"Dancing."

Zack just nodded. There were only ever four dancers for the shows at BlackJacks, and they were invariably the best of the best. Although they danced topless at some points during their show, it had nothing to do with stripping; it was moreso a cleverly choreographed erotic cabaret. In short, it was a class act. There was no private-dancing, or men touching them, or even talking to them. None of that bullshit.

They performed on stage a few times a night and rested in between. If they wanted to, they could socialise in the club, but it wasn't an obligation. They made great money. Basically it was a dream job and the envy of pretty much any girl in Roppongi. Except maybe the professional models, who didn't count anyway.

"What about you?"

"I'm between jobs at the moment, which is why I had time to come here."

"What were you doing?"

"I was managing the strippers at Cloud Nine Roppongi. I had a difference of opinion with Chad, and he fired me a couple of days ago."

"Oh yuck. That big American guy Chad?"

"That's the one."

She looked repulsed. "He is a pig of a man. Comes into Jacks sometimes, and seriously believes he's God's gift to woman-kind."

"That's definitely the guy."

"And what about when you get back?"

"I pick up my old job again."

"Which is?"

"Managing Bongoes."

She whistled in surprise. "Wow! That's a quick recovery."

"I was extremely lucky they had an opening." Zack nodded, more to himself than to her. "Timing, as they say, is everything."

By this time, the other customers had left without Zack even noticing. They were alone in the little restaurant. The harridan was bustling about cleaning up, eyeing them malevolently from time to time. Zack glanced at his watch. It was nine o'clock, and he was pretty sure there were no bars to go to.

Carla seemed aware of his uncertain frame of mind.

"Early to bed, early to rise in these parts it would seem, Zack." A playful smile accompanied this observation.

Zack had no idea what the smile meant. He chose to be proactive.

"Do you want to hook up tomorrow, and go for a wander?"

She paused, apparently weighing her answer carefully.

"I'd have to ask my boyfriend when he wakes up. I don't know what he wants to do." She looked at Zack with a slightly embarrassed expression. "He's sleeping at the moment."

Zack's face must have given away at least something of the extent to which his mind was reeling with disappointment. How *could* he have been so stupidly presumptuous? Of *course* she was here with someone. What a complete fucking *idiot* he was!

"Oh well, I guess that puts that idea to rest then," he said heavily.

Carla burst into laughter. "I'm kidding! I haven't had a boyfriend for six months now."

Watching her merriment, Zack couldn't help but laugh himself. She had nailed him good and proper.

"Well with a sense of humour like that, I can understand why."

Outside, the cold air quickly enveloped them, and they walked towards an ancient wooden bridge in silence.

"So going back to my question, would it be too much to expect a straight answer now?"

He looked sideways at her, watching the mist escape her mouth with each breath.

She smiled. "Zack, I enjoyed tonight. I'd be happy to hang out with you tomorrow."

A wave of relieved happiness swept through Zack. He couldn't believe it. Roppongi, and everything else seemed a million miles away. He hadn't had a *thought* about Crystal, or any of the other betrayals and shenanigans that were going on. If this chick wasn't a witch, she sure as hell cast a mean spell.

"Great. That's fantastic. Where are you staying anyway? I'll walk you back."

Once in bed, Zack lay awake for quite a while. He'd left her at the door of the little *Ichiban* guesthouse half a kilometre further up the road. They'd agreed to meet at Zack's place for breakfast at eight-thirty.

There was no doubt about it. She was something special. Jesus, he was even a bit nervous. He hadn't felt like that since the early days with Nurit.

* * *

Meanwhile, Carla likewise turned over the possibilities. She knew about Zack already. She knew his reputation around Roppongi for party antics and womanising. She had in fact met him about three years ago at a party in a cool but sadly short-lived club called Yin-Yang.

He obviously didn't remember. True to his word, he'd had eyes only for Nurit. She remembered thinking at the time that it was inspiring to still see genuinely committed couples going the distance in Roppongi.

And now here he was in *Nikko*. Alone. With her. What did she think about that? She didn't know really. Tomorrow would bring what it would bring. She set her alarm, and closed her eyes.

Twenty-four

The morning was bright and clear. Although it was still chilly, Zack took an outside table. He wanted to watch her walk down the hill. Although nothing had happened between them yet, he was sure there'd been a spark. No way did he want to fuck it up.

Christ, he thought, I'm like a love-struck teenager. For him this would usually have been a depressing realisation, but instead he felt extremely upbeat, more alive than usual. He caught sight of her as she rounded the bend, and kept his eyes on her through the mist rising off his tea.

"Morning beautiful."

She smiled that gorgeous smile and sat down. "Don't you mean beautiful morning?"

Goddamn she was quick.

"That too, if you like," he acknowledged.

She said nothing else, so he continued.

"If it's okay by you, I thought we'd indulge in a mellow day of tripping, and take the bus up the mountain. There's a lake and hot springs up there somewhere. Sound like a plan?"

"Sounds good. I'll have to go back and get my swimsuit though."

"So be it. Actually, we should do some of this now. I reckon a half to start, and then quarters as required after that. Cool with you?"

"Yeah, cool. I'll trust your judgment."

Zack looked at her reassuringly. "Don't worry. It's good judgment."

After sharing some toast, he tore one of the trips into two pieces, and they dropped.

"Every time I do this I'm astounded," Zack said, "that our perception of reality, whatever that is, can change so much by ingesting one tiny piece of paper. When was the last time you took acid anyway?"

Carla considered the question briefly. "Well, I haven't had any this time round. Just a couple of E's, so it must have been last time in Tokyo. A good couple of years. Shock, horror! You are a bad influence!"

Zack shot her a reproving look. "Carla, I don't want you to take it if you don't really want to. I just thought it would be a beautiful way to spend the day up on the lake."

"Relax Zack. I'm a big girl. I was kidding. And thanks for offering anyway. It'll be fun."

The mountain-bus picked them up at nine a.m. from Carla's hostel.

It was a stunning morning. Chilly, but the crisp, clean mountain air was suffused with bright sunshine. They were surrounded by rolling green fields and forest, which rose into imposing white-capped peaks. The sunshine reflected brilliantly off the glistening snow and ice, and occasionally you could catch a fleeting spectrum of colour in the swirling mists. Zack took a deep breath and looked at Carla.

It had been about forty-five minutes since they'd dropped, and Zack could feel the comfortably familiar tentacles of elevated perception entwining themselves into his senses, and slowly but surely, tweaking his world. He felt so calm, so peaceful. He closed his eyes briefly, savouring the moment. Really *being* in the moment. He wondered how she was feeling.

As if on cue, she answered him.

"This was a very good idea, Zack. I can't believe it's been so long since I did this." She turned and regarded him a little curiously. "Thank you again."

The bus continued winding its way up the mountain, affording them ever-changing views of the surrounding countryside. Zack loved that they were here off-season. In Tokyo, it was rare if not impossible to ever get a sense of nature, space and peace, and if they'd been obliged to share this experience with some noisy tour group today, it would not have had the same magic.

He looked out the window again, spied a herd of goats grazing near a tiny rustic cottage, and marvelled at the fact that a Tokyo *salariman* and whoever occupied that hut, lived only about two hours from each other. They might as well be on different planets.

He turned to Carla. "So how long have you been dancing anyway?"

She also twisted in her seat to better face him. "Oh, about since I could walk, I suppose."

"Just a beginner then?"

"Yep."

"What've you trained in? I mean ... what do you like most?"

"I guess my favourite is still classical ballet. That's what I always wanted to do. But y'know, I just love everything about dance. It's the most natural, honest form of expression we have. Dance doesn't lie. I think that's what I love about it most."

"What happened to the classical ballet? How the hell did you end up in Roppongi?"

Silence ensued. Her head turned away. Zack cursed inwardly. His phrasing of the question had been a little tactless; he suddenly felt like a trespasser.

"Hey, I'm sorry Carla. I didn't mean to pry. Or to upset you. Really ... it doesn't matter." He paused. "Don't worry about it."

She sighed. "No. It's not your fault, Zack. It's me."

So he waited. Wire fencing and signposts passed by the window as the bus continued its climb.

Eventually she spoke.

"My teacher was killed in a fucking stupid car accident. He ... I just felt like I had to get away." Her face was still averted.

Realising he was holding his breath, Zack slowly let it out.

"I'm really sorry to hear that Carla. I guess he must have been a huge influence on you."

"He taught me for twelve years. Since I was a child." Carla's eyes found Zack's once more. "He was the gentlest person you could ever meet."

They rode on in silence for a while, Zack feeling it was better to let that moment pass. Suddenly they jolted over a speed-hump on their way into the car-park, and the lake's vista opened up before them.

Carla half-rose from her seat. "Oh my God! I didn't expect anything like this!"

It was true. The lake was something from fairyland, fantastical. It was even more beautiful than he remembered. Suspended amongst the mist, the mountain peaks and the morning sun, it was a huge expanse of mesmerising, mirror-still water.

The bus stopped. "Come on, let's go." Carla was on her feet immediately.

Zack chuckled at her eagerness. "Carla, I don't think it's going anywhere in a real hurry."

The dark look she flicked him prompted a continuation. "But ... I guess we don't have a minute to lose."

"That's better you sarcastic git." She was off the bus in a flash. "We have to find a boat."

Zack quickly followed, and looked at her again. Her face had come alive, her cheeks flushed with excitement. Like a little girl in sideshow alley.

The mellowness of the acid creeping through his brain curtailed any vocalisation of his typical cheap shots. So for a moment, he found himself lost for words.

"Well come on, Zack! They must rent them. Where are they? You're the one that's been here before!"

"You know Carla. I have no idea where your boats will be, but let's go for a walk and find them."

It took a while, followed by some persuasion, but they finally found a place willing to let them take a boat out. Carla's proficiency with the language certainly helped. Ten minutes and 2,500 yen later they were floating serenely in the middle of the lake. Zack had assumed rowing duty, and once out there, he put the boat into a lazy spin before lying back on a couple of life jackets and closing his eyes to the sun.

The acid had really made itself at home, and whenever he opened his eyes he enjoyed sunbeams bouncing and clouds morphing. It reminded him of one time in Thailand when he and his brother Josh had dropped some phenomenal liquid acid and then played Frisbee on a deserted beach at low tide. It had been a gorgeous day, with low tide leaving a thin film of water on the flat beach surface. Sun, sky and clouds reflected brilliantly in this mirror, and catching sight of themselves in it, they appeared to be sky-walking in pursuit of the gleaming silver disc. Fascinated, they played so long they exhausted themselves.

Zack had often pondered whether sublime experiences like that happened *coincidentally* with acid use, or whether they happened all the time but went unnoticed. He now believed it was the latter. Perception, not actuality, was at fault. Hallucinogenics were, in his opinion, one of the most profoundly reverent ways possible to appreciate nature's wonders.

He recalled the excitement Carlos Castaneda's writing had provoked in him years before. At that time he'd been apprehensive to say the least, about hallucinogenic drugs, and Castaneda's concepts had been beyond both his experience and comprehension.

This realisation had only further heightened his desire to explore the mysterious worlds whose doors opened with psychotropic keys. Interestingly, up until then, he'd been successfully indoctrinated by governmental anti-drug propaganda.

Even some works of fiction he'd been exposed to as a youngster had instilled an unjustifiable terror of hallucinogens. He could still remember the book which first haunted his consciousness with the LSD bogeyman. S.E. Hinton's 'That was Then – This is Now'. An otherwise great book. A shame that thematically speaking, it might as well have been written by government anti-drug propagandists. The only good thing, he supposed …

His mental meanderings were interrupted by a jarring in his shoulder, and he half opened an eye.

"Hey tripper! You going all silent on me now?"

Carla was poking him, rather ineffectually, with one of the oars. Standing silhouetted against the sun, she looked sort of like an alien. Zack decided to try communicating.

"You look like an alien Carla. Why don't you lie down and chill out?"

"What do you mean chill out? We're going swimming."

Zack chuckled to himself. "Correction alien. *You're* going swimming."

Diving into the endless abyss of cold dark water that he envisioned beneath them was not currently top of his list of things to do. He didn't actually have a list. He had completely forgotten about the swimming idea. Then he remembered it wasn't swimming, it was hot springs they were supposed to be finding.

"Don't be such a pussy. And stop calling me an alien."

Zack started laughing, and found he couldn't stop. That's what he loved about acid. He'd never have called her an alien, even if he'd thought she looked like an alien, if he wasn't tripping.

"Why don't you just accept it Carla? You're a fucking gorgeous alien, and that's all there is to it. How many other people do you see who look anything like you?" He squinted at her through the sunlight.

She prodded him with the oar, frowned, said nothing.

He fended the weapon off. "I rest my case."

"Alright then, be a boring git."

He smiled. "Are you sure we know each other well enough to be recklessly insulting each other like this?"

"You started it."

"To be described as an alien," he said, half sitting up, "is surely one of life's greatest compliments. You'll realise that when you know me better." With that pronouncement, he sat up fully.

"My God … it moves."

"At least I'm from this planet."

"Ha ha! It's getting a bit tired now." Her tone bordered on irritation.

"Get used to it. Well, are you going in or not?"

"Will you save me if I get into trouble?"

Zack dropped his head for a moment. "I'd love to," he said, voice subdued. "But I can't swim."

Carla sat down heavily. "What! You can't swim! What d'you mean you can't swim? Are you fucking mad … coming out in this boat?"

"You were so keen for it. I just … well, I figured if anything happened, you'd save *me*. Wouldn't you?"

Despite his effort to remain po-faced, Zack couldn't help the edge of a grin creeping into his expression.

She spotted it instantly. "Zack … you are *such* an asshole."

Momentarily furious at having been taken in, she whipped off her dress and dived into the lake in one fluid motion.

Zack had but one stupefying second to see her in her swimsuit before she disappeared into the deep. "Shit," he whispered. Lounging against the rowboat's rails he watched her stroking expertly away, before turning around about fifty metres distant. She powered back at equally as strong a pace, pulling up just short of the boat, flicking water off her face, and glowering up at him. *God she was gorgeous!*

"How's the water?"

"Well Zack, they say true knowledge comes from experience."

'Touché."

"Are you really scared to come in?" A saccharine dig.

He responded in lofty tone. "What's scary is that you seem to believe infantile goading like that will persuade me to join you. But, I've decided to anyway."

Her smile of delight was swift, genuine, and already reward enough.

Off came his cargo pants and deck shoes. He let out a primitive howl, and dived out of the boat. His first impression of the cold, was of his balls being sucked up into his stomach in sheer, unadulterated shock.

Once he surfaced, time froze before he could breathe. When breath finally came, the oxygen it contained told his brain to get back in the boat. Quickly.

He became aware of Carla giggling hysterically, as she pulled herself in as well.

"What the fuck! That – water – is – freezing!" Zack could hardly get the words out. He looked at her disbelievingly. She had evidently faked her aquatic comfort for as long as it took to get him in as well.

Carla flopped into the boat looking invigorated. "I'm an alien ... remember?"

The weak sunlight took some time to defrost them, and neither spoke for a while. Zack eventually opened his eyes and reached out to touch her gently on the nose. Her eyes opened as if by magic. They seemed luminous.

"How are you feeling?"

"Zack, I feel absolutely fucking amazing. Time for another half I think."

He felt a surge of affection, and ferreted through his kit. "Your wish is my command m'lady. Are you sure you want a half? Or just a quarter?"

"Fuck it," she said. "Let's do another half. We're on holiday aren't we?"

Zack tore the trip in half, and leaned towards her. "Open wide."

She stuck out her tongue.

"Charming, I'm sure," Zack commented, popping the tiny piece of paper onto it. Mouth closed, she leant back, appraising him, as he dropped his own.

"Where do you get this stuff Zack?"

He lifted an eyebrow. "That's rather an adventurous question to be asking, don't you think?"

She shrugged. "I'm an adventurous girl."

And that's not all, Zack thought. She'd stretched out, and was leaning back against one of the lifejackets. The metallic-silver one-piece swimsuit glistened in the sunlight, and curved perfectly around her modest breasts. An aggressive pair of chilled nipples jutted provocatively through the material. Her long legs rested gently on Zack's seat. Wet hair clung sleekly to her head and neck, and her eyes seemed greener and brighter than ever. She was another good reason for believing that God was indeed, male.

"So you're not going to tell me?"

Zack realised her query had gone unanswered.

"I've got some good friends," he replied levelly. "Let's leave it at that for the time being."

"Whatever." She flexed her limbs and yawned contentedly.

Twenty-Five

Zack returned to Tokyo a changed man. He didn't know how things with Carla would play out. What he did know was that for the first time since Nurit, he was going to put everything he had into nurturing what had started between them in *Nikko*.

Carla was a revelation. The nervous twist in his gut reminded him how much he already cared about her. He loved that she hadn't yet let him sleep with her. "See how we feel back in Roppongi," she'd said.

The anticipation was energising. He felt more alive than he had in ages, as if previously he'd only been going through the motions of living his life. Could that be true? And if so, had he unknowingly been in that semi-anaesthetised state ever since breaking up with Nurit?

Sure, he'd had patches of emotion here and there, but this was different. His whole *being* was engaged. It was a palpable difference, and he was surprised, curious and a more than a little wary about where it would all lead him.

Zack's thoughts about Carla were interrupted by the train's arrival at *Shinjuku* station. This enormous transport nexus, used by over two million people daily, was virtually a wonder of the world. During rush hour it was like watching a colossal ant-hill angrily erupt. Now only three p.m, the busiest time of day was yet to come.

Zack knew he should just change platforms, take another train to *Hiroo* and then walk home. But, recoiling from the idea of burrowing further into the ant-hill so soon after *Nikko's* blissful solitude, he instead took the nearest escalator to street level. Commandeering the first passing cab, he directed it home to *Nishi-Azabu*.

Marshalling his thoughts and priorities, he dug the secret mobile out of his shoulder-bag and speed-dialled Lior. The phone rang once.

"Allo."

"Lior, *ma inyanim chaver shelli?*"

"Zack … 'ow are you … *hacol beseder?*"

"*Ken, en baiya biklal, ani mageesh tov meod.*"

"*Ezeh Ivrit,*" Lior responded, snidely complimenting Zack's elementary Hebrew.

Zack ignored Lior's baiting. "Are we in business yet?"

"I think maybe we stay out one more week. Then we see."

"Yep, fine … gives me time to settle back into the bar. Later Lior." Zack re-bagged the phone. Rarely did a phone-call between them last more than a minute.

So he needn't worry about drug-deals this week. That left two priorities: cementing his relationship with Carla and re-cementing his position in Bongoes. He was looking forward to getting on with both. The taxi pulled in to *Gaien-Nishi-Dori*, stopping outside the apartment block. Zack paid, and entered the building. His plan was to crash for a few hours, eat, and then make his way to Bongoes for Aya's going away party.

* * *

Not so far away, in *Shibuya*, the gangster's body spasmed as he climaxed. The young Filipina, eyes glazed, gulped reflexively then gagged as Max yanked her head towards him, forcing himself deeper down her throat.

Desperately wanting to please him, she continued her work and focused on breathing through her nose. She did not want to upset him again.

Spent, he sagged back into the leather lounge suite, pulling her with him. She felt his hardness begin to subside, but dared not take her mouth away.

"Keep it in there," Max murmured.

He reached to the coffee table, while the seventeen year old tried to make herself comfortable on the floor. The little brown bottle Max grasped was full of *Ice* crystals. Trickling a few of them into a glass pipe, he fired up a butane lighter.

Angelica looked up anxiously from between his legs, praying he would let her have some. Sometimes, when he was in a good mood, he let her have a lot. But Max finished the vaporised crystals in one long, slow toke and relaxed back onto the lounge. Aaaahhhh, that was better! The rush was magnificent. It made him feel like a king.

In a way, he thought, he was a king. He wished he was hard again right now inside this bitch's mouth. He idly stroked her hair, as he would a dog. She wasn't going anywhere, he thought. None of his bitches were.

"Max." Her whimpering voice came to him through his euphoric haze. "Can I ..." She trailed off, unable to finish the sentence.

He looked down and brought the pathetic bitch's cum-stained face into focus. She had taken her mouth from his cock, but was still kneeling in front of him. He always told them not to clean up until he said it was okay.

He smiled. "Yeah, that was good. Smoke some baby ... why not?" It amused him to get them so high they'd willingly do things he otherwise had to force them to do.

Reaching eagerly for the utensils, Angelica suddenly found herself on her back, gasping for breath. The kick had been short and sharp, hard into the sensitive underside of her left breast.

"Not like that you dumb bitch! Go get yourself cleaned up! And brush your fucking teeth. *Kyama*!"

His temper subsiding as quickly as it had flared, Max shifted his foot back to its resting place on the coffee table and reached for the stereo's remote, turning the heavy jungle music up a few notches.

Two hundred beats-per-minute of electronic drumming madness reverberated through the apartment as Angelica sponged his semen from her cheeks. She hoped she'd be able to swipe a few crystals for tonight. It made work so much easier.

When she'd left her family in Manila, Angelica had been promised hostessing and cleaning work, but the *Shinjuku* club she worked at was nothing but a brothel, full of other Filipinas like her, as well as a few South Americans and Eastern Europeans.

All the girls were contracted for a fixed wage and wheedled what extra money they could in tips from their customers. The cleaning applied to Max's personal apartment, as well as the cramped box she shared with five other girls. When she'd asked what they got paid for cleaning Max's apartment, they had laughed at her.

She'd wanted to run away. Christina had said to come with her, but at the last minute Angelica lost the courage to go through with it. And then Christina had died in Gas Panic 99. Everyone knew Max had killed her, but no-one said anything. No-one did anything. Angelica berated herself miserably. What had she been thinking anyway? She was alone. She had nowhere to go. Max would always find her, and he could get so angry sometimes.

She shuddered, thinking of her family, her little sisters. A tear slid down her face. She knuckled it quickly away, before hurrying back to the humiliating oblivion awaiting her in the lounge-room.

*   *   *

When Zack arrived at the apartment, James and Teri were just getting up.

"How goes it kids?" Zack said effusively. He was in a buoyant mood ... sleep could wait a few more minutes.

James, munching cereal, grunted something vaguely positive.

Teri cocked an eyebrow, before speaking. "Be better if the management at BlackJacks weren't such a bunch of fucking space cadets. I swear to God no-one knows who's supposed to be running that place. Everyone and their dog's a fucking manager."

James finished his mouthful. "How was *Nikko*? You're looking pretty good. Got a bit of sun, didja?"

"What can I say? It was awesome. I needed it more than I knew. The fact I met an amazing girl there didn't hurt either."

Teri lifted the other eyebrow. "An amazing girl, Zack? That's pretty expansive, for you." Glancing at James, she added, "Maybe Zack's human after all, sweetheart."

"So who is this chick mate? Japanese? *Gaijin*? What?" James stuffed another spoonful into his mouth and kept crunching away.

"Where's she working? In Roppongi?" Teri prompted, less casually.

Oh yes, very interested, Zack thought. "You know her actually," he teased.

"Really? Who?"

"Ahh, can't tell you yet," he said with a grin. "You'll have to wait a bit."

He slid open his bedroom door and leaned against the frame. "I'm crashing for a few hours, so it'd be great if you could keep the noise down. By the way, we're having a going-away party for Aya at Bongoes tonight. Come in after work. It should be a good one."

James looked up. "Who's we?"

"Oh shit, I forgot to tell you! I start managing Bongoes again on Monday."

Their joint look of incredulity was fun to watch.

"You jammy bastard," James finally commented.

"So I'll see you later tonight, hey guys?"

Grinning amiably, Zack slid his door shut, set the alarm for eight, and got his head down.

* * *

Over in Daikanyama, Hans studied Fumiko. Despite the chill in the apartment they were both filmed in sweat. Christ, she can fuck, he thought. She just loves it. The amount they'd been doing it lately was worth a call to the people at Guinness. Hans no longer worried about skipping the gym. He was getting more than enough exercise right here in this apartment.

Fumiko had unusually large breasts for a Japanese, and Hans knew she was proud of them. During sex she would often pull his hands to her breasts and knead them savagely. She liked it when he pinched her nipples hard, and squealed in mixed pain and delight as she ground his cock deeper inside her.

She wouldn't leave his cock alone; even after they'd finished their lovemaking, she'd go on stroking, licking, kissing and sucking, until it at least, was ready for another round. Hans had never had a lover as eager to please. After sex, she lit scented candles and performed *Shiatsu* on his still-tingling body, transporting him to another realm entirely.

Her English was limited, but he'd tried to get her to talk about her husband. Hans really wanted to know about their relationship. What their sex life was like. If they even had one. But every time he reached the same dead-end. She clammed up entirely.

"No speak about him," she would say. Over and over and over, until Hans had given up asking. What the fuck did he care anyway?

He glanced at his new Rolex. It was five o'clock. He'd better move. Work started at seven, and he had to get home, eat and dress before then. He suddenly realised how hungry he was, and evading Fumiko's clutches, rolled out of bed. There was also that party for Aya at Bongoes tonight. Zack was supposed to be back for it as well.

Hans wondered what Zack's plans would be now it was over for him at Cloud Nine. Would he stay in Roppongi? If so, doing what? Hans hadn't had a chance to speak with Zack before he'd disappeared into the countryside. But he knew Zack would turn up tonight for sure. He loved Aya like a baby sister.

*   *   *

Sofia dug her heels into the gelding's flanks, wheeled him around, then charged back to the other side of the field, leaving sod and dust in her wake. God, he had some power this one! A four year old, Midnight was being groomed for the Japan Cup, and was by far her most exciting mount ever. It was insane she was even being allowed to ride him, but Yamazaki-san had insisted. And he was a man used to getting what he wanted.

She knew little about him, except he was extremely rich. That much was obvious. He was also extremely old, which was the main reason she had let their friendship go this far. He had singled her out for special treatment from their first meeting in Casablanca. His English was good and he seemed genuinely interested in her life, concerned for her well-being and future.

From the outset, Sofia had thought his intentions entirely benign, almost grand-fatherly in nature. But now she was not so certain. Zack's cynical warnings haunted her. She couldn't quite figure why, but had a nagging suspicion that control of the situation was slowly but surely slipping away from her.

First there had been the gifts. According to Zack, gifts were a routine part of the hostessing game, so she'd accepted them graciously. But Yamazaki's latest offering had been Cartier jewellery. One night, after a hushed conference with Emiko, Casablanca's *Mama-san*, he'd taken her out of the club to a *Kabuki* performance.

This was a rare enough event in itself and had rattled her a little. In the limousine, he'd presented her with an emerald necklace and matching ear-rings, insisting she accept and wear them immediately. The night had been sublime, the *Kabuki* mesmerising, and he had returned her to the club without incident. Visiting Cartier the following day, Sofia had gone into shock after pricing her baubles at US$30,000. Her attempts to give them back had failed.

"If you like them, you must keep them," he had said.

How could she win that argument? Of course she bloody liked them. What girl wouldn't? Since then, the jewels had resided in a safe deposit box at Mitsubishi Bank in *Omotesandō*.

The thing really bothering her though, was his recent suggestion she live in Japan *with him*. Weeks before that, she and Hans had stopped paying rent for their apartment. Yamazaki-san was taking care of that. She was also routinely picking up about a thousand dollars *a week* in tips from him. Together with other tips, drink-backs, salary from the club, not to mention the gifts, the money she was accumulating was simply mind-boggling.

Back in Eilat, it had never occurred to her that Zack could have been *under*-representing the craziness of this place. But she was living the evidence of that truth. It was like being in a dream world. The goal-posts were ever-shifting and the world as she'd previously known it ... had ceased to exist. And now this charming but antique gentleman seriously believed she might stay in Japan *with him*! The whole thing was too ludicrous for words.

"Sofia."

Startled by the call, she saw Yamazaki beckoning from the veranda. She cantered Midnight across, pulling him up barely a metre from the veranda's railing.

"What do you think of him?" Yamazaki peered at her over round, rimless spectacles.

"Yamazaki-san, he is magnificent. Thank you so much for letting me ride him. It really has been a privilege."

"You ride with great confidence and it is a pleasure to watch you Sofia. As it always is, whatever you are doing." An indulgent smile played around the edges of his surprisingly fleshy lips.

Sofia reverted to her hostess mask. "As always, you are very kind to me, Yamazaki-san."

"Perhaps you would like to shower and change before my driver takes you back to the city?"

Sofia silently breathed a sigh of relief. She had been afraid he would ask her to stay the night.

"Yes, that would be good. Thank-you."

Yamazaki gestured to a middle-aged Japanese woman who had appeared noiselessly behind him. "Miho will show you the way."

Sofia dismounted. An equally telepathic stable-hand magically appeared, took the reins from her and led Midnight away.

Kicking off her boots, Sofia followed Miho into the house. She collected her day-pack from the divan on the way through.

The bathroom was immaculate. Modern, yet incorporating exquisite elements of Japanese culture, both in the tiling designs and various objet d'art unobtrusively set into wall niches.

Sofia peeled off her sweaty clothes and rolled them up neatly, ready to re-stow in the day-pack. She looked at herself in the mirror. Given that she was still hot from the ride, her nipples were surprisingly erect. It had been some time since she'd had sex, and in that moment she realised the riding had made her horny as hell.

Well, that was nothing that couldn't be fixed in the shower she thought, as she slipped under the steaming jets. Soaping herself thoroughly, Sofia caressed a nipple with one hand, while the other slid between her legs.

Closing her eyes, she moaned gently as her probing fingers increased their urgency. Her orgasm came quickly and powerfully. Relieved, Sofia finished showering as fast as possible. She couldn't wait to get out of this place and back to Roppongi.

Yamazaki meanwhile, had gone swiftly to his bedroom and switched on his massive, wall-mounted television. By the time he'd stepped out of his Gucci loafers and Savile Row flannels, Sofia's wet, naked body filled the sixty-inch screen in glorious technicolour.

He hastily lowered his conservative white Y-fronts. Leaning back on the enormous bed, one hand grasped his long-dormant penis as Sofia began lathering herself. His hand working hard, Yamazaki felt his heart begin to pound, his breathing getting louder and faster.

Using the remote, he split the screen and zoomed in on Sofia's face and the place her hand disappeared between her legs. The bathroom's high-powered extractor fan ensured he could see everything with crystal clarity. Her breath was coming in high-pitched gasps. Yamazaki's penis had thickened perceptibly.

At the precise moment of Sofia's orgasm he zoomed in exclusively on her face, eyes closed, mouth open, pink tongue glistening. How he loved watching their expressions! Yamazaki as good as felt his penis inside that mouth, being licked hungrily by that pink tongue.

He looked down as his dick twitched before emitting a thimbleful of greyish fluid. Yamazaki let out a gasp of triumph before collapsing, exhausted but elated. They had come together!

What a woman was Sofia, what a thoroughbred! His wrinkled face creased into a satisfied smile. It was much better than he'd dared hope. And soon, very soon, she would be his, permanently.

Twenty-Six

The unwelcome jangling of the primitive alarm clock unsympathetically separated Zack from his dreams. He yawned deeply and stretched whatever muscles that would. Shunit's head appeared in the doorway.

"*Ahh ... bokker tov chamoodi.*"

"*Ze erev tov ... lo?*"

"*Lo bishvilcha ani choshevet.*"

"*Ulay zeh nachon Shunit ... aval ma ani yodea? Ani rak mefager me Australie ve at ga-ona me Israel. Ma ani yachol oseh?*"

Shunit considered this a moment. "*Ze nachon meod meod ani yoda-at, aval ata rak talmid shelli, az zeh beseder. Ken?*"

"*Shachtsanit!*" Zack retorted.

"*Ze lo nachon,*" she reproached him, in feigned distress. Then, straight again, she asked, "*Ata rotzeh café nudnick?*"

"*Ma at choshevet makshefah katana shelli?*"

"Such rudeness to me, the polite Israeli girl! You might to get nothing Zack. *Kloom, kloom, kloom!*" Singsong threat delivered, she disappeared into the kitchen.

Shunit was a cool chick. Zack always loved their little Hebrew exchanges. He knew his Hebrew wasn't improving at all in Japan this visit, but at least it was getting oiled from time to time. It had been a great stroke of luck being able to move in with her.

"Hey Shunit," he called. "You should come out with me tonight. It's Aya's going away party down at Bongoes."

"And you are going back to work in there ... yes?"

"Yeah, that's right. I start back there on Monday. Cool huh?"

"Is a danger for you I think Zack. Already you partying too much."

On his way to the shower, he ambled past Shunit in the kitchen, clad only in his underwear.

"Eeeyaarghhhh." Shunit made faces and backed away with her hands in the air.

Zack turned and moved lecherously toward her, leering and rubbing his crotch perversely. "Yes that's right. I know it's hard to control yourself. After all, you're only a woman, Shunit. Just relax baby, and go with your instinct."

He looked ridiculous, and Shunit burst into laughter. When he got too close, she squealed and ducked around him back into the bedroom and slammed the door, still laughing.

Her muted voice came through the door. "*Ezeh magill Zack! Chaval al azman.*"

"Thanks for the coffee Shunit." He picked up his mug and took it with him to the bathroom.

An hour later, they left the apartment. After wrapping Aya's present, Zack had grabbed a handful of ecstasy and trips from the stash, just in case the evening went in that direction. It probably would. One of each were part of Aya's gift anyway. She was fully into the dance-party scene, so would definitely appreciate them. He was also fervently hoping Carla would stick to her word and put in an appearance after work.

"You are quiet tonight Zack," Shunit commented, as they walked up *Roppongi-Dori*.

"Just thinking Shunit, just thinking."

"And what is Mr. Roppongi thinking about so deeply?" she chided gently.

Zack debated with himself briefly, how much to tell her about Carla.

"Well, I've met this girl."

This revelation did not surprise Shunit. "Mmmm ... and?"

"I think I really like her. I mean ... *really* like her. Like ... hasn't happened since Nurit."

Shunit was paying attention now. Because of Zack's history with Nurit, they joked about Israeli women all the time.

"Who is she, this girl? Is she coming tonight?"

"Her name's Carla. She's a dancer at BlackJacks. She's Canadian. And yes, she said she'd come in to Bongoes and meet me after work."

"Interesting." Shunit exaggerated her Israeli accent, rolling the 'R' heavily like a Russian, and accenting each syllable slowly. "Well, we will see what will 'appen. Relax, Zack *chamoodi*." She reached over and rubbed him affectionately on the neck, as they continued up the hill towards the crossing.

At nine-thirty, Bongoes was only moderately busy, which was par for the course. The place wouldn't really take off until after midnight. Zack manoeuvred them through the crowd. There were even a couple of stools spare, so he pulled one out for Shunit, before continuing to the back of the bar. He nodded a greeting to the kid Jarrod, but hadn't seen Aya yet.

"Aya ... where the hell are you?"

Something burst out of the stock-room and charged towards him, whooping wildly. Zack took a step back. He was looking at a savage. Before he had time to move, the thing launched itself onto him and wrapped him up in a huge hug with both arms and legs.

"Jesus fucking Christ, Aya. You're scary!'

Zack hugged her tight, then lifted her up and off him, setting her down gently on the floor. "Well, I can see you're in good form! Folks are in trouble tonight."

She was fully kitted out in an extremely sexy squaw's outfit, complete with braided hair and a long feathered head-dress. Her face was painted, and in her right hand was a replica tomahawk. Aya loved dressing up for parties, and Zack had always wondered where she got all this stuff from.

She poked him on the forehead with her tomahawk-free hand. "It's not fair you know."

Zack looked at her blankly.

"How come you start working here again just when I'm leaving? We would have had so much fun."

"Sorry babe." He shrugged an apology, leaned forward and kissed her on the nose.

She heaved a melodramatic sigh, then marched into the bar.

"Hey Aya. What about your present?" Zack pushed the small package across the bar.

She turned back excitedly, snaffled it and squirrel-like, disappeared back into the stock-room.

Zack moved in behind the bar. "How's it going Jarrod? Got everything under control?"

The kid nodded at him, but didn't speak.

"I assume Steve told you I'm starting Monday."

Another nod.

Zack really hoped he wasn't going to have a problem with this kid.

"Look. I understand you're disappointed mate, but I hope we can get along okay. I'm a pretty easygoing guy. We should be able to have a hell of a lot of fun."

Jarrod finally managed to raise a smile, and put out his hand. "Yeah, fair enough Zack. I hope so."

They shook on it.

"Can you tell Aya we need some more vodka Zack? The way it's going down tonight you'd think we had a bar full of Russians."

"You make some shots for us, and you've got a deal."

The kid nodded and grinned. "You got it boss."

Zack hoped it would always be that easy.

He took a drink to Shunit, who was fending off the attentions of a drunken suit. Then he went to find Aya. She was still in the stock-room, sitting on a couple of boxes of Corona. When she looked up at him he could see she'd been crying. Jesus Christ, he thought. What was going on now?

"Aya," he whispered gently. "What's up baby?" He noticed the bracelet he'd given her was on her wrist.

She spoke in a quavering voice. "Zack, I'm going ... to miss ... this ... place so much. How am I going to live without it? And thanks so much for the bracelet. It's really beautiful."

She wiped the tears from her eyes. Zack, on the contrary, was smiling.

"What are you laughing at, you bastard? You're meant to be sorry too!"

"Well Pocahontas, your war paint is running."

"Oh Fuck! Fuck, Fuck, Fuck!"

Within seconds a small mirror appeared from somewhere in the folds of her animal skins. Zack took advantage of this distraction to push another little packet into her palm.

"Oh Aya, These are yours too, for later." He grabbed the vodka, and was gone before she could speak.

The clamour in the bar had risen a few decibels. Dumping the vodka, he shouted to Jarrod, "Who's coming on at ten?"

"Urban, I think"

"Durban? Who the fuck's Durban?"

Jarrod was shaking a cocktail to death. "Not Durban ... Urban. Maybe you haven't met him?"

"What's his last name? Sprawl? Renewal? Decay?"

Jarrod acknowledged these quips with a tight smile, before turning away to dispense the cocktails.

Zack downed a large swig of Corona, and realised he might need to move onto Jack Daniels sooner rather than later. What sort of a name was Urban anyway?

He felt someone pinch his arse, and turned to see Aya wink at him as she scooted back into the bar, war-paint restored. Jarrod pushed shots into Shunit, Aya and Zack's hands, then cut the music.

He whistled to grab everyone's attention.

"Everybody, tonight is a bad night and a good night. Aya's leaving us, but Zack's coming back to the fold. So, ladies and gentlemen, let's drink some goddamn alcohol."

He amped the music back into 'I Love Rock'n'Roll' and the crowd ignited. Zack nodded his approval. This kid was going to be okay.

A cacophony of whooping and cheering ensued. Everyone clinked glasses and downed shots. Belatedly, Zack remembered Shunit's situation with the suit, and set off to save her. It was going to be a long night, but already he could feel that unmistakable Roppongi vibe lifting him back into the groove where he was simply unstoppable.

Dyson hooked a long arm around Zack and pulled him aside. "Hey Zack. Where you been? Is everything okay?"

"Yeah mate, everything's cool. Life's a fucking roller-coaster at the moment though."

"I heard you're coming to work back in this madhouse. You happy about that?"

"Yeah I'm stoked actually." Zack was yelling, his mouth centimetres from Dyson's ear. "I thought that cunt Chad had fucked me good and proper, until Steve let me know there was a space here. I'm looking forward to cutting loose a bit actually. Get out of the Cloud Nine suit and tie y'know."

Dyson nodded. "What about the rest of it? That still workin'?"

"Yeah. We just gotta lie low at the moment. As you know, the cops are coming down hard after those kids died."

Dyson wrinkled his brow. "Who's putting shit like that out anyway?"

"Don't know mate, but I've got some people on it. We think it's the Africans; we'll soon know."

Zack finished his Corona, and beckoned Aya.

"JD and dry sweetheart?" she queried with a wink.

"Mind-reader." Zack smiled. "And get a Boddingtons for Dyson would you babe?"

Dyson was headed into the loo. "You want me to leave you one Zack?"

Zack didn't hesitate. "Yeah, do that mate. Thanks."

Drink in hand, he gravitated to the cubicle entrance so he'd be next in line when Dyson came out. It could be a tricky business, doing lines without standing out like dog's balls. He felt pretty comfortable about this crowd though. No one here that didn't really fit.

"Zack. These fucking guys never – get – any – better. What is wrong with them? Can't they just to be normal?"

It was Shunit, biting off each word with sharpened teeth; evidently, she had already met her soul-mate for the evening.

"If you give me a moment darling, we'll fuck off out of here and go for a nature walk. I've just got a bit of hoovering to do first." Zack gestured to the toilet behind him.

Jarrod had moved the music onto some cruising Tom Petty tunes. Pretty good call for a kid his age. Zack took a slug of his JD and winced a little. Aya certainly wasn't messing around tonight. Was there *any* dry ginger in there, he wondered?

Dyson exited the loo and Zack slipped in behind him like a flash.

183

"Hey Zack." Dyson grinned. "Might be a bit iffy in there ... sorry 'bout that."

The stench suddenly hit him. Christ, what a stink! Zack spun around.

"You arse is sick Dyson! Did one of your boyfriends' gerbils die up there?"

But it was an old-skool practical joke, and Dyson beamed at him, totally unrepentant.

"Oh don't worry," Zack added. "You'll pay for that mate."

Disgusted, Zack took a deep breath, and entered. A large line was sitting on top of the cistern. Dyson hadn't even bothered to cover it with the tissue box. Zack whipped the cut-down straw out of his pocket and quickly hoovered the line. He checked his reflection briefly for any leftovers, flushed the toilet, and stepped back into the crowd.

Aaahhh, that was nice. Unfortunately his drink would taste shitty for a while though. He put his arm around Shunit, and pulled her into the privacy of the tiny stock-room.

"It looks to me like you need a nudge in the right direction my sweet. I figure you should probably have half a trip now, take the E later on, and top up with the other half sometime after that. What do you reckon?"

He produced the trip and tore it in half. "In fact, I'll share this with you now."

Shunit hesitated only briefly. "*Ata meshuga chamoodi.*" She took the half and popped it in her mouth. Zack did likewise. They left the stock-room, and were fortunate enough to regain their stools at the bar.

Zack raised his glass and grinned at her. "Just like old times hey Shunit? Cheers!"

She looked at him fondly. He really was a soul to cherish. "*L'chaim chamoodi*, and thanks to you for dragging me out tonight. I mean, I am 'ere in Tokyo, this crazy exciting city, and still I am coming to be an old woman. Thanks to God you are 'ere sometimes."

Aya splashed down some more kamikaze shots for them. Shunit protested that she'd drunk enough for the time being. Zack decided to let her off easily. Israelis weren't really a drinking culture. And she didn't get out that much anyway, so her tolerance was low. There was no point turning her into a dribbling mess before midnight; she'd be floating along on the trip shortly anyway. So he drank hers as well as his, then suffered the customary parting jibes as he shuffled the pair of them through the melee of drunken revellers. Aya was pushing the pace a bit quickly for his liking tonight. She held her liquor well for a wee lass, but he wondered how she'd be doing at six a.m. Bongoes would be open until at least then.

Twenty-Seven

Zack felt fantastic. After Bongoes' sweaty heat, it was a relief to get fresh night air on his face and in his lungs. He jigged down the road a bit, then returned to Shunit.

"Where to baby? Roppongi is our oyster. Tomorrow is Sunday. Let's cruise."

"What about the Déjà Vu? It is still open these days?"

Zack had been thinking of going to Lexington Queen. The Lex, renowned as a celebrity and model bar, had always been good for a laugh, especially when tripping. But maybe Déjà Vu? He hadn't seen Mark lately, and the music would probably be better than the Lex's as their trips kicked in.

"Yeah, why not? It's been a while," Zack agreed.

Up the street to Almond, right towards Tokyo Tower, a quick foray into a 7-11 for his favourite BlackBlack chewing gum. He gave one pack to Shunit. "Getting ready for later darling," he explained. The last couple of times he'd taken E, there was no gum around and he'd spent half the night grinding his teeth.

They crossed the road opposite the recently opened Paddy Foley's. This mocked-up Irish kit-bar, sadly a major hit with many ex-pats, had apparently stolen some of Bongoes' early evening business. Having been there himself, Zack had to concede that if nothing else, their Guinness *was* excellent. Shunit grabbed his arm and they wove their way through the crawling traffic.

Out front of Déjà Vu, he nodded casual greetings to the familiar flotsam and jetsam hanging around. Inside, it was pumping. A deep techno vibe pulsed through the space. Zack was loving this freedom, of being out at a time when he'd usually be working. Shunit's hand in his, they undulated through the crowd towards the bar, behind which Zack saw Mark. By the time they got to him, a fresh JD and dry was waiting.

Zack surveyed the scene whilst waiting for Shunit's vodka and lime to arrive. It looked like being a pretty big party tonight. The walls were festooned with all manner of fluorescent paraphernalia. Every stool had been removed to maximise partying room.

The crowd was that classic funky Roppongi blend. Under thirty-five. Japanese, Japanese-Brazilian, African-American, Nigerian, North American, European, Australasian. The proverbial melting pot. Still relatively early, there was room to move. After two a.m, all the *hostess-club* crew would arrive. That's when things would really take off.

Zack collared Mark as he whizzed by behind the bar.

"Hey mate," he shouted. "What's going on tonight?"

Mark pushed sweat-soaked hair out of his face. He looked pumped.

"Tsuyoshi's playin' at Bar Isn't It at four this morning. It's gunna go absolutely fuckin' mental up there."

He rummaged in his pockets and thrust some cards at Zack.

"Here's a buncha passes … s'posed t'be 4000 yen in … they'll getcha infa fifteen hunjy."

He quickly re-scanned the bar area. At least five people waiting – not patiently.

"I gotta get movin' mate. Give us a nod when yas need sumfink."

"Thanks mate," Zack replied, but Mark was already gone.

"*Ma zeh?*" Shunit yelled.

Zack showed her the discount passes and raised his eyebrows. "Cool huh?"

She kissed him on the cheek. "Let's dance," she mouthed.

She grooved over to the dance floor, slipping into the throng easily. Her lithe body immediately synched with the music's tribal bass-line. Zack leant back on the bar, feeling the LSD tweaking his consciousness. Eyes shut, he let the music claim him, reaching far back into that primal past all humans shared.

As if embedded in human DNA, the experience was utterly familiar, coming at him from a place he knew well, but could never quite remember. To Zack, it always felt like an affirmation of self.

Like many, Zack had been a sceptic when he'd first checked out the rave scene with its inextricably linked drug-experience. He had scoffed at the notion that ravers danced within the music and *for themselves*, utterly transcending the typical alcohol-driven mentality of dance being solely a pre-mating ritual. And that if it was true, it must surely just be the drugs fucking with their heads.

But he'd been dead wrong. Zack now well-knew the difference dance party experiences had made to how he perceived people, the planet and life in general. Time in the party scene had changed his life and his awareness significantly for the better.

And he was not alone: multitudes of others had validated what he'd felt. Apart from the general euphoria of a great night out, most people he'd met routinely spoke about revelations of self, stress release, improved communication, increased affinity with nature, and better overall connections with the people around them.

The experience invariably reached into long-hidden recesses, effortlessly demolishing prejudices and other barriers constructed by social conditioning. But the main point, Zack believed, was that it made people think about *who they really were* and *what they really wanted out of life*.

On Ecstasy or LSD there was no hiding from those questions, and perhaps even more importantly, no *wanting* to hide from those questions. That alone was a huge gain of inestimable worth.

It was unfortunate that some found it difficult to reconcile their newly acquired wisdom with the shortcomings and challenges of modern society. Such casualties tended to over-embrace the party scene, allowing it to completely *become* their life, rather than using it periodically for release and self-development.

On the well-worn travel paths of South-East Asia, examples of this effect were commonplace. Zack conceived of them as the modern equivalent of the hippy burnouts of the sixties and seventies, and he often thought it would be interesting to see what became of their subculture as time went by.

Opening his eyes, Zack took another sip of his drink. The DJ was really kicking some class tunes in here tonight. Checking the dance-floor for Shunit, he spied her waving him over. He sashayed across, leaving the remnants of his drink on the bar; he wouldn't be needing JD for a while.

"*Az ya-alla Zack, chamoodi* ... you 'ave to dance with me baby!"

They danced. Zack let the music take him. Paradoxically, this was a profoundly empowering experience, a feeling of being totally engulfed by something far bigger than himself. Zack danced with his eyes closed, only occasionally opening them to feed off the euphoric faces around him.

Strangers and acquaintances alike gave knowing nods and smiled encouragement. Zack beamed back at them. Seeing Shunit radiating affection at him, he blew her a kiss. They were all headed for the same place tonight and it was the right path to be on.

He loved watching Shunit on the rare occasions she came out. She always had so much fun he didn't understand why she didn't do it more often. Maybe that was her secret though. Small doses. He made a mental note to ask her later.

Moving to her, Zack kissed her on the forehead before returning to the bar. It was getting too crowded on the floor. He finger-signed a 'W' to Mark and waited. Déjà Vu was now so packed the post two a.m. crowd might not get a look-in. Zack had to concentrate hard to focus on his watch-face, and grinned to himself. Time, literally, was blurring. It was one a.m.

Looking up, he was a little startled to see Ban staring at him from a booth. Fuck! Zack hadn't noticed him before. Hadn't seen him for a while, in fact. He was sitting with three black guys. Nigerians maybe, Zack thought. Definitely Africans.

Odd really. Iranians and Africans weren't Roppongi's natural bedfellows. Another funny thing. Zack was sure he'd seen these particular guys before somewhere. But where? Oh well, maybe it would come to him. He headed to their booth without hesitation.

"*Konban-wa* Ban-san." Zack, hands clasped, made a small mock bow and gazed benevolently around the table. The individual on Ban's left was astonishing looking. He was immaculately clothed, in stark contrast to the looser style of dress preferred by the resident ravers. His sharply defined features could have been chiselled out of polished onyx. An obsidian God, Zack thought.

Suddenly it hit him.

That night at Las Chicas! With Sofia, Shunit and Hans.

Images streamed into his mind's-eye as if someone had flicked the lever on a floodgate. The obsidian God had been standing at the bar, and later, it had been his buddies who hadn't returned Zack's friendly greeting in the adjoining section.

The buddies were run-of-the-mill dodgy-looking Nigerians, but there was something special about this other fucker. He had a presence, and as he looked up from the table, Zack saw that he knew it.

His body emanated an understated violence … and his eyes glittered like black sapphires. He reminded Zack of a coiled king-cobra: dangerous, taut with latent energy. This was an individual used to being taken very seriously.

Zack noted the economy and grace of movement as he leaned forward slightly to extend a finely manicured, elegantly bejewelled hand.

As they shook hands, he heard Ban say, "This is Max."

"And you are Zack. It is a pleasure to finally meet you. Ban has told me a great deal about you."

I bet he has, Zack thought.

Zack released his grip. The skin had been soft and, yes … strangely sensuous. His voice was a smooth baritone, and reminded Zack of rich dark chocolate. Only the faintest Nigerian accent remained. It had been all but obliterated by well-rounded English vowels and clipped consonants.

Educated abroad. Somebody had thrown money at this guy early on.

Zack permitted his own facial expression not a hint of recognition. But he indulged his penchant for flippancy.

"Just over on holiday, hey Max? Well you've got a great guide here. Ban knows the place like the back of his hand. What do you think so far?"

Max's eyes held Zack's. He looked a little disdainful, but curious nonetheless. "I think it has a lot of potential, Zack. I'm even considering setting up a business here."

Although he spoke softly, and in spite of the thumping music, Zack somehow had no trouble hearing him. Max's buddies shifted uncomfortably in their seats.

"Good for you," Zack responded cheerily, switching his gaze to the buddies. "Not dancing tonight guys?" he asked offhandedly. "Oh by the way, Zack's the name."

He deliberately reached in front of Max and shook the hands of his flunkies, who until then had been ignored. They mumbled their names, both failing spectacularly to hide their discomfort at Zack's deliberate bonhomie.

Fucking amateurs, Zack thought. It was surprising Max kept them around. Maybe good help was in short supply for him in Tokyo. This was all very interesting, *and not just a little unnerving. Who the fuck was this guy?*

Max spoke again. "Maybe we'll dance a little later at Bar Isn't It. You are going, aren't you?" A twisted half-smile accompanied this comment.

"Yeah, I am planning to." Zack feigned a yawn, then added, "Should be a good night with Tsuyoshi playing, don't you think?"

Max nodded. "Perhaps I can offer you and your friends some passes." He reached inside his jacket.

Zack whistled theatrically through his teeth and raised an eyebrow. "You're not doing too badly for a tourist, are you Max?"

Max shrugged. "I am lucky enough to have some very good friends here."

"Well, that's kind Max, but I've already been blessed by my own good friends. Thank you anyway." Zack smiled sunnily at all of them.

From Max, the barest inclination of his head. His hand returned to its drink. Still no-one else had spoken a word. Zack was all too aware of Max's increasingly malign gaze.

Wanting more information, Zack pushed the dialogue again. "What about you Ban? You kicking on?"

"Yes Zack, but I will be in Flower, or what is it they call it now?"

"Geoid," Zack answered. "Covering the bases hey?"

"Something like that. How come you're not working tonight?"

Zack ignored the question. "Did you know Flower got busted a little while ago? Not drug-busted exactly, but some lunatic apparently ran amok with a gun."

He turned to Max. "Can you imagine that? Running around in Flower with a fucking gun?" Still no response.

Zack ratcheted his performance up a few notches. "Cops were over the place like a rash. There sure are some crazies out there huh?" He grinned amiably at Max.

From the corner of his eye, he spotted Shunit at the bar. It was an opportune exit cue. "Gentlemen, it's been a *real* pleasure, but I must rejoin my friend. See you later perhaps."

Max smiled thinly. "I'm sure you will, Zack."

Zack edged through the bodies towards Shunit. *Fucking hell*! Every instinct told him something was rotten in the state of Roppongi. That guy was serious fucking trouble. Zack urgently needed to know what was going on, and where this motherfucker fitted into the picture. If he had to pick two words to label Max, they would be 'dangerous' and 'psychotic'.

Zack needed information fast. He had a sickening feeling however, that he would already know most of the answers. Wrapping Shunit in a welcoming hug in response to her exhilarated mood, he took a swig from her water and thought rapidly. Not wanting to be seen leaving straight away, it would have to be business before pleasure.

He signalled Mark over. "Hey mate, I need a favour."

"Yeah, name it."

"Don't look now, but over my left shoulder there's a freakishly good-looking black guy in the booth with Iranian Ban."

Gratified at Mark's unwavering eye contact, he continued. "I have to check him out. I want you to find out everything you can about him. When you've seen him – how often – who he hangs with – how he acts – whether he gets fucked up – if he's a fighter. All that sort of stuff. But make it discreet. My feeling is he's one dangerous motherfucker. Can you do that for me? It's really important mate."

Mark nodded instantly. "Consider it done guvna."

"Thanks," Zack replied. "Shunit and I are hitting Bongoes again. We'll probably get a crew together for Bar Isn't It about three-ish."

Mark wiped his brow with a bar-towel. "I'm jealous mate. Iss gunna be fuckin' rockin' in there ... an' I'm stuck wiv viss fuckin' lot."

"I'll be in the same boat soon enough mate. Tomorrow's my last night of freedom before I start running Bongoes again."

Mark did a classic double-take. "You're doin' what?"

Zack grinned. "That halfwit Chad fired me from Cloud Nine, so I had to find another job."

"An when did all this fuckin' 'appin?"

"Just this week. I've been up in *Nikko* chilling out for a few days. It's a long story. I'll tell you later."

"Damn-fuckin'rightchoowill."

"Anyway mate, gotta go. Don't forget our ebony friend over there, okay? And thanks for the drinks."

Holding Shunit's hand again, Zack threaded them a path to the exit.

He raised the water bottle to Max on the way through, mentally filing the reptilian flicker of response.

"What do you think?" said Ban, turning to Max.

Max ignored him. He was contemplating. Having now met Zack face to face, he understood how he had achieved his position of strength in Roppongi. Zack had a supremely laid-back confidence and an expert sense of people.

Max recalled his decision to approach their booth. No hesitation. No fear. The way he had countered their squat power-base with easygoing yet intelligent banter. How he had effortlessly exploited Henry and Oju's juvenile discomfort. The way he had deftly ignored and innocuously parried Ban's clumsy attempt to put him on the defensive.

Oh yes, Zack Morrissey could prove a formidable adversary. But Mr. Morrissey would soon have to reconsider his options.

The world according to Max was coming his way.

Twenty-Eight

Shunit had of course been oblivious to the dark machinations inside Déjà Vu. Her growing enthusiasm for the night was infectious, and it took Zack only a few minutes to discard his unease.

They dropped another half a trip each. Then, hand in hand, they more or less skipped their way back to Bongoes like a couple of little kids. Their antics attracted bemused stares and smiles as they frolicked through the thronging street crowds and dodged traffic on *Gaien-Higashi-Dori*.

Turning the corner towards Bongoes, Zack could already hear 'Devil Inside' by INXS blaring out of the powerful speakers.

Déjà Vu dance electronica to Bongoes rock. What a contrast!

The place was so packed that people had overflowed into the chilly air outside, and were drinking on the street. That was another anomaly about the Japanese. They were so anal about some things, but when it came to street-drinking, and even underage drinking, the police didn't appear too fussed. He forced a path through to the back of the bar, and was immediately collared by Steve.

"Ahhh, just the man I want to see. Feel like starting work tonight?" Steve clapped an arm around his shoulder.

Zack grinned, but his heart sank. The last thing he wanted to do now was work. "You're fucking kidding me aren't you?"

"Oh okay then, I'll let you off. I suppose you're going to that party tonight yeah?"

Zack relaxed. "Yep, really looking forward to it actually. My last night of freedom."

He turned and pulled Shunit into a small space beside him. "Steve, you haven't met Shunit have you? Shunit … Steve."

"So Shunit, how do you know this maniac anyway?"

"Oh, I am stupid enough to make him my flatmate. What to do?"

Steve pulled a face. "Jesus! I always wondered who those brave people were."

"Yeah, yeah! Everyone knows if you weren't married you'd be gagging for me Steve. In the meantime you've given me a job just so you can get close, haven't you?" Zack edged camply towards him, puckering up. "C'mon, give me just one little kiss, handsome."

"You are a truly sick man, Mr. Morrissey! Excuse me while I find some decent customers to talk to." To Shunit, Steve added, "Nice to have met you Shunit. And good luck with Transgender-Man here." Without waiting for an answer, he disappeared into the melee.

Zack glanced around the bar and nodded greetings to a number of familiar faces. God, he was going to have to get au-fait with all the regulars again. Figure out who was spending and who wasn't. Whose tab you could let run and whose you had to call in. Who the troublemakers might be. Who was selling drugs through the bar.

Well, he knew the answer to the last one!

His eyes stopped on the surfie-looking guy behind the bar with Jarrod. He must be the infamous 'Urban'. Zack realised he had seen him before, working the bar at Sports Café. From memory he had been okay. And now he was working here. Oh well, time for a re-introduction. Zack took a few steps into the bar entrance-way, a move guaranteed to annoy almost any bartender in the world.

Catching Jarrod's questioning eye, he winked and put his finger to his lips in a hush sign. Then he yelled at Urban. "Hey, any chance of a drink in this fucking place mate?"

Urban turned, with a half smile on his face. "Are you talking to me?"

"Are you a fucking bar-tender?" Zack barked abrasively.

Before he could say anything, Zack barked at him again.

"Jesus mate, I haven't got all fucking night. Just get me a JD and dry and a vodka lime and soda wouldya."

Urban came up to him. "Listen pal ... I don't know where you get your bloody attitude from, but if you swear at me one more time, you won't be drinking in here at all. Take it easy, okay!"

Zack exploded. "TAKE IT FUCKIN' EASY? Who the fuck are you to tell me to take it easy, you pussy-whipped faggot motherfucker. Just get me the fucking drinks!"

It took all Zack's willpower to keep a straight face. He could see both Jarrod and Steve behind Urban, desperately trying to contain their laughter.

Urban's face was deep red. "That's it mate," he blustered. "You're getting nothing from me. In fact, you're out of here."

"Out of here my arse! Get me the fucking manager you tosser. Where's the manager?" Zack already knew Aya was having a sleep out the back.

Urban looked around to Jarrod for some assistance. Steve had ducked out of view. To his credit Jarrod had a straight face again, and pretended he'd just noticed the problem. "What's up, Urban?"

Urban leant over and spoke into his ear. "This guy is the rudest motherfucker I've met since being in Tokyo. I want to throw him out, and he wants to see the manager. Who's manager at the moment, for fuck's sake?"

Jarrod looked at Zack, and was unable to hold his laughter any longer. Urban swivelled to see Zack doubled over with mirth as well.

"What the fuck?" he exclaimed helplessly.

Jarrod recovered long enough to say, "He's the manager, Urban. His name's Zack. Shit that *was* funny. You should have seen your face."

Zack had his hand out, and between gales of laughter, managed to greet Urban. "Let's hope that's as bad as it ever gets between us," he joked. "Good to meet you mate. I thought you were going to swing at me there for a moment."

Urban shook Zack's hand somewhat sheepishly. "Wow Zack, you really wound me up. I'm pretty calm usually."

Zack patted him on the shoulder reassuringly. "Lucky for me I guess, but don't worry about *your* temperament. I'm a world-class annoying bastard when I want to be."

Steve had made himself visible again. "So, you must really be looking forward to working with Zack, huh Urban?"

Urban eyed Zack carefully for a moment before replying. "Well, if that's any indication, it's probably not going to be boring!"

A bunch of people were waiting for drinks. Zack nodded in their direction. "I'll let you get on with it," Zack said. "Make us all some shots when you can. Something with vodka … do up a large shaker."

Urban got to it. Zack organised drinks for Shunit and himself, then grabbed a stool at the top of the bar. Jarrod had slipped some Chemical Brothers into the mix, and Zack closed his eyes again, savouring the atmosphere.

God, it was *great* not to be working! And it was amazing how much at home he always felt in this bar. It was like having his very own lunatic lounge-room in Roppongi.

He blessed the powers that be for having slotted him back in here after the Cloud Nine debacle. Well, Chad could go fuck himself. Zack would persuade all his ex-stripper-chicks that Bongoes was where they wanted to drink after work.

They would come to him. He could visualise it already, the girls strutting their stuff on the bar. It would be brilliant! The customers, and therefore Steve, would love him for it.

A pair of cool hands slid over his eyes, and a voice whispered in his ear. "Hello pretty boy, you going to sleep down here?"

He knew it was her. She was early. He pivoted on the stool to flounder in those mesmeric emerald eyes. His stomach flip-flopped. "I was really hoping you'd come."

"I said I would." She smiled. "I even got off early tonight."

He leaned forward and kissed her. She kissed him back, and he relaxed a bit. He had wondered if it would be awkward for her in the Roppongi environment.

Carla eyed him speculatively. "Did you mean what you said up there in *Nikko*?"

Zack didn't hesitate. "Every word."

"Okay then, let's give it a go."

Zack's heart soared. "You've got no idea how much I wanted to hear that."

The shots arrived. He introduced Carla to Shunit and the Bongoes crew. Shunit sneaked in a little Hebrew commentary: "*Ezeh cussit, chamoodi,*" and raised an eyebrow in approval.

Zack sat Carla down on his stool. "You want half a trip? I've got a few E's as well for later. We're heading to the party at Bar Isn't It pretty soon. Tsuyoshi's set starts around four."

Carla nodded, and Zack surreptitiously passed her a half from his wallet. She slipped it straight onto her tongue.

"What do you think of my new home?" Zack prompted.

Carla took a sip of the drink that had arrived, and studied him amusedly over the rim of the glass. "Let's just say I'm much happier you're working here, than being surrounded by forty hungry strippers every night."

Zack thought of clouds and silver linings. It was most unlikely Carla would have given their relationship the same chance if he'd still been working at Cloud Nine.

"Yes, I am too. For some reason it seems like I'm supposed to be back here." Gently massaging one of her shoulders, he continued. "And for the first time in a while, everything feels pretty much as it should."

Shunit joined them and the drinks kept flowing. Jarrod was doing a killer job on the music; aware half the bar was pre-lubricating for a dance party, he'd switched the usual eclectic Bongoes mix to a dance emphasis. It was going down a treat. Zack had caught his eye a few times and given him the thumbs up.

Sofia and Hans came in together at two-forty-five. "Hey everyone, how's it going?" Sofia spoke for them both.

Zack quickly introduced them to Carla, and noted Sofia's intensive appraisal of the new woman in Zack's life.

"So let me get this straight," Carla said. She pointed at Shunit. "You're Israeli." Shunit nodded.

Carla turned to Sofia. "And you're Swedish." Another nod. "And you Hans, are …"

"Dutch," Hans answered.

Carla swivelled towards Zack.

"And these," gesturing to Hans and Sofia, "are the ones you met in Israel, whereas you met Shunit the Israeli, here in Tokyo."

"Correct," Zack replied.

"Okay, I think I'm with the programme."

Shunit shrugged and smiled. "What I can say? Everybody love my crazy little country."

It was time to go. Mark had given Zack six passes, so he left one with Jarrod with instructions to give it to somebody worthwhile. Then they polished off their drinks and sallied forth into the night.

Twenty-Nine

Zack bought a bottle of water on the way, gave Sofia and Hans a couple of E's, and they all dropped as they wandered up to Bar Isn't It. Zack felt good about tonight. The girls had fallen back into their own group, and Zack walked ahead with Hans.

"So how's my favourite Dutchman going?"

"Really good actually mate. This Japan trip is turning out unbelievable. Making the bucks. Getting laid. Having fun. Time goes so fucking fast though."

Hans paused for a moment to glance behind them.

"Who the hell's this chick anyway? She's a drop-dead stunner."

"Well mate, believe it or not … I've sort of fallen for her."

Hans laughed out loud. "Yeah righto, Zack."

"No mate, no shit. I'm taking it really seriously. Nobody's more surprised than me!"

Hans looked hard at Zack to see if it was a wind-up, then realised he was serious.

*   *   *

Meanwhile, Carla had been worried that Zack's female friends might make her feel a little uncomfortable, but she'd been wrong. These girls were gems, both full of honest wisdom and cynical barbs about Roppongi, the work, the lifestyle. And it was obvious they both loved Zack to death.

He certainly had something that inspired people's friendship, she thought. Maybe it would be okay being with him. She'd had enough of living like a nun anyway. She'd missed the buzz of being out with friends. Something about Zack had given that desire back to her. She'd just have to make sure it didn't get too out of hand.

Sofia and Shunit were dying to know how she and Zack had met in *Nikko*. So she told them about the little restaurant. And what he'd said. And what she'd felt. Cracking up laughing, they had assured her that was vintage Zack.

Carla had a feeling it would be fun to get to know these girls; both had a certain worldliness. More importantly, she had immediately felt comfortable in their company.

*   *   *

"So this is love you reckon?" Hans queried.

Zack hesitated, wondering what to say. "Well, I don't know yet really. But whatever it is, it's different to anything else I've felt lately. There's really like, a chemistry, you know. The other difference is that I *want* to commit myself this time. You know. Really put in the hard yards and see where it goes."

Hans jumped around a couple of oncoming Japanese girls, then stuck his hand out towards Zack.

"What?" Zack asked, perplexed.

"Shake it," Hans insisted.

Zack took the proffered hand and shook it, still not comprehending.

"That's the first time in ages I've heard you really being serious about something."

"What the bloody hell are you talking about?" Zack looked at him in amazement.

"Well, usually with you everything is a joke, or half a joke, or not worth worrying about anyway. Nothing really seems to *touch* you, because everything always *works out* for you. Even when it goes wrong, it still somehow works out okay. It's almost like you already know that things will be fine … so you don't have to worry about them like other people do."

Zack listened, still amazed, and said nothing.

Hans was frustrated. It was *difficult* trying to explain this stuff to Zack. And why did he feel guilty even saying it?

He tried again.

"What I'm saying Zack, is that it looks like this chick has touched you … you know … for once you *give a fuck* about what's going to happen. And believe it or not, I'm really happy to see that … for you."

It had been quite the speech. Zack hadn't a clue how to respond to it, so he said nothing. Then the girls sneaked up and jumped on their backs. And the moment was gone.

* * *

Like many clubs in Tokyo, Bar Isn't It was a strange set-up. The building looked like an office complex, with a lift to take patrons up a couple of floors. Then the space opened right up. It was definitely one of the more impressive club layouts Zack had seen.

Two levels opened up into a large dance-floor underneath a stunning atrium with a stained-glass dome at one end. Platforms abounded, and a raised stage was central to the dance-floor. It was a very versatile space; Zack had seen it used for everything from fashion shows to comedy nights to blues concerts.

But it was at its best when taken over by the dance-party crowd. And that's what tonight was all about. They handed over their passes with fifteen hundred yen, and went quickly inside.

It was a veritable assault on the senses. First was the tribal pulse of the music. Deep, vibrant and uplifting. They were greeted by a wonderland inhabited by fantasy. Angels mixed with Devils. Superheroes were massaged by Pixies. Caligula tended to Cleopatra. And Tinkerbell brushed past Zack on her way to the toilet.

Fluorescent wands, clothing, jewellery, light-sabres, painted faces, and glitter were out in force. And the venue itself! Zack turned a complete circle and took it all in as they made their way to the bar. The promoters had been seriously busy!

Glowing fish with vivid colourings rippled their way through aquamarine walls of phosphorescence. Incandescent orbs were invisibly suspended from high ceilings. Invisible machines produced kaleidoscopic iridescent bubbles. A circular screen above centre-stage depicted brain-melting imagery. And lasers, lights, strobes and smoke-machines occasionally turned the landscape into something resembling an alien space-station at war with another planet.

Even by Tokyo standards, this design obliterated all remnants of reality. Zack hadn't seen anything this elaborate since Cirque du Soleil. Cognisant of the work that had gone into this place, he felt almost guilty having used the discount passes. This party would go into orbit tonight, and might well not return.

They found themselves a platform near the bar and the dance-floor. He grabbed Carla and hugged her close, her back to his chest. Hans disappeared to organise drinks.

Zack whispered into Carla's ear. "You've picked a good one for your first night out in a while sweetheart. What do you think?"

Carla was looking around disbelievingly. "I thought we put in a bit of effort with our show at Jacks. But this ..." She absorbed her surroundings in wordless appreciation. "This must have taken days to set up. It's just incredible."

Zack pulled her closer. He felt like he *never* wanted to let this girl go, and the E hadn't even kicked in yet. The trip was running through him nicely, but not too full-on. He wondered how she was feeling. Sofia and Shunit had already started their dancing games not too far away, effortlessly picking up their double-act from where they'd left off at Las Chicas.

"Look Carla, we'll make this platform home-base tonight, okay? We'll get separated at some stage. Just check back here if we lose each other alright?"

Carla swivelled her body around in Zack's arms. "I'm a big girl Zack. Don't worry too much about me." She kissed him on the nose and gave him a reassuring hug, as Hans returned laden with beers, alcoholic lemonade, and water.

They were all happy to chill out on the platform for a while. Carla and Hans started chatting. Zack gave up trying to involve himself in their conversation. The music made it impossible. His gaze roamed freely.

Dance-parties always reminded him of his time with Nurit, mainly because she was the first person he'd started going to them with, back in the very early days of the Ministry of Sound in London. But the other reason was because of the extraordinary popularity of the rave scene with Israelis. There was something deeply spiritual about the connection most Israelis had with the dance-party experience.

Zack remembered his time in Goa a couple of years previously. Israeli television had done a melodramatic exposé on what was happening to Israel's youth in places like Goa and Thailand. They'd secretly filmed a number of dance parties, snaring some very confronting footage of really drug-fucked Israelis. They'd also elicited many very unflattering comments about the Israeli Defence Force, Israel's political situation in general and the excessive demands the troubled country placed on its youth.

As it turned out, a number of these kids were from well-to-do, politically connected families. So these attitudes, coupled with the hedonistic and obviously mind-altering drug experiences their kids were so obviously loving in these exotic locales, did not go over at all well back home. So much so in fact, that their frantic parents actually banded together, chartered a jet, and flew in to 'rescue' them!

It didn't get much funnier than that, Zack reflected. A swarm of uptight, anxious, paranoid Israeli parents halfway around the world … descending on a place like Anjuna beach … trying angrily to locate their wayward children, who in any case, had already left, because they did not want to *be* found.

Their reluctance to be caught was unsurprising, given that many of them had only recently finished their national service and had certainly earned a break from the stress caused by the collective mindset of Israel's elites.

Zack had his own theories for why young Israelis tended to lose the plot a lot more than most other nationalities in places like Goa and Koh Pha Ngan. Basically, they completed twelve years of school, and were then shunted straight into the military; three years for guys and two for girls. By the time they left the army most of them would've been lucky to have even smoked a bit of pot.

Most of these kids were understandably desperate for their own space, and for some non-regimented adventure, where they wouldn't be expected to perhaps kill people. They just wanted the freedom to do their own thing for the first time in their entire lives; to not have to do anything at all if they didn't want to.

A pre-requisite for accomplishing this involved getting away from the control-structures, specifically parents, who invariably wanted to launch their progeny straight into university, or the family business, or whatever.

So when these kids finally escaped to such chilled-out party places, and combined that desperation for release and recreation with high-potency smoke and powerful hallucinogens like trips and mushrooms, the results were actually pretty predictable.

The problem was essentially threefold. One, they weren't used to the drugs to start with. Two, in a classic over-correction, they took too much of everything, too often. And three, because of the powerful need to escape the perceived pressures of their lives, the drugs made them question the basis, truth and worth of their own reality to date. This last stage was the most worrying aspect of the breakdown process.

Zack knew at least five Israelis who had completely and utterly lost the plot in this respect. One had been a good friend of Nurit's. He knew she was still receiving psychiatric help to this day.

Apparently, a few psychiatrists in Israel now even specialised in helping returned Israeli youth go through the readjustment process after their overseas adventures. It was now well-recognised as a 'syndrome'.

That was one thing he would always be thankful for. His parents, and the head-space they had helped him develop. Although they had split while he was in his second year of Uni, it was definitely for the best. Now his Dad lived in England, his Mum in Australia. Neither of them hassled him about his lifestyle, and his mother had even visited him last time in Tokyo, as well as in Nepal of all places. She'd also caught up with Josh in London and France and Portugal.

She seemed fascinated with their friends, their unorthodox experiences, and the travelling lifestyle in general. It was so different to what she had known growing up, and Zack thought she probably appreciated the chance to live a little of it now with her sons.

He knew she enjoyed telling her curious friends the stories of her adventurous sons roaming exotic destinations around the globe. He smiled, imagining her spinning these yarns to her arty wine and cheese circle.

"Hey, what are you looking so smug about?"

Carla pushed him, then lunged to grab him back as he pretended to slide off the platform. She pulled him up, and together they gravitated out to where Shunit and Sofia were having so much fun. He clowned around in the middle of the three of them, mimicking their dancing styles, before closing his eyes and slipping into his own. He was already tripping, so it was going to be a pretty smooth transition into the E anyway. He felt awesome. His body was auto-piloting the groove of this music. The unmistakable first twinges of the E nudged his soul.

Opening his eyes, he looked around. The girls each had completely different dancing styles. Sofia was hard and energetic. She bounced and shadow-boxed, skipping and darting about the place like a psychotic ferret. Shunit was half that pace and in perfect sync, but a whole lot more chilled. She used her entire body in sinuous movements that complemented the rhythmic flow of the music.

Carla matched Shunit's more laid-back pace, but it was easy to tell she'd had formal dance training. She incorporated a mishmash of countless learned routines and choreographed steps into an effortlessly natural expression of her mood.

Zack loved what she was wearing tonight. Sexy, cream, knee-high lace-up boots, a cream soft leather miniskirt and matching mid-riff bodice. She looked fucking incredible ... created for the dance floor. Catching him watching her, she gave him a smile. She knew how she looked.

Zack's face was one huge grin. Things were blurring around the edges, and he knew the E had arrived in full. He swooped across to Hans, hitting him at waist height and had him upside down in a fireman's carry before he knew what was going on. Zack spun him around a couple of times before dropping him on his feet in the middle of the girls. As he turned around, a girl ran up and pushed him in the chest. She was shouting at him.

"So you two idiots are still clowning around together?"

Zack re-focused and looked again at the pretty little face, but couldn't quite register where he knew it from. Then he was gobsmacked at what his brain came up with. It was SIMONA ... fucking SIMONA from Eilat.

"SIMONA," Zack roared, gathering her up in a massive hug. Hans and Sofia had also seen her, and were jumping up and down with delight. Shunit and Carla looked at each other and shrugged.

Zack was vaguely aware the music had been ratcheted back and that Tsuyoshi was being introduced. It was obviously about four o'clock.

"When did you get here? What are you doing here? How long have you been here?" Simona was deluged with questions as the lapse in music momentarily made conversation easier. In typical Gallic fashion, she put up her hands in mock defence.

"I got 'ere just two days before. Fuck, you are all here together! I just don't believe zis." She hugged them all again. Her face was shining with happiness. "I just have nothing to take yet! Do you know … ?"

Zack put up his hand to cut her off and produced another pill. He gave it to her with a ceremonial flourish. "It's a gift Simona. Welcome to Roppongi."

"Zack, *merci, merci*! I don't know what to say." Her eyes were wet with gratitude and excitement. She downed the E with a gulp of water. "Look at this timing! Tsuyoshi is coming on … wooooo-hoooooohhh!"

Simona screamed in pure elation, and hugged every one of them, including Carla and Shunit. Zack looked around the group. Everyone laughing and smiling like lunatics. Friends having fun. That's what it was all about. Then Tsuyoshi kicked his set into gear and the night went stratospheric.

It was probably about an hour later. Zack was on one of what he called his 'missions' around the venue. Rather than dancing in one place, he liked to cruise around vibing to the music, snaking through the crowd and checking everyone out. He grinned at people as he zoomed past. The E was superb. He could feel his positive energy streaming out of every pore in his body.

Then he saw Max standing at the bar. The black man's posture was rigid, completely at odds with his environment. Zack could actually *feel* the negativity emanating from him. Except it wasn't just negativity, but something worse. A sort of calculating malevolence.

Deciding to ignore him completely, Zack had almost passed by when a hand shot out and grabbed him on the shoulder. Immediately, he straightened up to his full height, turned, and brushed the hand easily away. He continued dancing on the spot whilst gazing nonchalantly at the man in front of him.

"Still not dancing Max? How can you not dance to this?" Grinning deliberately, Zack gestured at everything around him. Surreptitiously he scoped the room for the minders. They did not seem to be around.

Fuck! He hated situations like this when you were in the middle of a good E. It was such a pain in the arse to have to deal with loser energy like this. Max was beginning to thoroughly piss him off.

Max spoke. "You think you're so fucking cool, don't you Zack?"

"Funny," Zack said. "I was just thinking the same about you." He raised his eyebrows. "Fancy that."

Max leaned towards him. "I'm not going to fuck around with you Zack. The time for games is over. I am going to give you one chance though: to partner with me. What do you think?"

Zack continued vibing along to the music. "What ... like a dance partner? I'm very flattered Max, but there's two problems with that. One: I dance alone, and two: I'm not gay. There are heaps of gayboys in Roppongi though mate. Pretty boy like you should be able to strap one of them on *no problem*."

Zack grinned again and turned to move off.

"Listen, you fucking smart-arsed little shit." Max spun Zack around by the arm. Zack instantly broke the hold, and took a step towards Max.

"No, *you* listen black man! Don't *ever* lay your fucking hands on me. And don't *ever* tell me what to do! Just for the record, I don't like your face, I don't like your attitude, and I don't give a fuck about you, your friends, or whatever twisted shit is going on in that head of yours. You'd be best to just stay the *fuck* away from me and do your own thing! Is that clear enough, or do you want me to spell it out for you?"

They were now face to face, and Zack realised the sonofabitch had a good two inches on him. He checked Max's glacial expression for signs of imminent conflict, but all he saw was ice. Max took a hit from his cigarette, and looked away from Zack, exhaling over the bar.

"I'm sorry you feel that way Zack, but maybe now is not the best time for you to understand what is going on here."

He stubbed out the half-smoked cigarette, moved unhurriedly out of Zack's body space and headed for the door. Zack did nothing more, except watch him leave.

Jesus fucking Christ! What was it with that guy? And where were his fucking flunkies?

He had to remember to speak to Mark soon about this motherfucker. Something in the Roppongi universe was seriously adrift. Having dealt with a lot of weirdos and freaks in his time, you got a nose for types. And his initial impressions of this guy were being confirmed in spades. Zack pardoned himself the pun. Max was one frightening individual. So controlled. So calculating. And unbelievably arrogant.

Zack didn't like it at all. Worse, it was ruining his night. He'd been flying high on his E, but now this drama had lodged itself in his psyche. The happy vibe was gone, replaced by something darker. Suddenly he needed his friends. He felt cold. *Fuck! Why did this have to happen tonight?*

His rhythm gone, Zack walked slowly back to the platform. Carla took one look at him, and came straight over. She held him gently on the sides of his head, her eyes seeking his.

"What's wrong Zack? What's happened?"

Fuck, it was that obvious, Zack thought. *Impossible to hide something like that on E.* "Nothing really; come with me to the chill-out room would you? I just need to relax for a bit."

They lay back on a couple of beanbags. Zack rested his head on her chest, and closed his eyes.

"So what's wrong, Zack? Are you going to tell me?"

Opening his eyes, he was pinned by her clear green gaze. Zack smiled. "Now you *really* look like an alien ... your pupils are huge."

"Don't change the subject, you little shit."

"Funny ... someone else just called me that."

"So are you going to tell me what's going on, or not?"

Zack sighed. "I just had a nasty conversation with someone, and I want to be near you so I feel better. That's about it really."

She stroked his forehead. "That's it? No more details?"

"No. No more details ... not right now anyway. Now's not the time to talk about it, trust me."

She looked at him a little more firmly. "You're going to have to start *trusting me* sometime you know."

Zack pulled her face closer to his. "I do trust you babe. One hundred fucking percent. I just don't want to lay any of this ridiculous bullshit on you. It's depressing to think about it now. Can you just let it go for the moment ... as a favour ... please?"

She put her lips gently on his. "Okay Zack." Her words were as soft as the kiss which followed.

Zack let the sensations of the kiss permeate his mood. As he relaxed, he felt the music re-enter his being. Anyway, for some reason he had a feeling there would be no further threat tonight.

He was amazed at himself really. Firstly that he had let that Nigerian motherfucker get this far under his skin. It must just be the E, he thought. And secondly how he already felt so used to being with Carla. There had been no real awkwardness at all ... it was almost second nature. Was that a good or a bad thing, he wondered. He opened his eyes again to remind himself how beautiful she was.

Steady as a tractor-beam, her green eyes regarded him intently. Her face appeared almost ethereal, floating above him.

He smiled again as he looked up at her, an utterly genuine smile full of warmth and affection.

"You are so unbelievably fucking gorgeous! How can I lie here for even one second and think I've got problems when you're next to me? It's just self-indulgent fucking crap."

Jumping to his feet, he pulled her up with him. "C'mon, Tsuyoshi's playing. Let's party!"

Thirty

It turned out Zack was right. He did not see Max again that night, or for that matter, all the following week. It had been an eerie week nevertheless. Not seeing the guy around was somehow bugging him more than if Max had been in his face again. Well, at least Zack had an ace up his sleeve now: he had used the time for due diligence and called in a few favours. With any luck though, he wouldn't have to use it – it was by no means a risk-free play.

Maybe after their last encounter Max would just back the fuck off and leave him alone. Maybe. His mind kept going back to the party, the way Max had acted, and what had been said. Zack hated not being the protagonist; being reactive was just not his nature, and it made him uncomfortable. He had no idea what Max's next move would be, and being on the back foot with a situation like this did not sit at all well with him.

He was chilling out in Bongoes, methodically cleaning the CD collection. Urban was out shopping for bar supplies. It was early Thursday evening. He'd been edgy all week. He was, however, pretty sure he'd successfully hidden it from Carla. Jesus, she was really something, that girl.

Zack was convinced he was already as much or more in love with her than he'd ever been with Nurit. She was so beautiful, so talented, yet there wasn't a hint of the crap that was part of the package with most other Roppongi chicks.

She'd said to him on the Sunday following the party, 'Just be straight with me Zack, and we'll be okay.' He had no intention of letting her down. But somehow, he had to get this Nigerian monkey off his back.

In spite of the recent slowdown in distribution, his offshore account was sitting pretty at US$32,000, and the way things were shaping up, he might be able to bump it up to around $100,000 before he left. This sum did not include the $15,000 of legitimate earnings he had in his Citibank account. It had been a good five months.

Zack had never dreamed he'd be able to put away so much cash, so quickly. He could only hope the coming months would be as rewarding. Then, some well-earned time off. Ideally with Carla in South-East Asia somewhere: the perfect post-Tokyo pick-me-up. Or maybe South-East Africa for a change. He really fancied Madagascar for some reason. Well, they'd go somewhere anyway. The world was their oyster after all!

He still couldn't believe it was Christmas next week. It had sneaked up so damn quickly. The next fortnight would be party-time, which meant he would be doubly busy. 'Business' had of course taken off again, as people frantically got their drugs of choice organised for Christmas and New Year celebrations.

He'd been invited to the Christmas function at the Australian Embassy on the twenty-third, and was enthusiastically looking forward to it. It fell on a Wednesday, and he'd made sure of having that night off. Carla had managed to organise the same, so they could go together. Hans was coming too, although he obviously couldn't bring his Japanese 'girlfriend'.

Apparently it was still going strong between them. Zack was quietly chuffed that things had turned out so well for Hans over here. He hadn't been at all sure that they would. Hans could be quite dour sometimes, and this was a personality trait that did not usually fit in too well with the Roppongi party zone.

Though truthfully, that was what Zack liked most about him. He was solid. Zack appreciated his unyielding honesty – especially here in Roppongi – a place where lies and superficiality ruled. A place where it became almost too easy to let go of things like ethics, morals, and truth. In a sea of bullshit, Hans was a grounding influence, and it made him happy to think they'd be best of friends for a very long time.

When he looked up and saw Max standing in the doorway, Zack wasn't quite sure whether he grabbed the bottle of Galliano first, or hit the speed dial to Steve's mobile. Either way, both things happened, as he watched Max pace slowly into the bar towards him.

His stomach did a flip-flop. Everything was happening in slow motion. *Answer your fucking phone Steve for fuck's sake!* The long, insanely slow rings of Steve's mobile mocked him, and then he heard the answering service kick in.

Fuck Fuck Fuck!

He turned to keep his eyes on Max's progress towards him. *At least the arrogant fucker wasn't with his goons.*

"Yeah, Steve, Zack here."

Zack paused as if Steve was answering. "Yeah, sorry mate. Look, I've got some potential trouble here in the form of that big Nigerian gangster Max." Another pause. "Yeah mate, that's right. The one I pointed out to you before. Anyway he's here right now, and I thought you should know about it in case anything goes down." Another pause. "Oh, you're on your way? Cool. See you shortly. Thanks mate."

Folding the phone back into his pocket, Zack hoisted the club-like bottle of Galliano up beside the till. He fixed his eyes on the impassive black face approaching him.

"Needless to say, I've missed you Max. What are you doing here, in my lounge-room?"

A thin smile was the only answer, as Max slid onto a bar-stool.

Max inclined his head slightly, indicating Zack's firm grip on the bottle of Galliano.

"It looks like you've already decided for me Zack." Another smile. "But Galliano is a little sweet for my tastes these days."

Zack leaned across the bar. "Look Max. We've been flirting around for what, about a month now, and we both know we don't want to fuck each other. So what gives, black man? Why are you in my face *again*?"

The Nigerian's expression hardened, his eyes drained of any humanity whatsoever. He seemed almost resigned to what he was about to say. But his voice was deadly.

"Zack, you have a lot of guts. You have a lot of charisma, and you even have a certain style." His eyes narrowed. "I can use those abilities in my team. That is the main reason you are not in a hospital, or a morgue, yet."

Another smile, almost wistful, creased his unusually narrow lips. "Under other circumstances, we could have been friends. Who knows?" He shrugged. "Perhaps we still can. You and I: we are not so different you know." Another pause. "Except, I am willing to have you killed. And you are not strong enough to kill me."

He shrugged again. "Do you know where you are Zack? Really?" Raising his eyebrows to accentuate the question, Max flicked his eyes towards the doorway. "Roppongi, Zack. It's a jungle out there. The only question is, are you going to kill, or be killed?"

Apart from that door-wards glance, his glittering reptilian eyes never left Zack's.

Zack knew he should be scared. Perhaps more scared than he'd ever been. But to his surprise, all he felt was a quiet rage. The arrogance of this patronising motherfucker was breathtaking. How dare he stroll into this bar, and presume the power of life, death and choice over Zack? Bowing to him was inconceivable. Zack steeled himself for the performance that Max's visit necessitated. This could get ugly.

"Are you finished Max? Because Steve will be here any moment, and I want you to hear what I have to say before then."

The gangster nodded politely. As if they were perhaps enjoying a civilised debate, over afternoon tea.

"The first thing is that I appreciate your courtesy in explaining all this to me. It has done me the immeasurable favour of confirming exactly where we stand with each other. The second thing I want you to know, is that you know almost *nothing* about me, whereas *I* know what colour underpants you wear on a Tuesday."

Max raised an eyebrow and smiled patronisingly.

Zack paused and returned the smile. This would be interesting. "Henry Maximilian Obitawanu, born 2nd July 1965 to diplomatic parentage in Guildford, Surrey." Zack enunciated each part of the name slowly, for maximum effect.

The visceral shock Max suffered at this statement of fact was undeniable. His arrogant mask faltered. Zack took enormous pleasure in continuing.

"Mostly successful academically, but always struggling with authority, little Henry excelled in sporting events ranging from football, to rugby, to individual athletics. Groomed for a diplomatic post, he graduated to the London School of Economics, where he studied International Politics and Trade. Subsequently returned to his family's Victoria Island estate in Lagos in 1993. Became involved via rampant government corruption in black marketeering of everything from petrol to prostitution to drugs, until things started to go sideways in ninety-six. Exited the country firstly to London, then attempted to enter Chicago. Refused entry to the USA for reasons unknown, and subsequently turned up in Tokyo."

Max lowered his head threateningly. "You are a dead man," he said softly.

Zack ignored him and continued. He was enjoying himself. "Currently travelling on a false passport in the name of Edison Opatuku, he is powerfully connected at the Nigerian Embassy in Tokyo, but does not have diplomatic status in Japan, and therefore has to watch his fucking step a little more than he's used to."

Zack lowered his head, level with Max's. "Don't you, *Henry* my boy?"

Max shifted his gaze to the wall, not meeting Zack's eye.

"Needless to say *Henry*, I have left a dossier containing this juicy information, along with a summary of everything else I know about you and your activities, with two people. The first is a very close friend of mine in London, with whom I speak weekly. The second is with another friend at the Australian embassy here in Tokyo, along with my will and other personal effects, and is to be opened in the event of my death or disappearance."

Max was now looking at Zack with pure animal hatred. Zack noted with satisfaction his previous confidence had all but disappeared. So he pressed his advantage.

"Something else you should know, fuckhead, is that if anything happens to me, I have already arranged and paid to have you killed."

So what if it was a lie? On the strength of everything else, he doubted Max would disbelieve him.

"In fact, when I explained the situation to my friends here, they offered to do it for nothing. Funnily enough, they don't much like you either. So I would suggest, Maxi-babe, that it is very much in your interest to make sure I *don't* trip and have a fall anytime soon."

Zack paused, to better emphasis his last point.

"And one more thing. If I think you are making my life difficult in any way, *even for a second*, I'll have the Japanese Immigration service chewing your arse out on false documents charges quick-time. As I understand it, those guys aren't renowned for their tolerance of document-forging Nigerians."

Max's expression was unreadable, but Zack knew, that he knew he'd just been fucked, big time.

Zack rapped his fingers on the bar. "So now we understand each other better, why don't you just fuck off out of my bar and my life altogether."

At that moment Urban walked in, singing the tune 'I'm Too Sexy' by Right Said Fred, and dumped a load of groceries on the bar. "Fuck me! It's cold out there. They reckon it'll snow for sure this Christmas."

Max leaned over the bar and hissed at Zack. "I should have had you killed straight away, you little fucker. Remember this day Zack. Your life will turn to shit, and then you will die. Painfully. You will die with me laughing in your stupid fucking face."

Max was apoplectic with rage, and it seemed his face had become even darker. He got to his feet, and moved towards the door.

"Stupid?" Zack retorted mockingly. "I think we both know who's stupid. Know your enemy Max, and never, ever, underestimate him. You arrogant piece of shit. Fuck off."

Max stalked from the bar without another word.

The nervous energy of the moment suddenly overcame Zack. He started trembling uncontrollably. Quickly pouring himself a healthy JD over ice, he raised it in Urban's direction and announced, "Knowledge is power."

Urban looked completely flummoxed. "What the fuck just happened here?"

The Jack Daniels blazed a trail down Zack's parched throat, and he forced out a strained smile. "Well, I told you I was world-class at pissing people off, didn't I?"

Refusing to satisfy Urban's curiosity any further, Zack returned his attention to the CD collection. He was quietly pleased with how that little showdown had gone. Max was now on the back foot, and that could only be a good thing.

Zack would have to watch his step though. It was still a game, but the doubling cube was now in play.

Thirty-One

The bubbles of the spa-bath leapt purposefully upward, and Carla wriggled in pleasure as they tickled her skin and relaxed her body. She was as happy as she could remember ... certainly happier than she had ever previously been in Roppongi.

Zack continued to be a revelation. For reasons of privacy, on the morning following the party they had gone back to her place and stayed more or less in bed until Monday afternoon when Zack had to get ready for work. They'd made love, eaten, drunk wine, made love, slept, then talked ... and talked ... and talked.

The fact Zack had reiterated his desire for a full-time commitment, and in Roppongi of all places, surprised her. They were both fully cognisant of just how difficult a road that could be. But perhaps because of that awareness, she felt a quiet confidence that they could maybe pull it off.

Zack had apparently very much had his fill of the casual sex aspect of Roppongi, and told her she could trust him implicitly. She believed him. Furthermore, he'd gone almost as far as saying he was in love with her. She was sure only a deep-rooted instinct for self-protection had stopped him.

Only one thing about Zack frightened her. His obvious connection with Roppongi's drug scene. His access to drugs was seemingly without limits, and she knew that could only mean he was connected at a significant level. So far he had brushed off or deflected her probing in this regard, and she could understand why.

But she knew her relationship with Zack would be all or nothing. It was a package deal. Was she ready to accept the associated risks, most of which she couldn't even see? Tough call indeed.

*   *   *

In *Shinjuku*, Angelica crouched sobbing in the bathroom, and listened helplessly to Max raping her friend Sylvana. A pillow had muted the original screams. Now all Angelica could hear was Max's rhythmic grunting and Sylvana's whimpering. She had never seen him anything like this. He had stormed into the apartment, his face twisted in such demonic rage that Angelica had instinctively crossed herself. It made no difference: he'd slapped her so hard that she landed next to the bathroom door about ten feet away. Terrified, she had scrambled inside on all fours, then reached up and locked the door.

Leaning over the toilet bowl, she spat out a mouthful of blood and vacantly observed it discolour the water below. She wiped her bloody finger on the rim. Would the Virgin Mary ever help them? What did God want her to do? How could she ever speak to her family again? Her very soul burning in shame, she rested her bleeding face against the toilet bowl, closed her eyes and prayed while she wept.

* * *

Hans watched Fumiko across the dimly lit table. They nibbled at the unidentifiable salty snacks, sipped their drinks, each wondering what the other was thinking. He had decided to end it with her this coming weekend. The whole thing had simply become too full-on. Even his Japanese manager had passed comment on what had seemingly become a 'fatal attraction' scenario.

Funny, and sad, Hans thought, how fast attraction could turn to indifference, pity, and then contempt, when one partner in a relationship so obviously existed in a state of blind devotion to the other.

He now felt distinctly uncomfortable with Fumiko in any situation other than their sexual couplings. Then, the omnipresent tension dissipated at least temporarily, but always moved in as swiftly as a San Francisco fog once they lay sated. It was a suffocating tension, and gave their extra-coital interactions a forced quality.

If Fumiko noticed it, she had given him no sign. This level of denial had Hans worried. He would feel much more at ease if they simply addressed the issue. Having so far failed to do this himself, he supposed he was as much at fault as she.

Well, that would change this weekend. He had already planned the dénouement. He would change their usual meeting to a daytime rendezvous in *Yoyogi-Park*. He would then break it to her as gently as he could. It was not something he was looking forward to, but it had to be done.

* * *

Sofia lay in bed, pensively flicking through the muted TV channels. For the first time ever, she'd called in sick. Sick was right. Today, in his limo, Yamazaki-San had asked her to marry him. He had simultaneously pressed a case containing a matching Bvlgari necklace and engagement ring into her hands. What they were worth, she did not even want to think. Actually touching them had been out of the question. It would have made what was happening ... real.

She had actually *smelt* his age, as those leathery lips slithered across her cheek. She still remembered with clarity her involuntary shiver. Maybe he'd thought it was desire? She shivered again. She was very much on the Wonderland side of the looking-glass now.

In those few seconds the world had gone stark raving mental. What followed had been like an anaesthetised dream ... she could function only in slow motion, as if moving through some viscous substance. Her gaze seemed fixed on his wrinkled walnut of a head, his dead black eyes those of a shark.

She remembered vaguely jabbering something about it all being a huge shock. How she needed time to think. Christ, she had even stammered something about needing to talk to her mother. *Jesus fucking Christ!* What in God's name was she going to do?

* * *

The moment Sofia walked into the bar, Zack knew something was horribly wrong. She looked like shit for a start, and she'd definitely been crying. Not a trace of makeup on her, and he hadn't known Sofia to miss a night's work since she'd started in Tokyo.

It was only eight-thirty, and the bar had a smattering of post-work suits along with a couple of hostesses procrastinating about going to work. Given that Sofia usually lit up a room, the fact that no-one paid her much attention as she scooted up to Zack's end of the bar spoke volumes. Zack guessed that if he could see auras, hers would be non-existent at the moment. She looked *crushed*.

"Come here babe. What the bloody hell's the matter?"

Zack was genuinely unsettled. He wrapped her up in a big hug. Her body convulsed slightly against his and to his horror he realised she was sobbing. He held her a moment or two, then sat her gently back onto a stool.

She was a mess. He had never seen her like this. Maybe someone had died or something. It certainly looked like being one of those nights. First Max, now this. He waited.

Hunched over, she continued to sob.

"Do you want a drink?" he asked.

She nodded. "Just water."

Zack opened an Evian and pushed it in front of her, then popped behind the bar and selected about forty minutes worth of music. He bade the hostesses goodnight as they reluctantly left, then refilled a few of the suits' drinks. Returning to Sofia's side he noticed she had drunk about half the water, and seemed marginally more composed.

Looking at him clearly for the first time, she spoke.

"Zack, you remember that night on the yacht in Eilat, when you told us about this place?"

He nodded.

"Well, back then I didn't really believe you. Even though I didn't think it was in your nature, I thought you *had* to be exaggerating about this place."

She paused, and shook her head in apparent bewilderment.

Zack stayed silent, not wanting to break her flow now that she seemed ready to talk.

"This place is more fucked up than I could ever have imagined, you know. Describing this madhouse to anyone who hasn't been here would be practically fucking impossible."

Zack couldn't keep his mouth closed any longer. "Sofia. Can you perhaps just tell me what's upset you so much?"

"You know that old guy who I visited in the country a while ago?"

"Yeah, the eighty year old *Yakuza* guy or whatever he is."

Sofia nodded. "Well, he just proposed *marriage* to me this afternoon, and tried to force a matching Bvlgari necklace and engagement ring into my hands as he did it."

Zack expelled his breath in a soft whistle. This was interesting.

Sofia fixed him with a hard stare. "Zack, the stuff had to be worth well over a hundred thousand dollars. Maybe a quarter of a million for all I know."

"Shit babe, what the hell did you do?"

Sofia finished her water in a gulp. "I got out of the car. I can't even remember what I said really. It … it was just so disgusting Zack. He tried to kiss me …" She shuddered, and her voice trailed off.

"I think you need a proper drink," Zack suggested.

Sofia smiled weakly. "Yes, I do actually. Something with vodka."

"Your wish is my command m'lady." Keen to improve her mood, Zack theatrically mixed their drinks and served her with a flourish.

"Well it's a bit early for me of course, but to let you drink alone would be downright …" He paused, grinning. "Unchivalrous."

That got another little smile out of her. They sipped their drinks in silence.

When Jarrod arrived shortly afterwards, Zack told the guys he was taking a break to speak with Sofia in private for a while. He took up position on a stool next to her. "So what's your next move?"

Sofia ran her fingernails through her scalp distractedly. "Well, I can't ever see him again. Obviously."

"What about when he comes to the club?"

She hesitated. "Well … I'll just tell *Mama-san* that I won't see him anymore because of what happened."

Zack figured for a moment. She obviously hadn't thought this through at all. "Sofia, your club is literally about twice the size of a swung cat. Do you really think the two of you can be in there without confrontation if he is this obsessed with you?"

The tiniest twist of Sofia's lips.

"You can try it, but in these situations if the client is as mega-rich and powerful as this sick old bastard seems to be, the hostess always has to leave the club. It's a matter of face for the client and therefore necessity for the girl. No matter how nice you are, no matter how good a worker, no matter how pretty you are, you're still just a piece of flesh, and *gaijin* flesh at that. The club will never lose a customer like him over any hostess. It's that simple."

"You mean *I'm going to have to quit* … and go work somewhere else?"

Zack could see self-righteous indignation coming his way on an express-train. He worked hard to keep his tone compassionate, because what he had to say next, she would like even less. She was still staring at him expectantly.

"Sofia … just *think* for a second. Say you quit, and go to another club. It *might* take his secretary two phone calls to find out which one. He visits the club and requests you. The club will know who he is and what he is. How long do you think you'll last when you insult him and your new club, by refusing to sit with him?"

Judging by her expression, Sofia had slowly begun to grasp the reality of her position.

"But that's not …."

"Fair?" Zack finished for her. He shook his head impatiently. "Come on Sofia. You're in a patriarchal, misogynistic, xenophobic, practically caste-driven country with an organised crime system that would put most Fortune 500 companies to shame … and you want fair?"

Sofia's body slumped despairingly. Zack was immediately furious with himself. He really could be an insensitive shit sometimes. She was upset, fragile. She had come to him for comfort, and what did he do but rub her nose in her own naïvety. What an asshole. He put his arm around her reassuringly and went into recovery mode.

"Sofia, I'm really sorry for being such a prick. Maybe it won't work out that way. I can't help it. I'm just such a fucking cynic when it comes to this place."

He wondered how she'd react if she knew even a fraction of the deadly game he was playing out with the cute and cuddly Max. Compared to his daily Roppongi challenges, Sofia's immediate problem was small beans.

Sofia's head came up. "No. You're right Zack. Don't patronise me. It's okay. Regardless of anything else that's happened between us, there's always been one thing I liked about you. You call things as you see them. And, you're nearly always on the money." She looked calmer and more focused now. "That's why I came here tonight I suppose. I needed to hear it straight."

Zack saw what looked like relief in her eyes, so let her continue.

"You know, I just don't care about this game anymore, Zack. If I have to leave Roppongi earlier than I thought, then fuck it. I had to do a visa run in three weeks anyway. So what? Let's get drunk." She finished the remainder of her vodka, stood up and hugged him tightly.

* * *

A little later that evening, Hans swung the Honda Gyro scooter across the footpath and into the alleyway that ran alongside his building. He was tired. It had taken all his willpower not to end the thing with Fumiko in the club tonight. But that would have been unprofessional, and a nasty scene.

God she was hard work. The silences were deafening. Their next meeting would be *Yoyogi-Park* on Saturday and then it would all be over. He guided the Gyro into the little parking area next to the garbage bins, killed the motor and pulled off his helmet.

He did not see the two men step out of the shadows behind him. They were quick, brutal, and efficient. A leaden cosh thudded silently into his temple, and he fell heavily to the ground.

Thirty-Two

Wednesday, the twenty-third of December. Under the circumstances, the bonhomie and party-vibe surrounding Zack and Carla was suffocating in the extreme. The Australian embassy was abuzz with excitement, back-slapping, and general Yuletide good cheer. Zack took a swig of the specially imported Redback beer, but hardly tasted it. Hans should be here, sharing these beers with him. But as of now, Hans had been missing for six days.

Sofia had phoned Zack the previous Friday afternoon – the day after their heart-to-heart in Bongoes about Yamazaki's marriage proposal. She'd been worried that Hans had not returned home from work after Thursday night. This in itself would not necessarily have surprised Zack, and usually he would have teased her. There were times in Roppongi when he himself had not made it home for three or four days. That Hans's *scooter* had made it back to their building that night made things different. Why would he ride the scooter home and then just leave it there without even going inside?

When Hans had subsequently failed to materialise for work on Friday night, Zack and Sofia had become officially very worried. It was just way out of character. Bleary-eyed after barely a couple of hours sleep, they'd filed a missing persons report at *Nishi-Azabu* police station on Saturday morning. Apart from the name of the *host-club*, the only two things Zack could think of that would perhaps be of interest to the police, were Hans's affair with the married Fumiko, and the weird shit Sofia had experienced with her obsessive customer Yamazaki.

Sofia was a mess, and contributed almost nothing except to confirm that Hans had never been away for more than one night. Hans's sudden disappearance on top of the stress of the Yamazaki situation was almost too much for her. She had already quit work. With Hans missing, she was now unable to leave the country as she'd planned, and was living in unhealthy and morbid isolation in their silent apartment. Zack was worried about her. Everything was suddenly fucked.

He forced another swig of beer down, and glanced pensively around the room. Carla, attuned to his mood, watched him anxiously. They had moved across to an inconspicuous area of the enclosed embassy courtyard, away from the main crowd and the buffet.

The embassy function was something Zack would usually enjoy. It was a raucous, drunken affair consisting primarily of diplomatic staff, brokers, bankers, lawyers, and other assorted ex-pat businessmen. The absence of family for many of them added to the pent-up emotions which were inevitably unleashed by drinking to excess.

And it had long been customary for the manager of Bongoes to be invited as a gesture of thanks for the hospitality and parties they had provided all year. As his eyes travelled around the space, Zack noticed a plethora of Bongoes regulars and inwardly cringed. He was in no mood to be here, but putting in an appearance was practically mandatory. Aside from which, he had to see someone.

"Zack, why don't we just make the right noises and get the fuck out of here?" Carla whispered. "What's the point of staying?"

She hated seeing Zack's usually irrepressible personality mired in such darkness. He had been like this since Hans's disappearance, and the embassy's festivities only made his unease more apparent.

Zack knew Carla was hurting; he had been difficult lately. But the fact was he probably would have gone a bit mad if she hadn't been around the last few days. She was an angel, or the nearest thing to it in Roppongi. He took her head in his hands and kissed her firmly on the forehead, holding his lips there for some time. Then he met her gaze.

"Babe, I'm sorry as hell for everything at the moment."

Carla moved to speak, but he silenced her with his finger to her lips.

"We'll go soon, sweetie. I've just got to check a couple of things first." He forced a tight smile. "No matter how I seem right now, I want you to know that I am crazy about you. You are my angel." Carla had no time to respond before they were interrupted.

"Hey loverboy! Whattcha doin' hidin' over here? Don'tcha eat or somethin'?"

A hand clapped itself around Zack's shoulder. He already knew who it was.

Scotty was a big man with a ruddy complexion and hands like the side of a Hereford bull. About forty, he was originally from Mt Isa in rural Queensland. An unlikely beginning for someone who was now Executive Assistant to the Australian Ambassador to Japan.

But then, Scotty was a veritable sea of contradictions. His yokel speech patterns belied a razor-sharp intellect, and his folksy unthreatening country-boy approach invariably put just about anyone at ease; perfect for his line of work. Despite Zack's black mood, he was having that effect already. His gregariousness and enthusiasm were infectious.

"Merry Christmas Scotty, you goddamn yokel."

Zack turned to face him. They embraced and shook hands. Scotty's eyes wandered to Carla, who was resplendent in a shimmering silver evening gown.

"Scotty, this is my personal angel, Carla. Carla, Scotty. Farmer-cum-diplomat extraordinaire."

"Lovely to meet you, Carla. Welcome to the embassy. Good to have you here."

Carla's hand completely disappeared inside Scotty's great mitt.

"Good to meet you too," Carla replied, returning Scotty's thousand-watt smile.

"Ahh, a Canadian. Vancouver, is that right?"

Carla was momentarily stunned. "Umm, yes actually."

Zack murmured, "Told you he was sharp, babe."

"That's really impressive," Carla added. "Most people can't tell the difference from an American accent, much less differentiate between regions within Canada."

Scotty brushed some hair from his forehead. "Not that impressive really. We deal with them pretty frequently through the embassy, so I'm used to the accent."

An arresting-looking woman in a red gown had drifted their way. Scotty put his arm around her.

"Darlin', Zack you already know. With that fact in mind, I can safely introduce Carla as his better half." He winked at Carla. "Carla, this is my lovely wife Darlene."

"Pleased to meet you Darlene." Carla smiled dutifully.

Darlene gave Zack a cursory nod before turning her attention to Carla. "Sweetheart. My word ... aren't *you* gorgeous! And what a beautiful city you come from. Scott and I spent a couple of weeks in Vancouver back in '95. Delicious summer, magnificent restaurants, and fantastic shopping. I could easily live in that city."

She brought the champagne flute to her mouth and quaffed the contents, simultaneously beckoning one of the waiters for a replacement.

"Well, thank you that's ..." Carla's response was cut short by Darlene's attention to the arrival of the waiter.

Scotty caught Zack's pained expression, and raised an eyebrow in acknowledgment.

Darlene continued unfazed. "You will join me for a glass of champagne won't you darling? We'll leave this beer-swilling to the philistines in our midst. What do you say?"

"Well I ahh ..."

"Good that's settled then."

Plucking two champagne flutes from the platter, she proffered one to Carla.

Scotty flashed a split-second apologetic look at Carla. She caught it, somewhat taken aback. He disengaged his arm from Darlene's shoulders.

"Well this philistine needs a refill," he said. Looking pointedly at Zack's nearly empty bottle, he added, "You too, eh Zack?"

Scotty turned his attention back to Carla. "Carla, you wouldn't mind keepin' Darlene outta trouble for a moment or two wouldja? There's a couple of people I want Zack to meet."

A quick wink from Zack and Carla valiantly picked up the baton clean as a whistle.

"Oh sure. You guys take your time. I can tell Darlene and I are destined to be partners in crime at this party."

Darlene pounced on her new friend. "That's *right* darling!" she exclaimed delightedly, barely concealing a hiccup. "We'll be on the prowl together, won't we?"

Carla nodded limply, as Scotty and Zack peeled off toward the buffet.

"Jesus Scotty, she's getting worse. Are you guys okay?" Zack asked concernedly.

Scotty's face had saddened. "No mate, not really," he said heavily. "She's drivin' me crazy and this place is drivin' her crazy. She doesn't belong here. I dunno what's gunna happen."

Zack really felt for him. Momentarily his own gloom faded. Everyone had their problems, he thought. And the world wasn't waiting for anyone. It just kept on spinning. Beers in hand, they moved out into the reception area where it was quieter, and sat down on one of the lounges.

Scotty took a long pull on his Redback, and smacked his lips. "God it's good beer this stuff. We should've got it over 'ere ages ago. Beats that VB shit hands down."

He rested his head against the wall, eyes closed.

Zack's anxiety increased. Was everyone he knew going through a disaster at the moment? Scotty looked close to the end of his tether. "Mate, is there anything ... anything at all ... that I can do to help?"

After a long silence Scotty opened his eyes, and met Zack's gaze. "You're a good bloke Zack. I've always liked you. Always felt like I could trust you. And that's no small statement in this fucken madhouse."

He took a few mouthfuls of beer. His bottle was nearly empty again.

"No, there's nothing you can do mate. Nothin' anyone can do really. I'm gunna send 'er back to Queensland. Sadly, outta sight outta mind's about the best I've bin able to come up with. She's fuckin' up my career, sleepin' around, embarrassing me at functions, and drinkin' way, way too much."

Running a hand across his forehead, he took a quick breath.

"She's become a real fuckin' liability, and it's about time I faced reality. She's not gunna change. She's gunna get worse, and if I let it go, somethin' really bad is gunna happen. It's as simple as that." He sighed. "Today, I wish I had your life."

Zack almost choked on a mouthful of beer. "No you don't Scotty. My life is no fucking picnic at the moment. I need to speak to you about it actually."

Scotty straightened up a bit, seemingly happy to be able to focus on something other than his own problems.

Zack went on. "You know that envelope I left here at the embassy with you?"

"Yeah mate, what about it?"

"I just wanted to make sure it's safe, and that all the arrangements I made are still in place."

"Of course they are, mate. Why? You plannin' on jumpin' off a building or somethin'?"

Zack reply was terser than he intended. "No Scotty, that's not my nature. I have to know things are organised, that's all. If anything happens, and someone tries to tell you I suicided, or I have some weird accident, it's bullshit. You can be sure of that."

Scotty regarded him sharply. "You sure you're okay?"

Zack nodded, but didn't add anything.

"This wouldn't have anything to do with that Nigerian fella you spoke to me about?"

Zack hesitated. "It might. I don't know mate. I really can't talk about it right now. I just need to know we're on the same page with all that stuff."

Leaning towards him with two fingers pressed to his forehead, Scotty intoned, "Dib dib dib mate. Speakin' of the same page, you wanna do a cuppla lines?"

Zack looked around in surprise. "Here? Where?"

"In my office, you dill."

Scotty led Zack down a corridor to an elevator marked 'Embassy Staff Only'. With a swipe of his encoded ID card, it was summoned.

Once secure within his office, Scotty proceeded to cut up four chunky lines.

Zack observed in silence. At least he knew it would be decent stuff. Scotty had been a regular since Zack's last time in Tokyo. He surveyed the plush embassy office. It was certainly a novel environment in which to do drugs.

A cut-down straw magically appeared in Scotty's huge palm. He offered it to Zack.

They hoovered the lines and settled back into the luxurious Chesterfield furniture. Scotty sparked up a cigarette. "You still don't smoke, do ya Zack?"

Zack shook his head. "That stuff'll kill you Scotty. Smart fart like you should know better."

Scotty grunted indifferently. "Tell me the story with your new lady Zack? She's a bloody goddess! Not a stripper is she?"

Zack tossed him a withering glance. "Thanks mate. I'll let her know you thought so!"

Scotty merely chuckled at this empty threat, and gestured for Zack to continue.

"No. She's a dancer at BlackJacks. A dancer full-stop actually. She's classically trained. Her life-long ballet instructor was killed in a car accident. It messed with her head. So she went travelling and ended up here."

Scotty snorted. "Ended up here. Bloody hell! How do any of us end up here for God's sake?" Abruptly, he switched topics. "You know I'm gunna have to divorce her."

"Yeah mate." Zack nodded. "It looks that way. How long've you guys been married? Twelve years?"

Scotty pursed his lips, exhaling trails of cigarette smoke. "Thirteen in January, plus four years together before we did the deed. What a fuckin' shame."

He ran his free hand through greying hair. "My parents'll be devastated. They don't know a fuckin' thing. I've kept it all secret, just hopin' she'd come good. What a goddamn joke."

Suddenly he was on his feet. "Jeez I'm forgettin' me manners Zack. You want another coldie?" Scotty opened a wood-panelled fridge in the wall cabinet. It was fully stocked.

"Yeah, but I'll have a vodka, lime and soda if that's okay mate."

After the Charlie, it would be better than beer, Zack thought. He should really be getting back to Carla. But Scotty seemed to badly need the company right now. To tell the truth, Zack was touched Scotty had opened up like this with him today. A measure of the man's mounting desperation, he supposed.

"Scotty, there's something else I need to talk to you about."

"I'm all ears Zack. Anythin' I can do to help mate."

"I guess you haven't heard anything about this guy Hans Overmeyer, who's gone missing."

Scotty slipped Zack's drink onto a thick silver coaster on the coffee table and sank back into the lounge.

"Hans Overmeyer? Nup. Who is he anyway?"

"He's one of my best friends Scotty. A Dutch guy. We crewed for months on the same yacht in Israel. He went missing after work on Thursday night. Nobody knows where he is." Zack related the facts as concisely as he could.

"Shit, I'm sorry to hear that mate. You must be beside yourself. And the police haven't found anythin' yet?"

"If they have, they haven't told us."

"So this Hans guy. Was he into any dodgy shit or anything?"

Zack smiled a little. "Like me, you mean?"

Scotty grinned back, before raising his hands, palms outwards. "Well it has to be said, no?'

"No, he wasn't into any dodgy shit. He was just working over here. The usual things. Like I said, he was working at a *host-club* in *Ginza*. The only thing I can think of that could have anything to do with it is that he was banging one of his regular customers."

"So?" Scotty queried.

"She's married."

"Hmmm." Scotty took a deep drag on his cigarette and said nothing for a moment.

"Well, that's gotta be the cops' first lead. Find out who this chick is and more importantly, who she's married to. That's the info you want. If the cops give you any static, let me know. I'll figure out a way of making it official and see what I can dig out of them. Japanese officialdom can be obtuse as hell if they don't want to play ball for some reason."

"Thanks mate. I appreciate that."

They sipped their drinks in silence.

Then Zack decided to make a move. "I should really go and save Carla mate."

Scotty nodded sadly. "I just wish I could save Darlene."

"I'm sorry about you and Darlene. But you're right Scotty. The sooner you do something, the better."

Zack put his empty glass on a tray above the fridge. "Thanks for the lines by the way."

These words seemed to jolt Scotty from his reverie. "What about a couple for the road eh?"

He already had the familiar folded package out. It would be rude to say no.

"Yeah sure mate … cheers."

Scotty carved out four lines, and they disappeared as quickly as the first ones.

Whoooaahhh! Zack really had a buzz on now. He would need some chewing gum very shortly.

"Hahhhrrrhh! Those bastards hit the spot, that's for sure," Scotty wheezed.

As they re-entered the fray, Zack realised the lines had actually done him a power of good. He was feeling sort of normalised.

Carla was nibbling something over by the buffet, talking to somebody Zack didn't recognise. Darlene was nowhere to be seen.

Scotty squeezed Zack's hand. "I better find out what Darlene's up to mate. I'll catch you later." He moved off.

"Thanks mate … and take care hey."

Scotty waved an acknowledgment before continuing towards the main crowd.

Carla appeared at Zack's elbow. "Where the hell have you been? That woman was making me crazy! I could have strangled her. She's a fucking lunatic!"

"Well imagine living with it," Zack quipped. "Babe, I'm sorry about leaving you but I had no choice. Scotty's at crisis point with her and needed to talk, so we went to his office. Now I'm done here anyway, so unless *you* want to stay, let's go."

They went.

Thirty-Three

Zack and Carla exited the embassy into the freezing night, walked up the street, bought water and some chewing gum, then hailed a cab. The chill air entering Zack's warm and racing system made him feel slightly nauseous. It was only nine o'clock, and he didn't feel like going home.

He motioned the cab vaguely in the direction of *Roppongi Crossing*.

"Where do you want to go?" he asked.

She looked at him oddly. "Are you okay?"

"Scotty racked us up some lines in his office. I'm sort of flying a bit."

"You guys did coke in the Embassy! Un-fucking-believable."

"Let's go chill somewhere and have a drink, then maybe go to your place?" Zack suggested.

Carla sighed. "Yeah why not. Deep Blue?"

"Great idea!" Zack exclaimed. He didn't know why he hadn't thought of it. Deep Blue was a supremely beautiful bar-restaurant. And fortunately, most of Roppongi still seemed not to know about it. It was situated off *Gaien-Higashi-Dori* towards *Nogizaka* station, just down one of the side-alleys.

Directing the cabbie into the narrow alleyway, Zack paid the fare, and they swooped into the basement of the adjacent building. Once through the main entrance, they passed through a set of unobtrusive dark-blue floor-to-ceiling velour curtains. With the letters DB discreetly monogrammed in a raised circle on each curtain, the place radiated class. Deep Blue was like being inside a giant aquarium, except it was a bar. Gigantic fish tanks extended from waist height to ceiling almost everywhere you looked, even overhead in some places.

The entire space was suffused with a calming blue translucence which shimmered and shifted with the movements of the creatures within. A circular, cream-coloured bar finished in alabaster and mother-of-pearl occupied the centre of the room. Luckily, Zack had discovered this place within a week of being in Tokyo last time. Having hoofed it around Roppongi from one end to the other, asking for work in bars all over the place, he had eventually stumbled across Deep Blue. Being a fairly subdued venue, it hadn't been the sort of bar he'd wanted to work in, which was fine anyway because it seemed they only employed native staff for what was a mostly Japanese clientele. As a chill-out venue to kick back and relax in, it knocked the socks off anywhere Zack had ever been.

Recalling that job-hunting phase, which now seemed a lifetime ago, Zack remembered something else. It had given him his first taste of the deeply ingrained racism inherent in Japanese society. The search for work had taken him into clubs and bars of all descriptions, but it transpired many of these were not normally frequented by *gaijin*s. The reason for this was obvious; they were simply not welcome.

He had always conducted his job-hunting early in the evenings before places got busy. With some venues he'd walked into, Japanese staff had initially been so shocked at actually seeing a *gaijin* on the premises, that often they had been unable to speak. A sort of panicked facial expression ensued, before he was frantically told, '*Gaijin dame* – Japanese only,' with the forearms coming up in the customary cross to emphasise the '*dame*'.

Zack couldn't help but imagine the resulting public outcry were bars in Australia or Britain to adopt the same 'No Foreigners' policy. Of course it would never happen in either country these days. Certainly not so blatantly anyway; private clubs were invariably the 'civilised' way around the racism issue. Nevertheless, it exasperated him to see nations such as Britain and Australia idealistically pursue such admirable, ever politically-correct standpoints, but to then shrink from holding other 'beneficiary' countries to similar standards.

Happily, however, Deep Blue was not averse to foreign custom, and these thoughts quickly left him. He and Carla slipped off their shoes prior to being shown through to be seated. Pebbles crunched satisfyingly underfoot.

The entire floor consisted of a sea of white pebbles about half an inch in diameter, and little walkways of inlaid polished tree-stumps created an aesthetically pleasing mosaic between the tables, bar and toilet areas. Zack eschewed the stumps altogether and walked across the stones, enjoying the sensation of his soles being massaged through his socks.

They chose a low coffee table by the wall in the cushioned area near the bar, rather than sitting at one of the more formal dining tables. Another interesting Deep Blue feature was the music; beautiful, ambient stuff of varying ethnic origin, that Zack had never heard anywhere else.

"This was a great idea sweetheart," Zack murmured, as they sank heavily into cushioned luxuriousness.

Carla was not to be schmoozed so easily. "I still can't believe you were in there doing lines, while I had to talk to Miss Goony-Bird. How the hell could *he* ever have married *her*? It's just beyond me!"

Zack silently pulled a gram out of his pocket and slipped it into her palm. *No point in flying solo.*

Carla cuffed him not entirely playfully around the back of the head, and made for the toilet.

"Red wine okay with you, sweetie?" he called after her.

A nod, as she disappeared behind another monogrammed curtain.

After double-checking the wine would be served at room temperature, Zack selected a particularly delightful Californian Pinot Noir, and made himself even more comfortable. Red wine was another Japanese anomaly. Restaurants, bars and clubs routinely found it necessary to refrigerate otherwise perfectly acceptable bottles of red wine.

It seemed not to matter whether the venue was sophisticated or not. Some otherwise excellent restaurants in which Zack had eaten invariably served their red wines, of whatever variety, chilled. Tragically, it seemed to be a Tokyo-wide failing, of unknown origin or rationale. Just another of Tokyo's many unsolvable mysteries.

Things were a little different here though. Seeing the maitre-de expertly decant the wine, Zack's thoughts were free to return to the weighty matters he'd been relentlessly tortured by during waking hours the past few days. *Where the fucking hell was Hans?* He had gone over a million possibilities, permutations and combinations, but kept coming back to just two alternatives. Both of which made him feel very uneasy indeed.

Everything Zack and Sofia knew about Hans indicated he would not just disappear without telling them something. This seemed to point to him having been taken and detained against his will. If this was true, who would do such a thing, and to what end?

The first and most likely scenario in Zack's opinion was that it had something to do with Fumiko's husband, and he'd said as much to the police. No doubt they would currently be following that lead. The second, less likely scenario, made him personally feel much worse and he had kept it to himself.

What if Max was playing mind games with Zack via toying with his friends? If that was the case, all bets were off, Zack thought. Max would have ended both his own and Zack's Roppongi careers. Needless to say, Zack would quit immediately under that sort of pressure, but he wouldn't go down without permanently fucking up Max's game as well.

And that was mainly why he discounted the second possibility. He just didn't think Max was that stupid. Max hadn't become who he was by acting like a spoilt kid every time someone took some of his toys away: he was a thinker and a planner, a master of the dark arts.

Carla wafted ethereally across the room towards him, beaming. There wasn't an eye in the room, male or female, that hadn't stolen an admiring glance during her rest-room journey. She slipped the coke neatly back into Zack's pocket as she curled into the cushions next to him.

Zack presented her with a glass of wine. The glass itself was one of those huge, delicately blown bowls attached to an impossibly slender, long, elegant stem. It was a sublime vessel for a sublime recipient.

He raised his own glass. "Here's to getting Hans back from wherever he may be."

They gently clinked glasses. "Amen," said Carla softly.

She took only a small sip of her wine, before setting it down in exchange for some water.

"Got to get rid of this coke taste," she explained, unnecessarily.

Zack nodded, closed his eyes and drifted into the music. Carla snuggled in closer to him, and they stayed that way for some time. He opened his eyes eventually, when he'd finished the first glass of wine.

Leaning forward to replenish his glass, he dislodged Carla from her comfy position on his shoulder. "Sorry," Zack said, "but this wine's too good."

She blinked back to reality, looked at the wine glass in her hand, and finished the remnants. Zack re-poured for both of them.

"Zack, what do you really think has happened to Hans?" she murmured.

He let out a sigh. "To be honest sweetheart I don't even want to think about it, because whatever it is, it can't be good."

After swilling a mouthful of wine back and forth across his tongue, he added, "It's just a matter of how bad it could be."

He hunched his shoulders. "I can't help thinking that it must have something to do with this married chick Fumiko he was getting it on with. Other than that, I just don't know. This waiting, this … limbo of not knowing. It's really a nightmare."

Carla reached across and massaged his neck. Zack felt tears well inside him. He took her hand, kissed it.

"You've been such a superstar Carla. I don't know what I'd be doing if I didn't have you around." He brushed his free hand across his eyes. "Probably getting absolutely out of my fucking head by myself, instead of only agreeably out my head with you."

This amused both of them, and the tension evaporated slightly.

"You stop worrying, Zack Morrissey. There's nothing you can do right now, except be with me. So just be with me. I'm here, so you don't need to worry."

Zack kissed her again. "I know babe … I know." He forced another grin. "I think I'll go powder my nose."

Carla watched him crunch his way over the stones. Since Hans's disappearance, Zack had become much more vulnerable, much less defended by his well-practiced ploys of bonhomie. He was letting her in, ever-closer, and with each day that passed, she knew the bond between them was strengthening.

What a truly horrible thing this whole Hans nightmare was. Even though she'd only met Hans a few times, she felt awful, a sort of cold dread in the pit of her stomach. She shivered, and could only imagine what it must be like for Zack. Poor Sofia as well. The girl was a wreck.

Thirty-four

Zack looked askance at himself in Carla's bathroom mirror. A pale, drawn face, with heavily bagged eyes returned his stare. What a fucking Christmas! He shouldn't have worked last night, but he'd had no choice. All he'd done was drink and do lines: now he felt like shit.

Why Bongoes even opened on Christmas day was beyond Zack. It was a measure of the sorry loneliness of many of Roppongi's inhabitants that the bar took money at all. The fact they had nowhere else to go was more than a little depressing. But it also showed the famous bar was as good as family for many people, and you couldn't get higher praise for a hospitality venue than that, he supposed.

He'd been a miserable fuck all night, but the guys hadn't expected much else. They knew what was going on, so had been content to let him bar-back. They'd done most of the work themselves and left him alone. It was now just over a week, and still no word of Hans.

Zack felt as if his whole being was coming apart. Mechanical in both thought and deed, he was merely going through the motions of his existence. Not feeling, not seeing; a veritable ghost. Only Carla made him feel real. He glanced at her, still sleeping soundly. Having practically lived at her place for the last week, he almost didn't know what he'd do without her now, and that scared him. No option really. He *needed* to be with her, and they would have had no privacy at his place. Thank God that Lucinda, Carla's flatmate, spent nearly all her time at her rich boyfriend's pad.

The jangling electronica of his normal cell-phone bleeping sent him leaping silently across the room to pounce on it before it disturbed Carla. He moved quickly to the bathroom, closing the sliding door.

"*Moshi mosh.*" A strange Japanese voice.

"Hello," Zack said. "Who is it?"

"Zack-oh Morriss-oh *onegaishimasu?*"

"Yes, Zack here," he confirmed.

"Ah - Sakamoto-des ah *Nishi-Azabu* Police Station – you come to *Nishi-Azabu* Police Station, *hai*?"

The voice was metallic, clipped, and authoritative.

It must be Hans! Some news at last!

"*Hai, hai,*" Zack eagerly replied. "I come now, *hai, hai ... dōmo.*"

The simultaneous surge of adrenalin killed Zack's lethargy. He looked at his watch: 11.15. Headache forgotten, he threw himself under the shower, scraped his face quickly, and rugged up: it was sure to be cold outside. It took him fifteen minutes. Amazing the difference a sense of purpose makes, he thought. Carla was still asleep. He scribbled her a note explaining his disappearance, and left.

Outside he stopped dead in his tracks. Snow! It had snowed this morning! It was everywhere. The streetscape had become a fairytale kingdom. A magical sight. He couldn't help feeling it was some kind of sign. But of what? Picking his way carefully to the road, Zack hailed the first cab and jumped in.

"Police Station. *Nishi-Azabu onegaishimasu*," he intoned, Japanese-style. The driver nodded, repeated Zack's destination, and pulled out through a little snow-drift into the main flow of traffic.

Zack felt almost guilty at his exhilaration, but couldn't suppress it. He'd been so disconnected from everything except Carla for so long, that to feel anything else at all was a rush unto itself. He wondered what the police had discovered, why they wanted to see him. He forced himself to relax, despite the infuriatingly slow snow-bound traffic. Instead he tried to enjoy the surrealistic makeover the snow had given Tokyo's streets.

Aside from his and Sofia's visit to report Hans missing last week, Zack had visited *Nishi-Azabu* police station before. During his previous stint in Tokyo. On that occasion he'd been very lucky not to have been deported. Tired after work one night, he'd ridden on Nurit's Gyro scooter for a short distance on a footpath.

Big mistake. He should have walked it. Two policemen had almost bumped into him as they turned a corner from an alley into the footpath. Problems followed, and he was dragged off to *Nishi-Azabu* station. They wanted to see his identification, passport etc. Zack had been livid with himself. At that point, he'd only just started his new job at Bongoes, and had over-stayed his visa by three days. He had a lot to lose. If discovered, he'd be unceremoniously jailed and subsequently booted from the country.

To make matters worse, when searching him, they'd found seventeen fake telephone cards. Generally produced by Iranians, these were counterfeit cards that worked in Japanese public phones. They were totally illegal, but using them cut your international phone costs by about ninety percent.

The fact he'd talked his way out of that situation was something Zack had marvelled at ever since. He'd played the dumb-assed tourist, expressing righteous indignation when they tried to relieve him of the cards, claiming he'd bought them at *Ueno* market. Feigning disbelief, he'd made them explain to him three times why the cards were illegal.

No doubt somewhat dismayed by his obtuseness, they'd eventually presented him with a genuine card to show him the difference. To their abject relief, Zack had finally nodded magnanimously, saying, '*So desu, so desu. Wakarimashita, wakarimashita. Gomenasai.*' Then the cop who spoke the best English had asked Zack to follow him into another room.

What now, Zack had wondered. Amazingly, he had been obliged to watch the officer shred the illegal cards before his eyes, just so they knew that he knew they were not corrupt! How weird was Japan? *They* had felt obliged to prove themselves *to him.*

The worst was not over however. They *really* wanted to see his passport. Zack had then proceeded to talk some serious bullshit, running their questioner in circles for about an hour, whilst appearing to be as cooperative as possible. It was at the Indian embassy awaiting a visa stamp. He wouldn't be able to bring it in for at least a week, maybe two weeks. Blah blah blah.

They didn't really understand, and as far as he could tell, they eventually just got tired of him. Ultimately, to his relief, he had been handed the Gyro-keys and his personal effects at about six in the morning and informed he was free to go. It had been nothing short of a miracle.

These memories ricocheted around Zack's head as he stood on the footpath looking at the foreboding police building. What awaited him in there this time? He saw a solitary figure standing outside the station, and smiled despite himself.

Regardless of weather conditions, there was always one cop who stood guard outside the station, with of all things, a big stick to keep him company. Zack had long ago assumed it must be a traditional or symbolic requirement, because frankly he couldn't see a stick-wielding middle-aged cop being any sort of match for say, a nine-millimetre handgun.

Oh well, he thought. Time to go. He picked a gap in the traffic and made his way cautiously across the slippery road. Bowing slightly under the sentinel's watchful gaze, he swung open the doors and entered. There was a slight hush in the Japanese desk-staff's chatter, as they turned to see who might be about to share their gossipy insights. A fresh-faced boy who looked about fifteen but was probably twenty-four, detached himself from the group, bowed to Zack and said, "*Ohayou, hai?*"

"Sakamoto-san *onegaishimasu,*" Zack said.

At the mention of the name Sakamoto, the room fell completely silent. Zack took in this silence, before he was shown into an ante-room and asked to wait. The room was spartan: featureless, windowless, with a nasty fluorescent light, a round three-legged table and three metal chairs.

Zack sat in the chair facing the door, and waited.

The door opened after about five minutes. A man stepped in, shook hands, bowed, and sat down without saying a word. Zack quickly appraised him. He was not in a police uniform, but a suit. Zack had not seen him before. He had not been present when they reported Hans missing. Tall for a Japanese, the officer was rail-thin. His features were angular, but somehow delicate.

Zack put his age at about fifty-five, but you could have added or subtracted ten years and Zack would have been unsurprised if the resulting figure were accurate. With some Japanese people, their infamous inscrutability applied as easily to their age as to their character.

In keeping with most Japanese males in official positions, his hair was closely cropped; almost military, it was an even mix of cigarette ash and black. He wore frameless elliptical spectacles which drew attention to his odd, light-coloured eyes. Zack immediately noticed two other curiosities. The first was a pronounced 'U' shaped scar about five centimetres long just beside his left eye. The other was that a triangular piece of flesh was missing from mid-way up his right ear.

Given that ritualistic body modification was non-existent in orthodox Japanese society, Zack could only guess at what circumstances may have led to these permanent facial alterations.

Ail he knew was that this individual was no ordinary *salariman*. He had the air of a martial arts expert: quiet, understated fortitude. Just as the man appeared about to speak, he stopped himself, leaned back again and thrust his hand into his jacket pocket. Zack remained silent, continuing to regard the man with respectful equanimity. He wanted this unusual policeman to initiate the conversation.

Extracting a packet of cigarettes, the man proffered it to Zack wordlessly. Zack held up both hands, lowered them, said nothing. The man lit his cigarette, inhaled deeply, then exhaled into the corner of the room, like it was the freshest breath of air he'd had for days. His eyes finally came to rest on Zack.

"My name is Sak-a-mo-to." He pronounced the name slowly, with separated syllables. Zack recognised the metallic tone from his telephone summons and nodded in acknowledgement. Sakamoto's gaze stared into Zack's for some time as he took another deep hit from the cigarette. Zack wondered what he saw.

"We think we find your friend." A pause. "Han."

Zack didn't bother with a correction.

Sakamoto's eyes narrowed. "But he is dead."

The last four words came out in a dry rasp, and entered the room's atmosphere wreathed in a ghastly pall of smoke. The smoke seemed to hang, shroud-like, around the sound of those four words.

Zack tried to say something, but was unable to. He felt very strange. It was as if his mind had detached itself from the rest of him. He closed his eyes and tried to breathe, but his nostrils were full of the smell of those four words. '*But he is dead*' hung in the air with acrid morbidity. *Hans dead? It was ridiculous. How could Hans be dead? Why would be Hans be dead?*

A wave of nausea overtook Zack, and the cigarette smoke in this airless room was making him dizzy. Getting up, he walked unsteadily out of the room, across the lobby, and through the main doors onto the steps outside. There he sat down, and took in great gulps of the freezing cold air.

It was probably a mistake, he thought. They probably had the wrong guy. But somehow, he knew they didn't. He put his head between his knees and forced himself to breathe more slowly. Each breath caused him pain, because in his heart, he knew a man like Sakamoto would be right.

An involuntary sob escaped his body. Hans was gone. Zack had already known it, felt it, with prescient certainty. He didn't know how or why that could be, but this blank certainty had pervaded his sense of disconnectedness during the past week. He'd fought it. He'd deliberately refused to acknowledge it. Now he had no choice. This was really happening. It was time to face reality.

After another deep breath, Zack got to his feet and turned to find Sakamoto also standing outside the doors. The sentinel looked on with furtive glances of surprise, but quickly averted his gaze when Zack caught his eye.

"You want coffee maybe?" Sakamoto's voice seemed marginally more empathic.

"Yes, Sakamoto-san." Zack cleared his throat with a couple of small coughs. "That would be good."

He needed something anyway. Coffee wouldn't have been his first choice.

Thirty-Five

Sakamoto said not another word until Zack had taken a few sips of coffee. In the meantime, he continued to give the impression cigarettes were his lifeblood.

The coffee was a hot can from the machine in the street. Sakamoto had sent the desk boy. It was awful, but it was hot and sweet, and Zack's claggy dry mouth accepted the oily liquid gratefully.

"I sorry Zack-oh, but we must-oh identificate this-ah person." The inevitable had been said.

Zack smiled slightly, briefly. "Identify," he corrected softly.

Sakamoto paused. "Identify, yes. You can do this?"

Zack straightened, shocked. "What? Now? Where is he? He's not here, is he?"

He stared jumpily at Sakamoto. The concept of Hans as a corpse had been a badly formed piece of unreality, lurking at the far corners of Zack's mind. To think Hans's dead body might be nearby, simply around a corner and through a doorway, was unnerving. How the fuck had he died anyway? Someone must have killed him, Zack thought. Or maybe he had killed himself? Zack dispensed with this thought in the same second it came to him. It was absurd. Hans wasn't the type. He was the most sensible one out of all of them, for fuck's sake.

Sakamoto stood abruptly. "Come," he said severely.

Zack automatically got to his feet, and followed Sakamoto down a sterile hallway. He realised that without having made a conscious decision to do so, he was somehow on his way to identify a dead body. Not just *any* dead body. *Hans's dead body.* He plodded on mechanically, numbly, until he found himself outside with Sakamoto in the rear car-park of the station.

"Where are we going?" Zack asked. He wondered if his relief at the fact that Hans had not been sequestered in the police station's basement was obvious. Sakamoto made no sign of noticing. He might just not give a fuck, Zack thought.

"Please come," Sakamoto replied, simultaneously blipping the alarm of one of the half-dozen unmarked, anonymous-looking black cars in the compound.

Zack hesitated. He still couldn't believe he was a hair's breadth from making a decision to see Hans dead on a slab. For God's sake, it was twelve-thirty on Boxing Day.

Evidently having no trouble reading Zack's thoughts, Sakamoto squinted at him through the frigid sunshine. "Zack-oh. Is better for you ah-maybe ... than the girl, ah Sofie, I think."

"Sofia," Zack corrected him.

Jesus Christ! He had a point. Sofia was enough of a mess already without having to deal with Sakamoto taking her through something like this. Zack shut his eyes tight for a second, then opened the car door and got inside.

The first ten minutes passed in silence. Zack wondered if he was in shock. He didn't know. What did being in shock feel like anyway? What he did know was his body felt as if it belonged to someone else, while his mind was sluggish, reluctant to think about much at all. Oddly enough, when he did think, his thoughts were not of Hans, but of this strange Japanese policeman in the driving seat.

"Sakamoto-san."

The policeman grunted an acknowledgement but did not turn to look at Zack.

"How long have you been in the police force? If you don't mind me asking."

Sakamoto screwed his face up a little and squinted into the car's visor, as though trying to extract files from an unauthorised sector. It looked painful.

"Ah, I become police in 1962. Tokyo very different-oh."

"Your English is very good. Why is that?"

"Hinh hinh. Thank-you."

This stifled gurgle, which Zack interpreted as a wry chuckle was, apart from his smoking habit and the offer of coffee, the most human element Sakamoto had yet displayed.

"I study at Princeton in USA many years before," he added, without further prompting.

Interesting, Zack thought. "What did you study?"

"Ah you say ah... criminal psychology. And English, yes. I was USA three year."

Since the compliment regarding his English, Zack noticed Sakamoto seemed more willing to speak.

"Have you been back there since?" Zack asked.

"Ah, no."

"Not even for a holiday?" Zack pressed.

"Hinh, hinh." Sakamoto looked across at Zack for the first time, and shook his head once quickly.

Stupid question really, Zack thought. He was sure there mustn't be a Japanese equivalent for the word, 'holiday'. It wasn't in their psyche.

"How come you don't wear a uniform?" Zack was surprised at himself. The questions simply kept popping out, the verbal equivalent of automatic writing or something.

Sakamoto looked across at him again somewhat curiously, and there was a substantial pause before he answered."Different-oh depart-oh-ment-oh."

The former official distance was back in place, and the pause, together with Sakamoto's tone, suggested the shutters were down again. Never mind, Zack thought. What did it matter? It was unusual that Sakamoto had answered his questions at all. Reflecting on this, he decided the policeman had maybe wanted to make Zack feel more comfortable during what was a distressing experience.

Mulling Sakamoto's responses once again, and recalling the deference accorded him by the uniformed officers, Zack concluded he must occupy a very senior detective or consultant's position in the force. A thirty-six year veteran, qualified early on in criminal psychology at an Ivy League college. Jesus, the guy must be a few steps removed from God in the Tokyo police world.

An uneasy feeling gripped him, and something akin to a cognitive epiphany jump-started Zack's hung-over brain. If that was the case, what the hell was he doing ferrying a piece of shit *gaijin* like Zack, to what would for them usually be a routine ID?

The answer clubbed him in the head. It obviously wasn't a routine ID! Sakamoto must want to *watch Zack*. To study him! This realisation shocked him. What did someone like Sakamoto want with him? Why was it important to witness his reactions? Was he a *suspect*?

Zack straightened up a little in his seat and forced his brain to think. *Why* would they think Zack might have had something to do with Hans's death? He was now sure Hans must have been murdered. But how? And by whom? Zack suddenly wished he hadn't got so trashed last night. He hated his brain not working at full capacity when he needed it to.

* * *

The building was like a hundred thousand others in Tokyo. Nothing about it gave away the fact that it provided temporary accommodation for dead people. Except perhaps the sign, which was obviously in Japanese. Zack didn't know what it said. They had travelled for about twenty minutes. Traffic had been light, which given the amount of snow lying around, had made their journey easier. After their first conversational exchange, the rest of the trip had been talk free. All Zack knew was that they were in a place called *Kasumigaseki*.

He swung his door open and got out, his boots crunching ice clusters on the ground. There was a vast temperature difference between the car's interior and the open air. Zack put his exposed hands quickly into his pockets. Mist left his mouth with each hot breath.

Apart from feeling a little queasy, he was now about as ready as he ever would be for something like this. Sakamoto got out, re-blipped the vehicle, lit another cigarette. Zack found himself slightly touched. It could only have been out of consideration for him that the journey had not been a total Dutch-oven.

In Japan, so entrenched was the smoking culture, that non-smokers were almost regarded with suspicion. And the smokers generally didn't stop for anyone. With this in mind, Zack didn't mind a short wait in the cold whilst his chaperone fed his addiction. Sakamoto took a few long, deep tokes, then regretfully, as if snuffing out a friendship, stamped the remaining half out underfoot. Obviously, Zack thought, smoking would not be well received within the building.

Burying his hands into the pockets of his black military-style greatcoat, Sakamoto moved to the front doors of the building, rang the buzzer, and motioned Zack to follow. The door was opened by a young Japanese woman, who bowed deeply to Sakamoto before stepping away to allow them through.

They were in a small reception room like any other. *Manga* comic-books, along with various other waiting-room-style magazines, lay in ordered sections on and under a glass-topped rectangular coffee table. There was nobody else there. Sakamoto had moved across to the counter and was scribbling something into a book, whilst Zack studied the room. The girl retreated behind the counter, and having spoken briefly into the intercom, was now fishing around in a box for something.

Sakamoto turned to Zack. "We must-ah sign, Zack-oh."

As Sakamoto said this, a middle-aged Japanese man in thick black-rimmed glasses and a three-quarter length white coat appeared noiselessly in the foyer. He stood, waiting. He did not meet Zack's gaze. Zack moved to the register and made his mark in the appropriate places. In the meantime Sakamoto formally greeted the man; they exchanged a few terse sentences in Japanese.

The girl smiled shyly at Zack and handed Sakamoto two badges on which Zack assumed the *Kanji* symbols meant 'visitor' or 'guest' or something similar. After clipping their badges on, Sakamoto bowed curtly to the receptionist and followed their new acquaintance's lead back down the hallway from which he had appeared. Zack followed. Seeing the clinical looking guy in the white coat had rattled him a bit. Zack wiped sweat from his forehead. He could feel his heart beating faster ... *Hans was in here, on a slab.*

They walked about twenty metres before stopping at a lift. The doors opened smoothly, and their guide pressed B3. Zack noticed the buttons went down to B5: the building more underground than above it. How appropriate, he thought with a shudder. Being underground always gave him the creeps.

The doors opened. The trio stepped into what was a wider hallway, which seemed to be designed for large trolleys or the like. The man took them to the right, and as they walked, Zack became aware that something about the lighting here was different from the floor they'd just left. Concealed electrical systems hummed with subtle insistence, heightening Zack's impression of the building as a self-contained living organism, squatting, more than half buried in sodden ground.

They stopped beside a pair of grey, swinging double-doors, each with a small square window at about head height. The windows were reinforced with criss-crossed wire. Zack had always wondered why they did that. With a nod, the man went through, leaving Sakamoto and Zack standing outside.

"So, Zack. You are okay?" Sakamoto's pale eyes looked even stranger in this light. Perhaps he wore contact-lenses.

Zack snapped at him, suddenly angry. "Of course I'm not fucking okay, for Christ's sake!" Gesturing violently at the double doors, he heard his own voice echo around the humming hallways. It sounded weirdly shrill. "One of my best friends is maybe lying in there on a fucking slab." Zack took a deep breath and tried to get a hold of himself.

Sakamoto waited patiently, his eyes mostly on the floor. He glanced up briefly at Zack every now and then, until Zack, finally in near control of his voice, said, "Okay, let's do this thing."

Zack followed Sakamoto inside, and White-Coat hurried across to them from a curtained-off section on the other side of the room. He now wore dark green rubber boots. These complemented the rest of his outfit perfectly, Zack thought, as he took the place in. A pungent smell assaulted his nasal passages, the most overpowering component of which seemed to be antiseptic bleach.

White-Coat spoke briefly to Sakamoto in Japanese. Sakamoto merely nodded. They were in a large, predominantly white room full of stainless steel fittings and opaque green plastic curtains. The curtains were suspended from metal rods fastened to the ceiling. Three walls of the room looked more or less normal.

The one nearest to them however, on the left as they walked in, comprised two stainless steel blocks about two metres high by five metres long. These lay lengthways side by side, and fit perfectly along the room's width.

Each block comprised two rows of six metal-handled doors. Zack suddenly realised he was looking at refrigerated storage for twenty-four dead people.

White-Coat led them over to the second refrigerated block. The engraved tag in the metal above the door read B4. They must have been imported from an English speaking country Zack surmised. Probably the States.

With this thought, Zack realised his mind was doing all it could to avoid addressing the reality of where he was, and what was about to happen.

Sakamoto looked at him with raised eyebrows. "Zack-oh. You ready?"

Zack nodded, trying not to think.

White-Coat pulled B4's metal handle and the door opened. Reaching inside, he slid out the platform about a metre. Being one of the top row cubicles, it came out at lower chest height for Zack. A black, heavy-plastic body-bag lay on the metal surface. With a quick nod from Sakamoto, White-Coat unzipped it about half a metre.

The image before him seared itself into Zack's consciousness. His stomach and his mind rebelled in unison. Doubling over, Zack vomited violently onto the pristine antiseptic floor. He staggered away a few paces, struggling to steady his breathing, and wiped the sweat from his brow with his sleeve.

His mind was reeling. *Why? Why was this happening? It was monstrous!* He felt Sakamoto's hand on his shoulder and lashed out, beyond care. Spinning around, Zack grabbed the man by both shoulders, slammed him into the stainless steel doors, screaming the question at him.

"WHERE'S HIS FUCKING BODY, YOU ASSHOLE?"

The only thing in that bag was Hans's severed head.

Thirty-Six

The big screen in front of Fumiko was impossible to ignore. Their home-cinema system was state of the art: Toshiko never had anything but the best. Every pixel and sound of the amateur digital recording was larger than life. Tied to a wire fence, Hans slumped forward, Christ-like.

Two of Toshiko's men were taking turns hitting his face with a cosh. Hans was naked. Even covered in blood he was beautiful, she thought. The blood had trickled down each side of his chest, with rivulets making inroads across the sharply defined abdominal muscles of his stomach.

Fumiko was surprised at how calm she now felt. On the first screening, everything in her stomach had come up. She knew this because nothing else had come up during her attempts since. The dry retching had finally stopped, her panicked hysteria eventually dying away. But it had taken five or six screenings. Numbness and grief were her only companions now. She'd realised this was all of Hans she had left, so she watched, transfixed by pain. His, and hers.

She knew the video by heart now, had studied it intimately these past few hours. Every so often her husband barked, and the thugs would direct a few blows to Hans's lower sections. She supposed they were trying to get him to scream some more. It looked to be a futile goal, and she could see the thugs had started to lose their taste for this most savage of beatings.

Hans's original screams of fear and pain had soon turned to low accepting moans, but now even that sound was gone; there was just the grunting of men along with a dull thud each time their weapons hit flesh. Incredibly, Hans was still moving, still conscious.

"*Yamete!*"

She watched as her husband ordered his employees to stop. Toshiko approached Hans and threw a bucket of water over him. She didn't know if it was hot or cold. It cleared some of the blood anyway. She could see his face now. Toshiko barked another order and his men moved swiftly to cut Hans down.

He slumped to the ground, and as they dragged him to his feet, Fumiko could see her lover was sobbing. She could also hear him. His body shook violently, convulsively. It could have been anything ... cold, shock, fear; she would never know. Because the video was about to end.

But then it would start all over again. Hours ago, she had given up trying to escape her constraints but now flexed her hands again because she could feel them going numb. How many more times would he make her watch this? Why didn't he just kill her? That must be what he wanted, surely? Fumiko closed her eyes but briefly. The ecstasy that final release would bring was all she could think about. There was nothing left for her now. Not in this world.

They dragged Hans a short distance. The camera followed this movement and Fumiko closed her eyes again to say yet another small prayer. The men lifted Hans from the ground and slung him onto a waist-high bench. The bench was one of those long, thick, wooden types used for gutting fish. The men went about securing Hans to it.

She wondered which warehouse it was in: it could be any one of a hundred Toshiko owned. Her husband turned and glared into the camera. His eyes shone, almost messianically, and she no longer recognised the man she'd married years before. He wasn't there anymore.

"Honour!" Toshiko thundered at her through the camera.

The sword she did recognise. From the *Kamakura* period, it was more than seven hundred years old and had been in Toshiko's family for generations. A thing of exquisite beauty, it was so sharp that a piece of rice paper would be cut in two by merely falling onto the blade. The ornament usually never left their holiday home in *Kyoto*; it was only for special occasions.

It looked far more than ornamental in her husband's hands right now. Toshiko barked another order. One man moved to the gutting bench and turned Hans's head towards the camera. Although one eye was completely closed, or covered with blood, the other widened and darted about as he tried to see what was happening around him.

Although his body was still shivering, Hans didn't look as terrified as before, Fumiko thought, and she wondered if he might at that moment have thought the worst was over. The camera changed position slightly and zoomed in as her husband stepped towards the bench. By this time Hans's functional eye was fixed on Toshiko, mesmerised by the shiny sword. The penny having dropped, a grotesque fear now took over.

"Nooooo ... pleeaaaazzzzee ... noo ...hunh hunh hunh ... nooooh mooorre."

Hans's broken body instinctively tried to move, but the straps bit into his flesh; he was going nowhere. With a nod from Toshiko, one of the men pulled Hans by the hair, stretching his neck in a clean line. Seeing that gesture and response, Fumiko wondered whether her husband had executed people like this before.

She already knew he was an expert swordsman. He practised martial arts daily before commencing business duties, and she recollected tournament *Kendo* victories over men half his age. The *Samurai* sword he now held was very much an extension of his own body.

Had he been a killer when she married him? If not, when had he started? How many men had he killed or was he responsible for killing? How could she have married this monster, shared her heart, her bed, and her life with him? Fumiko had no answers for any of these questions.

Moving a few steps closer to Hans, Toshiko brought the sword down slowly in a graceful arc, resting the edge on an unbloodied section of Hans's neck. A small line of blood immediately appeared, and Hans's eyes rolled as grunting sounds of animal terror escaped his throat.

Toshiko removed the sword slowly and raised it high above his head, with the shaft kinked back at an angle. He had his line. Hans's body twitched and strained in terrified desperation; Fumiko knew he could see his death in her husband's eyes.

A blur of movement and the sword came down with dizzying speed. It appeared effortless, slicing as cleanly through Hans's neck as a razor through butter. His last scream died in his throat. Without the torso's support, Hans's head rolled forward, then rested, slightly askew on the bench. An initial blood spurt from his neck soaked the back of his head, before the rest spilled onto the gutting bench in ever decreasing pulses. Toshiko paused a moment, then calmly withdrew the sword from the soiled wooden surface.

As the camera zoomed in closer on Hans's now vacant expression, Fumiko watched her lover's blood spread across the bench like a dark oil slick.

Thirty-Seven

Zack sat alone on the floor beside the entry to the basement morgue, head in hands, elbows on knees. Sakamoto was in hushed conversation with White-Coat, who, after several furtive glances in Zack's direction, exchanged bows with Sakamoto and left them alone. *With Hans's head.* That image would stay with Zack forever.

Even though he knew they must have cleaned it up, the severed head was horrific. That it was Hans there was no doubt. The decomposition was not far gone enough to have erased all recognisable features on what now was nothing more than a lump of flesh, bone and brain. His skin was marbled white, but with an awful greenish pallor. And so wrinkled!

It was the twisted face of an old man, not Hans, potent, young and strong. Wizened sections of the face looked to have been eroded, and his eyes were missing. The yawning empty sockets had shocked him; there was something unearthly about a face without eyes. Zack felt drained, wasted. Nothing else could ever bother him; he had seen too much.

There was a sound. He looked up to see Sakamoto standing in front of him. There was a long silence, which Zack eventually broke.

"Why didn't you tell me?" More silence. "Why did you do that to me?" Zack's voice was flat, even, sterile. He just wanted to know.

Sakamoto cleared his throat uncomfortably. "I ahh, must-oh see. If you surprise or not. Maybe you-ah know something." He shrugged his shoulders slightly. "This was necessary. I sorry."

Zack looked at the policeman with undisguised contempt. "So Sakamoto, what do you think now? Do you think I had a fight with my best friend, things got a bit heated, so I killed him and *cut his fucking head off!*"

His voice had risen in intensity, and echoed loudly in the deathly quiet basement. He got to his feet without waiting for an answer. "Well you got what you wanted. I played your sick fucking game. Now get me the hell out of here."

Zack turned and strode back to the elevator. Sakamoto followed without another word.

Back in the car, Zack felt an extraordinary sense of relief. The not-knowing was over. He was also utterly convinced this monstrousness, whatever it was, had nothing to do with him. Even someone like Max wasn't psychotic enough to go around cutting the heads off uninvolved strangers whose only crime was being friendly with Zack. No. This was something altogether different. Thank Christ Sofia hadn't had to see that today! He could at least be grateful for that.

He wondered whether they'd investigated him at all: if Sakamoto had any inkling of Zack's Roppongi sideline? Was the fact he was close to Hans the *only* reason they had pulled that surprise stunt in the morgue? No wonder Sakamoto had wanted Zack to do the ID. They would never have had the balls to put a woman through something like that.

There would be no point anyway, Zack supposed. Not many women, least of all one like Sofia, would be capable of such an act. Zack suddenly realised he was scared. It had taken more than one man to abduct and kill Hans. The question was why? He felt quite light-headed.

Turning to Sakamoto he said, "I'm assuming you haven't found his body?"

Sakamoto started a little. Zack's sudden query after such a lengthy and stony silence had wrong-footed him. "No." He hesitated. "No body."

"Where did you find … his head?" *Surreal.* How incredible to be talking in this way about his best friend in Tokyo.

Sakamoto hesitated again, evidently considering whether or not to release this information. Finally he spoke. "Tokyo Bay." He simultaneously shot Zack a quick glance.

Ever the professional, Zack thought, remaining deliberately poker-faced. Nothing more was said for the remainder of the trip.

Once back at the station, Zack was required to sign a number of official documents attesting to the fact that he had positively identified the remains as belonging to Hans Overmeyer. The personal details section had already been completed, as Zack and Sofia had previously turned in Hans's passport. As he numbly signed the final page, Sakamoto spoke again.

"Zack-oh, we need-ah Han personal things. We must-oh contact family."

Zack realised what he was asking. They would need access to the apartment. Hans was no longer just a missing person. This was now a murder investigation. Someone had to tell Sofia first. Jesus! Better him than the police. He would have to do it today. Now.

He looked at Sakamoto wearily. "Give me two hours. I'll tell Sofia. I'll tell her to expect you. When, actually?"

"Five o'clock," Sakamoto replied. He looked pretty fed up too, Zack thought.

Zack's eyes narrowed. "And do me a favour," he said acidly. "Don't tell her anything you don't have to. It's going to be terrible enough as it is." Checking his watch he discovered it was two-thirty. He got up to leave.

Sakamoto nodded almost imperceptibly, then offered Zack his hand. Zack looked at the hand in surprise for a moment. Then he shook it firmly. Tears springing in his eyes, he hurriedly excused himself and walked out onto the street.

Turning left, he hastened down *Roppongi-Dori* towards *Nishi-Azabu* crossing. He would go back to his place first of all. He speed-dialled Sofia at home; it rang out. So he called her mobile.

"Hello."

"Sofia, it's me."

"I know. What's going on?"

She didn't sound too bad, Zack thought. "Where are you, babe?"

"I'm taking a walk in *Yoyogi-Park* right now. I had to get out of the apartment. This whole thing's driving me crazy. I've got that fucking lunatic Yamazaki phoning me non-stop. He's left about ten messages. Someone's following me. And I'm pretty sure someone's been spying on the apartment as well. I don't know who the fuck it is. I'm scared, Zack."

Probably Sakamoto's boys, Zack thought. At least he hoped it was.

"Watching the apartment? Really? Look Sofia, we should talk. Can you meet me?"

"What, now?"

"Yeah babe, now. How about you meet me right in front of the *Meiji-shrine*?"

"Oooh Zack, the *Meiji-shrine*. You going all spiritual on me?"

"Yeah, something like that. Look, I'll be there at three, okay? Can you be there by then?"

"Yes Zack, no problem. I'll be there."

As soon as Zack hung up, his phone trilled at him.

"Yeah, Zack here," he answered.

"Ho ho ho, big bro! And a merry Christmas t'you, y'ugly bastard. How's tricks?"

Jesus Christ, Zack thought. It was Josh, in a properly trolleyed condition. Zack calculated the time in France. Josh must not even have been to bed yet.

"Ahm, hi mate. Merry Christmas to you too. How's it going?"

"S'goin' fuckin brill. Wickid party last night on toppa the mountain. Snow-boarded into the village this morning. Wickid, wicked. Juss having a few morning tequilas with the crew. Heli-boarding trip this arvo. It is all cool."

Given Josh's condition, Zack found the idea of him boarding a helicopter at all, let alone jumping from it, onto a mountain, strapped to a snowboard, quite disturbing.

"Sounds like you'll need some kip before then bro."

"No, no, no. Sleeping 'snot required until tomorrow."

"Well, be a bit fucking careful okay."

Zack didn't want to cut Josh short, but he couldn't have this conversation right now. He hated lying to his brother, but he couldn't continue this conversation and *not talk* about what was happening here. Either way he had to lie, because now was simply not the time to bring Josh down with the grim realities unfolding in Zack's world.

"Listen Josh, I'm going into a tunnel on the Underground. I'm probably going to lose you, so I'll wish you the best for the season and all that bullshit, and I'll call you back soon. We can talk properly then, okay?"

"Yeah, yeah, yeah, I've heard it all before. Alright brother, I'm going now. Have a good one. Adieu."

There was a click, then nothing. Zack looked disconsolately at his phone. He could tell he'd hurt his brother's feelings. Josh's use of 'adieu' rather than the more positive 'au-revoir' more or less confirmed it. He would have to explain, and soon.

Hailing the first cab, he directed it to *Omotesandō*. Fuck. This was without a doubt one of the all-time most cunted days of his life. It was hard to believe he'd only been out of bed four hours.

Sofia was sitting on steps in front of the famous shrine as he walked up the pathway from *Meiji-Dori*. Zack steeled himself for the task that lay ahead. He took a deep breath and covered the remaining distance between them.

"Hey pretty girl."

Sofia pushed her hands together at bosom-level, and gave him a little bow. "*Zack-san, genki desu-ka?*"

Zack wrapped her up in a hug. He had decided not to mess about. He was just going to tell her. Disengaging himself, he stepped back. "Not so good actually babe, not so good."

He took another deep breath. "I've got some really bad news sweetheart."

As soon as their eyes met, he could see she knew. Zack merely nodded a confirmation. Tears instantly formed in her eyes. He moved to hold her again but Sofia backed away, hands in the air.

"No Zack! How do they … know for sure? Maybe it's somebody else."

The hope in her voice broke Zack's heart, and he felt tears coming to his own eyes again. He forced himself to shut the door on her hopes. "No Sofia, I've seen him. I've just been with the police. It's Hans. He's dead, Sofia."

She still had her hands raised in futile defence. They had begun to shake. Tears squeezed out of her closed eyes as she continued to back away. Zack stood helplessly, able only to watch.

Sofia collapsed onto the steps. Legs clasped to her chest, face on knees, she rocked her body. Forward and back, forward and back, sobs punctuating each change of direction.

Zack sat close beside her, but left her alone. A few passers-by noticed the scene and whispered to each other, before hurrying on.

"How did he die?" Sofia's question came quietly, and without looking up.

"They don't know yet babe; they have to do an autopsy."

That wasn't a lie really, but Zack wouldn't hesitate to lie if he had to. Sofia didn't need to know the gruesome truth right now, if ever.

"Sofia, the police are contacting his family. They need to check his personal things from the apartment. They're coming at five, and I told them you'll be there to let them in and help."

The barest of nods.

"If you don't want to do it, I will. You can stay out until it's all over. But I don't want them to take any of your stuff by mistake; you know what I mean?"

She nodded again, then raised her head. The tears were gone. She looked to have settled.

"It doesn't matter. I'm getting out of here: I'll be packing my stuff as well. I'm going home for a while I think."

"Home?" Zack echoed. It was an odd concept for him these days. "What ... Sweden?"

"Yes."

They sat silently for some time. Zack had started to feel the cold, when Sofia spoke.

"What will you do?"

Zack hesitated. He didn't know really. As usual, he hadn't given his future much thought. His decisions always seemed to somehow make themselves.

"I don't know anymore, Sofia," he sighed. "Carla is the most important thing in my life at the moment. I want to stay with her, whatever it takes really. We'll have to talk about it. I think she feels the same way. I hope she does anyway."

Sofia looked at Zack, her face a mask of bitterness. "You guys should get out of here too. Roppongi is a bad place Zack. After something like this, it can never be the same."

Zack was about to speak, but she cut him off.

"You don't *need* to be here anymore! What do you want? *More money*? You should take Carla to meet your family or something ... or go and meet hers. Do something positive that involves getting the hell out of this demented fucking place."

Her words tumbled out. "You should trust me on this, Zack. I know you probably think I'm hysterical. And maybe I am. Who knows? Don't get me wrong. I'm glad to have experienced this Roppongi-world and I know shit happens, but I'm telling you ... it is time to *get out of here*."

Zack shivered, only partly because of the cold. "I'm fucking freezing Sofia. Let's get some soup or something."

He put an arm around her, they rose as one, and headed along *Meiji-Dori* to his favourite *tempura* restaurant.

Thirty-Eight

Outside Almond coffee-shop in Roppongi, Zack stood, still shivering with cold in spite of the recent *miso* soup, *tempura* and a warm train ride. Sofia had just left for home, after a quick hard hug goodbye. He'd offered to go with her, but she wanted to be alone. And after hearing about Hans, she was sure it had to be the police keeping an eye on the apartment. Zack had reluctantly let her go. Sakamoto was waiting for her, after all. He shivered again. The evening chill had set in with malice, and his clothing no longer seemed adequate. Grunting disgustedly, Zack capitulated to the cold and strode inside the garish pink and white striped cafe.

It was only his second time inside the place. For some reason, probably the prices and the bright lighting, *gaijin*s were rarely to be found in Almond, and this evening was no different. Zack grimly ignored the bowing smiling robots at the counter, and went to the far side of the room, plonking himself down at a corner table next to the window. Just a few minutes respite from the cold to make a phone-call to Carla. That's all he wanted from this overpriced coffee and cake shop. After the way he'd looked at them on the way in, he doubted they'd even approach him for an order.

"Hey babe," he said, when Carla answered.

"Hi gorgeous," came the reply. "Where have you been? And what's this sneaking out on me without even a goodbye kiss?"

She could have been teasing him. Or not. Zack couldn't tell.

"Don't start on me sweetie. We've got to talk. Today has been hell. What time do you start work?" He was talking too quickly. Too harshly. It was all wrong.

"Are you okay Zack? What's wrong babe? You sound awful."

Zack tried to stop the tears coming. But they came anyway. Hot and fast. Putting his head down, he turned away from the other tables. He tried to speak but failed, grunting something unintelligible instead.

"Zack, you tell me where you are right now! What's going on?" Carla was frantic.

"Hans is dead, baby. Hans is dead." Zack couldn't stop his sobbing. His breath was laboured. "They fucking killed him. The fucking murderers fucking killed him. He's dead Carla."

He stopped talking, his body jerking between sobs. Jesus Christ. Now he had the hiccups. Zack fought to get his shit together, mopping his face ineffectually with a waterproof sleeve.

"I'm coming (hic), to your place, now baby. (Hic), I just wanted to (hic), make sure you were (hic), home. I'll see (hic), see you soon."

"Zack where are ..."

He terminated the call, dropped the phone onto the table, and tried to bring his breathing back to normal. Then he picked it up again, and quickly texted Carla that he was coming to her place. Using paper serviettes, he dried his face, before visiting their toilet. Thankfully it was empty. Another mirror. Zack regarded his reflection, appalled.

Great fucking performance, Zack. Just fucking *great*. That's it mate. Wait until you get home and break it to her gently. Nah ... stupid idea. Why not just crack up on the phone into a dribbling bawling baby and blurt everything out like a fucking drama queen. Way to go. Asshole. Now she'd be out of her mind with worry. Zack slapped the wall hard with the palm of his hand, and felt it sting satisfyingly. At least that was a real feeling. What the fuck was wrong with him?

In the cab on the way to Carla's, Zack debated again if he was in shock. 'Shock' was something he'd always scoffed at. Some abstraction invented by cops and paramedics to justify treating people like retards. But he had no better explanation for his present state of mind. He felt very fragile, and surely needed a good night's sleep. He knew he'd be a disaster at work. He couldn't even imagine working. Smiling, and serving drinks? It was unthinkable. He got out his phone again, and called one of Steve's back-up staff in to cover for him tonight at Bongoes. His shift didn't start until ten, so it wasn't too tragic for the guy. Steve would be pissed off, but the evening would be slow anyway. Even if it was Saturday. Always was on Boxing Day. He'd call Steve and explain the whole story tomorrow. In fact, he might even take a few days off. He should, really. Well, he'd think about it tomorrow with a fresh head on his shoulders.

When Carla opened the front door, Zack saw she'd been crying. They stood for a moment, assessing each other.

"Give me a hug, hey baby? I need one." Zack's voice wobbled.

Tears welled in Carla's eyes, seeing her man, so un-manned.

"Don't you do that to me again, Zack Morrissey," she whispered.

Stepping forward, she pulled Zack inside and wrapped herself around him as tightly as she could.

Another whisper. "Don't do that to me again. You scared me Zack."

"I'm sorry, baby. I'm so sorry," Zack whispered back.

He buried his face in her neck, smelling her hair, her skin, a scent of jasmine and camomile. He felt that familiar tightness in his chest building, and struggled to keep himself together.

They hugged each other for a long time.

Thirty-Nine

Max sat in the hotel lobby-bar, waiting. It was two forty-five, Sunday afternoon. Henry and Oju stood a few paces away, watching him. Their new suits were chafing, and they shuffled their feet nervously. Usually so calm, Max was nervous and irritable, and they were not used to it.

Max impatiently swirled the remnants of his third Chivas Regal, and downed it. What the fuck was going on! For nearly an hour they'd been waiting for these slope-eyed cunts to admit them to the scheduled two o'clock meeting. They were playing with him, fucking playing with him! And fuck it, he couldn't do a thing about it. He just had to take it up the dumper like a boy-whore.

It was enough to drive a man mad! How was he supposed to build an empire here, when being treated like a fucking minion? Respect? They didn't know the meaning of the word. What was it with these fucking *Yakuza*? Didn't they understand he could help them? That working together they'd consistently access the whole market, not just bits and pieces of it from time to time? Fuck it, they'd *make* markets where none had been before, for God's sake! *It was all so clear to him.*

He just had to make it clear to them. That he was here to stay. That he was here to succeed. And that they could make huge money, risk-free, simply by empowering and assisting him. But he couldn't make his case sitting here on his own in a fucking hotel bar! Goddamnit! What the fuck were they waiting for?

Mako had been watching the three Nigerians since they'd entered the hotel. Well, since before then really. He knew when they'd left Roppongi, and how. The seemingly random taxi they'd taken was a plant, so as planned, he'd listened to their conversation in the cab. He knew Max had ignored the no-smoking sign and physically threatened the driver. The *Hausa* they had spoken had already been translated for him; that Max hated Japanese people came as no surprise.

Within seconds of Max having sat at the lobby table, a vase of fresh flowers had been placed upon it by a staff-member. Had the flowers been turned away, an ashtray would have sufficed. Allowed to remain, the vase's hidden microphone had transmitted nothing but silence, save the initial order of Chivas Regal. However, with the added benefit of video surveillance, Mako could see Max was a frustrated man in a strange country.

He took another sip of iced water and smiled. He was pleased his father had finally agreed to allow this meeting, and even happier to have been granted authority to run it. He'd asked for it specifically. Takahashi-san had come down hard on him recently, especially since his car accident in San Francisco.

He smiled ruefully. The F40 Ferrari was unfortunately a write-off, but Mako had somehow emerged from the wreck without a scratch. Somebody up there must like him. His father had taken it as a sign, a good omen, a second chance. Mako pursed his lips thoughtfully.

For someone with the business acumen and ruthlessness of his father, Mako found his random superstitious beliefs incongruous. No matter. It had certainly done his prospects no harm, although his leash had since been considerably shortened. Despite his recently curtailed freedom, Mako had enormous respect for his father. And once more it seemed well-founded.

Takahashi senior's judgment had been borne out with this Nigerian troublemaker. Three months they'd kept Max waiting for a meeting. And now, so close, he was waiting a little longer. Takahashi's ability to keep in touch with the little things was indeed remarkable. No ivory-tower syndrome there, Mako thought. His father remembered the streets from whence he'd come. Times may have changed, but the rules of the game remained the same.

A small cough from his right-hand-man, Harada-san, brought Mako's attention back to the monitor. The time-display read 14:55. It was enough. Mako nodded to the head of security, who bowed deeply. A similarly uniformed underling tapped a panel and an electronic door slid aside. Mako and his entourage of four exited and took the private elevator directly to the penthouse.

He breathed in deeply as they entered the sumptuously appointed top-floor suite. He'd always loved this hotel: it held good memories for him. He'd been twelve years old when his father had built it.

The suite itself was unbelievably lush. More luxury and beauty in one dwelling was probably not possible, Mako thought. The designer's brief had been simple: Louis XIV, spare no expense. With this in mind, for it to have escaped even a hint of Trump-esquian vulgarity was tribute enough.

Muramoto was the designer's name, and Mako thought it a great pity he was now dead, not least because he'd been such good friends with Mako's father. What he had achieved here was breathtaking.

The penthouse consisted of four double bedrooms with en-suite bathrooms. These were upstairs, along with quarters for a chef, butler and maid. The north-facing master bedroom featured a glass-enclosed balcony area for dining, above which lay an enormous tinted skylight with electronic shutters. Overlooking the pool-deck of the entertaining area downstairs, it also adjoined a drawing-room and study featuring state of the art computer facilities.

Downstairs, the main living room opened onto the pool-deck via exquisite remote-controlled French-doors. It abutted a formal dining room whose huge oval table comfortably sat twenty. Beyond lay the kitchen, in which more than a few Michelin-starred chefs had felt spoilt. No laundry space was required. A general laundry chute, as well as one in each bedroom and bathroom, deposited soiled laundry into five separate baskets in the hotel basement. These baskets were checked and their contents laundered, every thirty minutes. The servants were then buzzed, and laundered items would be returned to their room of origin.

The servants themselves were permanent residents, and ensured every aspect of the suite remained in immaculate condition. As a meeting venue, it could intimidate or impress in equal measure, depending on the guest. Today would necessitate a measure of both.

When the bell-hop arrived at Max's table and announced, "Follow me please. Takahashi-san is waiting," it was all Max could do not to strangle him on the spot. Seething, he got to his feet and followed as requested. Tweedle-dum and Tweedle-dumber fell into lock-step behind him.

The bell-hop stopped abruptly. He turned to face Max. "I'm sorry sir. My instructions are that you must come alone."

Max felt his blood rising, but was impotent in the face of this annoying insect. "Wait for me in the bar for an hour and a half," he ordered his underlings. "If I'm not back by then," and here he paused, pinning the insect with an icy stare, "you can have this *gentleman* escort you to me whether he likes it or not. Failing that, advise the embassy."

Max turned back to the insect. "Come on then. Now move it."

Unflappable and unperturbed, the bell-hop glided towards the private lift.

Max followed, and tried not to let the insect's Zen-like demeanour bother him. He was more curious about this hidden lift, which had suddenly materialised from behind a sliding electronic panel. He watched in fascination as a code was entered to gain access, not failing to notice the insect had discreetly shielded his view of the touchpad.

Max looked around the lift's interior. It was plush maroon velvet with a gold braid trim. Very regal, he thought. It reminded him of a private club he'd once visited in London. The instrument panel consisted of an LCD display and a *Kanji* inscription next to one green button. The insect pushed it. Before Max had time to puzzle over the lack of buttons, he realised they were moving, and fast. About fifteen seconds later the lift chimed and the doors opened.

Facing Max was a tall, silver-haired Caucasian man of about sixty. This was surprising enough. That the man was attired in livery, left Max temporarily gob-smacked.

"Good afternoon sir. My name is Albert. Might I take your jacket, perhaps?"

Max couldn't believe his ears! The man had a plum the size of Belgravia in his mouth. It was as if Max had stepped through the looking glass and into the Royal Box at Ascot. This chap would shame the Duke of Edinburgh's personal equerry! Max's dark mood suddenly fell away, forgotten.

He felt strangely disorientated. In the face of such formal British courtesy, his own public school training re-asserted itself reflexively.

"Ahm, yes," he heard himself say. "That would be lovely. Thank you."

"Not at all, sir."

The butler helped him out of his camel-coloured cashmere overcoat, folded it neatly over his arm, opened the polished rosewood double-doors, and showed Max through to the suite. Max gasped in spite of himself. He stopped dead, and gazed around the penthouse in awe. Artwork, statues, bookcases, furnishings and display cabinets complemented a living room which was at least three times the size of Max's entire apartment. Max recognised at least two paintings, a Rubens and a Titian. He had no doubt they were originals.

"Sir?" Realising he'd mislaid his charge, Albert had returned.

"Yes, of course." Max forced his feet to move, and followed the butler's lead.

"Mr. Takahashi thought you may wish to freshen up a little. I will be outside when you finish." Albert held open the door to a bathroom area, and gestured for Max to enter. Still stunned, he did so automatically. Albert withdrew, and closed the door.

Max leaned back against the closed door; he was still taking in the opulence of his surroundings. With a deep breath, he gathered his thoughts. This was unbelievable. Who the fuck was this Takahashi guy?

He had expected to be taken seriously by the *Yaks*, but not at this level. Well, not so soon anyway. They must hold him in higher esteem than he'd dared hope. How stupid he'd been. And how impatient.

Max cringed inwardly, remembering his undignified frustration in the lobby. That mustn't happen again. He shouldn't have been drinking either. Flicking on the tap, he washed his face with warm water, then rinsed it with cold to sharpen himself. Towelling his face dry, he peered in the mirror and muttered grimly, "This is it tough guy. Don't fuck it up!"

He looked around for a place to dispose of his towel. No basket was obvious. Then he saw the silver flap marked 'Laundry Please'. It was also denoted in five other languages. Max whistled in amazement, dropped the towel in, and listened to it disappear silently into the void. Another quick check in the mirror. Hard-faced, Max opened the door, ready for action.

Forty

"This way sir," said Albert.

Max fell into line once more. They proceeded through the massive living-room to arrive at another set of double doors. Albert opened them and ushered him through. He was surprised to see a youthful, handsome, impeccably dressed Japanese man sitting at the head of an enormous board-room table.

This man was flanked by another on each side, both of whom looked at least ten years older. Two others stood behind them, one in either corner of the room. Slight bulges on the upper left side of their jackets conveyed their function. Max forced himself to stay cool; this was the real deal.

Albert pulled out a chair situated half-way along the table and gestured for Max to sit. Max hesitated. Turning to face those at the head of the table, he bowed respectfully. Then he sat. Albert bowed, and left.

The young man obviously in charge leaned forward, forearms on the table.

"Our time is short, so I'll be brief. I am Takahashi. These gentlemen," nodding to his companions, "work for the organisation I represent."

He paused to let his words sink in. "I understand you have been seeking a meeting with us for some time." Pausing again, he interlocked his fingers, and leaned back. "I'll be blunt with you. I didn't want this meeting. I think it's a waste of our time. But others disagreed." He gave the slightest of shrugs. "So here we are." Removing his arms from the table he raised them slowly, palms up. "The floor is yours, Mr Obitawanu. What do you want?"

Max stiffened at the use of his real name, but then mentally side-stepped it. If that fucker Zack had discovered his identity, he shouldn't be too surprised that the *Yakuza* also knew who he was.

Takahashi then startled him with another abrupt statement. "One piece of advice. There is not a lot we don't know about you. To save yourself any, embarrassment ..." and here he smiled thinly, "I suggest you be completely honest today."

"I have no intention of being otherwise, Takahashi-san," Max said. He looked quickly at each face, and returned his gaze to Takahashi. "In a nutshell, I see an enormous opportunity in Roppongi."

He made deliberate eye-contact with each of his three hosts. "What I want to do is create and manage an organisation which centralises and controls Roppongi's entire drug trade."

Focusing his attention primarily on Takahashi, he launched into his speech.

"With due respect, I assume you are aware of how disorganised the flow of drugs into Roppongi is at the moment. There is no control. There is no consistency of product. Anyone can walk into the scene, and as long as they've got product, they can take their chances. They have only the police and their own stupidity to worry about. Plainly, this is not a good business model."

He paused to reconnect with Takahashi's offsiders. Who knew how much influence they might have?

"What we need is a monopoly. We need to take the amateurs and opportunists completely out of the equation. Make those half-baked idiots understand if they've got anything to sell, it goes through us, or it goes nowhere. They sell it to us wholesale if we want it, or they give up and get out. If they don't play ball, we apply whatever pressure is required until they do. Fear and respect. It is a powerful combination, gentlemen."

Max described a large circle with his hands.

"Roppongi is a huge, ready-made market, and it will be here indefinitely. We can feed it, sustain it, grow it! But before we can do any of that, we have to dominate it. That means closing out the competition."

Max brought his palm down flat on the table for emphasis. "And that, Takahashi-san, is where I need your help." He sat back in the chair, hands now resting in his lap, eyes on Takahashi.

"That's as may be, Mr Obitawanu," Takahashi said indifferently. "As they say in America, opinions are like arseholes: everyone has one." Elbows on the table, he looked coolly at Max over his arched fingers. "Assuming we even agreed with your … theory," the word was ejected distastefully, "I fail to see what you can offer us in return for any cooperation we may choose to provide."

The implication was plain, Max thought. They needed to know he could do the job, they needed to know what he wanted from them, and they needed to know how much money they would make.

"With respect Takahashi-san, I am very experienced in running operations much more complicated than this. In Lagos, I ran about five or six different operations simultaneously, city-wide. Drugs, guns, petroleum, chemicals, prostitutes, protection. You name it, I ran it."

Max held Takahashi's stare. "Given you know my real name, I expect you also know something of my background. You'll therefore know *why* I had to leave Lagos."

He clasped his hands in front of him, prayer-like. Then he laid them down and inclined his head towards Takahashi again.

"Takahashi-san, I need a project to work on here. I can't do it without order, organisation, and discipline. And for this I need your cooperation, plain and simple. This Roppongi project, as I've described it, would be a simple matter for me. You know it, and I know it. It will mean *less work* for your organisation, and the more I control things at street level, the greater the profit. All I need is your backing to establish credibility, open doors, and drive out the two-bit trash. Teach them a lesson if we have to. Perhaps even recruit some of them. However we decide to play it, we will dominate this market, and together, we can make a fortune. To put it bluntly, you and your people have nothing to lose, and everything to gain."

Max looked from face to face with what he hoped was a confident, determined expression. It was met with a prolonged silence.

Eventually, Takahashi spoke. "You've been in Tokyo some time now, doing this *assessment*. Have you identified those people you'd need to ... persuade, yet?"

The atmosphere had softened a little, Max thought. He might be getting somewhere!

"There are four or five of them," Max replied. "One by the name of Yitzhak operates out of Burlesque. Siri, whose territory is around Déjà-Vu. Hiro, who operates from the Sports Café. And there's Miguel the Colombian who deals at a number of venues."

Pausing momentarily, he added, "As you probably know, I've already successfully recruited the Iranians. And needless to say, the Nigerians are now a tight unit under my control."

"What about Zack Morrissey?" Takahashi asked. "He's doing more business than any of those other guys. We understand he's backed by the Israelis."

This took Max a little off-guard. His mind raced. How was he going to talk his way through this one? Goddamn them for being so well informed! He hated doing it, but he'd have to bluff.

"You'll have to forgive me Takahashi-san, but I don't know much about him. My understanding is he's a small-time social dealer, favours for friends, things like that. It's hard to see him being a risk to an operation like ours."

"Clearly then, you haven't done your fucking homework!" Takahashi snapped irritably.

The silence following this rebuke was suffocating. Max, sensing confrontation would not be a positive step, let the silence hang.

Takahashi made a decision. Narrowing his eyes at Max, he said tersely. "You will wait in the main salon. I will speak with my associates. Then we will decide on you."

The two bodyguards moved in unison and escorted Max to the adjacent room. Max looked from one to the other without reward; their stony expressions told him nothing. He sat in one of the lounges, trying not to think about what their presence in this room might mean.

Albert materialised. "Another drink, sir?"

Max nodded. "Yes. Thank-you." To hell with his previous self-admonition. He badly needed a drink. After Albert had delivered his Chivas and left the room, Max turned his attention to the various artworks surrounding him. Good versus evil was a recurrent theme. Angels and devils, the light and the dark, hope and despair. The saved and the damned.

Max had no doubt he was now in the devil's parlour. He tried to ignore the bodyguards, who were as still and silent as statues. Fifteen minutes of Max's life disappeared while he sipped his Chivas Regal. They took a long, long time.

Albert finally reappeared. "Mr. Takahashi will see you now."

Max rose to his feet. The bodyguards remained statues. He followed Albert back into the board-room and resumed his place.

The Japanese gang-lord was alone. Albert bowed once, and departed. Takahashi studied Max intently for a few moments before speaking.

"My associates are impressed with your ideas. Does that please you?" Without waiting for an answer, he continued. "I asked them why we should grant you, a *gaijin*, this privilege. What do you think they said?"

Max was unsure whether an answer was expected of him.

Takahashi got to his feet. "Nothing to say?" He strolled along the other side of the long table until he was standing directly opposite Max. "I don't believe it," he added. The words were sneering.

Max spoke. "I know I can do what I say, if I have your help. Maybe they believe me."

"Maybe they believe me?" Takahashi mimicked him mockingly, then fixed Max with a cold stare.

"We are going to give you a chance. Do you know why?"

Max's heart leapt. Success! He maintained a poker-face and shook his head, silence being more difficult to ridicule.

Takahashi walked back to the head of the table. "Because *maybe* you can do what you say. And *maybe* we can strike a mutually profitable deal." His jaw muscles twitched. He walked towards Max. "You were right when you said we have nothing to lose."

He stood next to Max. "We don't. But you Max," patting him lightly on the shoulder, "do. And you would do very well to remember that. If things work out between us, you'll be king of the streets. That of itself puts a large target on your back, and …"

"I can take care of my own security," Max broke in. The insult was too provocative to let slide. Who did this fucking guy think he was dealing with? Snow White?

Takahashi withered Max with a look of contempt bordering on disgust. He took two short paces and stood behind Max, and spoke to the back of his head.

Inwardly, Max froze. Takahashi's fingers rested with a gentle pressure, on his temples.

"*Gaijin.*" Takahashi's voice was deathly. "You will not make the mistake of interrupting me again." Max could almost feel a cold steel barrel at the base of his skull.

His apology was instant. "Forgive me Takahashi-san. It was a mistake," he said, keeping his head absolutely motionless.

Takahashi removed his hands. Then spoke again, still from behind Max's head. "Listen, and listen well my black friend. You will have your chance. You will be the front-man for this operation. The advantage for us is if anything goes wrong, *you* will take the fall. There will not be so much as a fingerprint of ours to be seen."

Takahashi moved a little, to lean on the table beside him. "And why do I know this? Because you are not a stupid man. If something goes wrong, and you talk, wherever you are, you will be dead within twenty-four hours. As will your men. I would suggest you ensure they understand that fact. You've played this game before, after all. Do you understand me?"

Still maintaining his forward gaze, Max was aware Takahashi had now appeared in the peripheral vision of his left eye. Pushing his chair back slowly, Max got tentatively to his feet and turned to face him. "Yes Takahashi-san, I do."

Takahashi's handshake was cool and dry. Max's palms were sweating. He felt like he'd gone ten rounds with a *sumo*-wrestler. "Takahashi-san, how should we contact each other?"

"*We* don't. Albert will give you a card on your way out. It has a number for Harada-san, my associate. Memorise the number, destroy the card. Call him in twenty-four hours. Use *only* public phones for such calls. You will deal only with him from now on, and you will follow his instructions exactly.

He will inform you regarding the terms of our arrangement. They are not open to negotiation. He will also monitor your performance. Anything you need, information, support, or otherwise, you will notify Harada-san. You and I will never meet again. If you by chance see me in public, you do not know me. Are we clear?"

Takahashi's eyes had the cold certainty that accompanies absolute power. They bored into Max, exploring, probing, seeking weakness. Max wanted to get out. Away from this clinical avatar.

"Perfectly, Takahashi-san. Thank you for your time. You won't regret your decision." He broke eye contact, bowed hurriedly and was about to leave when Takahashi spoke again.

"One more thing Max."

Max stopped, and met that gimlet gaze once more.

"You will leave Zack Morrissey *completely out* of whatever street-operation you decide to run in Roppongi. We will deal with him ourselves, in our own way. This is an order, non-negotiable. Is that clear?"

Max controlled his fury as best he could. *How could it be that this Australian fucker always seemed to slip out of his grasp?*

"Yes, Takahashi-san. Whatever you say."

With a wave of Takahashi's fingers, he was dismissed.

Behind him, the double-doors opened, and Albert appeared. Handing him a card Albert said, "This is for you. Follow me please, sir."

Max glanced around the room. The bodyguards hadn't moved. There was still no sign of Takahashi's two associates. In the elevator, he exhaled deeply. Jesus! What a fucking meeting. He didn't relax until the doors let him into the lobby and he saw the moron-twins. Scowling, he barked at them in *Hausa* and they moved to the forecourt for a cab.

Max stretched his muscles and rolled his head, sharply aware of the tension in his body. He really needed to fuck something.

Forty-One

Mako leaned back in the chair, kicked his shiny shoes off, and put his sock-clad feet on the boardroom table. He inhaled deeply from the Montecristo No. 2 cigar, a habit inherited from his father. Harada sat to his right, smoking a cigarette. Ishi was home with his wife. The bodyguards had gone bowling.

"He thought we were going to shoot him! I'm fucking telling you. He thought we were going to fucking shoot him!" Mako started laughing and couldn't stop. Pungent cigar smoke erupted from his mouth and nostrils, and coughing overtook his original guffaws.

Harada regarded Mako with a curious affection. "You should go to fucking Hollywood, you sick bastard. You're not a gangster, you're a fucking actor." He waggled his finger at Mako. "Why did your father choose me to babysit you? What did I ever do?"

Mako recovered himself, and took another long drag on the cigar. It had recently become a surrogate for other, more insidious narcotics. "Oh, c'mon Harada, lighten up. We've got him holding the bag we're shitting in. What more do we want? It was brilliant. Can't I have a little fun?"

"*You* don't have to deal with him every week," Harada muttered gloomily. "Why did you do that anyway? Offload him on me."

Mako raised his eyebrows in surprise. "Well I obviously can't meet with him! I can't stand the sight of him."

Sensing Harada's gloom may be genuine, Mako swung his feet off the table and sat properly. He did not want to get Harada off-side.

"Look. You don't have to deal with him forever. Set out the terms, meet him the first couple of times, then bump him to someone down the ladder who's hungry and wants to impress you. You know, delegate." Mako waved his arms around vaguely. "I don't know. Junicho maybe? Or Nori? Jesus, you know better than me. There must be half a dozen who'd want the job."

Harada knew Mako was right. He could give this job to any of ten subordinates on the payroll. But that wasn't what troubled him. It was Mako's fluidity. The way he improvised, adapting rules, procedures and situations to suit himself, sometimes purely for amusement value. Today he'd been brilliant, Harada had to admit. The whole set-up had been his idea. They now had this problematic Nigerian on a very tight leash, and on their terms. Considering the nature of the animal, this was nothing short of a small miracle.

But there was a difference between getting the job done efficiently, and getting it done flamboyantly. Mako's need for flamboyance, his showiness, bothered Harada; perhaps because it was so different from the traditional *Yakuza* style. He shot out a jet of cigarette smoke. Who knew, he thought, maybe he was just getting old. But there was one question he definitely wanted answered.

"Why did you protect Zack from this project the savage is going to run in our name? If there is a benefit for us there, I can't see it."

Mako smiled. "Call it instinct Harada-san. What interests me is whatever Zack must have on this monkey." He continued breezily. "Zack should be his biggest target, but Max didn't even mention him. On the contrary, he tried to play him down."

Harada said nothing, indicated nothing.

Mako tapped the side of a temple with his fore-finger. "Zack is a fucking piece of work, I tell you. He's somehow got Max compromised. But I wonder how?"

"Maybe it's Zack who should be fronting this operation?" Harada speculated.

Mako erupted into laughter; cigar smoke billowed throughout the room. "I'd take him on in a heartbeat. But it's impossible. For two reasons. First, he would never do it. He's too much of a loner. Zack's not the sort to take direction. And second, he's basically too nice a guy. It's not his style at all, playing the heavy, making threats, hurting people."

He launched himself upright.

"Zack doesn't do business that way. He's a gentleman." He paced around the table. "He might *look* like a Roppongi party-boy, but he's a professional. Maybe he is *tight* with the Israelis, but he's no gangster. He just has some fun, makes friends, tries not to make enemies, does his business and gets out. He'll be gone in under six months … he told me himself. In and out. No complications. No obligations. Nice, sweet and easy."

Mako exhaled another pall of blue smoke. "Sometimes, I envy him."

* * *

Zack was sipping a fabulous Australian Shiraz, fireside, at Las Chicas. Carla snuggled next to him on the leather lounge, her head resting in his lap. He'd taken indefinite stress-leave from Bongoes until after the New Year. When Steve had heard the details of Hans's death, he'd been more than understanding. He had also promised not to say anything, but Zack knew the Bongoes staff would have put things together by now. Word would get out it was his friend Hans.

After all, it had finally featured in the papers.

Gaijin Murdered – Severed Head Found In Tokyo Bay. Police yesterday confirmed a severed human head was washed up four days ago in a deserted section of Tokyo Bay. The discovery was made by a local fisherman. Pending notification of next of kin, no information has been released as to the identity of the man, who is believed to be a Caucasian in his late twenties or early thirties. Despite an intensive search operation, no other body parts have been recovered. Notwithstanding this, it is believed a positive identification has been made. Another police statement is expected shortly. Anyone with information which may assist police in this investigation should contact Superintendent Sakamoto of the Homicide Division at Nishi-Azabu Police Station.

Zack stroked Carla's hair and watched the flames dance between the fake logs of the open fire-place. No matter how he tried, he could not rid himself of the image of Hans's severed head. It haunted him.

He kept wondering about those last moments. How scared Hans must have been. Had he seen it coming? Or had he been blindfolded? Was he even conscious? Did they torture him first? Sickening, sickening thoughts; they recycled themselves endlessly through Zack's over-active mind.

"When's your visa up babe?" he asked.

Carla stretched, and turned her head to look up at him.

"End of January ... why?"

"Want to introduce me to your folks?"

As if jolted by electricity, she sat up, twisting so she faced Zack, her eyes drilling his like lasers. "Are you serious? Don't bullshit me Zack! You said you wanted to stay until at least June."

Zack put his wine down and took her hand, holding it tightly. "I don't think I can do it anymore babe. I need to get out. Sofia's right, it'll never be the same again. I can't just carry on like nothing's happened."

Carla's eyes sparkled. "So, you want to do the family thing hey? You must be serious about us, *ay mate!*" She accentuated the Canadianism playfully.

Zack smiled. He couldn't imagine ever getting tired of this woman. She was a jewel. He cradled her head gently and kissed her for a long time.

Carla hugged him so hard he gasped.

"I love you, Zack Morrissey," she whispered in his ear. "I love you."

Getting his wind back, Zack held her tight. Once again he felt tears welling in his eyes.

"I love you too, babe."

Forty-Two

Zack had awoken, alone, in Carla's bed. Under the circumstances, he felt almost buoyant; akin to a successful escapee. Having made the decision to abandon the good ship Roppongi, the angst and sense of foreboding which had been dogging him, had partially lifted.

He still felt jaded and empty, but freer. And oddly, somehow *cleaner*. He wondered what had taken him so long. Why had that simple decision to *get out*, seemed so *difficult*?

He suddenly couldn't wait to leave this place far behind him. Roppongi now seemed very different. Brooding, dark ... and malevolent. But really, he knew Roppongi hadn't changed. It was just him. The way things look depend on the eyes doing the looking. And his eyes had seen enough. He knew Roppongi was over for him this time, probably forever.

Contemplating the day ahead brought him back to earth. It would be a demanding day. Hans's parents were arriving from Holland and Zack was to meet them at ANA Hotel at five in the evening. It was now nine-thirty. The telephone conversation with them had been short, but awful; one of the most awkward and painful conversations he had ever experienced. Kristiaan and Annemieke.

He didn't know them, had never met them. What was he supposed to say to them? He really didn't know. So, unusually for him, he had said very little. They had both been on the line, on separate extensions. In tightly controlled short sentences of heavily-accented English, they explained how Hans had told them so much about his 'great friend Zack'.

Hans's mother kept appending comments onto her husband's sentences, and then catching her breath sharply, before lapsing into a miserable silence. Then they all rushed to speak, only to stop again. More silence. Zack was sure he'd heard muffled sobbing. Excruciating was the only word; how do you speak about the unspeakable?

Zack knew Hans would never have come to Tokyo if it hadn't been for him, and he guessed they probably knew that too. He couldn't help wondering how much they blamed him. This ever-present thought had not made the conversation any easier for him. Eventually he said, "Look, this is really hard on the phone. Can we talk at the hotel?" Mercifully, they had agreed.

Realising he had tensed up and was holding his breath, he exhaled slowly, stretching deliberately and rolling from side to side. He eyed the note next to his side of the bed again. Carla had gone for a run at about eight-thirty. He hadn't heard her leave; she moved like a cat after all.

The fact it was freezing outside never affected her motivation. And afterwards, she would go to the gym. He shuddered inwardly at the thought. She was a machine. The girl ran ten kilometres practically every day! He would forever be in awe of that sort of discipline.

His own days of running to the Egyptian border-town of Taba and back to the Eilat Marina, and in forty-five degree heat no less, seemed a lifetime ago. He knew the road back to health for him post-Roppongi was going to be painful. But at least he was in nowhere near as bad a shape as he'd been last time around, and that fact alone made him feel a little better. Perhaps he and Carla would fast and cleanse in Thailand before they headed to Canada. Why not, he thought?

On a whim, he decided to see how Sofia was doing. She would probably appreciate the support, today especially. Punching her number on the speed-dial, he heard her phone ring, and imagined what it must be like for her in that empty apartment, alone, waiting for Hans's parents to arrive to get their dead son's things. No wonder she was going home to Sweden; she would be gone within days. Home to family and familiar things. Things she could trust.

"Hey Zack. Wow, this is early for you. I don't think I've ever spoken to you in the morning in Tokyo." Her voice had a dreamy quality, and she sounded very tired.

It was probably not far from the truth, Zack thought. Often, at this hour, he wouldn't even have gone to bed yet.

"I know babe, but I want to see you. I want to see how you're doing. I know you're by yourself." He paused. "I wanted to say I'm sorry. It's been a horrible time. And, I haven't been there for you as much as I should have."

Sofia laughed oddly. "You never were, Zack."

Zack felt a chill in his stomach. He forced his voice to remain even, and sympathetic. "What do you mean Sof?"

"Oh, forget it," she replied.

A lengthy silence ensued. Then Zack spoke.

"I'm meeting Hans's parents today at about five, before they come to the apartment. I wanted to make sure you're ready for that." He took a breath or two before going on. "But like I said before, you don't have to meet them if you don't want to. It's not like a duty written in stone or anything. I can handle it."

"*Kötthuvud!*" she cursed. "No, I'm not ready for that Zack! I hope I'm never ready for anything like that. But of course I will meet them. It's the least I can do. They will be going through seven kinds of fucking unimaginable hell. They are going to need some goddamn help here."

Zack wondered what manner of insult *Kötthuvud* was, but didn't really care. She was pretty strung-out. It wasn't about him. She was under a lot of stress. They both were.

"Let's get together Sof. Have some food, and just talk. It'll do us both good."

"Okay Zack." No enthusiasm. A short pause. "Where?"

Zack chose to ignore her apathy. "How about the Denny's up from *Omotesandō* towards *Shibuya*?'

"Okay. See you there in thirty minutes."

Left with the sound of static, Zack appraised his phone before putting it back on the bedside table. Sofia, he concluded, was in a bad way.

He rolled speedily off the bed and into a lightning-fast shower, finishing with a burst of water so cold it should have frozen in the pipes. Leaving Carla an explanatory note, he found his skin was still tingling from that frigid blast as he stepped from the apartment building.

Forty-Three

The young Japanese-Brazilian nicknamed Ebi was bound, naked, and suspended upside-down from a chunky length of chain. The room was effectively sound-proofed. But even so, he was gagged. His eyes bulged with terror. Although his body rocked languidly from side to side, it was screaming at him in pain. He was certain these men were going to kill him.

Max, who had just arrived, regarded him with disgust.

"Unhhh – uhhhgg – jhngggnn."

"Shut up, you fucking *bitch*," Max cursed. He flicked a glance towards Henry and Oju, his contemptuous expression intact. They shifted uneasily under his gaze. Although they had been told nothing so far, they sensed something important had changed, that Max was different. Somehow even more dangerous than before.

A sickly, foetid smell hung in the air. Glancing back at the dangling skinny body, Max recognised the smell as burnt hair and skin, sweat and urine, and God only knows what else. Henry was still holding the lit cigarette which he'd periodically been poking into various parts of this kid's anatomy. Max blinked twice. This part of the game had begun to repel him. Once upon a time he used to enjoy it.

"Get rid of that fucking cigarette," he snapped. "And get the gag off."

Once the gag was off, the prisoner sucked in a lungful of the foetid air and started begging rapidly in Japanese.

Max bent over and silenced him with a hard slap to the side of his face. "Shut that gibberish you fool."

The kid zipped it.

The impact of the slap had swung the boy's face away from Max's line of sight, so he motioned to the moron-twins, who moved across and held the boy firmly so his upside-down face was towards Max.

"Don't speak, just listen," Max instructed the terrified youth. "You probably don't feel this is the luckiest day of your life, do you?"

Walking behind the torturers, Max increased the boy's fear-level simply by disappearing from view. Henry and Oju stayed perfectly still. They had done this routine many times before. The boy's body tensed in anticipation of more pain. But none came.

Max reappeared in front of him, and crouched down, their faces more or less level. Max fixed a cold stare on Ebi's terrified eyes and went on softly.

"But you are mistaken my friend. It really *is* your lucky day. Today is the day you start your new job."

Max stood up. "I am leaving now. Once I am gone, these two are going to cut you down and let you go. You are now an employee of our organisation. From now on you'll do *exactly* as you're told. If you don't, we'll kill you. But not before we have a little more fun, like today. This type of fun can go on for days."

He jerked his head towards his two silent assistants. "These two love to have fun. And even though you think you're hurting now, believe me when I say there exists a level of pain you cannot even begin to imagine."

Max paused before adding, "And you aren't even close to that level yet." He let this possibility sink in to the damaged boy's fragile psyche before continuing.

"As of now, you have two jobs. One is to help us with our objectives in the drug trade here in Tokyo. In that, you will merely follow orders. The other is that of messenger. You will tell all your street-dealer friends about your experience today with us. Show them the evidence if you have to. Like you, they will either join our organisation, run away, or die, painfully. It's that simple. There will be no second chances. From this moment all street scumbags are part of my organisation. Or you do not exist."

Max stopped. The youth's haggard face told him everything he needed to know. For Ebi, Max was Satan incarnate. To ensure the kid was comprehending English, Max pushed the end of his boot against his forehead and rocked him gently.

"Do you understand what I am saying?"

The boy struggled against gravity, to nod. Unsure of whether he was even supposed to speak, he replied, "Yes," in tremulous English.

That was enough for Max. He knew this boy now understood his immediate future perfectly. It had been his experience that extreme pain and the possibility of death were generally rapid and effective educators. Max issued a final command to the moron-twins.

"He's got work to do. Cut him down. Clean him up. Give him his clothes and let him go. I am going out. I will call you later if I need you."

Max strode from the stinking room. Taking the stairs two at a time to street level, he breathed the chill smoggy air outside with some relief. This takeover was going to be even easier than he thought. With the backing of the *Yaks*, he was effectively omnipotent in this town.

And when that little bastard started telling his story, no one in their right mind would dare challenge him. Roppongi's streets would be his, and he could start building the empire outwards from there, using the exact same tactics.

Max surveyed the freezing streetscape, looking for a cab. There was only one irksome thing still niggling him. Zack. A cold fury churned inside Max as his mind replayed how Zack's very existence had significantly embarrassed him in his recent discussions with the *Yakuza* boss.

And now he'd actually been *ordered* not to touch Zack! So, having been granted the power he'd sought, he was unable to use it on Zack. What an infuriating impasse. He snorted disbelievingly, and breathed a jet of vapour into the freezing air.

That he was even obliged to speculate how close Zack had come to thwarting his partnership with the *Yaks* bothered him more than he cared to admit. Finally he spotted a cab edging its way down the frozen street and hailed it.

Once in the cab, his mind settled somewhat. He had his mandate, and playtime was most certainly over. Shortly, even those arrogant, slant-eyed fuckers ordering him about would have no reason to doubt his abilities.

And there was always more than one way to skin a cat. In fact, it would be a pleasure to design a more elegant solution for Mr. Zack Morrissey.

Forty-four

Carla studied Zack's note briefly and tossed it back on the bedside table before peeling off her clothes and entering the shower. She'd had a moment of panic when realising Zack was no longer in her apartment. Why, she wondered? *Stupid*!

While the stinging hot water cascaded over her, she reflected on her run. Probably twelve kilometres, she thought. And she hadn't even felt it; today she had run like the wind! She was *buzzing*, endorphins and adrenalin coursing through her body. How much of this feeling was from the run, and how much was from the new direction in her life? Taking this next step with Zack had changed everything: she felt phenomenal, supercharged.

Carla had already decided she wasn't going to wait. If Zack was happy to go early, she wanted to get out of Roppongi as soon as possible. She had made enough money for the time being, and she was pretty sure Zack had too. They could go to Thailand for a while, catch some sun, then head to Vancouver. She couldn't wait to introduce Zack to her family. If it was up to her, they would stay for Roppongi's New Year's party, then skip town as soon as possible. With a jolt, she realised New Year's Eve was Thursday night. Only a few days away!

She'd heard there was going to be a dance party in a half-completed building in *Shibuya* somewhere. The location was never announced until the last minute. The crew putting on this party went by the moniker 'Subterranean', which she guessed was a play on the 'underground' theme.

Their specialty was organising very cool parties in unlikely, semi-industrial spaces. Despite the extra planning challenge, they always seemed to pull off something extraordinary. People talked about their parties for weeks. DJs were even lining up to play for free just to get better known by the Subterranean guest-list. It was a hot ticket for sure.

The fact these parties were secret, unsanctioned affairs, outside the world of Roppongi's well-known clubs and bars, only added to their mystique and appeal for 'industry-folk'. All the BlackJacks girls had been talking about it for weeks. With all that had been going on, Zack may not have heard about it yet, but she knew she wanted to take him there. He needed something like this right now. To maybe find some final magic together in Tokyo before they left.

* * *

Across town, Zack paid the cab and walked briskly up the stairs into Denny's. Instantly enveloped by the familiar and somehow comforting aroma of fried food, he paused for a moment, pondering why he'd chosen Denny's today. Given the overall horribleness of his life at the moment, could it be that he was subconsciously looking for reassurance? Even from something as banal as fast food?

Zack immediately banished the thought, and deliberately shook those feelings off as he spotted Sofia in a booth on the far side of the room. The last thing she needed at the moment was to sense unease or any sort of insecurity *in him*. Zack decided that for her sake, he should be as strong as possible until she left for home.

Drawing nearer to Sofia's table, Zack felt his apprehension grow. She was sitting side-on to him, concentrating intently on the table-top. She appeared to be doing something with her hands. When he reached her, his heart sank, but he nevertheless slid quickly into the opposite side of her booth.

Zack's mind reeled. How long since he'd last seen Sofia? Two days? Three? Surely not more than that! How was this sort of catastrophic change possible in such a short time? He wondered when she'd last slept.

When she met his eyes across the table, Zack knew that her ghoulish appearance would remain with him for the rest of his life. Haunted was the only word which came to mind. He struggled to reconcile the sight in front of him, with the girl he'd once made such thrilling love to back on the *L'Chaim* in Eilat.

This was not that girl anymore! Her hair was lank and dirty. Pulled to one side, it was a straggly mess which hung mankily across her right cheek. Whatever makeup remained, was patchy and smeared. Her eyes were ringed at the bottom with sleepless dark circles, the mascara streaked; the effect was gothic.

The Eilat Sofia had been a goddess: confident, golden-skinned, glamorous and full of life. This Sofia was a vacant-eyed, chalk-skinned wraith.

"Cat got your tongue Zack?" she offered, with an unsettling, forced grin. "How's tricks?" The chuckle which followed this very un-Sofia utterance was ghastly.

Glancing downwards, he noticed she had poured most of the sugar onto the table in a large pile. She was arranging then rearranging it in patterns with her forefinger, sometimes also utilising the back of her teaspoon. He guessed the teaspoon had arrived with the mug of hot chocolate which was now congealing, untouched, near the edge of the table.

Zack reached for Sofia's right hand and held it gently, but firmly enough to stop her tracing out her sugar patterns.

Her body stiffened at the contact, and she looked blankly at the table, pointedly refusing to meet his gaze.

By way of a prompt, he squeezed her hand a little. "Sofia, why didn't you call me?"

What happened next was so unexpected it was truly frightening.

Half-rising from her chair, Sofia let out a shriek and with her free hand, punched Zack full-force in the face. He recoiled against the back of his seat. It would not be until much later that he would grasp just how shocked he had been by her violence.

Right now, all he knew for sure was that he knew nothing about this girl sitting opposite him. His shock and fear must have immediately shown in his face, because suddenly Sofia's mask slipped. Then she disintegrated. Her head fell into her hands onto the table and the tears came, thick and fast, in waves punctuated by a guttural sobbing.

Zack's shock continued unabated. He had literally watched it happen. Her whole face had collapsed in a second! Later he would swear it was almost as if some kind of demonic entity had left Sofia in that moment.

He stayed glued to his seat. An unknown instinct compelled him not to act as he normally would have. So he did not move to comfort her, or put his arms around her. He just stayed where he was, tried to regroup, and let her cry it out.

In that moment Zack was thankful the restaurant was so deserted at this time of day. There were only three other occupied tables in a sea of fifty or so. Regardless, he did see the restaurant manager lift a phone and look in their direction. Zack waved a finger at him and mouthed, 'No,' whilst firmly shaking his head.

The manager weighed the situation, looked around the restaurant again as if to assess whether this malady could perhaps be contagious, then gave it up. The phone disappeared. Zack breathed a quiet sigh of relief. Police would be an added complication they could probably do without right now.

He looked across at Sofia. For the moment, the storm appeared to have subsided.

"Sofia?" It was barely a whisper.

"I'm so sorry Zack. So sorry." Her muffled words emerged from a rumpled mess of head, hands and hair, all of which were still on the table.

"C'mon Sof, sit up sweetheart." Zack proffered a napkin. "Wipe your eyes with this hon. You'll feel better, believe me."

She righted herself and mopped at her eyes with the napkin. "Roppongi is bad news Zack. Why did you bring us here?"

She sounded very, very tired. But the *fury* was gone. She seemed more resigned than anything else right now. Finally, she looked at him.

Zack almost wished she hadn't. Her eyes spoke of a pain so terrible and raw that he wondered how much he wanted to know. "What happened to you, Sofia? You haven't *told* me anything!"

"People are just sick here Zack. Roppongi is a very sick place. Hans is gone; nothing *good* happens in this place." She seemed to be lapsing into her former state, and Zack wanted desperately to get her back.

"Sofia, *please!*" Zack raised his voice in pure frustration. "Tell me what the fuck is going on with you!"

She looked at him venomously. "He fucking *filmed* me Zack!" Her words came out like frozen bullets. She continued before he had a chance to fathom what the hell she was talking about.

"That sick old fuck actually *filmed* me! In the shower. He has a vid-"

It was clearly too much, too soon. She broke down again, sobbing inchoately.

Finally, a picture was forming in Zack's mind. "Sof, are you talking about that old *Yakuza* guy who bought you all the gifts?"

She pulled her head up slightly so she could nod a confirmation.

Zack breathed a little easier. Now he had something of a handle on what he was dealing with. It looked like this thing, whatever it was, in combination with Hans's murder, had pushed Sofia right over the edge.

"Tell me exactly what happened."

Sofia took another napkin and noisily blew her nose before mopping once again at her racoon eyes. She seemed marginally more together.

"Short story Zack. I went horse-riding at his country place. I can't remember whether I told you that before or not. I was worried he was going to try to make me stay overnight, but he didn't. I was hot and sweaty from the ride. He had the maid show me to the bathroom so I could shower and change before having the driver take me back to Roppongi. I was so relieved, I didn't give it a second thought. But now I know *why* he did that."

She had her head in her hands again.

"He fucking filmed me in that shower, Zack. And *even worse*, I got myself off while I was in there." She pounded the side of the table with her little fist. "Stupid! He must really have thought it was his lucky day."

Zack felt saying nothing was the best option.

"I would never even have *known* about it! Except a preview arrived under my door yesterday."

"Why would he send it to you?" Zack, momentarily nonplussed by this revelation, was thinking out loud. Then he got it.

"Wait a minute. I bet you don't see your face or anything which would identify the place, and the video is real short. Like, under thirty seconds short."

Her face became animated. "That's unbelievable! How do you know that Zack?"

He evaded the question. "Sofia, when was the last time you saw him?"

"That creep? I haven't spoken to him or seen him since he proposed marriage to me. That sick fuck."

"Sof, he just wants you to know that he's got the video. There's enough there for *you* to know what it is, but he's edited it so there's nothing to incriminate him or his place. My guess is he wants to see if it will give him some leverage over you. Maybe he wants you to think he'll release the video on some porn site or wherever, if you don't see him. Who knows?"

"See him!" Sofia snorted. "I'm getting the fuck out of this madhouse. There's no chance he'll ever see me again."

Glimpses of the Sofia he knew were reappearing. She was getting stronger just talking through it. So he kept going. Stay on the positive, he thought.

"I'm pretty sure he won't release anything, Sofia. Guys like that usually prefer to keep their pleasures private. And you're obviously someone he thinks very highly of."

"Thinks highly of!" Sofia spluttered.

Her face could hardly express the madness she obviously felt Zack's comment implied.

"You know, that's a perfect example of what I'm talking about!" she snapped. "Roppongi is the only fucking place I've ever been where that comment actually makes perfect sense."

Zack could see her point, but he was not going to debate it with her now. "So when's your flight out of here? You must be looking forward to seeing your folks."

This abrupt change of course took her by surprise. She had to think for a few seconds.

"Ahhm ... third of January. My plan was to stay for that Subterranean New Year's party, then collect my stuff and leave this twisted fucking place. But now, if I could change my flight I'd go home tomorrow. The sooner the better."

Given what he'd seen today, Zack thought so too. He had heard Subterranean were doing something cool for New Year's, but that was of secondary concern right now.

Then he saw a waiter clearly torturing himself about whether to approach their table or not. Zack was starving, so beckoned him across. He didn't need a menu to know what he wanted: an orange juice, a triple-espresso with cream on the side, and a full American breakfast with hash browns.

"Do you want something?" he asked Sofia. "Maybe another hot chocolate?" Indicating the now nearly solid lump that she hadn't touched, he ventured a small grin.

She rolled her eyes at him, and ordered a Diet-Coke.

With the waiter gone, Zack reverted to business. "Why don't you see whether you can change your flight. I think it's a good idea."

She raised an eyebrow. "Trying to get rid of me now, are you?"

Given what had just happened, it was a feeble attempt at a joke and they both knew it.

"Sofia, what do you want me to say? Look at the state you're in. You can't seriously be telling me you're staying here for a fucking party!"

He snapped his fingers for effect. "You are *over* this place Sofia. There is n*othing* keeping you here. You don't *need* to be here anymore." Softening his tone, Zack added, "Take the money and run Sofia. Chalk it up to a well-paid experience. Just change your ticket and go, for God's sake. Please tell me you'll go and change your ticket *today*."

Sofia studied the table, mute.

"What about Hans's parents? I'm supposed to meet them."

Zack could tell she was just treading water now, so he moved forward patiently. "Sof, do you honestly think it's going to help them to see you like this? Yes, or no?"

Reaching across, he took both her hands in his. "You know the answer to that, just like you know you should get your arse out of here and back to Sweden pronto. Why are you making me work so hard for this?"

There were tears in her eyes again, and Zack cursed himself for being so blunt. But he could see no other way.

Then she got to her feet. Zack braced himself for another punch, or for her to just walk out. Instead, she came around the table and pulled him up by the hand. Then she pulled him in close and hugged him tight.

Forty-Five

Fumiko lay on the lounge-room floor, looking at the intricate patterns within the unlit crystal chandelier, and speculated about what her husband had planned for her. She had now been a prisoner in her own home for seven days. Or was it eight? She didn't know anymore.

Apart from wondering what they were waiting for, what was mostly bothering her was the insistent buzzing noise she could hear in her head. It was always there now. Like a buzz of static on a radio, that varied a little in intensity from time to time as you turned the dial. She had tried, but been unable to pinpoint exactly when this noise had arrived. It was almost as if it had always been there, but somehow below the threshold of her hearing.

At first she'd guessed it must have been from the medication, but she had stopped taking that days ago and the buzzing was still with her, just as insistent. Nothing stopped it. She had put her head under water, stood on her head, shaken her head, held her breath, popped her ears, and even knocked her head against the wall a few times. The buzzing however, continued implacably.

She closed her eyes for a moment and her thoughts drifted. Images of her youth flitted by: happier times. She remembered being ten years old with her big sister Megumi. It was the first week of April, cherry blossom season. The family were holidaying in *Kyoto* and they had just finished a picnic by the canal near the Philosopher's Path.

Both girls had their special cherry blossom holiday treats, large red and white swirled lollypops. Together they ran excitedly along the path holding them like precious batons, while their parents hurried after them shouting warnings about not going too fast. Eventually they had flopped under one of the hundreds of trees lining that beautiful place, and together, rested on a bed of fallen blossoms whispering urgent secrets to each other during the time it took their parents to catch up.

When she opened her eyes there were tears in them. She blinked them angrily away. Apart from the time she had recently spent with Hans, that was surely one of her last truly happy memories. Shortly after that, her childhood had died in high-school; even Megumi stopped talking to her for a while because she was always getting teased so much.

Physically, she had developed early, and more fully than her schoolmates. School was a barbaric place, full of cruelty, taunts, and brutality which nearly always went unnoticed by those in charge. She couldn't wait to leave, and had done so at the earliest opportunity.

Everything about *Osaka* seemed to suck the life out of her. So to her parents' disgust and disappointment, she added the decision to move to Tokyo to her list of sins. She had quickly found her path in the *mizu-shōbai*, and it was this path that had ultimately led her to Toshiko. She had only seen her parents four times since then. One of those occasions was of course seven years ago, at her marriage to Toshiko.

She allowed herself a smile. Ironically, this had been the only time she had seen her father happy since she was a child. After the wedding she had not of course, had to work. But Toshiko was away on business all the time, and he had quickly tired of her in the bedroom. Having few friends, visiting her old industry for kicks had seemed like an exciting idea. This of course, had led her to Hans. Beautiful, strong, decent Hans. She wrenched her memory away from him, flinching with the effort.

What did Toshiko think was possible at this point? Did he plan to kill her too? He couldn't keep her prisoner forever, insulated from the world, her family, and her few friends. Could he? Surely not. So, what then?

She doubted she would have the opportunity to find out. He was due to visit her any moment now; the guards had told her to be ready to talk with him. It would be his second visit. The first was during a haze of medication which those same guards had forced on her during the first few days. Prozac, Librium, Valium, Xanax, and probably even Ecstasy she thought, had been forced into her one way or another.

It was as if Toshiko intended to pharmaceutically erase from her psyche, the madness which had taken place. Pacify her. Bring her back. Or perhaps drive her mad? Did he really think it could work? Or whether by now, in his madness, he too was vainly clutching at straws. Perhaps he was seeking to punish her even more than he already had.

She had vomited most of the drugs up anyway. Not even on purpose; it had just come back up by itself. The guards, disgustedly, had cleaned up the best they could, which she remembered had amused her at the time. To save themselves the trouble in future, they had even laid down a plastic groundsheet in case she threw up again.

The absurdity was beyond belief. This man who was her husband was completely insane, a cold-blooded killer, yet was apparently concerned about the state of his living-room carpet.

Her musings were interrupted by the click of the door being opened. She sat up and shook off her torpor; for what was to come she would need her wits about her. The room was quite dark, and although her eyes were now accustomed to it, she guessed he was waiting for his own to adjust. She was counting on it, in fact.

Another click. The door was now closed behind him. He was dressed in cream chinos and a blue blazer. She couldn't see his feet because of the sofa, but he'd almost certainly be wearing his dark green Gucci loafers.

It was almost impossible to think this impeccably dressed, mild-mannered looking man was personally responsible for the horrific things which had burned into her brain for hours in front of that screen. How could they be one and the same person?

Would he decide to turn the lights on? She readied herself and got to her feet. She could now see him clearly as he blinked in the twilight of this room. She waited. Another click. Followed by another.

Toshiko cursed the useless light-switch in frustration. Fumiko smiled inwardly. Some hours ago, she had removed all the light globes in this room. As he squinted in her direction, she waited until she was sure he had seen her.

The first shot tore through the centre of Toshiko's chest and embedded itself in the solid door he had just closed. His right hand came up from slightly behind him. At first she thought it was a natural reaction to clutch at his chest. But no, he was holding a gun! The realisation stunned her. *He had come to kill her!*

"*Satsujin-sha,*" she hissed at him. The second shot passed through his stomach. Toshiko's expression was one of complete bewilderment. He looked dazedly down the front of his Oxford shirt and observed for himself the two holes in his body spouting blood. The handgun fell from his grasp as his body sagged with terminal realisation.

"Fumiko," he spluttered.

As he fell, he took the third shot in the face.

She walked warily over to him. He was no longer moving. It was done. She looked at the 'baby-Glock' in her hand. The irony was profound. Toshiko had given her the *Glock 26* some years back. He had even organised her lessons in its use. This had been a new, and for a time, interesting experience for her, but she had never liked the gun the way he seemed to. He had caressed it, disassembled it for her, shown how to oil it and put it back together. Less successfully, he had tried to get her into the habit of carrying it.

Long ago though, she had wrapped it in its oily cloth and put it in a box in the bottom drawer of the TV cabinet; she had not wanted the gun in their bedroom. She guessed she could thank her husband's maintenance skills for the gun still working at all after languishing in there for so long.

It had clearly never occurred to Toshiko that there could be any potential weapons in this room. Certainly none with which she could pose any threat to him. Pure dumb luck, she thought, had provided her with the opportunity she should never have had.

Why hadn't the guards come bursting in yet? The answer came immediately. What a joke, she thought. They were *expecting* to hear shots. The shots killing her. They were probably under orders not to come in until he called them. Now she understood the plastic groundsheet! Typical Toshiko. So measured. So planned. He didn't want an incriminating and unsightly mess on the carpet.

She glanced at the still figure of his body by the door. Too late for that now, she thought. A big bloody puddle was working its way slowly outward as it overwhelmed the absorption capabilities of lush baby-blue carpet. She marvelled at how little she felt for this man who was once her husband. Looking again at the groundsheet, she grimaced. How had she missed so obvious a clue? How could she have been so stupid?

She walked around it, humming quietly to herself. The humming reminded her of something. Of course! She gasped. The incessant buzzing noise had disappeared! Without it, the room was now very silent.

Glancing at the door with renewed purpose, she knew she must hurry. The guards wouldn't wait forever. But she was nearly done now. Only one last thing to do before leaving.

Forty-Six

Having persuaded Sofia not to meet Hans's parents, Zack had taken her to his place, watched her take a Rohypnol followed by a glass of water, then tucked her up in his own bed. Unusually for mid-afternoon, the apartment was lifeless. James and Teri were out; Shunit was nowhere to be seen. Zack wasn't too bothered. They all knew Sofia anyway, and would not necessarily be surprised to see her in Zack's bed when they arrived home. Regardless, he decided to text them an explanation. Also, one to Carla, in case inappropriate rumours started circulating. Roppongi was a disaster-zone for shitty gossip; that sort of additional complication was the last thing he needed at the moment.

Zack knew he too, should have a short siesta before going to meet Hans's parents. He anticipated it would be at least as bad and as draining as his morning session with Sofia, and he already felt wrung-out. But he knew he couldn't sleep right now. Massaging his temples, he closed his eyes and realised anew just how much he wanted to leave all this behind him. How did life get so goddamn complicated?

He was also angry with himself for having let Sofia down so badly, by not being there when she'd obviously needed his help. There just wasn't enough *time*, he thought. Jesus, it was only luck that he'd decided to catch up with her prior to the meeting today at all. Thank God he had! He shuddered to think of what a disaster it would have been for Hans's parents to have encountered her in that state.

He sighed, lay back on Shunit's bed, and waited a while. Tried to meditate and clear his head. His efforts proved worse than useless. Not only was he a 'Monkey' according to the Chinese horoscope, but in his current state he seemed to be trapped in 'monkey-mind'. Thinking about 'nothing' at present was much easier said than done.

So, once he knew Sofia was sleeping comfortably, he decided he might as well get to ANA Hotel early. Have a drink in the lounge while he waited; he had a feeling he would need more than just one to get through the rest of this day. Levering himself silently off Shunit's bed, he picked up Sofia's keys, put his gloves, beanie and parka on again, and went back into the cold.

Once on the street, and breathing steam into the freezing air, Zack decided to walk to the hotel. It would only take him about fifteen minutes. There was snow on the ground, but he didn't care. Flipping his parka-hood up to keep his ears warm, he walked to *Roppongi-Dori*, turned right and started trudging up the hill.

Arriving at precisely four o'clock, he went straight to the lounge-bar in the lobby. He couldn't help a sad smile. The last time he'd been here was with Dorit, both partying like rock-stars. He wondered how she was doing. Probably just great, he thought. Choosing a table against the wall, from where he could see everything, he ordered a double JD on ice. As he took the first sip, his phone rang. Carla.

Zack answered. "Hello my love. How are you doing?"

"I'm okay baby. Where are you? Are you alright?" She sounded more than a little concerned.

"I'm fine sweetie. I'm in the lobby of ANA, waiting to meet Hans's parents. It's already been one hell of a day."

"I got your message. What's going on?"

Zack took a deep breath and a sip of JD before replying. "Sofia's a train-wreck babe. She probably hasn't slept for days. Been taking anti-depressants. Totally spaced-out. She actually punched me in the face in Denny's. The manager nearly called the police."

"Oh Jesus, Zack. That's crazy. The poor girl must be out of her mind."

"Fortunately, after that she came back to normal a little. So I managed to talk her out of meeting Hans's parents. I gave her a Rowy to put her to sleep, so she'd be out of the way while I take his parents to the apartment. How was your day anyway?"

"Can you just *shut-up* for a minute!" Carla exclaimed. "*My day*, has zero relevance at the moment. Stop pretending this is even a half-way normal sort of conversation. Because it isn't, Zack!"

She clicked her tongue a few times, an unconscious habit of hers on the rare occasions she was stressed or annoyed. So he waited.

"Not that it's important at all," she said. "I'm going to dinner with the girls, then going to work. Why don't you stop by the club when you're done with this awful thing? Honestly, I don't know how you do it. It's absolutely too much."

Zack agreed. 'Too much' was probably why he'd already finished this JD and just signalled the waiter for another. "I know babe. But someone has to do it. And I was his best friend here." He took another breath. "I'd rather do it than have that clinical fucker Sakamoto take them over there. They don't deserve that."

"I know, I know. I just want this all to be over and for us to get out of here. I'm giving my notice. I want us out of here as fast as possible after the New Year's party."

"The Subterranean party?" Zack queried.

"Oh, so you do know about it. Anyway that's what I want Zack. Let's get out of here a few days into New Year. We don't have to go to Vancouver right away. We can holiday somewhere. Somewhere warm. Wherever you want. Let's talk about it later okay?"

"Okay sweetheart, sounds good to me. I'll stop by the club a little later and maybe we can grab a bite and a nightcap after you're done."

"Okay, just call me when you're on your way."

"Will do babe. Bye for now." Zack clicked off. His second JD was already half gone. He'd just ordered his third when he saw them. It had to be them, he thought. Half-rising, he gave a tentative wave.

They acknowledged it, and made their way towards his table.

Zack's stomach contracted at the thought of the conversation ahead.

Kristiaan and Annemieke were both tall. Giants effectively, in a country like Japan. Kristiaan had taken the lead and was weaving a path through the tables, Annemieke holding his hand.

Zack stood respectfully, and evaluated them closely as they drew near.

Kristiaan was wearing deck shoes, dark-blue jeans and a white Ralph Lauren Polo-shirt, tucked in behind a chocolate leather belt. He had what looked like a black cashmere sweater draped over his shoulders, and it was loosely tied in a cross at the front. His face was ruddy and handsome and he had a shock of dark hair paired with a virile-looking moustache.

Together, it was a look straight out of the seventies and Zack found himself wondering if it had been in place since then. His modern rimless rectangular spectacles with incongruously small lenses drew attention to intense, almost black eyes. This effectively completed the image of a well-to-do corporate type, of whom there were many in Tokyo. The difference, Zack thought, was that this man was here tonight because his son had been viciously murdered, for reasons unknown, by persons unknown.

Turning his attention to Annemieke, Zack could see she had clearly once been a stunning woman, possibly a model or an athlete. She moved with a dancer's grace, and was quite striking even now. Yet she had to be perhaps sixty or more?

She wore a crisp white linen blouse and an elegant long skirt of what looked to be very expensive earth-coloured suede, with black boots. Her face was wan, her eyes pale blue, and her expression drawn. Her hair, that distinguished platinum colour favoured by certain older women, was worn up in a tight bun, off to one side. From a distance she looked very classy.

They had arrived early this morning, and both Hans's parents looked tired. Zack could see Annemieke had applied heavy make-up to cover the black bags under her eyes.

Knowing how tiring that flight could be, he was glad he had suggested they rest for most of the day before this meeting. But now, he wanted to be done with this thing as soon as he could. They would finish their drinks, then go.

As soon as he was near enough, Kristiaan extended his hand. Zack reciprocated. It was a firm handshake. Zack motioned Kristiaan to a seat and then shook Annemieke's hand. She followed Kristiaan to the other side of the table. Then Zack too, sat down.

Kristiaan looked first at his wife, then focused on Zack. He spoke in a heavy voice.

"Zack, we … ahhh … both of us … want you to know we are grateful you are willing to see us." He paused. "To …. ahhm … help us, with this. This is not an easy thing."

A waiter appeared, and Zack was grateful for the momentary interruption.

"I'm sorry," Zack said. "But we should get this order out of the way though, so we are not constantly interrupted." He turned his attention to Annemieke. "Would either of you like a drink?"

Kristiaan eyed Zack's glass. "What do you have there?"

"Jack Daniels on the rocks," Zack replied.

"I'll have one of those then."

Annemieke then spoke. "Just sparkling mineral-water with a lemon slice thank-you Zack." Her voice was soft and smooth.

Zack relayed those orders, and the waiter nodded, bowed, and perhaps sensing the tension, swiftly left them.

"You're not having another?" Kristiaan enquired.

Gesturing to his half-full rock glass, Zack said, "I've already ordered, thank-you."

Kristiaan nodded. Clasping the fingers of one hand to the other hand in front of him, he glanced quickly again at Annemieke, and then turned to Zack.

"Let me cut to the chase Zack. I am very direct in most matters. This will be no exception."

"I appreciate that. Me too," said Zack.

"Annemieke and I are, very slowly, accepting the fact that our boy is gone." His eyes moved to his wife, then back. "I must tell you Zack, I hope you never have to suffer the pain of losing a child. This is still for us, like we are having a very bad dream. Hans was our only child, and now, we have lost him."

Zack could only nod. There was nothing to say.

"We need to know why, Zack. Do you understand me?"

Zack maintained eye-contact, and nodded again.

"Although we know *nothing* will ever bring him back, we intend to move *heaven and earth* to discover the *why*, the *how*, and the *who*, of his death. Do you understand what I mean by that?"

"Yes, I believe I do sir."

Kristiaan studied him briefly, then echoed his words. "Yes. I believe you do. You look like the sort of person who would understand the implications of that statement."

Zack had his doubts as to whether that observation was a compliment.

Kristiaan checked on Annemieke, before continuing. "Annemieke and I are not short of money, Zack. And if it is going to take money to discover the absolute truth of this matter, then you can be very certain that is an expense we mean to incur."

For emphasis, he elaborated slightly. "In this matter you can be sure that both time and money have very little relevance to Annemieke and me."

Zack found himself rapidly gaining respect for this impressively proportioned man; for the dignity and grace with which he was carrying himself and his wife in this conversation.

"What I mean to make clear to you, is that we are almost certainly going to need help, Zack. We do not know this place *at all*. It is as foreign to us as any place could be."

Truer than they could imagine, Zack thought.

"But as Hans told us many times, *you* know what is going on *in this Roppongi*. You know *how it works*, and more or less *why* it does what it does."

"Hans actually told you that?" Zack asked in surprise.

Annemieke spoke, adding to Zack's surprise. "For whatever reasons Zack," she said coolly, "Hans held you in very high regard. And, although his behaviour could sometimes be rash, he was far from stupid."

Kristiaan cleared his throat. Zack guessed it was to indicate his preference to take it from there. Accordingly, Annemieke relaxed in her chair, while Kristiaan took a healthy slug from his JD.

"What that means to us Zack, is that notwithstanding the competence or otherwise of the local police, at the moment you are our best hope. I am certain that without your assistance here, we will be lost. We hope very much, that you will help us with anything at all which might lead us to the truth of what happened to our boy."

Zack was genuinely shocked. He had no doubt their reference to money was primarily a general one, in the event bribes or other payments might be necessary to extract information which might not otherwise be forthcoming.

But he also believed it was intended as a deliberate enticement to sway him towards helping them, were he potentially wavering in this respect. He was affronted. Take money off grieving parents for trying to help them get to the bottom of Hans's murder? They obviously didn't think too much of him at this point. But then, why would they? They didn't know him at all.

Perhaps more likely was that they were playing their only trump card up front to ensure the best possibility of success. They clearly did not want to risk losing him as a potential ally in their quest. How long they had agonised unnecessarily over this very simple thing? He had to allay their concerns about that. Right now.

Silence prevailed while these thoughts ran through Zack's mind. He looked from one to the other as they waited expectantly. When he spoke, Zack focused on Annemieke. He didn't know why.

"Please understand that during the time I knew Hans, he was like a brother to me. Forgive me, but I am a little shocked that it had even crossed your minds that I might *not* help you with this."

Relief illuminated their faces.

"You can be very sure," Zack continued, "that I *will* help you to the limit of my abilities. But if you offer me even one single dollar for doing so, I will quit and leave you to it. I can't be any clearer than that."

Now facing Kristiaan, he said, "Don't get me wrong. Certain costs may have to be met, but just don't offer to pay *me*. Helping you however I can, is the *least* I can do. I only wish we had been able to get this much clear on the phone. It would have saved you worrying about something which to me was always a given."

It had been a longish speech. He looked up at them. The eyes of both had filled with tears. Kristiaan extended his hand again. Zack took it, and held it.

"Thank-you Zack. Thank-you so very much. You don't know what a difference that makes to us."

When Annemieke leaned across and put her hand on top of theirs, the emotion of the moment also overcame Zack, so when the waiter arrived with their drinks, all three of them were quietly crying together.

Forty-Seven

At one a.m, the Seventh Floor bar had eighteen people in it. Twelve guys and six girls. Four of the guys were Japanese, the rest foreigners. All the girls were foreign. Zack looked around the space unenthusiastically; he was running on empty.

After leaving Hans's parents, he had decided not to meet Carla at BlackJacks. Too many cheerful people to deal with. Instead, he was waiting for her to finish work and meet him here. When he'd walked in, Ranay had taken one look at him, raised his eyebrows, wordlessly got him his JD, and left him well alone.

Zack guessed his face must be showing the strain of the last eighteen hours. He imagined this was how a one thousand year old friendless vampire would feel: old, jaded, and questioning the point of it all. Seated on the corner stool at the bar, he was nursing his drink whilst disconnectedly observing the energies in the room. If he had ever experienced a more emotionally draining day than this one, he couldn't remember when that might have been.

His time with Hans's parents could have been worse, considering the circumstances. However, now that he had bonded with them and understood their expectations, he felt a bit less strung out. If he had to delay his exit with Carla in order to help them, she would be disappointed, but he was sure she would understand.

Zack's mind played back the evening which had brought him to this point. From ANA Hotel, they had gone to Hans's apartment in a taxi. Zack had felt strange, turning the key in the lock, and upon entry, had reached a little too quickly for a light switch. Jumpy. Not a good sign. Especially considering the amount of Jack Daniels he'd put down beforehand.

The apartment was remarkably tidy. Given Sofia's condition earlier, he had been half-dreading the mess that might await them. But she'd tidied Hans's bedroom, and put his few possessions into a couple of boxes. His clothes remained on the clothes-rail and in a small chest of drawers next to his bed.

Zack had no idea what the police might have taken during their evidentiary search when they'd first visited, but no doubt these items were fastidiously catalogued in a database somewhere. Kristiaan and Annemieke had an appointment scheduled with Sakamoto tomorrow, and would retrieve whatever they were allowed to then.

Zack also had no idea whether either of them intended to view Hans's remains. His head, he thought grimly, as that grisly image flashed once again through his mind's-eye. He hoped neither did. They knew Hans had been positively identified by Zack. They would of course not have any idea how horrible that experience had been, and Zack had no intention of telling them. He took small comfort from the fact they had not pressed him for details of the identification process. The original news item had, after all, been widely syndicated since then. They surely knew by now that they would only be burying a small part of their son's body.

At least, he thought, no-one else would ever have to suffer the shock he had suffered at seeing that chilling sight. Especially unprepared. Even though he understood the clinical investigative rationale behind Sakamoto's ploy, he doubted he would ever be able to forgive him for it. Not that Sakamoto gave two shits about that, he thought.

At the apartment Kristiaan and Annemieke conducted themselves with great dignity. Whilst Kristiaan sat cross-legged on the floor and carefully picked through the items in the boxes, Annemieke ran her fingers slowly along the hangers on Hans's clothes-rail, seemingly taking a mental inventory of her dead son's wardrobe, before sitting on his bed and simply watching Kristiaan. Zack excused himself, and pulled the door closed in order to give them some privacy. He sat in silence in the living room, keenly feeling the absence of a drink in his hand.

They remained in Hans's room for about thirty minutes, and Zack thought he heard Annemieke sobbing. But when they emerged, Annemieke was again composed. There was little else for them to see or do in this now ghostly apartment. So they left. Zack guessed they had been in and out in under forty minutes. On the street, Kristiaan told Zack he and Annemieke would return to the apartment after their meeting with Sakamoto the following day, to formally collect all Hans's belongings.

Zack hailed them a taxi and instructed the driver to ANA Hotel. He then watched their tail-lights disappear into the distance before hailing the next cab. It was bitterly cold, and as he had not eaten since breakfast at Denny's he auto-piloted into Roppongi for some food. Two glasses of red wine and a fettuccine carbonara later, he migrated to his preferred late-night habitat, the Seventh Floor.

Zack snapped his awareness back to the present. He wasn't expecting Carla to appear until two o'clock at the earliest. Maybe he should just quit this night, head back to her place, and crash. He changed his mind when Tanaka, his old Japanese pool-playing friend arrived.

Zack felt an unusual surge of enthusiasm. "Tanaka-san! *Genki desu-ka*? How are you my friend?"

"Zack-san." Tanaka inclined his head towards the pool table. "You not play tonight?"

Zack shook his head. "I'm too tired Tanaka. It's been a rough week."

Tanaka studied Zack a little more closely. "Zack, you looking old tonight. You should sleep."

Zack pulled him up a stool at the bar. "If you don't want to play pool straight away, you can keep me company. I'm just waiting for Carla to finish work."

Tanaka took the stool, signalled Ranay for his Tom Collins, and asked, "Girlfriend?"

"Yes. And," he added ruefully, "she's about the only good thing happening in my life at the moment."

Tanaka raised his eyebrows. "Sound serious Zack. What matter with you?"

How much should he tell the old fellow? As a rule, he never confided in anyone. But he would be out of this place very soon. And he felt like talking to someone. What harm could it do to level a little with Tanaka? The old bugger might even have some useful insights. Who knew?

So Zack talked. Not about everything, obviously. He left Max, and the drug-scene out of things. But he told Tanaka about Hans's murder. And about Sofia's misfortune with the *Yakuza* boss Yamazaki.

By the time he'd finished, Tanaka's face was grave. "So what you do now Zack?"

"Well, my plans are different now, Tanaka. I want to help Hans's parents find the truth if I can. After that, Carla and I are leaving as soon as possible. Two, maybe three weeks from now. Roppongi feels all wrong to me at the moment. One of my friends has been murdered. Another has had a mental breakdown. It just seems like there is no good reason to stay here any longer."

In response to Tanaka's impassive expression, Zack added, "I have a bad feeling now Tanaka-san. And it is not going away."

Tanaka appeared ready to respond, but at that moment Carla materialised at their sides. Surprised, Zack checked his watch. Two-fifteen! Whilst unburdening himself on Tanaka, the time had simply disappeared.

Carla quickly registered Tanaka but focused on Zack, looking him up and down. "Zack, do you have *any clue* what you look like?" she asked.

He turned to Tanaka, ignoring this comment. "Tanaka-san, this is my beautiful girlfriend Carla. And sweetheart, this is a good friend of mine, Tanaka. We've just been talking about Hans and Sofia."

Appraising Tanaka at greater length, Carla was frankly surprised Zack was talking to some old Japanese guy in a bar about those things. It seemed out of character. Then again, Zack looked terrible, as though he needed at least twenty-four hours sleep. She had to get him to bed.

Nevertheless, she addressed Tanaka courteously in Japanese. "Hello Tanaka-san. It's really a pleasure to meet you."

Tanaka bowed by way of a compliment, but replied in English. "Your Japanese very good, Miss Carla. And Zack is right. You are very beautiful lady."

Carla smiled warmly at him: he was quite charming. Too bad there weren't more like him coming to the club, she thought. But now wasn't the time for chat. She had to get Zack home to bed. It was difficult to credit the amount he'd had to endure today.

"Tanaka-san, thank-you so much for the kind words. But I have to steal him from you now. As you can see, he needs some sleep."

Zack didn't object, and got to his feet.

"Bye for now, Tanaka-san. If I don't see you again before we leave, good luck with everything. I very much enjoyed our time together in this place."

They shook hands.

"Thank-you Zack-san." Tanaka replied. "You too. Be careful. It can be dangerous out there."

Carla and Zack left.

A few moments later, Tanaka did the same.

Forty-Eight

It was Thursday morning, the last day of the year. New Year's Eve imminent. Zack was lying in Carla's bed, re-reading his favourite Paulo Coelho novel, *The Pilgrimage*. He had not left her apartment since they'd come here two nights ago. Zack knew *The Alchemist* was Coelho's best-known and best-selling novel, but it did not resonate with him as deeply as *The Pilgrimage*, which explored much darker mental and spiritual territory.

For Zack it had more validity, and was therefore a more interesting book. He looked forward one day to finding time to incorporate some of these more esoteric spiritual practices into his life. For reasons he would be unable to explain if asked, he felt he was more likely to find meaningful answers in those mysterious realms than anywhere else.

Except for the day he looked after Sofia, who was now safely back in Sweden, he hadn't spent time in his own apartment in days. Shunit, bless her heart, had rung to make sure he was okay. Apart from Carla's, hers was about the only call he'd answered recently. With the exception of Kristiaan and Annemieke, he was more or less ignoring the world for the moment.

So, with his plans having changed so fast, he'd called Lior to explain he was now out of the business. Lior, who'd been counting on Zack being key-man for another six months, was disappointed. Now he had to find someone to fill Zack's shoes: not an easy task. Lior had of course, already heard about Hans's murder. And when Zack filled him in on the details, he reacted realistically. If Zack didn't want to play anymore, that was his prerogative.

Zack had also tendered his resignation at Bongoes. Knowing well the circumstances, Steve, to his credit, had paid him out his final month in full. The cash was waiting for him in an envelope at the bar anytime he could drop by. So that was it, Zack thought; another irrevocable change of course. He was, once again, looking like a vampire. But one way or another he and Carla would be out of here soon, headed for Thailand's sunny beaches. At least he would be able to get some healthy colour back before meeting Carla's family in Vancouver.

He had not experienced Vancouver yet. Canada yes, but not Vancouver. Some years back, on a month-long road trip from New York City, he had spent time with Nurit in Quebec, Ottawa, Montreal and Toronto. They hadn't had time to go further, and had returned to NYC via Buffalo and Niagara Falls. From what he'd heard though, he expected to like Vancouver. Except for the winter, perhaps.

Zack had refused Carla's earlier invitation to the gym. She had tried her hardest to get him to come with her, suggesting a spa and sauna would do him good. As usual, she was probably right. But he had preferred to stay curled up in bed with a book. He felt like the inactivity and relative isolation was somehow doing him good.

Tonight however, was party night. Which was another reason Zack had holed himself up in Carla's apartment. A heady combination of New Year's Eve and Subterranean; the perfect party with which to mentally farewell Roppongi.

Over the last couple of days however, Zack had been seriously considering not going to the party. He had not voiced this possibility to Carla, and anyway, had eventually changed his mind. Carla had after all, been eagerly looking forward to it for weeks. With the singular exception of the party however, he intended keeping a very low profile until their final departure.

With that thought, Zack also realised he had not yet shared with Carla the probability that their exit from Japan would be delayed because of the commitment he'd made to help Hans's parents. No matter. That conversation would have to happen sometime tonight, he thought.

At about three p.m, Zack's first warning of the whirlwind headed his way, was some discordant singing coming from the hallway. Shortly thereafter, the apartment door burst open. Carla bounced into the room, with Astrid and Fortuna, two of the other three dancers in her BlackJacks cabaret-show. They had their arms around each other and were more or less moving as one unsteady unit.

"Free, free, free!" Carla was singing at the top of her voice. She looked to be in tremendous spirits.

Zack, now dressed in jeans, socks, a t-shirt and sweater, had moved from the bed to a beanbag on the living room floor. Having finished *The Pilgrimage*, he'd been reading *Men are from Mars – Women are from Venus*. It had been sitting nearby on top of the television, and he had picked it up absent-mindedly, expecting to dump it after a few moments.

But he'd become both fascinated and appalled by the notoriously successful self-help manual. Appalled, because it was the worst type of generalised self-help trash imaginable. Fascinated, because it staggered him how anything so bad could make its author a multi-millionaire.

The infamous Mencken quote came to mind: 'No one ever went broke underestimating the intelligence of the American public.'

The book effectively reduced the infinitely variable and complex nature of relationships between men and women to a series of stereotypical author-invented generalisations, then played those generalisations out, with accompanying suggestions that would ameliorate or rebalance the relationship. It was like watching a D-grade movie, and he'd simply not been able to hit the off-switch.

The girls had spotted the book in his hand, and he knew he was in for some punishment. They were quite a sight! Seventy-five percent of the BlackJacks dancers together in this small room. Three leggy stunners, all of whom knew how to move like cats.

Astrid was Danish if he remembered rightly, and Fortuna was unmistakably Italian. The contrast between the three was striking. Astrid was tallest – fair, blond, and pale-blue-eyed; an athlete. Fortuna was lithe, about the same size as Carla, but had mischievous brown eyes, a gypsy look, and a shock of unruly chestnut-coloured hair. She also had the largest breasts of the three.

And his darling girl was sandwiched between them, grinning like he hadn't seen in some time. A regretful expression came over his face; he had undoubtedly been grim company lately. Hoping to deflect their imminent jibes, he put the book aside. But it was too late.

It was like being under attack by Charlie's Angels.

"Men are from Mars – Women are from Venus!" they all shrieked accusingly, in a cacophonous sort of unison. Zack had an idea a few wines over lunch, might have contributed to their raucous behaviour. They disentangled themselves, Astrid and Fortuna collapsing onto the couch together. Carla bent down, squeezed his shoulders and kissed him hard on the mouth, then slipped into the kitchen and returned, opening a bottle of wine.

He grinned disarmingly. "Well, I've been a loner for a long time now. If I'm going to settle down with Carla I really need to learn how you girls think."

"Alone?" Fortuna scoffed, deliberately misinterpreting Zack's comment. "I don't think I've ever seen you alone Zack! That sounds like bullsheeeiit to me!"

The two girls laughed extravagantly, jostling each other in merriment.

"What are you celebrating anyway?" Zack asked.

Astrid looked at Carla with mild shock.

"You witch!" she exclaimed. "You didn't tell him yet, did you!"

Curious, Zack turned to Carla with an enquiring expression, but he intuited the truth. "Don't tell me you quit BlackJacks. Not on New Year's Eve!"

Carla's face confirmed it.

Zack's expression didn't change, but it was a different story internally.

Shit! That was a mistake, Carla! Damn it! He should have told her earlier they might not be rushing out of here in NY. But how could he have known she would do something as crazy as quitting before their famous NY Eve show? Too late now!

Shifting his weight off the beanbag, he sat up straight, crossed his legs and shook his finger at her. "They're going to *kill* you," he said emphatically. "What's his name that guy? Hiroshi, or something?"

"Yes!" Fortuna looked positively gleeful. "The manager, it's Hiroshi."

Zack turned again to Carla, who was now pouring the wine. Given his previous position at Cloud Nine, he had some sympathy for their manager Hiroshi. Losing one or more of his forty strippers without warning from time to time was one thing, but losing one of only four dancers integral to your acclaimed cabaret-show, and on New Year's Eve to boot, was something entirely different.

"Babe, I'm not joking. He is going to hire a hit-squad and take you out. He is going to have a nervous fucking breakdown."

She shrugged. "I know. But I don't care. We got paid last week, so I'll only lose a few days. I've just had enough."

She handed out the wines and plonked herself down next to Zack Raising her glass, she declaimed, "To my freedom!" They all drank, Carla downing hers entirely.

"And I say another toast," chirped Fortuna. "Long and happy lives to you and Zack, Carla. Much happiness to you both!"

Up with the glasses and down with the wine again. Astrid and Fortuna smiled broadly at each other as they observed Zack and Carla curled up together. It was abundantly clear they were delighted to see Carla, one of their own, so happy. Zack was touched by how much they loved this woman, with whom he too, had fallen very much in love.

Keeping the mood light however, he sighed dramatically. "Oh well, I guess we better do some lines then."

Astrid waved a finger at him. "You are a *very* naughty man Zack." Catching Fortuna's eye, she cautioned, "Don't *give* me that look missy. If we start doing lines now, you *know* tonight will be a disaster." Looking pointedly at her watch for emphasis, she added, "It's already four o'clock you know. We're *on* at nine." Astrid was doing her very best to look severe.

Fortuna leaned over and tapped her gently on the forehead. "But you already know, don't you my love, we are going to do it anyway."

Zack retrieved the stash, and cut out four healthy lines on the glass-topped coffee table. Christmas night at Bongoes was the last time he'd taken anything. For God's sake, that was only six days ago! It seemed like he had crammed a few years into the week since then.

On that day, he'd still been hoping against hope that Hans would somehow resurface. Although, in his bones, he'd known that would not happen. Never in his wildest imaginings however had he expected anything as chilling and shocking as what *did* come next. Zack had never before lost anyone close to him to violence. He still did not really know whether his psyche had fully assimilated the reality of Hans's murder.

"C'mon Zack, what are you waiting for?" quipped Fortuna.

He realised these heavy thoughts had stalled his line-sculpting progress, and quickly reverted to the task at hand. Passing a rolled one-thousand yen note to Carla, he pulled her close for a kiss.

"To our post-Roppongi future, my love," he murmured.

Her emerald cat's-eyes met his, holding all the world at bay. She kissed him again before lowering her head to vacuum the line in one fell swoop.

Astrid and Fortuna cheered her performance, and despite Astrid's token protests, they made short work of theirs.

Zack snorted his line, and lolled back into the beanbag to savour the buzz. This stuff had been scraped off a solid, moist rock of coke. It was probably as pure as you'd find anywhere in the world.

The difference between adulterated cocaine, or any drug for that matter he supposed, was the more one adulterated it, the more one warped the original intent of the drug, and thereby the integrity of the experience. Coke, for example, had never been Zack's favourite drug. Mostly because unless you happened to be in Colombia or somewhere else close to source, the experience was *always* compromised, and the degree to which that compromise worsened depended on how far down the supply-chain you happened to be.

The nature of this compromise, especially when combined with the law of diminishing returns when one did coke without inherent reserves of *natural* energy, was, in Zack's experience anyway, not worth the trouble. The end result was invariably an edgy, irritable mood combined with an inability to sleep, which was generally not conducive to anything positive, enlightening or fun.

But sometimes, as in this case, when the product was pure and clean, the experience could be close to transcendent. And whenever this happened, it reminded Zack why humans enjoyed taking drugs so much. After all, we've been doing it for a hell of a long time, he reflected.

There was a mountain of indisputable evidence that humanity had been 'doing drugs' of all sorts, for literally thousands of years. And the vast majority of this evidence pointed to the use of these substances as *sacraments*; as catalysts for philosophy, self-exploration, appreciation of natural forces, as well as various types of spiritual practice.

It seemed to Zack that the pettiness of contemporary control-hungry authoritarian systems was fighting against an eons-old desire which was demonstrably an integral part of humanity's genetic make-up.

Who knew? Perhaps that apparently hard-wired desire to indulge was there for a *reason*. Maybe it was in fact *integral* to humanity's ability to evolve into something better, something more advanced than its current level.

He sat up and cut another four lines onto the table. He had the whole rock to get through before they left the country; they wouldn't be taking it with them. Might as well get cracking ...

Forty-Nine

Having enjoyed a blissful afternoon of laughter, fun and indulgence, the group had eventually forced themselves to leave the apartment in search of food. Nobody was hungry of course, due to the coke, but being nothing if not a disciplined drug-user, Zack good-naturedly imposed dinner as a condition of Astrid and Fortuna continuing to indulge.

It had been very difficult to leave the warm bonhomie they'd generated in the apartment. No-one wanted to brave the harsh cold outside, even for a short while. Zack however, did not want to be responsible for sabotaging the entire BlackJacks New Year's Eve cabaret-show any more than it was already going to suffer because of Carla's unanticipated exit.

The journey had been comical. They'd exited the cab early because traffic was at a standstill. Then three of the most gorgeous girls in Roppongi had sashayed up the street, attached to Zack's arms. He'd attracted a gaggle of envious stares as they strode purposefully along Roppongi's sidewalks through the frigid Tokyo evening.

Post-dinner, they all reclined in comfort in a booth at Deep Blue. Zack had chosen Deep Blue again, simply because they could be fairly certain of not bumping into unwanted guests. If they'd chosen Charleston, the Hard Rock, or the Sports-Café, they'd have been over-run with unwelcome attentions instantly, and their blissful vibe would have quickly evaporated.

Dinner had been a scanty affair. Zack had eaten a dozen oysters Kilpatrick. Astrid and Fortuna had shared french-onion soup and spaghetti bolognaise, and Carla had chosen *tempura*. But the point was, they'd eaten. Especially Astrid and Fortuna, who by now were loathing the prospect of going through the motions at BlackJacks in the very near future. It was now eight o'clock, Zack noted, and time to get these girls on their way.

He raised his glass, for what seemed like the twentieth time that afternoon, and gazed around the booth at three exceptionally content women. He spoke with his hand literally on his heart.

"Ladies, I have to say, I could not even have *fantasised* a better lead-in to New Year's Eve."

The clink of glasses which followed was imbued with a faint despondency; all were aware their fabulous adventure was, until the *Subterranean* party anyway, drawing to a close.

"Thanks so much darling man. You are a gem." Astrid spoke with heartfelt appreciation. Adding, to Fortuna, "We both needed a day like this more than we knew."

Fortuna grinned knowingly and rolled her eyes at this.

Gesturing towards Carla, firmly nestled into Zack's shoulder, Astrid finished with, "You make sure you take good care of this one. We love her to death, as you know."

"Or we'll hunt you down and string you up!" Fortuna smacked the table for emphasis.

"You don't need to worry about that," Zack said quickly, with a kiss to the top of Carla's head. "We're starting a new adventure. And I'm going to give it my best shot."

"Well, we'll see you soon at Sub anyway," Fortuna added. She and Astrid gathered up their coats and bags, and after kissing both Carla and Zack, skedaddled at speed.

* * *

Forty-five minutes later, Astrid and Fortuna were calming an irate Hiroshi and readying themselves for work. Zack and Carla were relaxing back in her apartment and enjoying a few more tranquil lines.

"So what's the plan maestro?" Carla enquired.

Zack considered for a moment. "We'd better keep going, that's all I know. If we try to rest now, we'll completely lose our momentum."

"Fine by me," she replied. "Where to then?"

Zack was about to answer, when his phone rang. He looked at the phone flashing the name 'Mako' at him. That was unusual he thought. Mako, phoning on New Year's Eve. It could only be interesting. So he pushed the green button.

"Zack man, where you been? I been callin' you for three hours!"

"I went out for dinner and forgot my phone, Mako. Besides, I'm not really talking to most people at the moment."

"Right Zack. Listen, we have to meet *right now* my friend. It's really fucking important. I have some things I need to tell you – in person."

What on earth was Mako on about?

"You want me to meet you now, on New Year's Eve? I hate to tell you Mako, but your timing sucks!"

"You gonna have to trust me on this Zack. I'm gonna send a car to bring you to a place of ours. This meeting is for your benefit. And it's top-secret. Just roll with it, okay?"

Zack considered his options. There weren't any really. You didn't fuck around with guys like Mako when they were being serious. Carla was going to kill him, but he would have to make this quick detour before they went out together.

"Alright," he said resignedly. "I'll wait outside Almond at exactly nine-thirty in the freezing cold. If your driver isn't there by nine-forty, the meeting will have to be postponed. I don't have a lot of time, and it's fucking New Year's Eve for Christ's sake. I have to meet some people." He looked briefly at Carla. "And my girlfriend is going to kill me."

"Okay ... good ... nine-thirty. The driver will be waiting."

The phone went dead.

Carla regarded him quizzically. "What, exactly, am I going to kill you for?"

Zack's mind was elsewhere. Despite the inconvenience, he was curious. Mako Takahashi was a major-league player. His father was practically the Emperor of Japan, in the *Yakuza* context anyway. What did he want with Zack? Zack could only imagine he had some information about Hans. *For your benefit*, he'd said. What did that mean?

"Ahem." Carla expectantly drummed her fingers on the table-top.

"Well. As you heard, I have to go. Now," Zack said, standing up. "That was Mako. He's not somebody you dick around with. I like him actually. He told me he needs to meet me. Right now. He has some information he needs to explain in person. So I'm going, for about two hours I'd guess. Then I'll come back here and we'll head out to Sub. Okay?"

Carla didn't like it. Apart from the fact she was enjoying this day in a way they hadn't enjoyed things for a while, she didn't like it anyway. And she didn't really know why.

She screwed up her face. "Well baby, I could tell you I don't want you to go, but I know you'll go anyway. I've seen that look on your face before. Just promise me you'll be careful, okay? And come back as quick as you can."

Zack was studying his phone. He'd missed nine calls during the time they'd been out. Five were from Mako. That underlined it, he thought. It was obviously important.

He looked back at Carla. "I'm really sorry my love. It's the absolute last thing I feel like doing at the moment. But I don't see I really have a choice. And yes, I'll make it as quick as I can." He pocketed his phone, leaned across the table and kissed her gently on each cheek before brushing her lips with his.

"I'll be back before you know it," he said.

She bumped his forehead gently with hers. "Okay," she said. "Go."

He separated himself, and carved off some coke onto the coffee table. "Just so you don't lose your momentum while I'm gone," he quipped.

Fifty

As the taxi crawled its way the kilometre or so to *Roppongi Crossing*, Zack's mind was whirling. Partly, he realised, because of the drug-fuelled afternoon, but also because this turn of events was so unexpected. Rarely was he as completely baffled by anything, as by Mako's call. The reason for it. The urgency of it. The timing of it. Moments before taking the call, he could not have imagined any event which might have separated him from Carla on this particular evening. Well, he thought, he would soon have some answers.

The taxi dropped him in front of the famous pink and white café at precisely nine-twenty-four. The last time he had been here, Zack reflected, was when he had broken down in tears about Hans's death whilst on the phone to Carla. Tonight he had no intention of actually going inside the café.

Plunging his hands to the bottom of the pockets of his parka, and with its hood pulled up to protect his ears from the winter cold, Zack stood with his back to the glass wall of Almond. There he waited, watching the infamous crossing buzz with feverish activity, in expectation of the massive party ahead.

A few of his former charges from Cloud Nine were wrapped up in head-to-toe faux-fur coats, reluctantly handing out flyers. Empathising with them, he gave them a comradely salute. A dozen steps from them were similarly-attired girls from BlackJacks whom he knew only by sight. One of them, he didn't know her name, waved to him. He waved back, smiling.

About the same distance from their group, facing towards Tokyo Tower, were a few guys from Gas Panic and Déjà-Vu, also reluctantly handing out flyers during this quieter part of the evening. All of them wore 'hoodies' or woollen beanie-style caps, because it was freezing. In most cities, just based on appearances alone, you'd give them a ninety percent chance of being drug-dealers, Zack thought. But he knew they weren't.

They were just other *gaijin* travellers trying to cash themselves up here, and party a bit along the way. To further ward off the cold, a communal hip-flask materialised from time to time, and they took turns to charge themselves up. Zack smiled to himself. A few years previously, he had been part of that group.

Before managing Bongoes on his first Tokyo trip, he'd helped launch a little-known bar nearby. It had been a lot of fun in the three months it had survived. Due in equal measure to a lack of funding for essential equipment, and a lack of interest from the owner, Zack had happily jumped ship to Bongoes when he'd been head-hunted by Steve.

The other bar had shut down shortly afterwards. But during that three months, he remembered many hours of standing on this corner in winter. Hours that consisted of handing out endless flyers and trading jokes with other *gaijin* nightlife workers, as well as the never ending sea of people surging past.

Zack had discovered that not many people enjoyed doing 'flyer-duty' on the crossing, but he hadn't really minded it. There existed a camaraderie of sorts between the foreigners working here, similar to that on the Eilat Marina, which he had always loved.

But doing flyers in a harsh Japanese winter was undoubtedly hard-core. You could only stay out for an hour, or at the most two, before running back to the warmth of the bar to defrost. On the street, he had rapidly become addicted to the nearby vending-machine's cans of coffee, appreciated as much for their hand-warming capacity as the syrupy-sweet caffeine hit they provided.

The blast of a car horn punctured Zack's reverie, and he looked quickly to the right, down the smaller one-way side-street adjacent to Almond. A gleaming Mercedes limousine had pulled over, its hazard lights flashing. Zack ambled across, bent down to catch the driver's eye.

"Zack-san?" The white-gloved, bespectacled driver checked him.

"*Hai*," Zack confirmed. The rear door popped open, and he made a show of stamping his feet to clear off any dirt, before climbing into the leather-clad luxury cocoon which comprised the stretched rear compartment.

About fifteen minutes later, Zack had no idea where they were. It had taken too long already he thought. At this rate he was sure to miss sharing the witching hour with Carla; that wasn't what he'd wanted for tonight. But if this thing dragged on and she had to find her own way to the party, it wasn't the end of the world. He would just have to meet her there.

He glanced out the limo's window. If he had to guess, he would say they were somewhere near *Shinjuku*. But if that was true, they had come via a route Zack wasn't familiar with. Not that that meant anything. He was about to quiz the driver about how much longer this journey would take, when they pulled into the basement car-park of what Zack guessed was perhaps a ten-storey building. Having glimpsed some neon signs on its side before they'd been swallowed by it, he judged they were entering the sort of building populated by restaurants and nightclubs on various levels.

The driver stopped the car next to the elevator. "*Dai roku-kai*, Zack-san."

Zack's Japanese was sufficient to know that meant the sixth floor, so he thanked the driver and got out. He noticed the driver was already on the phone, no doubt advising his superiors of Zack's imminent arrival. Entering the elevator, he pushed button number six, and tried to remain calm as it swished up past the other floors.

The doors opened to an opulent lobby decorated in rich colours; gold, vermilion, and navy-blue. Zack paused a moment to take in his new surroundings. About four metres from him was a reception desk staffed by one man and two extremely beautiful Japanese girls. Before he could approach the desk, one of the girls stepped around from behind it and came towards him.

"Zack-san. Takahashi-san is waiting for you. Follow me please."

Her command of English was as impressive as it was surprising, Zack thought. He nodded, and followed her without replying.

They walked about fifteen metres to the end of the corridor, turned right and approached a room protected by a large padded door. It opened with a small whooshing sound; Zack guessed the room was probably sound-proofed.

He did a classic double-take when he stepped across the threshold. A full-size billiard table, with a set of snooker balls set up and ready to go. He looked around. This was a dedicated snooker-room, complete with a bar, Chesterfield lounges and an electronic scoreboard.

In addition to the sound-proofing, Zack reckoned the room was controlled for humidity, probably for the benefit of the table itself. Mako waved at him from the far end of the billiard table. He was alone. Zack's pretty escort smiled and bowed ... to him or to Mako ... it was impossible to tell. Then she left.

Zack hardly noticed her departure. The billiard table was a beast of extraordinary beauty. Not a modern version, but an ancient-looking English thing. He ran his eyes over its lines, the way a car buff might a vintage sports car. Zack admired its fat, ornately carved oak legs, thinking it might be more than one hundred years old. It had obviously been expertly restored, and perfectly maintained since then. If Zack was ever going to have his own billiard table, he would want one just like this.

"So Zack, how do you like it?"

Zack laid his hands on the edge of the table. "It is very beautiful Mako, but you already know that." He continued without pause. "I must confess I'm a little more interested to know what the hell I'm doing here with only two hours left until next year."

"Zack, Zack, Zack. Always so direct. That is not the Japanese way, you know." Mako spoke amiably as he approached. He was dressed in an impeccable tuxedo and upon reaching Zack, extended his hand in greeting. Zack shook it. This experience was quite different to their typically drug-fuelled adventures in places like the Seventh Floor.

The whole thing was surreal, Zack thought. *What was he doing here?* In his parka, jeans, boots and sweater, Zack felt out of place ... somehow *inappropriate*. It was as if he had walked onto the wrong movie set, into a film he knew nothing about. Yet he was still obliged to play his part, whatever that was. Right now, he needed information like he needed oxygen. But he kept cool, and said nothing. Just met Mako's eyes evenly, and waited for clues.

Mako gestured towards the table. "Let's play while we talk?"

It sounded like a question, but it wasn't. Zack knew it would be useless to argue. That did not, however, mean he had to go down without a fight.

"Look Mako, I like you. You know that. We've partied. We've had some fun times. But it should be obvious to you, that being here is not where I want to be right now. So I'd appreciate it if you'd just let me know what's going on. It might not be the Japanese way my friend, but recently some *Japanese ways* have really started to get under my skin."

"Come on Zack," Mako countered. "Relax a little. You'll thank me for it, I promise. In the meantime, let's play a quick frame." Mako raised his eyebrows and proffered a cue, before adding, "The way you play, it won't take long, I'm sure."

How long had it been since he'd played on a full-size table? At least two years, Zack thought. A seedy billiard-hall in Bangkok was the last place he could remember racking up a few frames of snooker. He and some Brits he'd dredged up on *Khao-San Road* had played doubles for a while, before challenging some of the local talent. It was actually a fun memory of his last night in that deranged city.

He closed the distance between them and took the cue. "Okay Mako, have it your way. Let's play." Zack could see that was the only way Mako was going to get to the point. He might as well get it over with. Regardless, if he hadn't found out what he wanted to know by the end of this frame, he would leave.

Mako chalked his own cue, placed the white ball on the line just to the right of the brown, and made his shot. The white clipped the right-side of the triangle of red balls, narrowly missed the corner pocket, returned diagonally across the table, clipped the blue, and ended up more or less where it started.

He grinned at Zack. "I'm a bit out of practice, as you can see."

"I don't know why that would be," Zack replied cuttingly. "You don't have much else to do, and you have this room whenever you want it." This provocation went unchallenged.

"I'm curious Zack," Mako responded. "What sort of information do you have on our Nigerian friend Max, that keeps him so docile where *your activities* are concerned?"

Mako had timed his delivery to coincide with the moment Zack made his shot. For his part, Zack could almost not believe he had heard Mako correctly, but knew that he had. It was too late though. He had played the shot. He watched impassively as the red ball wobbled in the corner pocket, and sat there like a cherry. This night of surprises just kept rolling on, he thought. It was *inconceivable* that Mako could know anything about that matter, yet he evidently did. Zack's mind raced some more as he turned over the possibilities and implications of Mako's bold opening question.

"I'm not sure I know what you mean by that Mako," Zack lied. "I sort of know the guy you're talking about, but what does he have to do with me?"

Mako gestured at the red ball Zack had just left next to the pocket and smiled knowingly at him. "My friend. If that were true, that red ball would be in the pocket, you would be about to sink the black and you wouldn't have had to come up with a plausible lie, because you'd be busy building a break of, ohhh, I don't know." He looked at the lay of the balls. "About twenty or thirty, I would guess."

Fucking smartarse, Zack thought. This smooth gangster was even smarter than he'd credited. All of what he'd just said was true. But Zack just shrugged, kept his poker face, and responded affably. "Maybe I'm not as good at this game as you think I am, Mako."

Mako moved up to the table to start making the break which should have been Zack's.

"I am not in the habit of underestimating people, Zack. It's something I learned very early on, from my father." Bending over, he sighted the red ball down his cue. "And I should add that it's really not polite to lie to your host, especially when he has invited you here for the express purpose of *helping you*."

Zack narrowed his eyes at this, and watched Mako take his shot. He played it perfectly. The red went down cleanly. Zack was pretty sure he'd even managed a little check-side to stop the white drifting too close to the black as it came back from the cushion. Not bad at all. He smiled to himself as he realised just how easily he was again slipping into the enjoyment of this game.

"I wasn't aware I needed anyone's help," Zack replied evenly.

"That, my friend, is exactly the point." Mako deftly pocketed the black. He straightened. "It is invariably the things we *don't know about*, which hurt us."

Zack had no ready reply for that observation. He moved around the table and retrieved, then replaced the black ball on its spot.

The door to the room whooshed open, the pretty hostess reappearing with two drinks, some snacks, a jug of iced water and two glasses.

Mako gestured towards the tray. "Jack Daniels and Dry right? Or some water if you don't feel like drinking." Then he eyed up his next target red. "Anyway," he continued, "maybe you do need help, or maybe you don't. My information says you do. So as I said, that's why I invited you here tonight."

"Well if you're right Mako, you're going to have to provide that help pretty goddamn quickly. I'm leaving any day now."

Zack's timing for this comment proved spot-on; he watched with satisfaction as Mako double-lipped the red off the middle pocket and left it sitting there.

Mako stayed in the same bent position, closed his eyes for a moment, then looked up over his cue at Zack. "You're leaving Roppongi?" He was clearly stunned by this revelation.

"Yes Mako, I am. A very good friend of mine was murdered. Maybe you heard? They cut off his fucking head," Zack replied with unstudied bitterness.

He slammed the red into the middle pocket with more force than was necessary, and screwed the white ball down the table for an easy black.

"On top of that, another very dear friend of mine has had a nervous breakdown *because* of that murder, not to mention the perverted *Japanese ways* of one of her clients."

Zack slammed the black into the corner pocket, screwing the white ball hard back into the remaining cluster of reds. After watching them scatter nicely, he again stared hard at Mako.

"So I have decided to get out of here with my girl, and go lie on a beach for a while."

Mako nodded, replaced the black on its spot, and eyed the table thoughtfully. He knew he was now in trouble with this game. "Yes. I heard about your unfortunate friend. I'm sorry, Zack." He pursed his lips pensively, before continuing. "Well, if you *are* leaving, perhaps what I have to say isn't so important after all."

Zack sighted a red to the corner. To be truthful, he interested in the game than he was in whatever Mako thought so important. The red went down, and as Zack was pink into the centre pocket, Mako spoke.

"Zack, I think you should know that our organisation has engaged the services of your friend Max to manage some operations for us at ground level in Roppongi."

Zack's stomach flip-flopped, and his brain struggled to process Mako's announcement. *It had to be a joke!* He could manage only the grimmest of smiles. His *flow* was officially interrupted, and he straightened up from his shot without taking it.

"Mako. Seriously. Please tell me you are joking."

It was clear from Mako's expression that he wasn't.

Zack found himself shell-shocked. Utterly speechless in fact. His mind was still on Mako's bombshell. The implications were truly frightening. He wondered if they had any idea yet just how big a mistake they'd made, and how long this arrangement had been in place. For no reason other than to explore that, he decided to level with Mako.

"Mako. If you forget everything else I say tonight, please do yourself a favour and remember this." Zack took a deep breath. "If you really think you have that fucking psychopath somehow on a leash or under your control, you're as thick as the legs on this table."

Zack put his cue back in the rack on the wall, and took an angry sip from his JD.

"I mean, I can see *why* you guys might *think* it's a good idea, but hiring that fucking animal is going to be one of the worst decisions you ever made. If you want to rectify it, then I suggest you nip it in the bud, and get some distance. However it is your *organisation* goes about doing that sort of thing."

Mako looked a little rattled by the venom in Zack's remarks. "I thought you only *sort of* knew this guy Zack." This cheap comeback sank without trace.

Zack regarded Mako scornfully. "Do you have *any idea* of the things he's done back in his own country? I bet you don't, do you Mako? The guy is a mass-murderer for Christ's sake! A psychopath. He enjoys it! *Fucking Max*! I know more about that guy than anyone else in Roppongi does. Thinking you, your organisation, or anybody else can actually *control* a guy like that is just *insane*."

Zack waved his arms in the air, trying to pluck an apt metaphor from somewhere.

"It's like … like dealing with a rabid dog. You don't know *when* he's going to bite you. You only know that he *will bite you*. You can't fucking *keep* a rabid dog, Mako. All you can do is *maybe* keep it at arm's length for a while."

A pause to catch his breath.

"And does that do you any good? No, it doesn't!" Zack slapped his hand flat on the table for emphasis, and pinned Mako with an unflinching glare.

"The only way to rest easy is to *get rid of it*. Put it out of its misery, and thereby prevent your own."

Mako had remained motionless and silent throughout Zack's angry rant. Zack walked past him and sank into one of the Chesterfield lounges, nursing his drink. At that moment his phone beeped. Carla. She was going to the party without him. She would see him there. Zack closed his eyes resignedly. He needed another line. Good idea. Force a change of gears.

"Mako, wanna do a couple of lines? I have some incredible stuff."

Wrong-footed by Zack's apparent mood-switch, Mako hesitated for a moment. "Sure, why not?"

Zack broke out the package and carved four large lines on the black table-top. Their game was forgotten for a moment, as Mako came over and sat down next to him.

Zack did a line, proffered the rolled up note to Mako, and swiftly texted a confirmation to Carla.

"You know Mako, I can't wait to get out of this place. My best friend's been killed, for fuck's sake. I still can't actually believe Hans *no longer exists*!"

He watched Mako vacuum his line, then continued.

"It's just crazy. With all this shit that's happened, I've totally had it. Roppongi's a cesspit. And after what you just told me, I want to get out of here *even faster*. That sick fuck was a handful even *before* you guys decided to back him."

"You don't need to worry Zack. You're protected."

Mako, line cleanly inhaled, was now in more relaxed mode.

"That's why I wanted to speak to you," he continued. "I needed you to see the bigger picture, and find out what you wanted to do. In the meantime I issued a protection order specifically for you."

Zack regarded Mako in silent amazement. This smooth-talking, movie-star-looking *Yakuza* gangster had surprised him yet again. What to say to that? It was a remarkably thoughtful and kind thing to have done. Perhaps unnecessary, given Zack's own insurance in that respect, but Mako of course knew nothing of that. He had just gone ahead and done it.

"Mako, I'm genuinely touched. I don't know why you did that, but whatever the reason, I'm grateful. It's very generous of you."

Mako raised his glass, a salute. "I like you Zack. Always have. You're smart. And you're a gentleman. Besides which, you're one hell of a pool-player." His face creased into a knowing smile.

Zack clinked his glass against Mako's. Mako's expression as their eyes met was that of a real brother. Zack nodded his appreciation, then bent over to snort his second line.

"I didn't want to see you get fucked up or dead for no good reason," Mako continued. "I'm happy you're leaving Roppongi. It's a good time for you to get out of here. The next few months could get a little ... untidy."

Zack passed Mako the rolled bill, and nodded again. "I would have to agree with you there my friend." Then, as a series of ugly possibilities played out in his mind, he hunched forward over the table, his voice full of concern. "I'll say it again, Mako. You need to solve the Max problem. If you don't, it will blow up in your face."

Zack followed this up by pouring them each a glass of iced water, and pushed Mako's along the table.

Mako pondered this advice in silence, then snorted his other line.

"I appreciate your assessment of this individual, Zack. You can be sure I will keep it in mind."

For his part, Zack felt he'd done all he could. It was no business of his anymore, he thought. If they wanted to dance with the Devil, that was their call. The *Yakuza* hardly needed someone like Zack to babysit them.

He rose, with a purposeful grin back on his face.

"Now, it was my shot I think. Ahh, that's right. Pink. Centre pocket. This could be a game-winning break coming up, my friend."

Zack pulled him to his feet.

And the game continued.

Fifty-One

Ebi hobbled as quickly as he could along the frigid street, the package in his pocket. He didn't care that it was New Year's Eve; he had nothing to celebrate right now. His feet still hurt. He just wanted to get this job done, and go back to watching movies and eating junk food in his apartment.

One of his torturers, the one called Oju, had phoned and instructed him to pick up and deliver a package. Told him it was high priority, and that if he fucked up, he'd better leave town or they would finish the job they'd already started on him.

Since his beating, Ebi had found walking difficult. And this cold weather didn't make things any easier. After Max had left the torture-cell that awful day, the two thugs had gagged him again, covered him with a blanket, carried him out of the sound-proofed room like a piece of luggage, put him in the boot of a car and dumped him in the street next to a nearby subway station.

Sprawled on the sidewalk in the freezing cold, he realised he was unable to feel his feet. No-one had helped him. In that very Japanese way, the passers-by had all consciously averted their eyes, walking around him like he wasn't there. Suffering acute pain, it was miraculous that he'd finally managed to hail a cab, and get it to take him home. On the way he had called the only person who he knew would help him. His sister.

His body was bruised, burned and beaten. But the problem was his feet. They had been starved of blood whilst he was chained upside-down. Much longer, and it would have been too late; he would have lost them. A life without feet. The involuntary shudder which followed, had nothing to do with the cold. Fortunately, with help, his blood had eventually started re-entering those starved vessels. But the pain which accompanied that process had eclipsed all that went before it. Without the help of his sister, he doubted he would be walking by now; she had literally saved him.

Her tears had come thick and fast when she'd seen what they'd done to his skinny boy's body. As she tended to him, they had cried together. She made him sit on the bed and repetitively massaged his feet with oils and tubs of warm water. She interrupted the massages only to periodically dry his feet, and work in a diluted form of tiger-balm oil. Then she wrapped them in warm towels, which she tied gently with cord above the ankles.

During these rest periods, he was required to slowly walk around the heater in the centre of the room. She had disinfected, applied salves, and bandaged his other wounds. All in all, it had taken about thirty hours of rest and careful foot-massage, accompanied by the sustenance of *miso* soup, *onigiri* and *ramen*-noodles, before he had been able to walk again.

And only then, only when she knew he was going to be alright, had his sister started berating him for his choice of lifestyle. Although they never usually spoke about it, he knew that she knew about his street-life; how he made his money. Now she could no longer hold her tongue, and he had neither the motivation nor energy to fight her.

She had more than earned the moral authority to castigate him. She was right. He had to get out. And he had already made his decision to leave Roppongi. Hopefully his grandparents in *Kyushu* would take him in for a while. *Kyushu* was also warmer. Most importantly, it was a place that monsters like Max and his henchmen would not come looking for him.

* * *

Basking in strategically placed candle-light and a smooth electronic tribal beat, Carla had now thoroughly explored the marvel which was the party-site within this unfinished building. The *Subterranean* crew had done it again!

Utilising four floors for their purpose, what they had achieved in this construction-zone was nothing short of masterful. Sturdy canvas wind-breaks were set up on two sides to shield the interior from the brunt of the prevailing chill winds. Gas-cylinders attached to flame-heaters were plentiful within. Lounge furniture and settees had been brought in and positioned appropriately. Rattan matting had been used extensively in conjunction with Moroccan-style cushions so party-goers could relax in comfort.

The bottom 'party-floor', which was actually the third floor of the building itself, comprised the main dance area. The DJs were pumping out some fast and furious tribal techno, the likes of which Carla hadn't heard for a long while, and consequently the dance floor was in full swing.

The quality of the sound-system was outstanding, and because there were really no walls to speak of, there was none of the reverb which was common in many clubs. Just clean, pure sound, radiating out of the building into the night.

The next floor up was a bar and lounge area, serving mixed drinks, beers, and water. Carla was on the floor above that where another set of DJs were spinning ambient tunes at a slightly less intense volume. The final floor had a large central fire roaring within two welded metal drums, and this chill-out area was surrounded by more rattan matting and cushions. Bottles of water were also available at a booth in the corner.

On each level, it was obvious significant effort had been put into visual effects, and numerous psychedelic artworks were complemented by UV-light for maximum effect. The many-armed Hindu goddess Kali featured prominently.

Carla had used her tour of the venue to try to distract herself from how annoyed she was with Zack. It hadn't worked very well. And she was out of drugs, which wasn't helping. Bloody Zack! He had abandoned her. On this night, of all nights! And right after they'd had such an amazing day. Damn him! What in hell could be so important that he was standing her up like this on New Year's Eve? The witching hour had come and gone, and she was still alone.

Not that it had been a big event here. The crew and the people who came to these parties were far too cool to engage in anything as cheesy as a New Year's countdown! She didn't care; she had wanted to kiss him as the New Year commenced, and say a little prayer for their future together. Slumping into an armchair, she looked disconsolately at Zack's last message. *'Sorry. On my way now babe. See you by 1.30. All my love. XOX'*

She jumped up as quickly as she'd sat down. Damned if she was going to feel sorry for herself. She was going to *party*! Let Zack get here when he damn-well liked. She headed downstairs to the main floor to dance.

*   *   *

Zack lay back in the limo, sipping a glass of red wine as they crawled through the packed streets. After finishing the frame of snooker, he had persuaded Mako to come with him to the *Sub* party. It had taken some doing. Mako had wanted to play him again to avenge the loss. But although Zack had hugely enjoyed their game, he simply pointed at his watch. At one o'clock, he was already two hours late.

And so it was, that as he was being chauffeur-driven to the *Sub* gig with the son of the biggest *Yakuza* boss in Tokyo, Zack finally relaxed. Life was still far from okay, but things were turning around. Only a few more details to sort, and he and Carla would leave this sinister place behind them, probably for good.

Mako took a long drag on his cigar, glanced at Zack, and forcefully jettisoned most of the smoke out the small gap at the top of the window. He suddenly had a lot on his mind. Zack seemed very sure they had made a mistake in dealing with Max. And as Mako well knew, when it came to people, Zack did not make many errors of judgment.

Consequently, Mako wasn't feeling half as smug as he had been after closing the deal with Max in his father's penthouse board-room. He had thought Harada's gloominess in their conversation afterwards was only because of the showy way in which he'd intimidated and overcome Max.

But perhaps there was more to it than that. Perhaps the older, more experienced man had sensed something dangerous and amiss, that he himself had not. Perhaps he was already talking to Mako's father, and deriding both the style as well as the judgment of Takahashi-junior. Just because Mako had not heard anything from his father yet did not mean things might not be seriously amiss.

* * *

Irritated, and in more than a little pain, Ebi passed three thousand yen to the doorman, gritted his teeth, and hauled his sorry carcass up the candle-lit stairwell. Unlike most of the clubs in Roppongi, where all the doormen knew him and he had more or less a free pass to come and go, this was a different type of event: the doormen were one-offs, with whom he had no relationship. So, not only was he being forced to do this delivery on a night he'd thought would be his own, but he was having to pay for the privilege! The sooner he was out of Tokyo the better, he thought. But in the meantime, he would just follow the plan, text Oju that the job was done, and get back to base.

* * *

Carla found herself revelling in the music, but not completely letting go. She felt edgy, and couldn't help looking at her watch. It was one-twenty. She sidled through the heaving, sweaty mass of dancers, making for the stairwell. Water. She needed more water. She realised she didn't want more coke now anyway. It was time for a change. She wanted to move into New Year's day on an Ecstasy buzz. Well, Zack would have something, she thought. He always did.

Cold water purchased, she was about to go downstairs, when someone touched her arm. A slightly built Japanese youth who looked vaguely familiar, was speaking to her. She bent down, to hear him better.

"Present from Zack," he said, pushing a small package into her hand.

Quickly transferring it to her purse, Carla shouted back. "Thanks! What is it?"

"MDMA, with bit of speed. It's good. Sorry for late."

Carla radiated delight. Zack! Trust him to have a delivery arrive ahead of himself. And he had anticipated her mood! This was his way of apologising. Bending down again, she spoke into the courier's ear.

"I know you, don't I?" she said. "I've seen you around."

Ebi hesitated. "Don't think so. They call me Ebi. I just know you from BlackJacks. I see your show once. You very beautiful."

Carla beamed a full wattage smile directly into his face. He was really a sweet kid, she thought. Feeling much happier in light of this unexpected result, she kissed him on the cheek. She couldn't help wondering how he'd got the marks on his face. They looked painful.

"Thank-you Ebi," she said.

Ebi watched her walk across to the Portaloo toilet facility. She was really very nice, he thought. Not just beautiful on the outside.

*   *   *

Zack was on the stairs when he heard the screaming. He and Mako were ascending from the main dance floor to the bar floor. What the hell was going on, he wondered. At the top of the stairs, he noticed a crowd to his left. Near the Portaloos. Several girls were screaming hysterically and staring in horror at something on the floor. A guy who Zack guessed was the bartender shoved him aside as he came rushing through with a bucket of water. Instinctively, Zack followed him through the crowd to discover the cause of the drama.

In that moment, Zack's life moved into a different dimension of time and space.

He saw Carla on the floor.

His Carla.

On the floor.

Spasming wildly.

Legs splayed ... jerking.

Mouth open. Closed. Open. Closed.

White spittle foaming on her chin.

Eyes rolling.

Fighting for breath.

Zack roared, throwing people out of the way. Kneeling at her side, he felt reality crumbling into little pieces.

Her eyes opened.
She saw him.
She saw him.
She was scared.
But she saw him.

Zack felt panic rise in him. *This could not be happening!*

There'd been nothing wrong with her when he'd farewelled her four hours ago. She'd been fine! Something had gone horribly wrong. *Where to start? What had she taken?*

He grabbed a sponge from the bucket of water. Pressed it to her face.

Her head rolled. Her body twitched.

More water to arms and neck. Cool her down.

A low moan escaped from her body. An unearthly keening sound.

"It's okay baby! It's okay. We're gonna get you out of here."

He wiped drool from the side of her mouth and splashed more water on her face.

Her eyes closed again. *Maybe because of the water?*

He half-lifted her from the floor, cradling her head in his lap. Squeezing out the sponge, he wiped her face dry.

"Baby! Open your eyes! Who did this to you? What did you take? Tell me! I need to know what you've taken. Help me sweetie!"

Zack was frantic. Shouting at the top of his voice. Fighting against the heavy bass.

Carla's eyes opened.

She saw him.

She tried to speak. But her voice was barely a whisper.

Zack leaned down close.

"My heart, Zack. My heart … it's … going so fast."

Her voice had a dreamy quality. *He was losing her!*

Zack shook her and splashed water on her face. He had to find out what she'd taken. Now.

"Baby, help me. Please help me! Who gave you this stuff you took? Where is it?"

Her eyes fluttered closed, then opened again. She gasped for air.

"Can't breathe. Zack, help me. Help me!"

Zack picked her up bodily and moved her to the nearest couch, scattering people on their way. He sat her up, then propped her with cushions, and desperately tried to get her to respond.

She looked ghastly. No colour.

Her eyes opened. He took her hand, squeezed it hard.

"Baby, please help me! Who gave you this stuff?"

Her eyes closed again. But she pulled his hand to her breast, attempted to speak, and failed.

Zack could feel a lump. He pushed his hand under her bra, and extracted a small plastic pack of white powder. *The stash!*

She was trying to speak again.

"Sweet boy ... funny name."

"What was his name, baby? Tell me his name," Zack implored.

"They ... Ebi," she whispered. "Sweet boy. Scars."

Her eyes opened, and she looked at Zack for the last time. She saw him.

"I love ... you. Zack."

He felt her fingers curl around his.

Then she closed her eyes, and let go.

Carla was gone. And Zack's world went with her.

Fifty-Two

Zack sat cross-legged on the floor next to a vending machine in the hospital waiting room, his head in his hands. He was practically catatonic. He felt like a little child again. Adrift in a sea of madness. He no longer knew what to do. He could not move. He could not *feel* anything. And worst of all, he was unable to *think*.

Carla was dead. His beautiful girl was dead. *It just made no sense.*

He still could not really believe she was gone. It felt like a very bad movie. Or a nightmare that he might soon wake from.

It was officially over during the ambulance ride. Mako had got an ambulance there in under five minutes – it was a *Yakuza* special. It made no difference. They had given up CPR, taken off the respirator, and pulled the sheet over her beautiful still white face.

At that moment, an enormous and unspeakable rage rose in Zack. It was such an overwhelming feeling that he bowed his head between his knees for the rest of the journey. He forced himself to look inwards and focus on his breathing. He simply did not trust himself to interact with the paramedics who had failed to bring her back to him.

Carla was dead.

His fist was clenched around the small bag of white death. *What was this stuff?*

Carla was dead.

If only he had got there earlier ...

Carla was dead.

If only Mako hadn't called him ...

Carla was dead.

If only he hadn't answered his phone ...

Carla was dead.

If only he had said no to Mako ...

Carla was dead.

Carla was dead because of him. Why hadn't he been with his girl?

Mako had silently watched him sitting like this for more than an hour. They were not waiting for anything else, except for Zack to begin to function again. In an hour or two it would be daylight. He wanted to help Zack somehow, but how? Zack had not looked at him. Had not said one single word since issuing that anguished howl at the moment Carla had died in his arms at the party. When the ambulance arrived, it had taken four people to get him to let her go.

So when Zack spoke suddenly and clearly, it was a little disconcerting.

"Mako, would you drive me to *Nikko*? I need to think, and I want to do it there."

Zack hadn't raised his head, but Mako was relieved to hear him speak at all. He also had a feeling his answer would probably determine whether he'd ever see Zack again.

"Sure Zack. Of course ... anything."

Zack's red, puffy eyes met Mako's for the first time since the arrival of the ambulance at the party. "Okay, let's go."

Mako rose from his seat, putting out a hand. Zack gripped it, stood upright.

"You want to go home first? Get some things maybe?"

"No home. No people." Zack's face was a stone. "Get some cash. Then drive."

"Okay Zack. *Nikko* it is."

The driver was waiting outside. They got into the rear compartment once more. Mako instructed the driver to find a cash machine.

Cashed up, and clear of the city, Zack promptly went to sleep. Mako, wide-awake, wondered why, of all places, Zack had chosen *Nikko*. The little town was one hundred and thirty kilometres away. He opened the fridge-compartment in the console, poured himself a tonic water, and guessed he was fortunate Zack hadn't said *Kyoto*.

Given the hour, traffic was sparse and they made good time.

Zack woke shortly before their arrival and directed the driver to the *Chuzenjiko Onsen*, situated on the lake at the foot of the extinct volcano. Once they had pulled up, he turned to Mako.

"Mako, my friend. I have never asked you for anything. But I am asking for your help now. I can do these things without you if I have to, but it will take me more time and I just don't know how much of that I have."

"Tell me, Zack. We will do everything we can to help. You should know that."

"I need you to do three things," Zack said, reaching into his pocket, pulling out the packet of white death. "First. This is what they killed Carla with. I need you to get it analysed. Someone professional. It's a poison. Find out what kind."

Gingerly, Mako took the package.

"Second. There is a small-time dealer. Street name is Ebi. From memory he's a Japanese-Brazilian kid. Hangs around Déjà-Vu. He gave Carla this stuff. Hunt him down and find out the *who* and the *why* of this delivery."

Zack pressed his fingers to his temples. "Be *harsh* if you have to be. Whatever it takes."

He eyed Mako accusingly. "I think you will find your new *business partner* killed her, Mako."

Mako opened his mouth to protest, but Zack cut him off with a wave of his hand.

"Third. Call me when you have the answers. And don't lie to me about this, Mako. If you hadn't fucked up and brought that psychopath onto Team *Yakuza*, I am pretty sure Carla would be alive right now." He looked hard at Mako. "*I* might not be, but *she* would be. Trust me, Mako. I know how his mind works."

Mako opened his mouth, but was cut off again.

"Let me finish. If I'm right, continue as normal. Don't give any hint that you suspect him or that anything might be wrong. And obviously, I am off the radar as of now. This stays between us. That's all I ask. Can you do those things for me?"

A nod from Mako was sufficient.

"I need these answers in the next forty-eight hours, Mako. That's enough time for you to do what needs to be done. Don't string it out. Not for any reason at all. Otherwise I will assume the worst, disappear, and get things done myself."

Zack's face was haggard, his voice bitter. "So if you really want to help me brother, for the sake of the beautiful innocent girl who's just been murdered for no reason, please fucking help me."

Without a backward glance, Zack got out of the car and made for the hotel.

Fifty-Three

The room-bell made a harsh buzzing sound, jerking Zack from a deep dream. He instinctively rolled himself to a seated position and rubbed his eyes before blinking several times and glancing around the room.

The buzzer sounded again.

"Okay, that's enough," Zack shouted. "Who is it?"

Barring hotel staff, he knew it could only really be one person. God, he must have been deep under, he thought. Closing his eyes, he strained to remember some more of the dream. It seemed important, and in a few moments it would probably be gone.

"Open up Zack, it's me. Mako."

Mako? So he'd come back in person, instead of just phoning? Weird.

Zack's mind flashed back to the dream. He'd been chasing Carla through a broken-down building. It was a dark dangerous-looking place, but she had seemed completely unconcerned. She was laughing, teasing, and looking back at him as she ran. Then she waved, and flitted around a corner. Zack had sped up and reached the same spot within seconds, but she was nowhere to be seen.

He had stood there, flummoxed, looking in all directions. That she was gone was impossible. Then he heard her laughter again. But he couldn't see her. The way the sound echoed around the space meant he couldn't tell where she might be. That was the last thing he remembered before hearing the buzzer. He had been left standing in that place, frustrated, alone, and scared.

Pushing himself up off the bed, he warily opened the door. Mako was dressed immaculately in a dark-grey suit and crisp white shirt, with a bodyguard at his side. Zack peered up and down the hall. There was no-one else in sight, so he assumed the driver must be waiting in the car.

He stepped aside. "Come in Mako."

Mako moved inside, surveying the room with distaste. Zack knew he was accustomed to much more salubrious environments. Whether his expression was for the décor in general, or because it would have to be the setting for the conversation which would ensue, Zack couldn't tell, and didn't care anyway.

The bodyguard stayed in the hallway. Zack nodded respectfully to him and closed the door.

Mako leaned over the bed slightly and tested the firmness of the mattress. Thinking the better of it, he moved to the far wall, and seated himself on the chair by the window, crossing one leg over the other.

"How are you doing Zack, my friend?" He regarded Zack with a measured gaze.

Zack pulled a couple of pillows against the wall, sat cross-legged on the bed, and leaned against them. Popping the top on a bottle of water he took a long swig, before answering. "I'm okay. What have you got?"

"It was cyanide Zack. Practically pure. No doubt at all he intended Carla to die."

Zack bowed his head.

"The kid didn't know anything. He was just doing as he was told. We found him hiding with his grandmother in *Kyushu*. He was terrified. He thought *Max* had sent us to kill him."

Mako stopped in response to Zack's questioning expression.

"Sorry. There's a back-story. Only last week, Max's boys stripped him naked, hung him upside-down and tortured him with cigarettes and beatings. I saw the scars myself. He nearly lost his feet as well. Delivering that package was the last job he did for them before running."

Zack pondered this. *'Sweet boy. Scars.' Carla's last words were engraved in his memory.* So the kid, too, was just another victim. And it sounded like he had already suffered enough.

"We left him in *Kyushu*," Mako added. "His grandmother is so fierce we thought about recruiting her."

When Zack didn't register his wry quip, Mako adjusted his tone.

"We can pick him up again if you want Zack, but there's no point. Well, not until later perhaps. He might be useful in another way. Things are moving faster than any of us might have imagined."

Zack gestured for more information. "How do you mean?"

Mako ignored the question. "You need to come to a meeting Zack. Tonight. We have to leave soon. Trust me, it is a meeting you want to have. But I can't say any more than that right now."

Zack stared at Mako incredulously. "Let me get this right. You want me to come back to Tokyo, now, unprepared, for a mystery meeting, with unspecified people, for an unknown purpose?"

Mako knew how it sounded. So he said nothing, waiting for Zack's next thrust.

The words were bitten off precisely. "You know me more than a little by now Mako. *What in the motherfucking world* makes you think I would agree to that?"

Mako, frustrated, folded his arms, and jiggled his leg impatiently. His tone was mocking. "What's your plan, Zack? You're gonna kill this guy?" He waved his hands around in the air and pulled an imaginary gun. "Like some bad-arsed gangster-dude?"

Zack spoke coldly, as Mako finished his theatrical putdown.

"Firstly Mako, I don't see how any of that, is any of your business. Secondly, under the circumstances, I can *really* do *without* your fucking *sarcasm, my friend.*"

A heavy silence ensued.

Eventually, Mako leaned forward, clasping his hands together for emphasis. "Zack. Listen to me. Since I left you, I have hardly slept. Many things have happened. Things that have surprised me. And things that have surprised even *my father.*

It may interest you to know that he has interrupted a golfing holiday in Hawaii with his best friends, to fly back for this meeting tonight. We might have fucked up by dealing with the Nigerian, but now, I am *helping* you. *We*, are *helping you* Zack. You owe it to yourself, and to us, to attend this meeting."

Mako checked himself. "No, that's wrong actually. *You owe it to Carla*, to attend this meeting."

Zack had no ready response. His brain was several seconds behind Mako's words, trying to process their meaning.

Mako's father? What in hell was going on? In what possible way, could someone like Mako's father, be remotely involved in this? Let alone for it to be important enough for him to cut short an international golfing holiday!

Mako pressed the advantage he felt. He had known it would not necessarily be easy to get Zack to come. "I'll be blunt Zack. There are some people who like you. Powerful people. And given how you probably want to deal with this ... well, there is a better way."

Zack still said nothing. Whatever reservations he'd had about going to the meeting had vanished. His curiosity was more than piqued. If even half what Mako said was true, there was nothing that would now keep him from attending.

Mako, unaware of Zack's mental turnaround, opened his hands and placed them palms up, in a resigned form of offer. "Come to the meeting tonight and talk things through, Zack. Then you can do whatever you want." He knew the last part of that statement was not entirely true, but by then it would not matter. Zack would have changed his mind anyway.

They both waited in silence, just looking at each other.

"Okay Mako, you've persuaded me," Zack said matter of factly. "Let's go."

With that snap pronouncement, Zack got up. He gathered his few belongings together, simultaneously marshalling his scattered, multi-tangential thoughts. Then they walked outside to the waiting vehicle.

What next?

Fifty-Four

After returning from *Nikko*, Zack had spent the last couple of hours in the sanctuary of Mako's penthouse apartment, reading. The book was the latest from Bret Easton Ellis: *Glamorama*.

He'd read it when it first came out last year, but something had compelled him to pull it off the shelf again. Given his overall state of mind, and the surreal madness engulfing his life, it felt sort of appropriate.

Putting the book aside for a moment, Zack walked across the room to the floor-to-ceiling windows and looked down. He was about a zillion floors up in a building somewhere in *Shinjuku*. The mass of Tokyo's enormous metropolis sprawled into the distance.

How must it be, to live like this, Zack wondered. In a cocoon, above it all. Interacting with the seething mass of humanity below only when you chose to. Completely insulated by luxury: Ferraris, Limousines, Drivers, Butlers, Maids, Bodyguards. Apartments like this one.

Picking through *Glamorama* had again repelled, yet fascinated him. The human condition was so ruthlessly observed and exposed: it was like watching a sociological train-wreck in slow motion. You were hypnotised, spellbound. Nearly all its pitiless observations about human nature were accurate.

Acknowledging these nihilistic truths led to one becoming utterly dispirited about humanity per se. The perspective and style of writing made it possible to not only understand extreme superficiality, but worse, and completely against your will, to empathise with psychopathic mindsets.

The novel was a yawning abyssal vacuum of morality, intelligence, compassion, taste, and humanity. It sucked you into that void, held you prisoner and forced you to bear witness to the lives of appalling people it was impossible to care anything about. It was a good book, he thought, to give someone who could only manage 'borderline suicidal'. If anything would push them over the edge, *Glamorama* would.

When he'd last read it, he remembered wondering what the author was like in real life. Whether that seemingly irretrievable cynicism was real, or feigned; and if real, whether he was actually able to enjoy life anymore, especially having now garnered the sort of fame which was the only currency his own depraved characters seemed to respect.

Roppongi was surely the real-world playground for characters such as these, he thought. That was becoming ever-clearer to him. And now that he was once more centre-stage in this fucked-up movie, he wondered what that said about him, an habitué who had formerly been so comfortable, so at home here.

His brief respite in *Nikko* over, the train was picking up speed again. This tranquil moment observing Tokyo from above was merely another lull, before another inevitable storm. But it wasn't even his movie anymore. If it ever had been, he thought despairingly.

The director, whatever that creature was, had irrevocably shifted gears; clearly no longer cared about Zack's pitiful existence. Zack himself no longer knew his lines, or what he was supposed to do. All he really did know was that he wanted to see Max die, preferably painfully. Then he would figure out the rest, for whatever it was worth.

Zack heard the fridge open. Mako was in the kitchen on the other side of the cavernous space between them. "You want something maybe?" Mako held the door open.

"Diet-Coke, ice and lemon if you have it. Otherwise, just water. Thanks Mako."

While Zack waited for Mako to get his drink, he reflected on what lay ahead this evening. Once he had agreed to come, Mako had refused to be further baited regarding anything else about tonight's meeting. Only that it was important for reasons which apparently went beyond Carla, and that it would probably offer potential solutions which Zack should at the very least be aware of.

One reason Zack had started reading *Glamorama* earlier was to take his mind off the subject of the meeting; otherwise he would only torture himself by speculating fruitlessly about it.

Mako appeared at his side and passed him the Diet Coke. They stood by the windows, looking out over the city.

"Why are you, *the collective you*, helping me, Mako?" Zack asked quietly.

Mako sighed heavily before speaking. "It seems events have overtaken all of us Zack. It looks like we … me actually … made a mistake. A serious mistake. That mistake has now affected you, it has affected us, and it is still out there, affecting things. It needs to be dealt with properly, for the good of all of us."

Zack looked sideways at Mako, mentally willing him to continue.

Mako obliged. "So as it happens, our *interests* seem to coincide."

He sipped his Scotch.

"This meeting tonight is a very big deal, Zack. You will see something no gaijin has ever seen before. I am telling you this for your own good. I myself, still cannot quite believe this meeting is really going to happen. Even moreso, with you present. It is a great honour. You will understand why, afterwards."

Zack, ever wary of undeserved flattery, wondered how much of this was just some kind of sales pitch. *But for what?* Perhaps Mako thought Zack might yet change his mind?

But his expression was earnest. "Zack, I urge you to put aside your rage, hatred and desire for vengeance *for the time being*. In the meeting, behave respectfully, and rationally. If you *can* do that, it's very likely we will all walk out of there with a solution which works, and we can live with."

Mako drained the rest of his scotch before finishing.

"If you *can't*," he spread his arms wide, "whatever happens next will be completely *out* of my hands." A nod. "We leave at eight-thirty. Be ready."

Not needing a response, Mako dropped his glass in the sink, returned to his bedroom, and closed the door.

Zack looked at the closed door and returned to the sofa. Pondering Mako's pronouncements, he very deliberately put *Glamorama* back where he found it on the bookshelf.

If he was going to read at all, he would read something else; he did not want Easton Ellis's morally vacuous psychotic characters seeping into his mindset before the meeting.

Fifty-Five

As the limousine pulled into traffic, Zack stared indifferently at the multitudes on the other side of the bullet-proof glass and felt as ready as he ever would, for what lay ahead. As he saw it, he had nothing to lose by attending this meeting. Whatever its outcome, if it wasn't to his liking he could always revert to Plan A.

As an aside to this, he also thought he was starting to have a better understanding of why extremely wealthy people often acted as badly as they did. He had only been in Mako's cocooned environment for a short period of time, but he was already feeling more dissociated from the world at large and from the people often disdainfully referred to as 'the great unwashed'.

Admittedly, this feeling of dissociation could be due to the fact he was, and had been for some time, operating under a great deal of emotional stress. But he still felt the idea had validity, regardless. Such dissociation from the *everyday*, could only lead to the feeling that you were indeed somehow *better* than the rest. And once that illusion set in as part of your psyche, it became your reality, after which anything became possible.

With this thought he suddenly realised the insidious themes from *Glamorama* had not left him so easily after all.

The car slowed; Zack looked out and up. The landscape was familiar; they were entering the same building where he'd visited Mako last time, when they'd played snooker.

When Carla was still living, breathing, dancing, and laughing.

Could that really have been only a few short nights ago? He knew it was, but it seemed like a parallel universe now. It was eight-forty-eight when they exited the car and entered the elevator. This time Mako inserted some sort of security key and they did not stop at the sixth floor, but went all the way to the top.

As the doors opened they were met by a uniformed attendant, who took their coats. Mako walked smartly down the corridor to the right and stopped outside a set of thick wooden double-doors. Zack was close behind him as he knocked.

"Are you ready Zack?" Mako's gaze was unusually intense. "Remember: respectful and rational."

He opened the doors and they went in.

Zack didn't know what he had expected, but he could hardly have been more surprised by what he saw.

His worst envisioning had included the possibility of Max being in this room. Thankfully, that was not the case. Inside this old-style boardroom were three elderly Japanese men sitting around the end of the boardroom table. Zack already knew two of them. He could only guess that the third must be Mako's infamous father, the *Oyabun*, Takahashi-san.

Zack's surprise came from the identities of the other two men. The one seated at the head of the table was none other than Tanaka-san, his Japanese pool-buddy from the Seventh Floor. And to Tanaka's right sat the policeman, Sakamoto-san.

Mako guided Zack to the chair beside Sakamoto, then spoke. "Zack, you already know everyone here except my father, Takahashi-san." Pausing, Mako looked at Takahashi senior. "Father, this is my friend, Zack Morrissey."

Mako bowed deeply to his father and the other two men. Zack, still somewhat stunned at how things were unfolding, dumbly followed suit, then sat meekly in the proffered chair. Mako also took his seat.

What the hell was going on here? This made no sense! No sense at all.

Looking at Zack's bemused expression, Mako realised it was probably time to give him some context. It had after all, been Tanaka-san's strict instruction not to give Zack any foreknowledge of the participants. In telling Zack about his father in order to ensure his attendance, Mako felt he had breached sufficiently little of this instruction.

"Zack, you already know Sakamoto-san. Tanaka-san is his boss."

Zack's mind, already reeling, was pushed to another level. *His pool-playing, gambling friend Tanaka-san was Sakamoto's boss?*

This was crazy. He was falling through the looking-glass at speed now. Tanaka-san, that harmless, charming, funny little guy from whom Zack had cheerfully taken winnings at the Seventh Floor, was a cop! And not just any cop! He was in charge of a hard-head like Sakamoto? It was unfathomable!

So despite the money he had taken from Tanaka, it looked like Zack was the one who'd been 'played'. And now he was having a meeting with two very senior Japanese police-officers, the most powerful Yakuza boss in Tokyo and his son, in one of the board-rooms of a building which seemed to be Yakuza headquarters! Why would these people ever choose to be in the same building, let alone the same board-room?

Still bewildered, Zack surveyed the room and blinked once or twice, to check he wasn't hallucinating.

At that moment, Tanaka stood, leaned across the table, and extended his hand to Zack. Zack reflexively stood, and shook it.

"Zack. I ... for all of us," Tanaka gestured with his head to Takahashi and Sakamoto, "very sorry ... for your girlfriend. For Carla. Is very sad." He clasped his hands, almost as if to pray. "When I meet her ... I think she ... very nice lady. Very smart lady."

Zack bowed his head and felt tears coming to his eyes at these heartfelt words and at Tanaka's very Japanese pronunciation of Carla's name. Holding the tears back, he raised his head. "Thank-you Tanaka-san. I appreciate that. Very much." He composed himself as they resumed their seats.

Tanaka opened the meeting. "Zack. We know the facts. We know what happen."

Tanaka motioned to Takahashi, whose English, when he spoke, was as perfect as his son's, although with less of an American accent.

"Zack. My son has explained how these events came to be. And my old friend Tanaka-san here, has also explained the misfortune which befell your friend Hans. But I will leave that strange, and somewhat incredible story, for him to tell."

He picked up the smouldering cigar in front of him, took a deep pull on it and sent smoke spiralling into the air between them. "I must say Zack, I was curious to meet you. I had heard about you, of course, from my son. But I wondered how it could be that a *gaijin* who has been in this country barely six months has been central to so many extraordinary events in just the last few weeks."

He tapped some ash off the cigar. "Right now Zack, you must be wishing you never came back to Japan." Takahashi's black eyes bored through the blue-grey pall of cigar-smoke into Zack's.

Zack held his gaze, poker-faced, entranced by the certainty with which this man carried what was obviously absolute power. Zack had the strong impression that as a consolation for having his holiday interrupted, Takahashi was somehow deriving *amusement* from this situation.

"It seems things have not turned out so well for you, or your friends."

Zack felt as if he were dreaming again, and let Takahashi's tastelessly understated observations roll over him.

"I am an old man Zack. Right now, I should be relaxing and drinking Pina-Coladas with old friends in Hawaii. But as you can see, I am not."

Gesturing towards Tanaka and Sakamoto, Takahashi continued. "Instead, I received a mix of good and bad news, the combination of which was sufficient for me to fly back to Tokyo, where I am catching up with an *even older* friend, and his famous protégé, here in my own building." He chuckled slightly at some private amusement. "But my work here is done."

He turned his focus to Mako. "I would like to think my *son* can continue to represent our interests here." He got to his feet. So did the rest of the room.

Takahashi bowed curtly but deeply to both Sakamoto and Tanaka, bidding them farewell in Japanese. He nodded to Mako and to Zack, before pinning Zack with that predatory stare.

"Zack, you are young. You have borne witness to rare people and rare events. It is important that you find the lessons, and take them with you when you go."

Takahashi then left the room.

With his exit, it seemed to Zack that a great pressure had also left the room. Involuntarily, he exhaled, as though he'd been holding his breath unawares.

Across the table, Tanaka chuckled. His eyes sparkled merrily as he looked at Mako. "Your father, Mako. Still the same. Never change."

Mako agreed, reluctantly. "It is never ... easy."

Zack finally found his voice. "Does anyone feel like telling me what is going on here?"

Mako exchanged a glance with Tanaka before speaking.

"Tanaka-san and my father have been, well, friends. Since they were boys." Mako raised his eyebrows. "As you can see, their life-paths have diverged considerably since their school days. But it is fair to say that both have reached the top of their respective professions. They are like opposite sides, of the same coin."

A memory flashed into Zack's mind of the night at the Seventh Floor when Mako had come in whilst Zack had been playing pool with Tanaka. He remembered the strange energetic shift, and how Tanaka had left before finishing the game. So that was it. They knew each other! And had clearly known each other for a very long time.

"Okay, I get it," Zack said. "But why this meeting? Why now?"

Mako looked to Tanaka for guidance.

"Mako-san, you English so much better than this old man. Tell him."

So Mako continued. "Tanaka has decided it is time to clean up Roppongi, Zack. There has been too much trouble. It looks very bad for his department."

Things were becoming clearer to Zack. *This meeting was a professional courtesy, between old friends!*

Mako was still talking. " ... first Hans, now Carla. And they are just the people *you* know Zack. Tanaka tells me there have been at least a dozen other deaths these last few months. It cannot continue like that. It does not look good for Tanaka. And it's not good business for us."

Not good business? Carla's death. Hans's death. Not good business? Zack could hardly believe what he was hearing. He felt his anger rising and looked across at Tanaka.

He was surprised to find Tanaka studying him intently, and as Mako's brutally candid explanation continued, it seemed Tanaka was reading Zack's mind because he shook his head minutely, and closed his eyes for a moment.

Zack recalled Mako's words ... *'respectful, and rational'* and wondered whether it was Tanaka who had provided those words. Right now, his old friend seemed to be a kind of sage.

" ... and our Nigerian friend is responsible for the vast majority of this mess." Mako paused. "It seems old habits, die hard."

Zack acknowledged Mako's final comment, calmed himself, then addressed Tanaka. "Tanaka-san. Based on what Takahashi-san said, do you have any more news about what happened to Hans?"

Tanaka gestured to Sakamoto, who shifted in his seat and cleared his throat with the sound that was now familiar to Zack.

"Hinh. Hnhh. Yes. The man who killed Hans is Japanese. He is dead." The statement was typically blunt.

Although it appeared Sakamoto had finished, Zack knew there was more to come. He waited.

"His wife. She kill him. The wife. She also, is dead. Maybe she kill herself." Sakamoto glanced at Tanaka. "We think so."

Zack raised his eyebrows at Sakamoto. Was there more?

"Hnhh. Your friend have ahhh ... rerayshonship with her ... ahhm ... before."

Zack winced at the completely unnecessary final word.

Sakamoto leaned back, arms folded impassively. Zack observed that his short speech had required a disproportionate amount of effort.

That instant, Zack felt a weight lifted from him. *Hans's death had nothing to do with him! It was gruesome and terrible ... but it wasn't his fault. Thank God!*

He sank back into the luxurious leather chair, his clenched fists easing open on his thighs, his eyes closed. A few seconds passed in silence. Then Zack's eyes opened and sought Sakamoto's.

"His parents know this? You've told them?"

This time Tanaka chose to answer. "Yes, Zack. We tell them yesterday." His lips compressed before he continued. "Hans's parents. They take his ... ahhh ... remains. They go home, tomorrow."

Zack sat, picturing Kristiaan and Annemieke. At least they were going home with closure, he thought grimly. That was a commodity he would like some of.

As if picking up on a cue, Mako said, "Zack, now we must talk about Max."

"Just a minute Mako." Zack held up a hand. "Your father mentioned good news. What was that news?"

Mako looked quickly at Tanaka, who gave a nod. "The man who killed Hans was a *Yakuza* named Toshiko. He is an ..."

Mako backed up and corrected himself. "He *was* ... an enemy of our family. He was a big problem for my father for many years. It is an incredible thing, but because he killed Hans, his wife somehow managed to kill him. The way he died ... a *Yakuza* ... killed by a woman. His own wife. My father finds it ironic and, I'm afraid, amusing."

That explained the chuckle, Zack thought. Incredible was the word alright.

"But to return to the matter at hand, Zack?" Mako said, "I must now say some things you might not like." Gesturing towards Tanaka and Sakamoto, he explained that he would do the speaking because he had the best English. Anything needing clarification would be discussed amongst the three Japanese and then reiterated for Zack in English.

Mako cleared his throat and began. "As I said, you are probably not going to like this my friend, but once you hear what I have to say, you will realise that realistically, like us, you have no other option. The main thing you need to understand is that what I will explain to you now has already been planned and agreed between our organisation and Tanaka-san; it is not open to negotiation by you or anyone. We are telling you about it only because we believe you want to hunt Max down and kill him. If you were to attempt that, it creates a problem for all of us."

Mako checked Zack's expression. It was unreadable. "If I was you," he went on in a less formal tone, "I would want to do the same."

Another glance at Zack. "But my friend, we are all in agreement that there has been quite enough, shall we say, *disorganised* killing going on lately."

Poker-faced, Zack listened, absorbing and processing the Japanese blueprint.

"Our plan simply cannot work with you running around like some sort of wild-man vigilante, trying to kill Max. Therefore, you cannot be permitted to follow that path. We forbid you to take action of your own against Max."

He weighted his next words with significance. "For *us* it would be better if you left Japan immediately. But we will not *force* you to do so. However, if you wish to remain here during the clean up Tanaka-san will direct, you must go into complete hiding. We will help you with that."

Zack folded his arms, lowered his eyes.

"If you choose to stay here and *do not* stay in hiding and *do not* follow our instructions exactly, one of our organisations will pick you up, and you will be deported from Japan on the first available plane."

Mako let some seconds elapse after this ultimatum. He concluded his oration in a more conversational tone. "Put simply Zack, we need some space to dismantle the problems Max has created for us. Tanaka-san and I both give you our word that Max will *not* be walking away from his many crimes."

Zack was conflicted. He knew now he had been tricked into this meeting. And that annoyed him. But he also felt relieved; he was not going to have to fight this battle all by himself. That path clearly no longer existed for him. He couldn't conceivably remain operational in Tokyo if *either* the police *or* the *Yakuza* were seriously on his trail. But with both allied against him, it was a logistical dead-end. Zack realised he'd been well and truly snookered.

He looked back at Mako, then to Tanaka. "Okay, you've got me. You all know I won't try to fight you. That would be crazy. And I'm not crazy. Not yet, anyway." He sighed, looking at all of them in turn. "But I do want to know the plan. I think I deserve that much."

Mako deferred to Tanaka. This decision was clearly in his court.

Tanaka put his hands flat in front of him on the table. "Okay Zack, we will tell you."

Fifty-Six

Max stalked around his apartment in frustration. On the surface, everything was good. But he was worried: two things were bothering him. One was a small thing, but the other? Well, it was more serious.

The girl had died of course, as planned. Which was good. But then the courier had mysteriously disappeared. His phone was out of service, and they couldn't find him anywhere.

Max wanted him dead, had planned to have him killed the following day. It was a long-time habit of Max's to never leave anything which could link such jobs back to him. But the courier had vaporised almost instantly. And worse still, Zack too, had vanished. It had been over two weeks now. The moron-twins were on rotating shifts outside Zack's apartment, but so far there was no sign of him.

Max forced himself to sit down. He lit a cigar and tried to relax. Perhaps he should be grateful Zack was gone. But instinct told him otherwise. What was frustrating him was that he couldn't do anything about it. How did you fight an enemy you could not find?

The main thing was that business was looking good. His army of street-dealers was taking shape nicely. And he was rapidly firming up his regular deliveries to various bar and club owners as well as private high-net-worth individuals.

As far as he knew, there was nobody on Roppongi's streets who now openly opposed his rule. It was a good result, he thought, and one that had taken remarkably little time to accomplish.

It was just the Israelis now. They had gone into lockdown. But when they tried to continue supplying product clandestinely, they would be met with an iron fist. The rest of the bit-players had fallen into line. Anyway with time and effort, he knew the Israelis would fold. They had to.

After all, he had the big guns, and those big guns were very happy with his work. He would talk to Harada soon about getting some extra help with the Israeli problem. Max had recently revised his opinion of the respect the *Yaks* were capable of showing him.

Harada had yesterday phoned him personally, to express their satisfaction at his progress. As a reward for Max's hard work, Harada explained they were going to allow him access to a drug pipeline beyond compare. Max could hardly believe he had been so successful, so quickly. It was better than his wildest dreams.

To think that now he wasn't even going to have to actively source product, or worry about lines of supply. He merely had to distribute the product, via an absolute monopoly, to the hordes of eager users Roppongi so readily provided. He had become the king in a very short time. All his hard work and risk-taking was about to pay off, big-time.

Very soon he would be meeting Harada face to face, to take delivery of the first of several large and varied shipments. They had asked him what he needed, and he had told them. All the boxes of his order had been ticked, including, to his elation, the weaponry. As of tonight, he could put the word out on the street that supply and security was guaranteed.

Roppongi's drug-fiends would get as much as they wanted of whatever they wanted. He was even going to relax the prices, for a while anyway. Draw the punters in, then lock them in. It was a tried and tested strategy.

Max had also decided to get more heroin onto the streets. He had invariably found this the most useful drug for enslaving people. And Max wanted more girls in his stable. He was bored with the current crop, and was sure their customers felt the same way.

Taking another pull on the cigar, he mellowed a trifle. This game was all about control, he thought. Control was what it took to be successful. It was always going to be a jungle out there. And jungles inevitably needed a strong hand.

Life in Roppongi was about survival of the fittest, and he was determined to stay the fittest for a very long time. Stubbing out his cigar, he headed to the bathroom to get ready. Today was a big day, and he wanted to be sharp.

One hour later, he was sitting in the back of the hired BMW, with Henry at the wheel. They were parked across from the elevator on the third floor of the agreed multi-storey car-park, waiting. Max found himself unexpectedly excited. This first shipment alone would net him $100,000 personally, and it would be just the first of many such shipments. And he would of course grow the current market.

Who knew what might develop? If he continued to impress the *Yaks* in Roppongi, maybe they would give him additional fiefdoms to rule? Outsourcing seemed to be the key to success these days; why should it be any different in this business?

The elevator doors opened and he saw Harada exit and come towards him. Harada joined Max in the back seat.

"Congratulations Max-san." Harada grinned warmly. After shaking Max's hand, he passed him a bright yellow envelope sealed with a red gob of wax.

Max looked at him blankly.

Harada casually waved a hand. "Open it later. It is a gift. A token of our appreciation and continued support. We have much success ahead of us."

As Max tucked the envelope into his jacket pocket, Harada continued matter of factly. "Once I leave, you will pop the trunk of this car. A dark-blue Mercedes will arrive. It will stop in front of your car. A man will transfer two boxes to your trunk. They will leave. After that you are to wait three minutes before driving to the safehouse."

Max nodded. "I understand, Harada-san."

Harada patted Max on the shoulder, opening the door to exit.

"Harada-san." Max's expression was one of gratitude. "I want to thank you once again for this opportunity. You will not regret your decision."

"I think you are right, Max-san," Harada replied smoothly. He stepped from the car, and vanished down the nearby stairwell.

Within a minute, the Mercedes arrived. The driver waited, a security guard stood sentry, while a hefty chap deposited the cargo into the BMW's trunk.

Max's excitement grew. It was really happening! His exultant mood so took him, that he couldn't help sharing his pleasure with Henry. As the Merc pulled away, Max punched him softly on the shoulder and whispered, "We've made it this time Henry! And this is just the beginning."

When the elevator doors opened in front of them, Max, engrossed in his plans for greatness, did not immediately see the eight heavily-armed, military-style officers striding purposefully towards their vehicle. Two levelled their weapons at Henry and Max, while others motioned for them to get out. In typical Japanese style, one officer carried a digital video camera, recording everything as it happened.

It took Max fully five seconds, to realise this was really happening, and happening to him. Everything slowed to snail's pace, and Max could feel his life slipping away, as events and forces beyond his control took over and imposed themselves on his reality.

Henry was already out of the car, hands above his head. Max watched incredulously as Henry lay down on the cold concrete and was restrained with flexi-cuffs.

Max looked to his window. The guns were still levelled at him, and the officers were now yelling at him. In a daze, he clicked open the door and slowly levered himself out of the car.

They had fucked him. Those double-dealing, back-stabbing, slanty-eyed Japanese animals had fucked him!

As this realisation enveloped him like a funeral shroud, his mind fought against the truth.

Why? He had done nothing wrong! In fact he had done everything right. Textbook.

Max felt himself being forced roughly to the ground, a boot on the side of his throat. His arms were twisted up behind his back and secured.

Then he was manhandled into the rear of a police vehicle. In front of him was a metal-reinforced Perspex grid. Swivelling to follow the police movements through the window he saw them search the BMW, placing its cargo onto the pavement and hood.

The two boxes were unceremoniously ripped open, the camera greedily recording the contents. Max saw weapons and drugs. Everything he had asked for, and probably more.

But why?

His vehicle started moving, and quickly traversed the distance to the ground floor exit. Max saw another armed policemen at the barrier ahead.

At a signal, the policeman activated the barrier control.

It was then Max saw the other person in the booth.

It couldn't be! This could not be happening!

As the car approached the barrier, Zack's face became clear.

His eyes were locked on Max, and the two had eyes only for each other as the car passed through. For a split second, they were less than a metre apart.

When he saw what Zack was holding, Max's mind rebelled. *Impossible!* But there it was.

Zack was slowly waving it at Max. Backwards and forwards it went.

The object was unmistakable.

It was an envelope.

A bright yellow envelope.

The same bright yellow envelope Harada had just given him.

It was still in his jacket pocket.

'Open it later,' Harada had said. *'It's a gift.'*

Fifty-Seven

Zack stood atop the windy knoll, hugged his jacket tighter around him, and stared into the distance. In every sense of the expression he had come a very long way to be here. Squinting against the breeze, he could see water to the north and the west. Bringing his gaze down a little, all he could see were graves. There were thousands of them.

Vancouver's Mountain View Cemetery unfolded in all directions. He fingered the bottle in his pocket. Six months ago it would have contained Jack Daniels, or something similar. But he was past that now. He wasn't what he would call 'better'. But he was alive. And he was clean. He hadn't had a drink or done drugs for more than six months. In short, he'd got through the bad times. He'd stopped hating himself. He'd stopped punishing himself.

It had taken a while.

Zack's eyes wandered to a small child about a hundred metres away. She was standing with a woman who was probably her mother, he thought. Or maybe an aunt. The woman had a dark purple umbrella open, even though it wasn't raining. He watched the woman gesture to the girl to put the small bunch of flowers she held on the patch of stone in front of them. He wondered fleetingly what their sad story might be.

Zack knew he would never actually forgive himself for what had happened to Carla. How it had happened. Why it had happened. He just couldn't. She would always be with him. But he also now knew she wouldn't have wanted him to squander his life in a violent death-spiral of self-destructive obliteration.

That realisation had, ironically enough, come to him in a moment of lucidity during one especially severe bout of self-destructive obliteration. In that moment it was almost as if he could hear her voice … at once scornfully admonishing him for his stupidity, and then pleading with him to save himself.

He'd been in Bangkok at the time. The perfect city in which to drown oneself in wretchedness. When he'd woken the next day it was with a single thought.

If he stayed in this city, it would happily kill him.

Looking back with a clearer head, he guessed that's probably why he'd chosen it when quitting Tokyo.

He'd been permitted to visit Max in jail prior to leaving. However, the satisfaction of seeing that scum raging at him like a caged beast had speedily dissipated. He supposed that putting someone like Max more or less permanently behind bars *was* a kind of service to the world at large.

But it was not enough. Nothing ever would be. Nothing would bring her back. Nothing could make it better. It had been a senseless waste brought on by a colossal error of judgment. His judgment. She had died because of him: because of his selfishness, and his hubris. He'd been too fucking arrogant to see it coming. He replayed those events over again, as he'd done endlessly since then.

It had been impossible for him to attend Carla's funeral.

Following the official notification by Japanese police, her parents had arrived swiftly in Tokyo to claim her body and try to understand the nature of the tragedy which had befallen them. But Zack couldn't see them, couldn't help them. He'd been obliged to remain underground, in the shadows. At that time, putting Max behind bars or seeing him dead, had been his top priority.

Zack knew Carla's folks had even suspected him, Zack, of killing their daughter. Tanaka and Sakamoto had told him this much. He'd been wounded by this, but not really surprised. He didn't blame them. Why wouldn't they suspect him? They didn't know him.

They had actually put significant pressure on the two policemen to locate Zack for questioning. But given the overall plan Mako and his father had already hatched with the police, there was a bigger game unfolding.

Sakamoto had stonewalled them, playing for the time they needed for Max to be entangled in a net he couldn't escape from. Zack could not even begin to guess at how frustrating this time would have been for them. But his remaining hidden had been a necessary cruelty; there had been no other way to ensure justice would be done for their daughter.

He had watched them during their time in Tokyo. Being in hiding, he'd had nothing better to do, and it had taken his mind off the tension of waiting for the Max trap to spring. Zack had maintained an altered wardrobe: unshaven, head-gear, dark glasses, and Roppongi was a no-go zone. He had changed his mobile number, and only three people knew it: Tanaka, Sakamoto, and Mako.

From the night of Carla's death, he had expunged himself from the Roppongi landscape. Zack knew the sort of vacuum his complete effacement had left after Carla's death. It was easy to imagine the feverish speculation whizzing around the Roppongi rumour-mill during that time.

The only person he'd felt particularly sorry for was Shunit, and before changing SIM-cards he had texted her a solitary message with his email address, letting her know he was fine and would contact her later.

Tanaka would surely have horse-whipped him had he known that one night, whilst enhancing his anonymity with a hat, scarf and funky eye-wear, Zack breached Roppongi's outer territory in order to have dinner just a few tables away from Carla's folks.

It had not taken him long to regret the idea. Carla's mother Vivien had spent most of the evening staring into a jug of iced water, hardly touching her food. Terence had eaten with a mechanical stolidity, as if seeking reassurance in a habitual process. They had exchanged no more than three sentences throughout the entire meal. Zack could see they too, like Hans's parents before them, were utterly broken.

It had been heart-wrenching to watch, and incredibly difficult not to go to them. But to do so would have been folly. What would he have said? What *could* he have said? For them, Zack was nothing but a spectre who was responsible for their only daughter's death, and who was now haunting their grief with his elusiveness.

Zack winced at the memory; he could only hope they had thought better of him after Max was arrested and then convicted of Carla's murder. But he doubted it. After all, their only daughter was gone, and Zack was just another player in a series of events they would never fully know about, let alone understand. Maybe a time for talk would come one day, he mused. Maybe one day he would visit them, beg their forgiveness, and explain some things. If they would let him.

Zack swayed in the raw wind. To be honest, he had no idea whether it would do anyone any good. Did he want to do it just for himself? Could it do any harm to set the record straight? Could it really ever do them any good to know how close they had been to having both him and Carla safely together with them in Vancouver? To perhaps taking Zack in as their son-in-law?

These were now unanswerable questions. Zack had absolutely no idea. These days he felt a peculiar lack of ability to properly judge things or make good assessments. He no longer had confidence in his capacity to understand situations, read people, or reliably predict behaviours and outcomes.

The brutal reality, was that he doubted Carla's parents would ever be able to look at him without blaming him. Therefore, following up with them was an idea which would have to keep for another trip.

This trip was for Carla. Just Carla.

He dropped his eyes again to the headstone in front of him.

Carla Louise Verity De Lange
b. 2 November 1973 – d. 1 January 1999

Our beautiful graceful dancer, cruelly and abruptly taken from us on foreign shores. Your life-dance ended far too soon, but you will be forever dancing in our hearts. Carla, we loved you so much. You will be with us always. Your father Terence, your mother Vivien, and your brother Benjamin.

Finally, Zack knelt in front of the tombstone, and ran a hand tentatively over the silvered inscription. As he read it and his fingers traced their way over this, the full-stop on Carla's life, Zack felt himself breaking. He let his tears come freely, until they came no more.

When he had recovered, he caught his breath, sat back on his haunches and wiped his wet face with the back of a jacket-sleeve. He looked around. There was no one in sight.

Taking the bottle from his jacket pocket, he placed it carefully on the ground, then withdrew a small garden trowel from his other pocket.

He had written the final draft of this letter a couple of weeks previously. Over the time he'd gathered these thoughts, the original drafts had been recorded on various bits and pieces of paper, and with his crossings-out and emendations, were generally a mess.

So he had visited a stationery shop and bought some elegant cream vellum, which he was certain Carla would have liked. The letter was now scrolled neatly within the clear glass bottle, which he'd then sealed with the original stopper and a little clear epoxy.

After again checking he was unobserved, Zack dug up the earth in front of Carla's headstone. It was densely packed, and harder to dislodge than he expected. It took him five minutes of solid work to excavate a suitable dwelling place for his offering.

Zack was surprised how much this exertion cost him; he'd really worked up a sweat. In spite of himself and the occasion, he had to suppress a smile at the thought of being apprehended digging in a cemetery by the Canadian authorities. That certainly was a scenario Carla herself would have absolutely hooted at.

Done. He wedged the bottle firmly into the base of the hole. He kissed his fingertips, then touched them to the bottle.

"Carla. My beautiful girl." Zack's voice was tremulous. "Please forgive me. I would have done anything to save you. But I was too stupid. You know it already, but it was you who saved me. You saved me twice, my love. In Roppongi, and again in Bangkok."

He blinked back tears.

"Because of you, I am different. *Everything* is different. I will always love you Carla, and you can be sure I will see you on the other side."

The lump in his throat hurt; he concentrated fiercely on compacting the freshly dug earth back in on top of the bottle. Once it was at its prior level, he stood up and scuffed it roughly, camouflaging it with leaf litter. Stepping back, he realised it had started raining.

The woman with the umbrella had been right after all. Or was she a pessimist by nature? Maybe, like Carla had been, she was a local who knew the area well.

The thought lingering with him, Zack retrieved the trowel and huddled inside his jacket. Then he moved. He made his way through the misty grey rain, out of the cemetery, and into a much less certain future.

For Carla

I'm so sorry, my love. I'm so sorry your life was cut short by my stupidity. I'm so sorry for all the pain I've caused your family, and the many other people who loved you and are keenly feeling your loss in their lives. I'm so sorry that I didn't protect you.

Well, where to start? This letter has been a difficult thing for me to write. It has taken a long time. And you already know, I wrote it as much for myself as I did for you.

The pit which I inhabited for a while was a very dark place. And looking back, it seems that focusing on what I wanted to tell you gave me some of the rungs I needed to climb out of it. So please bear with me, my love.

First, I thought you'd be happy to know that I am out of that pit. I finally climbed out of it and saw the sun again. Before leaving Thailand I went back to the Spa in Samui, and fasted for a month. Got rid of all that poison from inside me. I never thought I would be able to fast that long, but the same extreme voice which has driven me in other less healthy directions in the past, positively screamed at me to cleanse and fast for a month. So I did. It's the first time in my life I had visions without the assistance of my favourite chemicals! But at that point I was clean, which was a good start for what came next.

After the fast, the Vipassana retreat in India was easier than I expected. I hadn't been speaking much for a while anyway. The hardest thing for me was the sitting still and meditating. I still have a monkey-mind and especially given what's happened, I'm going to need a bit more practice to quiet it on demand. After I finished the ten days, I stayed on in a simple bungalow nearby, and helped the monks with their gardening each day. They were surprised at first, but then accepted it. Maybe they could tell I needed it. Or maybe they just appreciated the help! First time I ever gardened in my life. They taught me a lot. I used to think gardening was boring; only for old folks or simple-minded rural types. But I was wrong about that too (don't worry, I've added it to the long long list of things I've been wrong about).

It took weeks until it dawned on me that I felt different. Not happy, or anything like that, but different. Certainly I felt better than before. My body was different. My energy was different. And then I realised how far I'd come since almost drugging and drinking myself to death in various holes in Bangkok. There are an awful lot of lost souls in Bangkok – the hungry ghosts. I'd never really seen it that way before. Or maybe this time it was a matter of like attracting like. All those lost souls, but you found me there didn't you, you clever creature!

In my different self, I knew it was time to leave the monks. I don't know how I knew, but there it was. Time. To. Go.

And then the oddest thing struck me. I had no idea where to go! I had been on the road for almost ten years. During that time the next destination had nearly always become obvious to me. Just as Thailand was obvious (for all the wrong reasons) in Tokyo, and just as India became obvious when my time in Thailand drew to a close. But this time I had nothing. I sat down that day with not the faintest clue about where I would go, or what I would do next.

So I went 'home'. I spent more than a few days in Australia for the first time in over seven years. Put a fair bit of effort into helping Mum with her garden (much to her surprise!). And so, my beautiful girl, that's where I've been until I flew here to see you. I told Mum pretty much everything that happened. It helped to talk through some of the stuff which had been roiling around in my head to that point. She's a good listener. I think she could see I needed time and space. She gave me plenty of both anyway, bless her.

I won't lie. I'm a little scared about what comes next. I can't do the bar thing anymore. That life requires a certain type of person. And I'm not the same person who crashed into you in a noodle-bar in Nikko. One way or another, I'm pretty sure that Zack died the same day you did, my love. He was arrogant; full of certainty, bravado and hot air. And most of the time it worked. Until it didn't.

After all the madness that's happened, I guess you'll laugh if I tell you I'm still thinking of going to South America. But I really am. I've always wanted to, and given I can't think of anything else right now, maybe that's the best idea?

I wish so much you were here with me Carla, to help me figure some things out. I'm winging it, and really have no clue what to do next.

Anyway, let me tell you how things ended up in Tokyo. It's like this. If Max is going to kill me, he'll have to do it from behind bars. He received a combined jail-sentence of forty-one years. Tanaka pulled some strings and made sure they fast-tracked the judicial process. So, there are even more charges pending. In addition to his other activities, Max apparently ran a brothel full of sex-slaves. And not so long ago, as a warning to the others, he killed one of them for trying to escape. The same way he killed you.

So, between the drugs we ensured he was caught with, two confirmed murders, various firearms offences, passport fraud, and the kidnapping and torture of the Japanese-Brazilian boy who unwittingly gave you the package, the judges had more than enough reasons to put him away for a very long time. Japan isn't big on parole anyway, so that, together with the help of Tanaka's contacts, means Max shouldn't be seeing daylight for at least thirty-five years.

Did it make me feel any better? Yes. But not for long. I had the satisfaction of calling in on his jail cell shortly before I flew out of Tokyo. He's a truly scary guy Carla. After some pacing and ranting and raving, he told me, very calmly, that 'his people' would find me and 'gut me like a fish'. His exact words.

I told him he was one of the stupidest gangsters I'd ever met. And that I hoped he liked taking it in the ass. Told him he'd never be able to go home to Nigeria, because they kill homosexuals there. Then I blew him a kiss, gave him the finger and left him there.

So right now it's a fair bet there are more than a couple of Nigerian gangsters trying to sniff me out and make a mess of me. In which case there's always the possibility I'll be seeing you sooner, rather than later. But at least that's not my own wish now, if you know what I mean. I'm going to try to live my life, such as it is. As fully and for as long as I can.

I know I didn't have to confirm for him, my involvement in his demise. Mako was against it – he couldn't see the point. And I know you're probably angry with me for that decision. Yes, I could have left him guessing. But, I wanted him to know why, Carla. I wanted him to know what tipped the balance. I want him to see my face, every single day he rots in that cell, and know why I helped put him there. Sorry, but I've rolled those dice and I'll take my chances.

I loved you, Carla. You saved me in Roppongi except I was too dumb to see it. And when you found me in that hellhole in Bangkok, you saved me again.

In my life, I've always been looking for the lesson.

Meeting you, falling in love with you, then losing you like I did?

I don't know if I found the lesson yet, but I'm looking. And for once, I'm looking with a clear head. And maybe, just maybe, there's nothing more to it than that.

Rest in peace, lovely girl. I'll see you when I see you.

All my love, always.
Zack

Afterword

Roppongi is, first and foremost, a work of fiction. It draws upon the many and varied characters I met not only during my time in Tokyo, but on my travels generally. And although *Roppongi's* themes necessarily include racism, misogyny, violence, criminality, and a range of flawed characters of varying ethnic origin, it is not my intention for any of these depictions to stereotype the races, nationalities, or genders in question. *Roppongi's* characters were drawn and evolved as they did purely for dramatic effect, nothing more. If I had felt obligated to pull punches for the sake of political correctness, *Roppongi* would not have been half as enjoyable a journey as it was (to read or to write!). Those readers who experienced the Roppongi life will no doubt understand. For those who didn't, I'm afraid you'll just have to give me the benefit of the doubt.

Care to Help?

If you enjoyed *Roppongi*, please visit Amazon, rate the novel highly and post a review! If you do write a review, please do me a favour and also email it to: **reviews@roppongithenovel.com**.

As you may know, this is my first novel, and I would very much appreciate your help in publicising it as widely as possible. If you have any general queries, please email me at: **info@roppongithenovel.com**. If you have any feedback, please email me at: **feedback@roppongithenovel.com**. Your interest, comments and opinions are valuable, and will greatly help me to successfully promote the novel.

Below I have made a list of the many different ways in which anyone who wants to help me, can. Some of them (especially the online ones) require very little time and effort on your part, but with the power of the internet and social media, even these seemingly 'little' things can now make a huge difference to how rapidly a book gains traction worldwide. If you've enjoyed this book, *please talk about it, show it to your friends, and encourage people to buy it*. Please spread the word as widely as you can. Your goodwill will make a huge difference in how far this book travels!

Roppongi is also available as an eBook (Kindle). As a marketing strategy, I am focusing all my efforts on promotion of the book through Amazon (**www.amazon.com**). This (together with your favourable ratings and reviews) helps drive the popularity of the book upwards on the biggest book-seller in the world, and makes it increasingly visible to those who may want to read it. Accordingly, Amazon is where folks need to purchase their copy of *Roppongi*. Click through to Amazon's *Roppongi* page from the 'Buy' page on the *Roppongi* website. Thanks!

Here are ten very simple things you can do to help both now and in the future!
1. *Roppongi* has a Facebook page: Roppongi - The Novel. You can click to this page from the *Roppongi* website. Please LIKE this page, and suggest to all your friends they LIKE it also.
2. Recommend the *Roppongi* website (www.roppongithenovel.com). Link to it from your website, blog, Facebook page, etc. Tweet about it. If I write a Facebook post, re-post it or link to it. Feature a quote you like from the book's publicity on your website or Facebook page. Or tweet the quote.

In short broadcast the *Roppongi* info far and wide!

3. Facebook – Twitter – Blogs etc: Promote *Roppongi* to anyone and everyone: *"Check out the cool new novel 'Roppongi' that Nick Vasey just published! See more info and BUY IT NOW at:* www.roppongithenovel.com*."* Post this as your status update on Facebook and re-post it as often as you like!

4. Help me with the media and PR. If you know of any newspaper or magazine editors, radio producers or hosts, TV show hosts or producers, columnists, bloggers, etc, promote *Roppongi* to them. Or simply tell me about them, introduce me, and I'll take it from there.

5. Write a Facebook Note about *Roppongi* and share it with all your friends. Suggest to your friends they re-post your note and *Roppongi* status update.

6. Write a review and submit it to Amazon, as well as to any other online book review sites such as: BN.com, GoodReads, Library Thing, and other reader social networks. Don't forget to include the link to *Roppongi's* website! And send me a copy at: **reviews@roppongithenovel.com**.

7. Send me your feedback please! Was it a good read? Did it move you to tears or laughter? Did you learn something new? Did you remember stuff you'd forgotten? I would love to hear what you think so please send all feedback to: **feedback@roppongithenovel.com**.

8. Do a video review of the book and post it on YouTube and other video sharing websites.

9. Movie Rights? Do you have film connections? If, like me, you think the novel would make a great movie and you have a connection to an A-list actor or producer who might be interested in making the movie, hook me up with your connection. Just remember the six degrees of separation. Someone you know, or know of, might be that crucial link *Roppongi* needs. Take a punt, and help make *Roppongi the Movie* a reality!

10. Ask me how else you might be able to help. You may have skills, contacts or knowledge which can help me. Talk to me and let's find out! Add 'troglodyte-downunder' to your Skype contacts and get directly in touch with me.

Thank-you for reading *Roppongi*, and know in your heart that any support you offer will be sincerely appreciated. Really.

Foreign Dialogue - Translated

Chapter 4: *Bokker-tov chaverim shelli.*
Good morning my friends.

Chapter 11: *Bokker-tov Yitzhak ... ma-inyanim*
Good morning, Yitzhak.
"*En baya*, Zack,"
No problem, Zack.

Chapter 15: *Chaval al azman ... schteim trippim*
In Hebrew slang this is an expression of disbelief (akin to 'I have no words') – in this instance in relation to the fact that the person has taken two acid trips.
En brera.
No choice.

Chapter 18: *Ata rotzeh café nudnick?"*
Do you want coffee, 'silly pest'?
"*Ken makshefah katana shelli ... toda rabah.*
Yes, my little witch – thanks very much.

Chapter 25: "*ma inyanim chaver shelli?*"
How are you, my brother?
" ... *hacol beseder?*"
... everything okay?
"*Ken, en baiya biklal, ani mageesh tov meod.*"
Yes, no problem at all, I feel very good.
"*Ezeh Ivrit,*"
What Hebrew!

Chapter 26: *Ahh ... bokker tov chamoodi."*
Good morning my cutie/sweetie.
"*Ze erev tov ... lo?*"
It's good evening, no?
"*Lo bishvilcha ani choshevet.*"
Not for you, I think.

"*Ulay zeh nachon Shunit ... aval ma ani yodea? Ani rak mefager me Australie ve ata ga-ona me Israel. Ma ani yachol oseh?*"
Maybe that's right Shunit, but what do I know? I'm just a retard from Australia and you are a genius from Israel. What can I do?
"*Ze nachon meod meod ani yoda-at, aval ata rak talmid shelli, az zeh beseder. Ken?*"
That's very very right I know, but you are just my student, that's okay. Yes?
"*Shachtsanit!*"
Liar!
"*Ze lo nachon,*"
That's not right.
"*Ata rotzeh café nudnick?*"
You want coffee 'silly pest'?
"*Ma at choshevet makshefah katana shelli?*"
What do you think my little witch?
Kloom, kloom, kloom.
Nothing, nothing, nothing.
"*Ezeh magill Zack! Chaval al azman.*"
How disgusting Zack! No words for that!

Chapter 34: "*So desu, so desu Wakarimashita, wakarimashita. Gomenasai.*"
Okay, okay, I understand. I'm sorry.

Glossary (most references sourced courtesy of Wikipedia)

Akasaka – Japanese – a suburb adjoining Roppongi, in which the ANA Hotel is located.
Aoyama-Dori – Japanese – the next major street which runs perpendicular to Omotesandō, at the opposite end from where Omotesandō intersects with Meiji-Dori.
Basta – any type of street vendor's stall which is selling something other than food, typically jewellery, clothing, sunglasses, designer rip-offs etc.
Bindi - traditionally it is a dot of red colour applied in the centre of the forehead close to the eyebrows, but it can also consist of a sign or piece of jewellery worn at this location.
Chamoodi – Hebrew – loosely translates as 'cutie'.
Charedim – Hebrew – 'the pious', usually used to describe Orthodox Jews.
Chuo (line) – Japanese – is one of the major trunk railway lines in Japan, but in this case applies to a small section of the Japanese subway operating through the regions of Chiyoda, Shinjuku and Shibuya.
Chuzenjiko Onsen – Japanese – Chuzenji Lake's shores, near Nikko, are mostly undeveloped and forested except at the lake's eastern end where the small hot spring town of Chuzenjiko Onsen was built.
Dame – Japanese – is an informal term with many meanings. It can mean 'no' or 'it's bad' or 'it's not possible' or 'you can't do that' etc. It is a word that signals a 'no' answer.
Do-itashi-mashite – Japanese – means 'you're welcome'.
Doves – English (slang) – a particular 'brand' of Ecstasy reputed for its strength and purity, originally made famous in the UK around 1990.
Esser – Hebrew – means the number 'ten'. It is also used colloquially to signify a person or thing being 'good', 'great', or 'excellent'.
Ezeh magilim – Hebrew – the word 'ezeh' in front of any other Hebrew word emphasises even more, the meaning of that word. In this case, 'ezeh magilim' roughly means 'how disgusting they are'.
FUBAR – commonly used slang acronym for the phrase 'Fucked Up Beyond All Recognition'.
Fuji – Japanese – short version of 'Mount Fuji', the famous mountain in Japan.
Gaien-Higashi-Dori – a major street which intersects with Roppongi-Dori to form the famous 'Roppongi Crossing' intersection.
Gaien-Nishi-Dori – a major street which crosses Roppongi-Dori in the area of Nishi-Aazabu.

Gaijin – Japanese – literally means 'outside person'. Common Japanese word used for any non-Japanese person.
Gaijin-House – Japanese – A larger 'share-house' usually with four or more bedrooms, typically shared by a group of gaijins living and working in Japan. Usually rented to residents on a per-room basis.
Genki – Japanese – a popular word in Japan meaning happy, lively, fun, or enthusiastic.
Genki desu-ka – Japanese – the question form of the above definition, typically meaning: 'are you feeling good, happy, lively, enthusiastic,' etc.
Ginza – is a district of Chuo, Tokyo, famous as one of the most luxurious shopping districts in the world.
Glamorama – is a novel by American writer Bret Easton Ellis, published by Alfred A. Knopf in 1998. Unlike Ellis's previous novels, *Glamorama* is set in and satirizes the 1990s, specifically celebrity culture and consumerism.
Glock 26 – The Glock 26 is a 9×19mm "subcompact" variant handgun designed for concealed carry, and was introduced in 1995, mainly for the civilian market.
Goman – Japanese – 50,000 (fifty thousand).
Gomenasai – Japanese – means 'sorry'. Used as an apology.
Hai – Japanese – means 'yes'.
Hausa – Africa - is the Chadic language with the largest number of speakers, spoken as a first language by about 25 million people, and as a second language by about 18 million more, an approximate total of 43 million people.
Harajuku – Japanese – is the common name for the area around Harajuku Station in the Shibuya area of Tokyo.
Hiroo – Japanese – a neighbourhood in the Shibuya district of Tokyo.
Host/Hostess Club – Japanese – are a common feature in the night-time entertainment industry of Japan and east-Asian countries and other areas with a high east Asian population. They employ primarily female staff and cater to males seeking drinks and attentive conversation. The more recent host clubs are similar establishments where primarily male staff cater to females clientele. Host and hostess clubs are considered part of mizu-shōbai or 'water trade' in Japan.
Ice – a highly potent crystalline form of methamphetamine, also commonly referred to as 'crystal meth', 'meth', 'crystal', 'ice', 'p', 'shabu' or 'glass'.
Ichiban – Japanese – means 'one'. Also commonly used colloquially to mean 'number one', 'first', or 'the best'.
Ichiman – Japanese – the number 10,000 (ten thousand). Common use 'ichiman yen', or 10,000 yen.

Kabuki – Japanese – A form of traditional Japanese dramatic theatre with highly stylized song, mime, and dance, now performed only by male actors.

Kabukicho – Japanese – is an entertainment and red-light district in Shinjuku, Tokyo which is the location of many hostess bars, host bars, love hotels, shops, restaurants, and nightclubs, and is often called the 'Sleepless Town'.

Kamakura (period) – Japanese – is a period of Japanese history that marks the governance by the Kamakura Shogunate, officially established in 1192 in Kamakura by the first shogun Minamoto no Yoritomo.

Kanpai – Japanese – a toast, the Japanese equivalent for 'Cheers!' (Sometimes spelled incorrectly as 'kampai', due to the difficulty some people have with pronouncing the 'n' sound next to a hard consonant.)

Kanji – Japanese – are the adopted logographic Chinese characters 'hanzi' that are used in the modern Japanese writing system along with hiragana, katakana, Indo Arabic numerals, and the occasional use of the Latin alphabet (known as 'rōmaji').

Kasumigaseki – Japanese – literally 'barrier/gate of fog' is a district in Chiyoda Ward in Tokyo. It is the location of most of Japan's cabinet ministry offices.

Ka-wy-ee (phonetic) – spelling is actually 'kawaii' – Japanese – an adjective (literally, 'lovable, 'cute', or 'adorable'.) The term 'kawaii' has taken on the secondary meanings of 'cool', 'groovy', 'acceptable', 'desirable', 'charming', and 'non-threatening'.

Kendo – Japanese – meaning "way of the sword", is a modern Japanese martial art of sword-fighting based on traditional Japanese swordsmanship, or 'kenjutsu'.

Khao-San Road – is a short street in Banglamphu, central Bangkok. Full of cheap accommodation and drinking options, it is popular with international backpackers.

Kiddyland – Japanese – a giant toy store on Omotesandō in Harajuku, Tokyo.

Kirin – Japanese – a brand of Japanese-brewed beer.

Kobe – Japanese – is the fifth-largest city in Japan and is the capital city of Hyōgo Prefecture on the southern side of the main island of Honshū, approximately 30 km (19 mi) west of Osaka.

Koh Samui – Thai – meaning 'Butterfly Island', is an island in the Surat Thani province of Thailand, off the east coast of the Kra Isthmus, not far from the mainland town of Surat Thani.

Konban-wa – Japanese – means 'good evening'.

Kötthuvud – Swedish – curse meaning 'meat-head' or 'idiot' or similar.

Kyama – a curse in the Hausa language similar to damn or shit.

Kyoto – Japanese – formerly the imperial capital of Japan, Kyoto is a city in the central part of the island of Honshū. It has a population close to 1.5 million.
Kyushu – Japanese – is the third largest island of Japan and most south-westerly of its four main islands.
L'Chaim – Hebrew – a toast literally meaning 'to life'.
La Foret – a large shopping mall on Meiji-Dori in Harajuku.
Mama-San – Japanese – typically used to describe the female owner or manager of a hostess club.
Manga – Japanese – means 'comics'. In the West, the term 'manga' has been appropriated to refer specifically to comics created in Japan.
Mastoolim – Hebrew – a group of people who are stoned, drunk, or otherwise wasted. In this case, the name of a bar in Eilat.
Matok shelli – Hebrew – literally means 'my sweetie' (matok-sweetie, shelli-my).
Meidi-Ya – Japanese – a convenience supermarket very near Roppongi Crossing, often used by bar-staff to obtain supplies (lemons, limes, cherries, straws etc) for the bar.
Meiji / Meiji-Dori / Meiji-shrine – Japanese – the Meiji period, also known as the Meiji era, is a Japanese era which extended from September 1868 through July 1912. It also refers to a street in Tokyo (Meiji-Dori) and a shrine on Meiji-Dori in the Shibuya area of Tokyo.
Meiji-Jingumae – Japanese – used to describe a small area around Omotesandō. Is also a train station near Omotesandō.
Meishi – Japanese – means 'business card'.
Miso / Miso-soup – Japanese – is a traditional Japanese seasoning produced by fermenting rice, barley and/or soybeans, with salt and the fungus 'kōjikin', the most typical miso being made with soy.
Mizu-shōbai – Japanese – or the 'water trade', is the traditional euphemism for the night-time entertainment business in Japan, provided by hostess or snack bars, bars, nightclubs and cabarets.
Moshi mosh / Moshi moshi – Japanese – used to say 'hello' when you talk on the telephone. It is also used when you want to get someone's attention.
Nikko – Japanese – literally 'sunlight' or 'sunshine', and is a city in the mountains of Tochigi Prefecture, Japan.
Niman – Japanese – 20,000 (twenty thousand)
Nishi-Azabu – Japanese – is a district of Minato-ku, Tokyo, Japan, which was a part of the former Azabu Ward. Nishiazabu borders Minami-aoyama on the north and west, Hiroo on the south, Motoazabu on the southeast, and Roppongi on the northeast.

Nogizaka / Nogizaka Station – Japanese – is located on the Tokyo Metro Chiyoda Line in the Nogizaka district of Minato Ward of Tokyo. It is a popular tourist destination because of the shrines, museums, and parks located in the area.

Ohayou / Ohayou gozaymashita – Japanese – the shorter form means 'good morning' informally, and the longer form is more respectful.

Omotesandō is an avenue, subway station and neighbourhood in the Minato and Shibuya wards in Tokyo stretching from Harajuku station, the foot of the famous Takeshita-Dori, to Aoyama-Dori where Omotesandō station can be found.

Onegaishimasu – Japanese – means 'please'.

Onigiri – Japanese – also known as 'omusubi' or rice-ball, is a Japanese food made from white rice formed into triangular or oval shapes and often wrapped in 'nori' (seaweed).

Osaka – Japanese – is a city in the Kansai region of Japan's main island of Honshu, the capital city of Osaka prefecture. Located at the mouth of the Yodo River on Osaka Bay, Osaka is the third largest city by population after Tokyo.

Oyabun – Japanese – head of a Yakuza family, basically a Japanese counterpart to a 'Don (head of Italian/Sicilian mafia), the Oyabun is the father figure, superior to the Waka-Gashira (second in command).

Paris (perfume) – a scent by Yves Saint Laurent. Launched in 1983, Paris is classified as a refined, flowery fragrance. This feminine scent possesses a blend of mimosa, orange flower, rose, moss, sandalwood, and amber.

Ramen – Japanese – is a Japanese noodle dish. It consists of Chinese-style wheat noodles served in a meat or fish-based broth, often flavoured with soy sauce or miso, and uses toppings such as sliced pork, dried seaweed (nori), kamaboko, green onions and occasionally corn.

Roppongi – Japanese – The name 'Roppongi' appears to have been coined around 1660, and literally means 'six trees'. It is a district of Minato, Tokyo, Japan, famous as home to the rich Roppongi Hills area and an active night club scene. Many foreign embassies are located in Roppongi, and the night life, which incorporates bars, nightclubs, hostess clubs, casinos, restaurants, strip clubs and cabarets, is popular with locals and foreigners alike.

Roppongi Crosseten – Japanese – Japanese pronunciation of the English phrase 'Roppongi Crossing' (see below).

Roppongi Crossing – the intersection of Gaien-Higashi-Dori and Roppongi-Dori, typically used to describe the place many people meet each other, when planning a night out in Roppongi.

Roppongi-Dori – the main street which runs through Roppongi in the direction from Akasaka to Nishi-Azabu.

Salariman/men – Japanese – refers to someone whose income is salary based, particularly those working for corporations. Its frequent use by Japanese corporations, and its prevalence in Japanese manga and anime has gradually led to its acceptance in English-speaking countries as a noun for a Japanese white-collar businessman/men.
Samurai – Japanese – is the term for the military nobility of pre-industrial Japan.
Satsujin-sha – Japanese – means 'murderer'.
Sentō – Japanese – is a type of Japanese communal bath house where customers pay for entrance.
Sephardi – Hebrew – essentially meaning 'Spanish', is a general term referring to the descendants of the Jews who lived in the Iberian Peninsula before their expulsion during the Spanish Inquisition. Sephardic Jews generally have a darker skin-colouring than their Ashkenazi (typically Eastern-European) brethren.
Shiatsu – Japanese – meaning 'finger pressure' it is a type of alternative medicine consisting of finger and palm pressure, stretches, and other massage techniques.
Shibuya / Shibuya Station – Japanese – apart from one of the 23 wards of Tokyo, the name 'Shibuya' is also used to refer to the shopping district which surrounds Shibuya Station, one of Tokyo's busiest railway stations. This area is known as one of the fashion centres of Japan, particularly for young people, and as a major nightlife area.
Shinjuku / Shinjuku Station – Japanese – is one of the 23 wards of Tokyo. It is a major commercial and administrative centre, housing the busiest train station in the world (Shinjuku Station).
Shuto Expressway – Japanese – is a network of toll expressways in the Greater Tokyo area of Japan.
Sumo – Japanese – is a competitive full-contact sport where a wrestler 'rikishi' attempts to force another wrestler out of a circular ring 'dohyō' or to touch the ground with anything other than the soles of the feet. The sport originated in Japan, the only country where it is practiced professionally.
Tempura – Japanese – is a dish of seafood or vegetables that have been battered and deep fried.
The Alchemist - is an allegorical novel by Paolo Coelho, first published in 1988.
The Pilgrimage - is a 1987 novel by Brazilian novelist Paolo Coelho. It is a recollection of Paulo's experiences as he made his way across Northern Spain on the Pilgrimage of Santiago de Compostela in 1986.
TV Asahi-Dori – Japanese – a major street which intersects with Roppongi-Dori in the vicinity of Nishi-Azabu.

Ueno – Japanese – is a district in Tokyo's Taitō Ward, best known as the home of Ueno Station and Ueno Park, as well as the Ueno market.
Yaks / Yakuza also known as 'gokudō', are members of traditional organized crime syndicates in Japan. The Japanese police, and media (by request of the police), call them 'bōryokudan', literally 'violence group', while the Yakuza call themselves 'ninkyō dantai', 'chivalrous organisations'. The Yakuza are notoriously known for their strict codes of conduct and very organized nature.
Yamete – Japanese – means 'stop' or 'stop what you are doing'.
Yokohama – Japanese – is the capital city of Kanagawa prefecture and the second largest city in Japan by population after Tokyo and most populous municipality of Japan. It lies on Tokyo Bay, south of Tokyo, in the Kantō region of the main island of Honshu.
Yoshinoya – Japanese – is the largest chain of beef bowl (or 'gyūdon') restaurants (a Japanese fast-food chain), which was established in Japan in 1899.
Yoyogi-Park – Japanese – is one of the largest parks in Tokyo and is located adjacent to Harajuku Station and Meiji Shrine in Shibuya.

Made in the USA
Charleston, SC
16 January 2012